Tales for Twilight

Watch the candles lit by fright
One by one through the black night.

—from 'The Drum' by Edith Sitwell

Tales for Twilight

*Two Hundred Years of
Scottish Ghost Stories*

Edited by
Alistair Kerr

This hardback edition first published in 2021 by Polygon,
an imprint of Birlinn Ltd.

Birlinn Ltd
West Newington House
10 Newington Road
Edinburgh
EH9 1QS

www.polygonbooks.co.uk

1

ISBN 978 1 84697 526 4

British Library Cataloguing-in-Publication Data
A catalogue record for this book is available on request
from the British Library.

Typeset by 3btype.com, Edinburgh

There came a ghost to Margaret's door,
With many a grievous grone,
And aye he tirled at the pin,
But answer made she none.

'Is this my father Philip?
Or is't my brother John?
Or is't my true love Willie,
From Scotland new come home?'

''Tis not thy father Philip,
Nor yet thy brother John:
But 'tis thy true love Willie,
From Scotland new come home.'

'O sweet Margret! O dear Margret!
I pray thee speak to mee:
Give me my faith and troth, Margret,
As I gave it to thee.'

'Thy faith and troth thou'se nevir get,
Of me shalt nevir win,
Till that thou come within my bower,
And kiss my cheek and chin.'

'If I should come within thy bower,
I am no earthly man:
And should I kiss thy rosy lipp,
Thy days will not be lang . . .'

—'Sweet William's Ghost', Thomas Percy

Contents

Introduction

Come on, sit down: come on, and do your best
To fright me with your sprites; you're powerful at it.
—*The Winter's Tale*, Act 2, Scene 1
Shakespeare

I SHOULD BEGIN by explaining what this book is not: it is *not* yet another collection of ghostly legends and traditions of old Scottish castles, replete with breathless first- or second-hand accounts of 'ghoulies and ghosties and long-leggedy beasties and things that go bump in the night'.

I believe the stories presented here are more interesting than that. They are works of fiction, products of their authors' vivid imagination, although a few of them might be loosely based on authentic folk legends or attested hauntings. The authors include such renowned wordsmiths as Robert Louis Stevenson, Sir Arthur Conan Doyle and Muriel Spark, as well as others who are less familiar, or who chose to be anonymous. The criteria for inclusion were that the story should be well-written, scary and that the author and/or setting should be Scottish. 'Scottish' has been loosely interpreted to include such expatriate Scots as Guy Boothby. Likewise, Algernon Blackwood, who was born in Kent of distant Scots descent and who later worked in North America, but studied for a short time at Edinburgh University and whose story, presented here, is set in Edinburgh.

These fifteen stories cover two centuries: from 1820 to 2020. The majority are from the Golden Age of ghost-story writing: the Victorian and Edwardian eras. That period ended abruptly with the outbreak of the First World War, although the ghost story was soon resurrected, reinvented, and, especially in Scotland, recovered much of its popularity. That Golden Age overlapped with the Golden Age of detective and mystery writing; many authors – Conan Doyle, for example – wrote both detective and ghost stories. The demand for ghost and mystery stories extended far beyond Scotland to the rest of the United Kingdom, the USA and elsewhere. Although any collection of Victorian or Edwardian ghost stories is likely to include one or two tales by Scottish writers, they are outnumbered by the many non-Scots who also produced brilliant ghost stories during this period, including Charles Dickens, Sheridan Le Fanu, Henry James, Rudyard Kipling and M. R. James.

That begs the question: is this new anthology justified? Are Scottish ghost stories truly in a class of their own, or were they simply part of a wider literary phenomenon? I believe that both suggestions are true: yes, that flowering of Scottish ghost stories was part of an international trend; and yes, Scottish ghost-story writers tend to have special qualities that set them apart. The next questions are 'which' and 'why'? But first, let us look at the common factors.

The two pioneer ghost-story writers – famous for other achievements – who ushered in the new story form were both Scottish: James Hogg and Sir Walter Scott became known and admired far beyond their homeland. Their two tales in this anthology are 'Strange Letter of a Lunatic' (1827) by Hogg and 'The Tapestried Chamber, or The Lady in the Sacque' (1828) by Scott. Hogg's story is unusual in that there are two 'ghosts': one is clearly the Devil himself, who ensnares the narrator by means of a pinch of magical snuff; the other is the narrator's diabolical double, who gets him into trouble. The story, which has an affinity with Hogg's famous novel, *The Private Memoirs and Confessions of a Justified Sinner* (1824), is a reworking of the Romantic theme of the doppelgänger, although it also draws on a Scottish tradition of devilish visitations and witchcraft, which was still alive in the nineteenth century. By contrast Scott's skilful tale is a conventional ghost story, involving a wicked ancestor who cannot rest because of her evil career. Thanks to Hogg and Scott, the literary ghost story got off to a flying start. The Golden Age would soon follow.

The nineteenth century saw the first great wave of globalisation, which brought unprecedented prosperity to the United Kingdom, including Scotland. It was partly based on advances in technology, notably in the fields of transport and engineering. Other factors included the dramatic expansion of the British Empire and of the English language; the growth of mass literacy through better education; and new developments in printing technology and publishing. At a time when there were no cinemas, radio, television or online amusements, all of these factors resulted in a burgeoning demand for fiction as entertainment. That included long novels, which could be serialised, and short stories, especially ghost, detection and mystery stories.

To meet this demand a shoal of literary magazines came into being. They published short stories, reviews, articles and serialised novels. Virtually all of them have now disappeared but some, like *Blackwood's Magazine* (1817–1980) and *Chambers's Edinburgh Journal* (1832–1956), flourished for well over a century. Not a few were founded by Scots and were published in Edinburgh or Glasgow rather than, or as well as, in London. Highly influential in their day, they achieved a wide circulation beyond the British Isles. Each issue would be read and enjoyed in New York, San Francisco, Toronto, Bombay, Calcutta and Sydney within days or weeks of its publication. British daily newspapers, too, were keen to publish serialised novels and short stories. Starting in the 1820s, *The Scotsman* and other Scottish newspapers, as well as a few Irish and English ones, began to commission and publish a regular Christmas ghost story for their readers' enjoyment. This custom was to continue for many years. In this tradition, Ian Rankin's ghost story 'I Live Here Now' was published in the Christmas edition of *The Spectator* for 2020.

The proliferation of publications led to a notable expansion of the profession of 'man of letters': someone devoted to literature in all its forms, who combined the function of author, playwright or poet with those of editor, reviewer, critic, sometimes also of publisher or journalist, and who made a reasonable, albeit hard-working and multi-tasked, living by doing so. Many Scots found it a congenial career.

There were women of letters, too. Because they were excluded from most of the learned professions until after the First World War, well-educated women of limited means – often with family responsibilities – responded to this opportunity. One example is the prolific ghost-story writer, Margaret Oliphant of East Lothian, who was happily married for a short time but soon found herself a poor young widow with children to support and educate.

Mrs Oliphant became a successful author and influential critic, whose admirers included Queen Victoria. She was able to send her sons to Eton on the proceeds of her writing and reviewing, much of which appeared in *Blackwood's Magazine*. She wrote damningly about Thomas Hardy's novel, *Jude the Obscure*, but praised the artless spontaneity and simplicity of Queen Victoria's *Leaves from the Journal of Our Life in the Highlands* in February 1868. In private she did not rate the literary merits of the Queen's journal quite as highly as she appeared to, but Mrs Oliphant's flattering review resulted in a generous fee of £100, and she was later awarded a Civil List pension. Despite Mrs Oliphant's private reservations, Queen Victoria's book became a best-seller.

There was a brisk demand for ghost stories in such magazines, and a significant number of ghost stories from the Victorian age and later are now known to have been written by women, although – unlike Mrs Oliphant – they did not always choose to advertise their gender; 'F. G. Trafford', for example, was in reality the Irish author Charlotte Riddell. Others preferred to remain Miss, Mrs or Lady Anon.

The classic modern ghost story evolved out of the Romantic or Gothic tale of terror around the time of Queen Victoria's birth in 1819. One of the earliest examples was Scott's aforementioned 'The Tapestried Chamber', set in an ancient, picturesque English castle and recounted by a modern general who has the misfortune to pass a night in the haunted chamber. By contrast, the Gothic terror tale, which was often set at a distant date in history or in an exotic location, continued to flourish separately through the nineteenth century. Those terror stories are of mixed quality. It can sometimes be hard for us now to understand their evident popularity: in J. B. Priestley's words, they 'strain so much towards horror that they come close to absurdity'. Matthew Gregory Lewis's OTT horror story, 'The Anaconda', set in Ceylon (now Sri Lanka), is an example of this genre. The fact that anacondas are native to South America, not Asia, further detracts from the tale – which is not included in this collection.

By contrast, the best ghost stories are both understated and firmly grounded in the author's present time, although they normally refer back to earlier events and personalities. They contain circumstantial detail, including authentic fragments of history, biography, archaeology and details of décor, food, drink, landscape and dress, so that readers may easily read themselves into the plot. In M. R. James's words:

> some degree of actuality is the charm of the best ghost stories; not a very insistent actuality, but one strong enough to allow the reader to identify himself with the patient; while it is almost inevitable that the reader of an antique story [*a story that takes place purely in olden times*] should fall into the position of a mere spectator.

What James meant by 'actuality' was a backdrop of contemporary Victorian or Edwardian convention, prosperity and peace: for example, an old college, manor house or rectory. There are flowers in the conservatory; the cat is dozing by the fire; there is the comforting prospect of afternoon tea or evening dinner and the certainty of a life to come. Then something shocking, untoward and mysterious starts to happen; the past is coming back and it may prove to be dangerous . . .

For ghost-story writers of the Golden Age, certain things in Scotland and the wider UK were, or seemed to be, unchanging and would remain so for many years to come. They included such institutions as marriage, the law, the church, the universities, the gentry, the nobility and the monarchy. They provided an orderly, stable, even humdrum, context into which the supernatural could suddenly and dramatically intrude.

By contrast, another quite different factor of the success of the ghost story was nostalgia for the vanishing past. Although the Victorian era might seem to us a period of enviable stability, compared with the wars and revolutions of the twentieth and twenty-first centuries, that was not necessarily how the Victorians themselves perceived it. On the contrary, every few years a new and disconcerting development or discovery in science, technology, politics, economics or philosophy would threaten to disarrange their universe; this would plunge them into excited, often acrimonious, discussion, which they pursued publicly in magazine columns, in the daily press, in learned debate and occasionally in Parliament. The Oxford evolution debate of 1860, for example, seemed to shake the foundations of revealed religion. It moved many Christians to re-examine their beliefs, and the shock waves that it generated have still not completely subsided. To some believers Darwin's theories are still controversial. Whether they welcomed change as progress or feared and distrusted it, the Victorians had become aware that – for all kinds of reasons – their generation was becoming more cut off from their collective past than any previous one had been.

When they looked back, even at the recent past of the eighteenth century or the Regency, both within living memory into the late Victorian period, it already seemed picturesque and remote. Many Victorians felt uneasily like emigrants on a ship bound for Canada or New Zealand, taking a final look at the receding figures of friends and relations on the quayside in the knowledge that they would never see them again. From time to time the death of a distinguished survivor from that earlier period – for example, the Duke of Wellington (1769–1852) or Dr Martin Routh (1755–1854), the President of Magdalen College and the last man in Oxford to wear a wig, tricorne hat and knee-breeches – would generate a mood of profound, reflective melancholy: a page of history had turned and nothing could turn it back.

The death in 1824 of Peter Grant, who was the last survivor of the 1745 Jacobite Rising and had fought at Culloden, provoked a similar reaction in Scotland, where he passed away at the age of 110, an unrepentant Jacobite to the last. The royal House of Stuart had meanwhile become extinct, but the future Queen Victoria was already five years old.

The outward and visible signs of change included improved means of communication and transport, as a result of which the very landscape was being transformed. When Victoria was born the stage coach was still the normal means of long-distance land travel; the journey along rutted and muddy roads from London to Edinburgh could take days. The attendant hazards included highwaymen: the last known highway robbery in the UK occurred in 1831. By the time of her death in 1901, fast and reliable railway trains criss-crossed the country, flying over immense viaducts and through tunnels. Inconvenient hills, houses and even ancient monuments had been removed to facilitate the railways' construction. The motor car had been invented, and within a very few years the first flimsy biplanes would start to appear in the skies. The pace of change was relentless. In Prince Albert's words: 'we are living at a period of most wonderful transition'. It was truly an innovative age, but it had been realised at a high psychological cost: the British past was fast becoming a distant and distinctly foreign country.

A. N. Wilson analysed this phenomenon, I believe correctly, in his 2019 biography, *Prince Albert: The Man Who Saved the Monarchy*: '[The Victorians'] . . . need to cloak modernity in fancy dress, to build railway stations in the manner of Gothic cathedrals, or to make brand-new schools look as if they had been built in the time of Shakespeare, is probably part of their jumble of uncertainties.' These uncertainties included troubling doubts about their origins, their status, the basis of their religion and where, exactly, their civilisation was heading.

Various responses to this perception included a revival of the academic discipline of history; new historical and archaeological research; and a fashionable interest in 'roots', heraldry and genealogy, which resulted, *inter alia*, in some ancient peerages being brought out of abeyance. Historical re-enactment extravaganzas such as the 1839 Eglinton Tournament; period costume balls, at least one given by Queen Victoria herself; and a vogue for historical paintings and costumed portraits, of which Robert Thorburn's portrait of Prince Albert in medieval armour is a well-known example, abounded. Likewise, there was an increasing popularity in the study of traditional folk music, songs, dances and legends, including ghostly legends; the revival of earlier styles of art and architecture, especially Gothic and Scottish Baronial; and an avalanche of historical romances inspired by Sir Walter Scott's *Waverley* novels, which had appeared between 1814 and 1832. Along with the parallel Victorian interest in spiritualism and psychical research, the ghost story, whether fictional or 'authentic', fitted easily into this picture. It seemed to suggest that, despite recent developments, the past – even the distant past – could still influence and interact with the present, albeit not necessarily in an agreeable or reassuring way.

Why and in what ways does Scottish ghost fiction differ from contemporary ghost fiction written elsewhere? First, because Scots tend to stand in a relationship to the past with which few English, or other, people readily empathise; they celebrate and identify emotionally with all their ancestors – good and bad, real and legendary – back to the earliest generations.

Second, because the Scots' historical experience was different from that of their neighbours. While the Scots, like the Welsh and Irish, had often been invaded by England, only one English invasion of Scotland, – that of Oliver Cromwell, starting in 1650 – was completely successful, and the results of that, both good and bad, were swept away at the Restoration in 1660. Although in reality the Middle Ages and certain other 'heroic' periods – the Jacobite rebellions of 1690–1745, for instance – were miserable and dangerous times in which to be a Scot, the tradition of Scotland's successful resistance to the invader allowed the past, particularly the medieval wars of independence, to be reinvented and romanticised as 'the brave days of old'.

It should be remembered that the Jacobite campaigns were not simply an English vs Scots contest, although some films portray them in that way. They were the final round in the long contest between progressive, Presbyterian Protestant, English-speaking Lowland Scotland, which supported the Hanoverians, and traditional, Catholic and Episcopalian, Gaelic-speaking Highland Scotland, which supported the exiled Stuarts. In the final battle at Culloden in 1746, most of the redcoats of the Government army were serving in Scottish regiments, which – apart from the Black Watch – did not then wear distinctive uniforms. (English regiments were also present on the Government side, while some French troops were fighting with the Jacobite army.)

Thanks to Sir Walter Scott and his imitators, the imagined, heroic version largely eclipsed the grim reality in the popular imagination. This influenced Scottish literature in general, including Scottish ghost fiction.

Third, there was a tradition of oral story-telling in Scotland that predated Sir Walter Scott and the classic ghost story by centuries. It can be traced to pre-literate times, when a good narrator, especially if he were also a poet, ballad singer or minstrel, was welcomed everywhere. A number of these old stories survive, usually in ballad form, and many of them deal with the supernatural. The tradition of telling ghost stories on winter nights, especially on Christmas Eve, survived within living memory: older family members would recite ghostly tales or poems to give their children, grandchildren, nieces and nephews an enjoyable fright. As a logical development, some ghost stories published as recently as the late nineteenth and early twentieth centuries were clearly written with the intention that they should be read aloud. Given this long-standing tradition, it was foreseeable that, starting with James Hogg and Sir Walter Scott and continuing all the way to Muriel Spark, George Mackay Brown, Ian Rankin and James Robertson, some of Scotland's finest modern writers should have risen to the challenge and tried their hand at writing ghost stories.

Another inescapable factor which makes Scotland, and therefore Scottish fiction, different is religion. In the sixteenth century, Scotland became Protestant. However, the precise form that the Protestant Church of Scotland should take – Episcopalian, with bishops and subject to royal authority, as in England, or Presbyterian, subject to no earthly Prince and without any hierarchy above the Parish Minister – was not settled until 1689 when, following a period of bitter and bloody conflict known as 'the Killing Times', Presbyterianism finally triumphed. That victory allowed the Kirk to impose a stern and conformist moral code on Scotland, drawing its intellectual sustenance from Calvinism, while making use of the extensive civil powers that the church enjoyed until well into the nineteenth century publicly to punish offenders against that code and to persecute and discriminate against Nonconformist religious minorities, especially Episcopalians and Roman Catholics, who were also politically suspect as potential Jacobites. Offenders included James Greenshields, an Edinburgh Episcopalian clergyman imprisoned in 1709, who had publicly used the Prayer Book in defiance of the orders of the local Presbytery and the Council. Another, in 1784, was Robert Burns, for fornication. Burns was fined and made to do public penance, only to re-offend soon afterwards.

All of this caused the themes of guilt, judgement, punishment and atonement to be central to many Scottish ghost stories. That, in my opinion, lends them an added edge and nuance. These influences are implicit in, for example, Hogg's 'Strange Letter of a Lunatic' and explicit in other ghost fiction, including other stories by Hogg.

There is a curious correlation, also to be seen in other societies than Scotland (colonial Massachusetts, for example), between religious extremism and superstition. Ironically, although the 'superstitious' Church of Rome had been banished, superstition continued to flourish vigorously in Protestant Scotland, including belief in diabolical visitations, witches and ghosts. The notorious Edinburgh warlock, Major Thomas Weir, was executed in 1670, more than a century after the Reformation, and the last witch trial in Scotland took place as recently as 1727. As Sacheverell Sitwell expressed it in his book, *Poltergeists*: 'Every religion, and all superstition, serve one another and are sealed in compact . . . And those who have used them, on purpose, have made it worse. Such are the hands that make a haunted place more frightening.'

The same themes are implied, rather than spelled out, in the later tales, for example in the anonymous 'A Tale for Twilight', written in the 1880s. Who was the mysterious, well-heeled Oxford undergraduate who found himself ill, alone and friendless, apart from his doctor and nurse, in Edinburgh in the winter of 1798? What was he doing there? Had he deliberately placed himself beyond the jurisdiction of English law? If so, from what disgrace or danger had he fled? Why was he hiding? The author does not tell us. As for the enigmatic veiled woman, whose nightly visitations were scaring him to death: was she the supernatural instrument of his punishment? We find out at the end of the story.

Scottish ghost stories written immediately before, during and after the First World War carry the same preoccupation with guilt and punishment, but in a different way. Science, including psychology, had started to influence ghost-story writers. An example is Algernon Blackwood's tale, 'Keeping His Promise' (1906), which perfectly conjures up a dreich winter's night in Edinburgh with its icy winds and horizontal sleet. Merely reading it can make you feel cold. It seems possible – even likely – that Field, who suddenly appears out of the night and imposes himself on his boyhood friend Marriott, an undergraduate of Edinburgh University, is a ghost. A dissolute young man, about whose recent disgrace Marriott dimly recalls having read or heard – 'drink, a woman, opium, or something of the sort' – Field seems to deserve punishment, as he would in a classic old Scottish ghost story. Moreover Marriott and Field, while schoolboys, had made a solemn compact that whoever died first should show himself to the other after death. But we are also presented with the possibility that Marriott might have imagined the whole strange episode. He has been working far too hard for his exams and neglecting his health: 'For some weeks now he had been reading as hard as mortal man can read.' Perhaps Marriott has simply flipped? A similar alternative explanation is proposed in other more recent ghost stories, for example those of William Croft Dickinson, although Dickinson always suggests, rather than spells out, a potential supernatural cause for the events.

Finally, to demonstrate that the ghosts are still with us, the contemporary crime-fiction writer Ian Rankin uses the Gothic convention of the ghost, especially in his novels *Black and Blue*, *Set in Darkness* and *The Very Last Drop*. In Rankin's works ghosts and skeletons are treated in a very modern way: as metaphors both for Detective Inspector John Rebus's guilt over his past mistakes and for Edinburgh's dark past. Rankin peppers his work with references to it: eerie settings, ghostly hauntings, the discovery of human skeletons, witchcraft and macabre crimes, and he draws parallels between modern crimes and sinister past events in the city's history.

That brings us back full-circle to the themes of sin, punishment and the related hauntings. As the Parish Minister explains in George Mackay Brown's 'The Drowned Rose': 'The earth bound soul refuses to acknowledge its death . . . It is desperately in love with the things of this world—possessions, fame, lust. How, once it has tasted them, can it ever exist without them? Death is a negation of all that wonder and delight. It will not enter the dark door of the grave. It lurks, a ghost, round the places where it fed on earthly joys. It spreads a coldness about the abodes of the living.' Sometimes the precise sin, crime or punishment is not explained, which can be more disquieting than, for example, 'The Tapestried Chamber', where the haunting has an explanation. In Muriel Spark's story, 'The Girl I Left Behind Me', we learn that a murder was committed but at the end of the narrative we are left guessing how and why.

In the words of Sacheverell Sitwell, 'We are now in the night world; the hauntings have begun.'

A.K.

Strange Letter of a Lunatic
to Mr James Hogg, of Mount Benger

James Hogg

Sir;—As you seem to have been born for the purpose of collecting all the whimsical and romantic stories of this country, I have taken the fancy of sending you an account of a most painful and unaccountable one that happened to myself, and at the same time leave you at liberty to make what use of it you please. An explanation of the circumstances from you would give me great satisfaction.

Last summer in June, I happened to be in Edinburgh, and walking very early on the Castle Hill one morning, I perceived a strange looking figure of an old man watching all my motions, as if anxious to introduce himself to me, yet still kept at the same distance. I beckoned him, on which he came waddling briskly up, and taking an elegant gold snuff-box, set with jewels, from his pocket, he offered me a pinch. I accepted of it most readily, and then without speaking a word, he took his box again, thrust it into his pocket, and went away chuckling and laughing in perfect ecstasy. He was even so overjoyed, that, in hobbling down the platform, he would leap from the ground, clap his hands on his loins, and laugh immoderately.

'The devil I am sure is in that body,' said I to myself, 'What does he mean? Let me see. I wish I may be well enough! I feel very queer since I took that snuff of his.' I stood there I do not know how long, like one who had been knocked on the head, until I thought I saw the body peering at me from a shady place in the rock. I hasted to him; but on going up, I found myself standing there. Yes, sir, myself. My own likeness in every respect. I was turned to a rigid statue at once, but the unaccountable being went down the hill convulsed with laughter.

I felt very uncomfortable all that day, and at night having adjourned from the theatre with a party to a celebrated tavern well known to you, judge of my astonishment when I saw another me sitting at the other end of the table. I was struck speechless, and began to watch this unaccountable fellow's motions, and perceived that he was doing the same with regard to me. A gentleman on his left hand, asked his name, that he might drink to their better acquaintance. 'Beatman, sir,' said the other: 'James Beatman, younger, of Drumloning, at your service; one who will never fail a friend at a cheerful glass.'

'I deny the premises, principle and proposition,' cried I, springing up and smiting the table with my closed hand. 'James Beatman, younger, of Drumloning, you cannot be. I am he. I am the *right* James Beatman, and I appeal to the parish registers, to witnesses innumerable, to—'

'Stop, stop, my dear fellow,' cried he, 'this is no place to settle a matter of such moment as that. I suppose all present are quite satisfied with regard to the premises; let us therefore drop the subject, if you please.'

'O yes, yes, drop the dispute!' resounded from every part of the table. No more was said about this strange coincidence; but I remarked, that no one present knew the gentleman, excepting those who took him for me. I heard them addressing him often regarding my family and affairs, and I really thought the fellow answered as sensibly and as much to the point as I could have done for my life, and began seriously to doubt which of us was the *right* James Beatman.

We drank long and deep, for the song and the glass went round, and the greatest hilarity prevailed; but at length the gentleman at the head of the table proposed calling the bill, at the same time remarking, that we should find it a swinging one. 'George, bring the bill, that we may see what is to pay.'

'All's paid, sir.'

'All paid? You are dreaming, George, or drunk. There has not a farthing been paid by any of us here.'

'I assure you all's paid, however, sir. And there's six of claret to come in, and three Glen-Livat.'

'Come, George, let us understand one another. Do you persist in asserting that our bill is positively paid?'

'Yes, certainly, sir.'

'By whom then?'

'By this good gentleman here,' tapping me on the shoulder.

'Oh, Mr Beatman, that's unfair! That's unfair! You have taken us at a disadvantage. But it is so like yourself!'

'Is it, gentlemen? Is it indeed so like myself? I'm sorry for it then; I'll take a bet yon rascal is the *right* James Beatman after all. For, upon the word and honour of a gentleman, I *did not* pay the bill. No, not a farthing of it.'

'Gie ower, lad, an' haud the daft tongue o' thee,' cried a countryman from the other end of the table. 'Ye hae muckle to flee intil a rage about. I think the best thing ye can do to oblige us a', will be to pouch the affront; or I sal take it aff thee head for half a mutchkin; for I ken thou wast out twice, and stayed a gay bitty while baith times. Thou'rt fou. Count thee siller, lad.'

This speech set them in a roar of laughter, and, convinced that the countryman was right, and that I, their liberal entertainer, was quite drunk, they all rose simultaneously, and wishing me a good night, left me haranguing them on the falsity of the waiter's statement.

The next morning I intended to have gone with the Stirling morning coach, but arriving a few minutes too late, I went into the office, and began abusing the book-keeper for letting the coach go off too soon. 'No, no, sir, you wrong me,' said he; 'the coach started at the very minute. But as you had not arrived, another took your place, and here is your money again.'

'The devil it is,' said I; 'why, sir, I gave you no money, therefore mine it cannot possibly be.'

'Is not your name Mr James Beatman?'

'Yes, to be sure it is. But how came you to know my name?'

'Because I have it in the coach-book here. See!—Mr James Beatman, paid *17s. 6d.;* so here it is.'

I took the money, fully convinced that I was under the power of some strange enchantment. And ever on these occasions, my mind reverted to the little crooked gentleman, and the gold snuff-box.

From the coach-office I hasted to Newhaven, to catch one of the steamboats going up the Frith; and on the quay whom should I meet face to face but my whimsical namesake and second self, Mr James Beatman. I had almost fainted, and could only falter out, 'How is this? You here again?'

'Yes, here I am,' said he, with perfect frankness; 'I lost my seat in the Stirling coach by sleeping a few minutes too long; but the lad gave me my money again, though I had quite forgot having paid it. And as I must be at Stirling to-day to meet Mr Walker, I have taken my passage in the Morning Star of Alloa, and from thence I must post it to Stirling.'

I was stupified, bamboozled, dumbfounded! And could do nothing but stand and gape, for I had lost *my* place in the coach, got *my* money again, which I never paid—had taken *my* passage in the Morning Star of Alloa, and proposed posting it to Stirling to meet Mr Walker. It must have been the devil, thought I, from whom I took the pinch on the Castle Hill, for I am either become two people, else I am *not* the *right* James Beatman.

I took my seat on one of the sofas in the elegant cabin of the Morning Star—Mr Beatman *secundus* placed himself right over against me. I looked at him—he at me. I grinned—he did the same; but I thought there was a sly leer in his eye which I could not attain, though I was conscious of having been master of it once; and just as I was considering who of us could be the *right* James Beatman, he accosted me as follows:—

'Yon was truly a clever trick you played us last night, though rather an expensive one to yourself. However, as it made me come off with flying colours, I shall take care to requite it in some way, and with interest too!'

'Do you say so?' said I; 'you are a strange wag, and I wish I could comprehend you! I suppose you will be talking of requiting me for the Stirling coach hire next.'

'Very well remembered,' cried he; 'I could not recollect of having paid that money, but I now see the trick. You are a strange wag; but here is the sum for you in full.'

'Thank you, kindly, sir! very much obliged to you indeed! Five and thirty shillings into pocket! Good! Ha! ha! ha!'

'Ha! ha! ha!' echoed he; 'and now, sir, if you will be so friendly and affable as to accept the one half of last night's bill from me, just the half, I will take it kind, and shall regard that business as settled.'

'With all my heart, sir! with all my heart, sir!' said I, 'only tell me this simple question. Do you suppose that I *am not* the right James Beatman, younger, of Drumloning? For I tell you, sir, and tremble while I do so, that *I am* the right James Beatman;' and saying so, I gave a tremendous tramp on the floor, on which the captain seized me by the shoulder behind, saying, 'Who doubts it, sir? No one I am sure can be mistaken in that. Come into the starboard chamber here, and let us have something to drink.'

I went with all my heart; but at that moment I felt my mind running on the old warlock on the Castle Hill; and I had no sooner taken my seat, than, on lifting my eyes, there was my companion sitting opposite to me, with the same confounded leer on his face as before. However, we began our potations in great good humour. Ginger beer and brandy mixed was the delicious beverage, and we swigged at it till I felt the far-famed Morning Star begin to twirl round with me like a te-totum. Thinking we were going to sink, I clambered above. All was going on well, but with a strong head-wind, and the ladies mortal sick. I felt quite dizzy, and the roll of the boat rendered it terribly difficult for me to keep my feet. The ladies began to titter and laugh at me. They were all sitting on two forms, the one row close behind the other, and looking miserably bad; and as one freedom courts another, I put my hands in the pockets of my trousers, and steadying myself right in front of them, began an address, condoling with them on their deplorable and melancholy faces, and advising them to go down below, and drink ginger beer mixed with a *leetle* brandy, and there was no fear; when unluckily, at this point of my harangue, a great roll of the vessel ruining my equipoise, threw me right across four of the ladies, who screamed horribly; and my hands being entangled in my pockets, my head top heavy, and my ears stunned with female shrieks, all that I could do I could not get up: but my efforts made matters still worse. The ladies at length, by a joint effort, tumbled me over, but it was only to throw me upon other four on the next bench, and these I fairly overset. Then there was laughing, screaming, clapping of hands, and loud hurras, all mixed together, for every person on board was above by this time. I never was so much ashamed in my life, and had no other resource, but to haste down once more to the brandy and ginger beer.

We drank on and sung until we came near the quay at Alloa. There were five of us; but I had not seen my namesake from the time we first entered, for he never molested me, unless when I was quite sober. But on calling the steward, and enquiring what was to pay, he told us all was paid for our party. The party stared at one another, and I at the steward; till a Mr Anderson asked, who had the kindness, or rather the insolence to do such a thing. The man said it was I; but I being conscious of having done no such thing, denied it with many oaths. Each of the party, however, flung down his share, which the steward obliged me to pocket. I felt myself in a strange state indeed, and quite uncertain whether I was the *right* James Beatman or not.

On going up to the Tontine, I found dinner and a chaise for Stirling ordered in my name; and, though feeling quite as if in a dream, I sat down with the rest of our boat party. But scarcely had I taken my seat, ere I was desired to speak with one in another room. There I found the captain, who received me with a grave face, and said, 'This is a very disagreeable business, Mr Beatman.'

'What is it, sir?'

'About this young lady who was on board. Her brother wants to challenge you; but I told him that you were a little intoxicated, else you were quite incapable of such a thing, and I was sure you would make any apology.'

'I will, indeed, sir. I will make any apology that shall be required; for, in truth, it was a mere accident, which I could not help, and I am truly sorry for it. I will make any apology.'

He then took me away to a genteel house out of the town, and introduced me to a most beautiful and elegant young lady, still in teens, who eyed me with a most ungracious look, and then said, 'Sir, had it not been for the dread of peril, I would have scorned an apology from such a person; but as matters stand at present, I am content to accept of one. But I must tell you, that if you had not been a coward and a poltroon, you never would have presumed to look me again in the face.'

'My dear madam,' said I, 'there is some confounded mistake here; for, on the word of a gentleman, I declare, and by the honour of manhood, I swear that I never till this moment beheld that lovely face of yours.'

The whole party uttered exclamations of astonishment and abhorrence on hearing these words, and the captain said, 'Good G—, Mr Beatman, did you not confess it to me, saying you were sorry for it, and that you were willing to make any apology?'

'Because I thought this had been one of the ladies whom I overthrew on deck,' said I, 'when yon unmannerly wave made me lose my equilibrium; but on honour and conscience, this divine creature I never saw before. And if I had, sooner than have offered her any insult, I would have cut off my right hand.'

The lady declared I was the person. Other two gentlemen did the same, and the irritated brother had me committed for a criminal assault, and carried to prison, which I liked very ill. But on being conducted off, I said, 'Gentlemen, I cannot explain this matter to you, though I understand well enough who is the aggressor. I have for the last twenty-four hours been struggling with an inextricable phenomenon—plague on the old fellow with the gold snuff-box! But I have *now* the satisfaction of knowing that *I am* the right James Beatman after all!'

There was I given over to the constables, and put under confinement till I could find bail, which detained me in Alloa till next day at noon; and ere I reached Stirling, Mr Walker had gone off to the Highlands without me, at which I was greatly vexed, as he was to have taken me with him in his gig to the braes of Glen-Orchy, where we were to have shot together. I asked the landlord when Mr Walker went away, and the former told me he only went off that day, for that he had waited four and twenty hours on a companion of his, a strange fish, who had got into a scrape with a pretty girl about Alloa, but that he came at last, and Walker and he went off together: this was a clinker. Who was I to think was the *right* James Beatman now?

I could get no conveyance for two days, and at length I reached Inverouran, where the only person I found was my namesake, who once more placed himself over against me, and still with the same malicious leer on his face. I accused him at once of the insult to the young lady, which was like to cost me so dear. He shook his head with a leering smile, and said, 'I well knew it was not he who was guilty, but myself; for saving that he was pitched headlong right upon a whole covey of ladies, when he was tipsy with ginger beer and brandy, he had never so much as seen a lady during the passage.'

'You sir,' said I. 'Do you presume to say that *you* were tipsy with ginger beer and brandy, and that *you* were pitched upon the two tiers of ladies? Then, sir, let me tell you that you are one of the most notorious impostors that ever lived. A most unaccountable and impalpable being, who has taken a fancy to personate me, and to cross and confound me in every relation of life. I will submit to this no longer, and therefore pray favour me with your proper address.' He gave me my own, on which I got into such a rage at him, that I believe I would have pistoled him on the spot, had not Mr Fletcher, the landlord, at that moment, tapped me on the shoulder, and told me that Mr Watten and Mr Walker wanted me in the next room. I followed him; but in such bad humour that my chagrin would not hide, and forthwith accused Mr Walker of leaving me behind, and bringing an impostor with him. He blamed me for such an unaccountable joke, a mistake it could not be, for I surely never would pretend to say that I did not come along with him. Mr Watten, an English gentleman, then asked me if I would likewise deny having won a bet from him at angling of five pounds. I begged his pardon, and said, I recollected of no such thing. 'Well then, to assist your memory, here is your money,' said he. I said, I would not take it, but run double or quits with him for the greatest number of birds bagged on the following day; for the real fact was, that neither trout nor bait had I taken since I left Edinburgh. Walker and he stared at one another, and began a reasoning with me, but I lost all manner of temper at their absurdity, and went away to my bed.

Never was there a human creature in such a dilemma as I now found myself. I was conscious of possessing the same body and spirit that I ever did, without any dereliction of my mental faculties. But here was another being endowed with the same personal qualifications, who looked as I looked, thought as I thought, and expressed what I would have said; and more than all seemed to be engaged in every transaction along with me, or did what I should have done and left me out. What was I next to do, for in this state I could not live? I had become, as it were, two bodies, with only one soul between them, and felt that some decisive measures behoved to be resorted to immediately, for I would much rather be out of the world than remain in it on such terms.

Overpowered by these bewildering thoughts, I fell asleep, and the whole night over dreamed about the old man and the gold snuff-box, who told me that I was now himself, and that he had transformed his own nature and spirit into my shape and form; and so strong was the impression, that when I awoke, I was quite stupid. On going out early for a mouthful of fresh air, my second was immediately by my side. I was just going to break out in a rage at this endless counterfeiting of my person, when he prevented me, by beginning first.

'I am sorry to see you looking so disturbed this morning,' said he, 'and must really entreat of you to give up this foolery. The joke is worn quite stale, I assure you. For the first day or so it did very well, and was rather puzzling; but now I cannot help pitying you, and beg that you will forthwith appear in your own character, and drop mine.'

'Sir, I have no other character to appear in,' said I. 'I was born, christened, and educated as James Beatman, younger, of Drumloning; and that designation I will maintain against all the counterfeits on earth.'

'Well, your perversity confounds me,' replied he; 'for you must be perfectly sensible that you are acting a part that is not your own. That you are either a rank counterfeit, or, what I rather begin to suspect, the devil in my likeness.'

These words overpowered me so much, that I fell a trembling, for I thought of the vision of last night, and what the old man had told me; and the thoughts of having become the devil in my own likeness, was more than my heart could brook, and I dare say I looked fearfully ill.

'O ho! old Cloots, are you caught?' cried he, jeeringly; 'well, your sublime majesty will choose to keep your distance in future, as I would rather dispense with your society.'

'Sir, I'll let you know that I am *not* the devil,' cried I, in great wrath, 'and if you dare, sir, it shall be tried this moment, and on this spot, who is the counterfeit, and who is the *right* James Beatman, you or I.'

'To-night at the sun going down, that shall be tried here, if you change not your purpose before that time,' said he. 'In the meanwhile let us hie to the moors, for our companions are out, and I have a bet of ten guineas with that Englishman.' And forthwith he hasted after the other two, and left me in dreadful perplexity, whether I was the devil or James Beatman. I followed to the moors—those dark and interminable moors of Buravurich—but not one bird could I get. They would scarcely let me come in view of them; and, moreover, my dog seemed to be in a dream as well as myself. He would do nothing but stare about him like a crazed beast, as if constantly in a state of terror. At the croak of the raven he turned up his nose, as if making a dead point at heaven, and at the yell of the eagle he took his tail between his legs and ran. I lost heart and gave up the sport, convinced that all was not right with me. How could a person shoot game while in a state of uncertainty whether he was the devil or not?

I returned to Inverouran, and at night-fall Mr Watten came in, but no more. He was no sooner seated than he began to congratulate me on my success, acknowledging that he was again fairly beat.

'And pray how do you know that I have beat you?' said I.

'Why, what means this perversity?' said he; 'did we not meet at six o'clock as agreed, and count our birds, and found that you had a brace more? You cannot have forgot that.'

'Very well, my dear sir,' said I, 'as I do not choose to give a gentleman the lie, against my own interest, I'll thank you for my money, and then I'll tell you what *I* suppose to be the truth.' He paid it. 'And now,' continued I, 'the d—l a bird did I count with you or any other person to-day, for the best of reasons, I had not one to count.'

At the setting of the sun 1 loaded my pistols and attended at the appointed place, which was in a little concealed dell near the corner of the lake. My enemy met me. We fired at six paces distance, and I fell. Rather a sure sign that I *was* the right James Beatman, but which of the I's it was that fell I never knew till this day, nor ever can.

These, sir, are all the incidents that I recollect relating to this strange adventure. When I next came a little to myself, I found myself in this lunatic asylum, with my head shaven, and my wounds dressed, and waited upon by a great, burly vulgar fellow, who refuses to open his mouth in answer to any question of mine. I have been frequently visited by my father, and by several surgeons; but they, too, preserve toward me looks of the most superb mystery, and often lay their fingers on their lips. One day I teazed my keeper so much, that he lost patience, and said, 'Whoy, sur, un you wooll knaw the treuth, you have droonken away your seven senses. That's all, so never mind.'

Now, sir, this vile hint has cut me to the heart. It is manifest that I have been in a state of derangement; but instead of having been driven to it by drinking, it has been solely caused by my wound, and by having been turned into two men, acting on various and distinct principles, yet still conscious of an idiosyncracy.—These circumstances, as they affected me, were enough to overset the mind of any one, and though to myself quite unintelligible, I send them to you, in hopes that, by publishing them, you may induce an inquiry, which may tend to the solution of this mystery that hangs over my fate.

I remain, sir, your perplexed, but very humble servant,
JAMES BEATMAN.

————•❧•————

This letter puzzled me exceedingly, and certainly I would have regarded it altogether as the dream of a lunatic, had it not been for two circumstances. These were his being left behind at Stirling, and posting the rest of the road himself; and the duel, and wound at the last. These I could not identify with the visions of a disordered imagination, if there were any proofs abiding. And having once met with Mr Walker, of Crowell, at the house of my friend Mr Stein, the distiller, I wrote to him, requesting an explanation of these circumstances, and all others relating to the unfortunate catastrophe, which came under his observation. His answer was as follows:—

————•❧•————

'SIR;—I feel that I cannot explain the circumstances relating to my young friend's misfortune to your satisfaction, and for the sake of his family who are my near relatives, I dare not tell you what I think, because these thoughts will not conform to human reason. This thing is certain, that neither Mr Watten nor I ever saw more than one person. I took him from Stirling to Inverouran on the Black Mount with me in my own gig; yet strange to say, a chaise arrived at the inn the night but one after our arrival with the same gentleman, as we supposed, who blamed me bitterly for leaving him behind. The chaise came after dark. Mr Beatman had been with us on the previous evening, and we had not seen him subsequently till he stepped out of the carriage. These are the facts, reconcile them if you can. Mr Beatman's hallucinations were first manifested that night. The landlord came into us, and said, 'I wat pe te mhotter with te prave shentleman' in te oter rhoom? Hu! she pe cot into creat pig tarnnation twarvel with her own self. She pe eiter trunk or horn mat.'

'I sent for him and he came on the instant, but looked much disturbed. On the 12th he shot as well as I ever saw him do, and was excellent company; but that night he was shot, as he affirms in a duel, and carried in dangerously wounded, in a state of utter insensibility, in which he continued for six weeks.

'This duel, is of all things I ever heard of, the most mysterious. He was seen go by himself into the little dell at the head of the loch. I myself heard the two shots, yet there was no other man there that any person knew of, and still it was quite impossible that the pistol could have been fired by his own hand. The ball had struck him on the right side of the head, leaving a considerable fracture, cut the top of his right ear, and lodged in his shoulder; so that it must either have been fired at him while in a stooping posture, or from the air straight above him. Both the pistols were found discharged, and lying very near one another. This is all that I or any mortal man know of the matter, save himself; and though he is now nearly well and quite collected, he is still perfectly incoherent about that.

'I remain, sir, yours truly,

'ALEXANDER WALKER.

'Crowell, *Nov.* 6, 1827.'

The Tapestried Chamber;
or, The Lady in The Sacque

Sir Walter Scott

THE FOLLOWING NARRATIVE is given from the pen, so far as memory permits, in the same character in which it was presented to the author's ear; nor has he claim to further praise, or to be more deeply censured, than in proportion to the good or bad judgment which he has employed in selecting his materials, as he has studiously avoided any attempt at ornament which might interfere with the simplicity of the tale.

At the same time, it must be admitted that the particular class of stories which turns on the marvellous possesses a stronger influence when told than when committed to print. The volume taken up at noonday, though rehearsing the same incidents, conveys a much more feeble impression than is achieved by the voice of the speaker on a circle of fireside auditors, who hang upon the narrative as the narrator details the minute incidents which serve to give it authenticity, and lowers his voice with an affectation of mystery while he approaches the fearful and wonderful part. It was with such advantages that the present writer heard the following events related, more than twenty years since, by the celebrated Miss Seward of Litchfield, who, to

her numerous accomplishments, added, in a remarkable degree, the power of narrative in private conversation. In its present form the tale must necessarily lose all the interest which was attached to it by the flexible voice and intelligent features of the gifted narrator. Yet still, read aloud to an undoubting audience by the doubtful light of the closing evening, or in silence by a decaying taper, and amidst the solitude of a half-lighted apartment, it may redeem its character as a good ghost story. Miss Seward always affirmed that she had derived her information from an authentic source, although she suppressed the names of the two persons chiefly concerned. I will not avail myself of any particulars I may have since received concerning the localities of the detail, but suffer them to rest under the same general description in which they were first related to me; and for the same reason I will not add to or diminish the narrative by any circumstance, whether more or less material, but simply rehearse, as I heard it, a story of supernatural terror.

About the end of the American war, when the officers of Lord Cornwallis's army, which surrendered at Yorktown, and others, who had been made prisoners during the impolitic and ill-fated controversy, were returning to their own country, to relate their adventures, and repose themselves after their fatigues, there was amongst them a general officer, to whom Miss S. gave the name of Browne, but merely, as I understood, to save the inconvenience of introducing a nameless agent in the narrative. He was an officer of merit, as well as a gentleman of high consideration for family and attainments.

Some business had carried General Browne upon a tour through the western counties, when, in the conclusion of a morning stage, he found himself in the vicinity of a small country town, which presented a scene of uncommon beauty, and of a character peculiarly English.

The little town, with its stately old church, whose tower bore testimony to the devotion of ages long past, lay amidst pastures and cornfields of small extent, but bounded and divided with hedgerow timber of great age and size. There were few marks of modern improvement. The environs of the place intimated neither the solitude of decay nor the bustle of novelty; the houses were old, but in good repair; and the beautiful little river murmured freely on its way to the left of the town, neither restrained by a dam nor bordered by a towing-path.

Upon a gentle eminence, nearly a mile to the southward of the town, were seen, amongst many venerable oaks and tangled thickets, the turrets of a castle as old as the walls of York and Lancaster, but which seemed to have received important alterations during the age of Elizabeth and her successor. It had not been a place of great size; but whatever accommodation it formerly afforded was, it must be supposed, still to be obtained within its walls. At least, such was the inference which General Browne drew from observing the smoke arise merrily from several of the ancient wreathed and carved chimney-stalks. The wall of the park ran alongside of the highway for two or three hundred yards; and through the different points by which the eye found glimpses into the woodland scenery, it seemed to be well stocked. Other points of view opened in succession—now a full one of the front of the old castle, and now a side glimpse at its particular towers, the former rich in all the bizarrerie of the Elizabethan school, while the simple and solid strength of other parts of the building seemed to show that they had been raised more for defence than ostentation.

Delighted with the partial glimpses which he obtained of the castle through the woods and glades by which this ancient feudal fortress was surrounded, our military traveller was determined to inquire whether it might not deserve a nearer view, and whether it contained family pictures or other objects of curiosity worthy of a stranger's visit, when, leaving the vicinity of the park, he rolled through a clean and well-paved street, and stopped at the door of a well-frequented inn.

Before ordering horses, to proceed on his journey, General Browne made inquiries concerning the proprietor of the chateau which had so attracted his admiration, and was equally surprised and pleased at hearing in reply a nobleman named, whom we shall call Lord Woodville. How fortunate! Much of Browne's early recollections, both at school and at college, had been connected with young Woodville, whom, by a few questions, he now ascertained to be the same with the owner of this fair domain. He had been raised to the peerage by the decease of his father a few months before, and, as the General learned from the landlord, the term of mourning being ended, was now taking possession of his paternal estate in the jovial season of merry, autumn, accompanied by a select party of friends, to enjoy the sports of a country famous for game.

This was delightful news to our traveller. Frank Woodville had been Richard Browne's fag at Eton, and his chosen intimate at Christ Church; their pleasures and their tasks had been the same; and the honest soldier's heart warmed to find his early friend in possession of so delightful a residence, and of an estate, as the landlord assured him with a nod and a wink, fully adequate to maintain and add to his dignity. Nothing was more natural than that the traveller should suspend a journey, which there was nothing to render hurried, to pay a visit to an old friend under such agreeable circumstances.

The fresh horses, therefore, had only the brief task of conveying the General's travelling carriage to Woodville Castle. A porter admitted them at a modern Gothic lodge, built in that style to correspond with the castle itself, and at the same time rang a bell to give warning of the approach of visitors. Apparently the sound of the bell had suspended the separation of the company, bent on the various amusements of the morning; for, on entering the court of the chateau, several young men were lounging about in their sporting dresses, looking at and criticizing the dogs which the keepers held in readiness to attend their pastime. As General Browne alighted, the young lord came to the gate of the hall, and for an instant gazed, as at a stranger, upon the countenance of his friend, on which war, with its fatigues and its wounds, had made a great alteration. But the uncertainty lasted no longer than till the visitor had spoken, and the hearty greeting which followed was such as can only be exchanged betwixt those who have passed together the merry days of careless boyhood or early youth.

'If I could have formed a wish, my dear Browne,' said Lord Woodville, 'it would have been to have you here, of all men, upon this occasion, which my friends are good enough to hold as a sort of holiday. Do not think you have been unwatched during the years you have been absent from us. I have traced you through your dangers, your triumphs, your misfortunes, and was delighted to see that, whether in victory or defeat, the name of my old friend was always distinguished with applause.'

The General made a suitable reply, and congratulated his friend on his new dignities, and the possession of a place and domain so beautiful.

'Nay, you have seen nothing of it as yet,' said Lord Woodville, 'and I trust you do not mean to leave us till you are better acquainted with it. It is true, I confess, that my present party is pretty large, and the old house, like other places of the kind, does not possess so much accommodation as the extent of the outward walls appears to promise. But we can give you a comfortable old-fashioned room, and I venture to suppose that your campaigns have taught you to be glad of worse quarters.'

The General shrugged his shoulders, and laughed. 'I presume,' he said, 'the worst apartment in your chateau is considerably superior to the old tobacco-cask in which I was fain to take up my night's lodging when I was in the Bush, as the Virginians call it, with the light corps. There I lay, like Diogenes himself, so delighted with my covering from the elements, that I made a vain attempt to have it rolled on to my next quarters; but my commander for the time would give way to no such luxurious provision, and I took farewell of my beloved cask with tears in my eyes.'

'Well, then, since you do not fear your quarters,' said Lord Woodville, 'you will stay with me a week at least. Of guns, dogs, fishing-rods, flies, and means of sport by sea and land, we have enough and to spare—you cannot pitch on an amusement but we will find the means of pursuing it. But if you prefer the gun and pointers, I will go with you myself, and see whether you have mended your shooting since you have been amongst the Indians of the back settlements.'

The General gladly accepted his friendly host's proposal in all its points. After a morning of manly exercise, the company met at dinner, where it was the delight of Lord Woodville to conduce to the display of the high properties of his recovered friend, so as to recommend him to his guests, most of whom were persons of distinction. He led General Browne to speak of the scenes he had witnessed; and as every word marked alike the brave officer and the sensible man, who retained possession of his cool judgment under the most imminent dangers, the company looked upon the soldier with general respect, as on one who had proved himself possessed of an uncommon portion of personal courage—that attribute of all others of which everybody desires to be thought possessed.

The day at Woodville Castle ended as usual in such mansions. The hospitality stopped within the limits of good order. Music, in which the young lord was a proficient, succeeded to the circulation of the bottle; cards and billiards, for those who preferred such amusements, were in readiness; but the exercise of the morning required early hours, and not long after eleven o'clock the guests began to retire to their several apartments.

The young lord himself conducted his friend, General Browne, to the chamber destined for him, which answered the description he had given of it, being comfortable, but old-fashioned. The bed was of the massive form used in the end of the seventeenth century, and the curtains of faded silk, heavily trimmed with tarnished gold. But then the sheets, pillows, and blankets looked delightful to the campaigner, when he thought of his 'mansion, the cask'. There was an air of gloom in the tapestry hangings, which, with their worn-out graces, curtained the walls of the little chamber, and gently undulated as the autumnal breeze found its way through the ancient lattice window, which pattered and whistled as the air gained entrance. The toilet, too, with its mirror, turbaned after the manner of the beginning of the century, with a coiffure of murrey-coloured silk, and its hundred strange-shaped boxes, providing for arrangements which had been obsolete for more than fifty years, had an antique, and in so far a melancholy, aspect. But nothing could blaze more brightly and cheerfully than the two large wax candles; or if aught could rival them, it was the flaming, bickering fagots in the chimney, that sent at once their gleam and their warmth through the snug apartment, which, notwithstanding the general antiquity of its appearance, was not wanting in the least convenience that modern habits rendered either necessary or desirable.

'This is an old-fashioned sleeping apartment, General,' said the young lord; 'but I hope you find nothing that makes you envy your old tobacco-cask.'

'I am not particular respecting my lodgings,' replied the General; 'yet were I to make any choice, I would prefer this chamber by many degrees to the gayer and more modern rooms of your family mansion. Believe me that, when I unite its modern air of comfort with its venerable antiquity, and recollect that it is your lordship's property, I shall feel in better quarters here than if I were in the best hotel London could afford.'

'I trust—I have no doubt—that you will find yourself as comfortable as I wish you, my dear General,' said the young nobleman; and once more bidding his guest good-night, he shook him by the hand, and withdrew.

The General once more looked round him, and internally congratulating himself on his return to peaceful life, the comforts of which were endeared by the recollection of the hardships and dangers he had lately sustained, undressed himself, and prepared for a luxurious night's rest.

Here, contrary to the custom of this species of tale, we leave the General in possession of his apartment until the next morning.

The company assembled for breakfast at an early hour, but without the appearance of General Browne, who seemed the guest that Lord Woodville was desirous of honouring above all whom his hospitality had assembled around him. He more than once expressed surprise at the General's absence, and at length sent a servant to make inquiry after him. The man brought back information that General Browne had been walking abroad since an early hour of the morning, in defiance of the weather, which was misty and ungenial.

'The custom of a soldier,' said the young nobleman to his friends. 'Many of them acquire habitual vigilance, and cannot sleep after the early hour at which their duty usually commands them to be alert.'

Yet the explanation which Lord Woodville thus offered to the company seemed hardly satisfactory to his own mind, and it was in a fit of silence and abstraction that he waited the return of the General. It took place near an hour after the breakfast bell had rung. He looked fatigued and feverish. His hair, the powdering and arrangement of which was at this time one of the most important occupations of a man's whole day, and marked his fashion as much as in the present time the tying of a cravat, or the want of one, was dishevelled, uncurled, void of powder, and dank with dew. His clothes were huddled on with a careless negligence, remarkable in a military man, whose real or supposed duties are usually held to include some attention to the toilet; and his looks were haggard and ghastly in a peculiar degree.

'So you have stolen a march upon us this morning, my dear General,' said Lord Woodville; 'or you have not found your bed so much to your mind as I had hoped and you seemed to expect. How did you rest last night?'

'Oh, excellently well! remarkably well! never better in my life,' said General Browne rapidly, and yet with an air of embarrassment which was obvious to his friend. He then hastily swallowed a cup of tea, and neglecting or refusing whatever else was offered, seemed to fall into a fit of abstraction.

'You will take the gun to-day, General?' said his friend and host, but had to repeat the question twice ere he received the abrupt answer, 'No, my lord; I am sorry I cannot have the opportunity of spending another day with your lordship; my post horses are ordered, and will be here directly.'

All who were present showed surprise, and Lord Woodville immediately replied 'Post horses, my good friend! What can you possibly want with them when you promised to stay with me quietly for at least a week?'

'I believe,' said the General, obviously much embarrassed, 'that I might, in the pleasure of my first meeting with your lordship, have said something about stopping here a few days; but I have since found it altogether impossible.'

'That is very extraordinary,' answered the young nobleman. 'You seemed quite disengaged yesterday, and you cannot have had a summons to-day, for our post has not come up from the town, and therefore you cannot have received any letters.'

General Browne, without giving any further explanation, muttered something about indispensable business, and insisted on the absolute necessity of his departure in a manner which silenced all opposition on the part of his host, who saw that his resolution was taken, and forbore all further importunity.

'At least, however,' he said, 'permit me, my dear Browne, since go you will or must, to show you the view from the terrace, which the mist, that is now rising, will soon display.'

He threw open a sash-window, and stepped down upon the terrace as he spoke. The General followed him mechanically, but seemed little to attend to what his host was saying, as, looking across an extended and rich prospect, he pointed out the different objects worthy of observation. Thus they moved on till Lord Woodville had attained his purpose of drawing his guest entirely apart from the rest of the company, when, turning round upon him with an air of great solemnity, he addressed him thus:—

'Richard Browne, my old and very dear friend, we are now alone. Let me conjure you to answer me upon the word of a friend, and the honour of a soldier. How did you in reality rest during last night?'

'Most wretchedly indeed, my lord,' answered the General, in the same tone of solemnity—'so miserably, that I would not run the risk of such a second night, not only for all the lands belonging to this castle, but for all the country which I see from this elevated point of view.'

'This is most extraordinary,' said the young lord, as if speaking to himself; 'then there must be something in the reports concerning that apartment.' Again turning to the General, he said, 'For God's sake, my dear friend, be candid with me, and let me know the disagreeable particulars which have befallen you under a roof, where, with consent of the owner, you should have met nothing save comfort.'

The General seemed distressed by this appeal, and paused a moment before he replied. 'My dear lord,' he at length said, 'what happened to me last night is of a nature so peculiar and so unpleasant, that I could hardly bring myself to detail it even to your lordship, were it not that, independent of my wish to gratify any request of yours, I think that sincerity on my part may lead to some explanation about a circumstance equally painful and mysterious. To others, the communication I am about to make, might place me in the light of a weak-minded, superstitious fool, who suffered his own imagination to delude and bewilder him;

but you have known me in childhood and youth, and will not suspect me of having adopted in manhood the feelings and frailties from which my early years were free.' Here he paused, and his friend replied,—

'Do not doubt my perfect confidence in the truth of your communication, however strange it may be,' replied Lord Woodville. 'I know your firmness of disposition too well, to suspect you could be made the object of imposition, and am aware that your honour and your friendship will equally deter you from exaggerating whatever you may have witnessed.'

'Well, then,' said the General, 'I will proceed with my story as well as I can, relying upon your candour, and yet distinctly feeling that I would rather face a battery than recall to my mind the odious recollections of last night.'

He paused a second time, and then perceiving that Lord Woodville remained silent and in an attitude of attention, he commenced, though not without obvious reluctance, the history of his night's adventures in the Tapestried Chamber.

'I undressed and went to bed so soon as your lordship left me yesterday evening; but the wood in the chimney, which nearly fronted my bed, blazed brightly and cheerfully, and, aided by a hundred exciting recollections of my childhood and youth, which had been recalled by the unexpected pleasure of meeting your lordship, prevented me from falling immediately asleep. I ought, however, to say that these reflections were all of a pleasant and agreeable kind, grounded on a sense of having for a time exchanged the labour, fatigues, and dangers of my profession for the enjoyments of a peaceful life, and the reunion of those friendly and affectionate ties which I had torn asunder at the rude summons of war.

'While such pleasing reflections were stealing over my mind, and gradually lulling me to slumber, I was suddenly aroused by a sound like that of the rustling of a silken gown, and the tapping of a pair of high-heeled shoes, as if a woman were walking in the apartment. Ere I could draw the curtain to see what the matter was, the figure of a little woman passed between the bed and the fire. The back of this form was turned to me, and I could observe, from the shoulders and neck, it was that of an old woman, whose dress was an old-fashioned gown, which I think ladies call a sacque—that is, a sort of robe completely loose in the body, but gathered into broad plaits upon the neck and shoulders, which fall down to the ground, and terminate in a species of train.

'I thought the intrusion singular enough, but never harboured for a moment the idea that what I saw was anything more than the mortal form of some old woman about the establishment, who had a fancy to dress like her grandmother, and who, having perhaps (as your lordship mentioned that you were rather straitened for room) been dislodged from her chamber for my accommodation, had forgotten the circumstance, and returned by twelve to her old haunt. Under this persuasion I moved myself in bed and coughed a little, to make the intruder sensible of my being in possession of the premises. She turned slowly round, but, gracious Heaven! my lord, what a countenance did she display to me! There was no longer any question what she was, or any thought of her being a living being. Upon a face which wore the fixed features of a corpse were imprinted the traces of the vilest and most hideous passions which had animated her while she lived. The body of some atrocious criminal seemed to have been given up from the grave, and the soul restored from the penal fire, in order to form for a space a union with the ancient accomplice of its guilt. I started up in bed, and sat upright, supporting myself on my palms, as I gazed on this horrible spectre. The hag made, as it seemed, a single and swift stride to the bed where I lay, and squatted herself down upon it, in precisely the same attitude which I had assumed in the extremity of horror, advancing her diabolical countenance within half a yard of mine, with a grin which seemed to intimate the malice and the derision of an incarnate fiend.'

Here General Browne stopped, and wiped from his brow the cold perspiration with which the recollection of his horrible vision had covered it.

'My lord,' he said, 'I am no coward, I have been in all the mortal dangers incidental to my profession, and I may truly boast that no man ever knew Richard Browne dishonour the sword he wears; but in these horrible circumstances, under the eyes, and, as it seemed, almost in the grasp of an incarnation of an evil spirit, all firmness forsook me, all manhood melted from me like wax in the furnace, and I felt my hair individually bristle. The current of my life-blood ceased to flow, and I sank back in a swoon, as very a victim to panic terror as ever was a village girl, or a child of ten years old. How long I lay in this condition I cannot pretend to guess.

'But I was roused by the castle clock striking one, so loud that it seemed as if it were in the very room. It was some time before I dared open my eyes, lest they should again encounter the horrible spectacle. When, however, I summoned courage to look up, she was no longer visible. My first idea was to pull my bell, wake the servants, and remove to a garret or a hay-loft, to be ensured against a second visitation. Nay, I will confess the truth that my resolution was altered, not by the shame of exposing myself, but by the fear that, as the bell-cord hung by the chimney, I might, in making my way to it, be again crossed by the fiendish hag, who, I figured to myself, might be still lurking about some corner of the apartment.

'I will not pretend to describe what hot and cold fever-fits tormented me for the rest of the night, through broken sleep, weary vigils, and that dubious state which forms the neutral ground between them. A hundred terrible objects appeared to haunt me; but there was the great difference betwixt the vision which I have described, and those which followed, that I knew the last to be deceptions of my own fancy and over-excited nerves.

'Day at last appeared, and I rose from my bed ill in health and humiliated in mind. I was ashamed of myself as a man and a soldier, and still more so at feeling my own extreme desire to escape from the haunted apartment, which, however, conquered all other considerations; so that, huddling on my clothes with the most careless haste, I made my escape from your lordship's mansion, to seek in the open air some relief to my nervous system, shaken as it was by this horrible rencounter with a visitant, for such I must believe her, from the other world. Your lordship has now heard the cause of my discomposure, and of my sudden desire to leave your hospitable castle. In other places I trust we may often meet, but God protect me from ever spending a second night under that roof!'

Strange as the General's tale was, he spoke with such a deep air of conviction that it cut short all the usual commentaries which are made on such stories. Lord Woodville never once asked him if he was sure he did not dream of the apparition, or suggested any of the possibilities by which it is fashionable to explain supernatural appearances as wild vagaries of the fancy, or deceptions of the optic nerves, On the contrary, he seemed deeply impressed with the truth and reality of what he had heard; and, after a considerable pause regretted, with much appearance of sincerity, that his early friend should in his house have suffered so severely.

'I am the more sorry for your pain, my dear Browne,' he continued, 'that it is the unhappy, though most unexpected, result of an experiment of my own. You must know that, for my father and grandfather's time, at least, the apartment which was assigned to you last night had been shut on account of reports that it was disturbed by supernatural sights and noises. When I came, a few weeks since, into possession of the estate, I thought the accommodation which the castle afforded for my friends was not extensive enough to permit the inhabitants of the invisible world to retain possession of a comfortable sleeping apartment.

I therefore caused the Tapestried Chamber, as we call it, to be opened, and, without destroying its air of antiquity, I had such new articles of furniture placed in it as became the modern times. Yet, as the opinion that the room was haunted very strongly prevailed among the domestics, and was also known in the neighbourhood and to many of my friends, I feared some prejudice might be entertained by the first occupant of the Tapestried Chamber, which might tend to revive the evil report which it had laboured under, and so disappoint my purpose of rendering it a useful part or the house. I must confess, my dear Browne, that your arrival yesterday, agreeable to me for a thousand reasons besides, seemed the most favourable opportunity of removing the unpleasant rumours which attached to the room, since your courage was indubitable, and your mind free of any preoccupation on the subject. I could not, therefore, have chosen a more fitting subject for my experiment.'

'Upon my life,' said General Browne, somewhat hastily, 'I am infinitely obliged to your lordship—very particularly indebted indeed. I am likely to remember for some time the consequences of the experiment, as your lordship is pleased to call it.'

'Nay, now you are unjust, my dear friend,' said Lord Woodville. 'You have only to reflect for a single moment, in order to be convinced that I could not augur the possibility of the pain to which you have been so unhappily exposed. I was yesterday morning a complete sceptic on the subject of supernatural appearances. Nay, I am sure that, had I told you what was said about that room, those very reports would have induced you, by your own choice, to select it for your accommodation. It was my misfortune, perhaps my error, but really cannot be termed my fault, that you have been afflicted so strangely.'

'Strangely indeed!' said the General, resuming his good temper; 'and I acknowledge that I have no right to be offended with your lordship for treating me like what I used to think myself—a man of some firmness and courage. But I see my post horses are arrived, and I must not detain your lordship from your amusement.'

'Nay, my old friend,' said Lord Woodville, 'since you cannot stay with us another day—which, indeed, I can no longer urge— give me at least half an hour more. You used to love pictures, and I have a gallery of portraits, some of them by Vandyke, representing ancestry to whom this property and castle formerly belonged. I think that several of them will strike you as possessing merit.'

General Browne accepted the invitation, though somewhat unwillingly. It was evident he was not to breathe freely or at ease till he left Woodville Castle far behind him. He could not refuse his friend's invitation, however; and the less so, that he was a little ashamed of the peevishness which he had displayed towards his well-meaning entertainer.

The General, therefore, followed Lord Woodville through several rooms into a long gallery hung with pictures, which the latter pointed out to his guest, telling the names, and giving some account of the personages whose portraits presented them-selves in progression. General Browne was but little interested in the details which these accounts conveyed to him. They were, indeed, of the kind which are usually found in an old family gallery. Here was a Cavalier who had ruined the estate in the royal cause; there a fine lady who had reinstated it by contracting a match with a wealthy Roundhead. There hung a gallant who had been in danger for corresponding with the exiled Court at Saint Germain's; here one who had taken arms for William at the Revolution; and there a third that had thrown his weight alternately into the scale of Whig and Tory.

While Lord Woodville was cramming these words into his guest's ear, 'against the stomach of his sense,' they gained the middle of the gallery, when he beheld General Browne suddenly start, and assume an attitude of the utmost surprise, not unmixed with fear, as his eyes were suddenly caught and riveted by a portrait of an old lady in a sacque, the fashionable dress of the end of the seventeenth century.

'There she is!' he exclaimed—'there she is, in form and features, though Inferior in demoniac expression to the accursed hag who visited me last night!'

'If that be the case,' said the young nobleman, 'there can remain no longer any doubt of the horrible reality of your apparition. That is the picture of a wretched ancestress of mine, of whose crimes a black and fearful catalogue is recorded in a family history in my charter-chest. The recital of them would be too horrible; it is enough to say, that in yon fatal apartment incest and unnatural murder were committed. I will restore it to the solitude to which the better judgment of those who preceded me had consigned it; and never shall any one, so long as I can prevent it, be exposed to a repetition of the supernatural horrors which could shake such courage as yours.'

Thus the friends, who had met with such glee, parted in a very different mood—Lord Woodville to command the Tapestried Chamber to be unmantled, and the door built up; and General Browne to seek in some less beautiful country, and with some less dignified friend, forgetfulness of the painful night which he had passed in Woodville Castle.

A Tale for Twilight

Anonymous

As far as I am myself concerned with the following facts, I am
fully prepared to vouch for their authenticity; but the reliance to
be placed on the other parts of the recital must be at the option
of the reader, or his conviction of their apparent truth. I am
neither over-credulous nor sceptic in matters of a superhuman
nature; I would neither implicitly confide in unsupported
assertions, nor dissent from well-attested truths; but at the same
time I must confess, that, although rather inclined to be a non-
believer, I have sometimes listened to details of supernatural
occurrences so borne out by concurring testimony as almost to
fix my wavering faith. It is now nearly thirty years since I was a
partial witness to the following circumstance at my father's
house in Edinburgh; and though, during that period, time and
foreign climates may have thinned my locks and furrowed my
brow a little, they have neither effaced one item of its details
from my memory, nor warped the vivid impression which it left
upon my recollection.

It was in the winter of 1798 the occurrence took place:
I remember the time distinctly, by the circumstance of my
father's being absent with his regiment, which had been ordered

to Ireland to reinforce the troops then engaged in quelling the insurgents, who had risen in rebellion in the summer of that year. There was an old retainer of our house who used at that time to be very frequently about us; she had nursed my younger brother and myself, and the family felt for her all the attachment due to an old and faithful inmate. Her husband had been a sergeant in the army of General Burgoyne, and was killed at the attack on Yalencia de Alcantara, in the early part of his late majesty's reign, when the British crossed the Portuguese frontier in order to check the advance of the Spaniards upon Alentejo; and perhaps this circumstance created an additional sympathy towards her in my mother's breast. I remember her appearance distinctly; her neatly plaited cap and scarlet riband, her white fringed apron and purple quilted petticoat, are all as fresh in my memory as yesterday, and though nearly sixty at the period I speak of, she retained all the activity and good-humour of sixteen. Her strength was but little impaired; and as she was but slightly affected by fatigue or watching, she was in the habit of engaging herself as a nurse-tender in numerous respectable families, who were equally prepossessed in her favour.

The winter was drawing near a close, and we were beginning to be anxious for the return of my father, who was expected home about this time, when old Nurse, as we always called her, came to tell us of an engagement she had got to attend a young gentleman who was lying dangerously ill in one of the streets of the Old Town; for at that time few of the fine palaces of the New Town had been even thought of, and many a splendid street now covers what was then green fields and waving meadows. She mentioned that a physician, who had been always very kind to her, had recommended her to this duty; but as the patient was in a most critical state, the manner of her attendance was to be very particular. She was to go every evening at eight o'clock to relieve another who remained during the day; and to be extremely cautious not to speak to the young man unless it was urgently necessary, nor make any motion which might in the slightest degree disturb the few intervals of rest which he was enabled to enjoy; but she knew neither the name nor residence of the person she was to wait on. There was something unusual in all this, and I remember perfectly well my mother desiring her to call soon and let her know how she fared. But nearly six weeks had elapsed, and we had never once seen or heard of her, when my mother at last resolved on sending to learn whether she was sick, and to say she was longing to see her again. The servant, on his return, informed us that poor Nurse had been dangerously ill, and confined to her bed almost ever since she had been with us; but she was now a little better, and had purposed coming to see us the following day.

She came accordingly; but oh, so altered in so short a time no one would have believed it! She was almost double, and could not walk without support; her flesh and cheeks were all shrunk away, and her dim lustreless eyes almost lost in their sockets. We were all startled at seeing her: it seemed that those six weeks had produced greater changes in her than years of disease in others; but our surprise at the effect was nothing, when compared to that which her recital of the cause excited when she informed us of it; and as we had never known her to tell a falsehood, we could not avoid placing implicit confidence in her words.

She told us that in the evening, according to appointment, the physician had conducted her to the residence of her charge, in one of the narrow streets near the abbey. It was one of those extensive old houses which seem built for eternity rather than time, and in the constructing of which the founder had consulted convenience and comfort more than show or situation. A flight of high stone steps brought them to the door; and a dark staircase of immense width, fenced with balustres a foot broad, and supported by railing of massy dimensions, led to the chamber of the patient. This was a lofty wainscotted room, with a window sunk a yard deep in the wall, and looking out upon what was once a garden at the rear, but now grown so wild that the weeds and rank grass almost reached the level of the wall which inclosed it. At one end stood an old-fashioned square bed, where the young gentleman lay. It was hung with faded Venetian tapestry, and seemed itself as large as a moderate-sized room. At the other end, and opposite to the foot of the bed, was a fire-place, supported by ponderous stone buttresses, but with no grate, and a few smouldering turf were merely piled on the spacious hearth. There was no door except that by which she had entered, and no other furniture than a few low chairs, and a table covered with medicines and draughts beside the window. The oak which covered the walls and formed the panels of the ceiling was as black as time could make it, and the whole apart-ment, which was kept dark at the suggestion of the physician, was so gloomy that the glimmering of the single candle in the shade of the fireplace could not penetrate it, and cast a faint gleam around, not sad, but absolutely sickening.

Whilst the doctor was speaking in a low tone to the invalid, Nurse tried to find out some farther particulars from the other attendant, who was tying on her bonnet, and preparing to muffle herself in her plaid before going away; for, as I said before, it was winter and bitterly cold. She could gain no information from her, however, although she had been in the situation for a considerable time. She could not tell the name of the gentleman; she only knew that he was an Oxford student; but no one, save herself and the doctor, had ever crossed the threshold to inquire after him, nor had she ever seen any one in the rest of the house, which she believed to be uninhabited.

The doctor and she soon went away, after leaving a few unimportant directions; Nurse closed the door behind them, and shivering with the cold frosty gust of air from the spacious lobby, hastened to her duty, wrapped her cloak about her, drew her seat close to the hearth, replenished the fire, and commenced reading a volume of Mr Alexander Peden's *Prophecies*, which she had brought in her pocket.

There was no sound to disturb her, except now and then a blast of wind which shook the withering trees in the garden below, or the 'death-watch,' which ticked incessantly in the wainscot of the room. In this manner an hour or two elapsed, when concluding, from the motionless posture of the patient, that he must be asleep, she rose, and taking the light in her hand, moved on tiptoe across the polished oaken floor, to take a survey of his features and appearance. She gently opened the curtains, and, bringing the light to bear upon him, started to find that he was still awake; she attempted to apologize for her curiosity by an awkward tender of her services, but apology and offer were equally useless; he moved neither limb nor muscle; he made not the faintest reply; he lay motionless on his back, his bright blue eyes glaring fixedly upon her, his under-lip fallen, and his mouth apart, his cheek a perfect hollow, and his long white teeth projecting fearfully from his shrunken lips, whilst his bony hand, covered with wiry sinews, was stretched upon the bed-clothes, and looked more like the claw of a bird than the fingers of a human being.

She felt rather uneasy whilst looking at him; but when a slight motion of the eyelids, which the light was too strong for, assured her he was still living, which she was half-inclined to doubt, she returned to her seat and her book by the fire. As she was directed not to disturb him, and as his medicine was only to be administered in the morning, she had but little to do, and the succeeding two hours passed heavily away; she continued, however, to lighten them by the assistance of Mr Peden, and by now and then crooning and gazing over the silent flickering progress of her turf fire, till, about midnight, as near as she could guess, the gentleman began to breathe heavily and appeared very uneasy; as, however, he spoke nothing, she thought he was perhaps asleep, and was rising to go towards him, when she was surprised to see a lady seated on a chair near the head of the bed beside him.

Though somewhat startled at this, she was by no means alarmed, and, making a curtsey, was moving on as she had intended, when the lady raised her arm, and turning the palm of her hand, which was covered with a white glove, towards her, motioned her silently to keep her seat. She accordingly sat down as before, but she now began to wonder within herself how and when this lady came in: it was true she had not been looking towards the door, and it might have been opened without her perceiving it; but then it was so cold a night and so late an hour, it was this which made it so remarkable.

She turned quietly round and took a second view of her visitor. She wore a black veil over her bonnet, and as her face was turned towards the bed of the invalid, she could not in that gloomy chamber perceive her features but she saw that the shape and turn of her head and neck were graceful and elegant in the extreme; the rest of her person she could not so well discern, as it was enveloped in a green silk gown, and the fashion at that period was not so favourable to a display of figure as now. It occurred to her that it must be some intimate female friend who had called in; but then the woman had told her that no visitors had ever come before: altogether, she could not well understand the matter, but she thought she would observe whether she went off as gently as she had entered; and for that purpose she altered the position of her chair so as to command a view of the door, and fixed herself with her book on her knees, but her eye intently set upon the lady in the green gown.

In this position she remained for a considerable time, but no alteration took place in the room; the stranger sat evidently gazing on the face of the sick gentleman, whilst he heaved and sighed and breathed in agony as if a nightmare were on him. Nurse a second time moved towards him in order to hold him up in the bed, or give him some temporary relief; and a second time the mysterious visitant motioned her to remain quiet; and unwillingly, but by a kind of fascination, she complied, and again commenced her watch. But her position was a painful one, and she sat so long and so quietly that at last her eyes closed for a moment, and when she opened them the lady was gone, the young man was once more composed, and, after taking something to relieve his breathing, he fell into a gentle sleep, from which he had not awakened when her colleague arrived in the morning to take her place, and Nurse returned to her own house about daybreak.

The following night she was again at her duty; she came rather late, and found her companion already muffled and waiting impatiently to set out. She lighted her to the stairs, and heard her close the hall-door behind her; when, on returning to the room, the wind, as she shut the door, blew out her candle. She relighted it, however, from the dying embers, roused up the fire, and resumed, as before, her seat and her volume of prophecies. The night was stormy, the dry crisp sleet hissed on the window, and the wind sighed in heavy gusts down the spacious chimney; whilst the rattling of the shutters, and the occasional clash of a door in some distant part of the house, came with a dim and hollow echo along the dreary silent passages. She did not feel so comfortable as the night before; the whistling of the wind through the trees made her flesh creep involuntarily; and sometimes the thundering clap of a distant door made her start and drop her book, with a sudden prayer for the protection of Heaven.

She was thinking within herself of giving up the engagement, and was half resolved to do so on the morrow, when all at once her ear was struck with the heavy throes and agonized breathing of her charge, and, on raising her head, she saw the same lady in the green gown seated in the same position as the night before. Well, thought she, this is unusually strange; but it immediately struck her that it *must* be some inmate of the house, for what human being could venture out in such a dreary night, and at such an hour?—but then her dress: it was neither such as one could wear in the streets on a wintry night, nor yet such as they would be likely to have on *in the house* at that hour; it was, in fact, the fashionable summer costume of the time.

She rose and made her a curtsey, and spoke to her politely, but got no reply save the waving of her hand, by which she had been silenced before. At length the agitation of the invalid was so increased that she could not reconcile it to her duty to sit still whilst a stranger was attending him. She accordingly drew nearer to the bed in spite of the repeated beckonings of the lady, who, as she advanced, drew her veil closer across her face, and retired to the table at the window. Nurse approached the bed, but was terrified on beholding the countenance of the patient: the big drops of cold sweat were rolling down his pale brow; his livid lips were quivering with agony; and, as he motioned her aside, his glaring eyes followed the retreating figure in the green gown. She soon saw that it was in vain to attempt assisting him; he impatiently repulsed every proffer of attention, and she again resumed her seat, whilst the silent visitor returned to her place by his bedside.

Rather piqued at being thus baffled in her intentions of kindness, but still putting from her the idea of a supernatural being, the old woman again determined to watch with attention the retreat of the lady, and observe whether she resided in the house or took her departure by the main door. She almost refrained from winking in order to *secure* a scrutiny of her motions; but it was all in vain; she could not remember to have taken off her glance for a moment, but still the visitant was gone. It seemed as if she had only changed her thoughts for an instant and not her eyes, but that change was enough; when she again reverted to the object of her anxiety, the mysterious lady had departed.

As on the foregoing night, her patient now became composed, and enjoyed an uninterrupted slumber till the light of morning, now reflected from heaps of dazzling snow, brought with it the female who was to relieve guard at the bed of misery.

The following morning Nurse went to the house of the physician who had engaged her, with the determination of giving up the task in which she was employed. She felt uneasy at the thoughts of retaining it, as she had never been similarly situated before; she always had some companion to speak to, or was at least employed in an inhabited house; but besides she was not by any means comfortable in the visits of the nightly stranger. She was disappointed, however, by not finding him at home, and was directed to return at a certain hour; but as she lay down to rest in the meantime, she did not awake till that hour was long past. Nothing then remained but to return for another night, and give warning of her intention on the morrow; and with a heavy discontented heart she repaired to the gloomy apartment.

The physician was already there when she arrived, and received her notice with regret; but was rather surprised when she informed him of the attentions of the strange lady, and the manner in which she had been prevented from performing her duty: he, however, treated it as a common-place occurrence, and suggested that it was some affectionate relative or friend of the patient, of whose connections he knew nothing. At last he took his leave, and Nurse arranged her chair and seated herself to watch, not merely the departure but the arrival of her fair friend. As she had not, however, appeared on the former occasions till the night was far advanced, she did not expect her sooner, and endeavoured to occupy her attention till that time by some other means.

But it was all in vain, she could only think of the one mysterious circumstance, fix her dim gaze on the blackened trellis-work of the ceiling, and start at every trifling sound, which was now doubly audible, as all without was hushed by the noiseless snow in which the streets were imbedded. Again, however, her vigilance was eluded, and as, wearied with thought, she raised her head with a long-drawn sigh and a yawn of fatigue, she encountered the green garments of her unsolicited companion. Angry with herself, and at the same time unwilling to accuse herself of remissness, she determined once again that she should not escape unnoticed. There hung a feeling of awe around her whenever she approached this singular being, and when, as before, the lady retired to another quarter of the room as she approached the bed, she had not courage to follow her. Again the same distressing scene of suffering in her unfortunate charge ensued; he gasped and heaved till the noise of his agony made her heart sicken within her; when she drew near his bed his corpse-like features were convulsed with a feeling which seemed to twist their relaxed nerves into the most fearful expression, while his ghastly eyes were straining from their sunken sockets. She spoke, but he answered not; she touched him, but he was cold with terror, and unconscious of any object save the one mysterious being whom his glance followed with awful intensity. I have often heard my mother say that Nurse was naturally a woman of very strong feelings, but here she was totally beside herself with anxiety. She thought that the young gentleman was just expiring, and was preparing to leave the room in search of farther assistance when she saw the lady again move towards the bed of the dying man; she bent above him for a moment, whilst his writhings were indescribable; she then moved towards the door. Now was the moment!

Nurse advanced at the same time, laid her one hand on the latch, whilst with the other she attempted to raise the veil of the stranger, and in the next instant fell lifeless on the floor. As she glanced on the face of the lady, she saw that a lifeless head filled the bonnet; its vacant sockets and ghastly teeth were all that could be seen beneath the folds of the veil.

Daylight was breaking the following morning when the other attendant arrived, and found the poor old woman cold and benumbed stretched upon the floor beside the passage; and when she looked upon the bed of the invalid he lay stiffened and lifeless, as if many hours had elapsed since his spirit had shaken off its mortal coil. One hand was thrown across his eyes, as if to shade them from some object on which he feared to look; and the other grasped the coverlet with convulsive firmness.

The remains of the mysterious student were interred in the old Calton burying-ground, and I remember, before the new road was made through it, to have often seen his grave; but I never could learn his name, what connection the spirit had with his story, or how he came to be in that melancholy deserted situation in Edinburgh. I have mentioned at the commencement of this narration that I will vouch for its truth as far as regards myself, and that is, merely, that I heard the poor old woman herself tell all the extraordinary circumstances as I have recited them, a very few weeks before her death, with a fearful accuracy. Be it as it may, they cost her her life, as she never recovered from the effects of the terror, and pined and wasted away to the hour of her death, which followed in about two months after the fearful occurrence. For my part I firmly believe all she told us; and though my father, who came home the spring following, used to say it was all a dream or the effects of imagination, I always saw too many concurrent circumstances attending it to permit me to think so.

Horror – A True Story

Anonymous

I WAS BUT nineteen years of age when the incident occurred which has thrown a shadow over my life; and, ah me! how many and many a weary year has dragged by since then! Young, happy, and beloved I was in those long-departed days. They said that I was beautiful. The mirror now reflects a haggard old woman, with ashen lips and face of deadly pallor. But do not fancy that you are listening to a mere puling lament. It is not the flight of years that has brought me to be this wreck of my former self: had it been so I could have borne the loss cheerfully, patiently, as the common lot of all; but it was no natural progress of decay which has robbed me of bloom, of youth, of the hopes and joys that belong to youth, snapped the link that bound my heart to another's, and doomed me to a lone old age. I try to be patient, but my cross has been heavy, and my heart is empty and weary, and I long for the death that comes so slowly to those who pray to die.

I will try and relate, exactly as it happened, the event which blighted my life. Though it occurred many years ago, there is no fear that I should have forgotten any of the minutest circumstances: they were stamped on my brain too clearly and burningly, like the brand of a red-hot iron. I see them written in the wrinkles of my brow, in the dead whiteness of my hair, which was a glossy brown once, and has known no gradual change from dark to grey, from grey to white, as with those happy ones who were the companions of my girlhood, and whose honoured age is soothed by the love of children and grandchildren. But I must not envy them. I only meant to say that the difficulty of my task has no connection with want of memory—I remember but too well. But as I take my pen my hand trembles, my head swims, the old rushing faintness and Horror comes over me again, and the well-remembered fear is upon me. Yet I will go on.

This, briefly, is my story: I was a great heiress, I believe, though I cared little for the fact; but so it was. My father had great possessions, and no son to inherit after him. His three daughters, of whom I was the youngest, were to share the broad acres among them. I have said, and truly, that I cared little for the circumstance; and, indeed, I was so rich then in health and youth and love that I felt myself quite indifferent to all else. The possession of all the treasures of earth could never have made up for what I then had—and lost, as I am about to relate. Of course, we girls knew that we were heiresses, but I do not think Lucy and Minnie were any the prouder or the happier on that account. I know I was not. Reginald did not court me for my money. Of THAT I felt assured. He proved it, Heaven be praised! when he shrank from my side after the change. Yes, in all my lonely age, I can still be thankful that he did not keep his word, as some would have done—did not clasp at the altar a hand he had learned to loathe and shudder at, because it was full of gold— much gold! At least he spared me that. And I know that I was loved, and the knowledge has kept me from going mad through many a weary day and restless night, when my hot eyeballs had not a tear to shed, and even to weep was a luxury denied me.

Our house was an old Tudor mansion. My father was very particular in keeping the smallest peculiarities of his home unaltered. Thus the many peaks and gables, the numerous turrets, and the mullioned windows with their quaint lozenge panes set in lead, remained very nearly as they had been three centuries back. Over and above the quaint melancholy of our dwelling, with the deep woods of its park and the sullen waters of the mere, our neighbourhood was thinly peopled and primitive, and the people round us were ignorant, and tenacious of ancient ideas and traditions. Thus it was a superstitious atmosphere that we children were reared in, and we heard, from our infancy, countless tales of horror, some mere fables doubtless, others legends of dark deeds of the olden time, exaggerated by credulity and the love of the marvellous. Our mother had died when we were young, and our other parent being, though a kind father, much absorbed in affairs of various kinds, as an active magistrate and landlord, there was no one to check the unwholesome stream of tradition with which our plastic minds were inundated in the company of nurses and servants. As years went on, however, the old ghostly tales partially lost their effects, and our undisciplined minds were turned more towards balls, dress, and partners, and other matters airy and trivial, more welcome to our riper age. It was at a county assembly that Reginald and I first met—met and loved. Yes, I am sure that he loved me with all his heart. It was not as deep a heart as some, I have thought in my grief and anger; but I never doubted its truth and honesty. Reginald's father and mine approved of our growing attachment; and as for myself, I know I was so happy then, that I look back upon those fleeting moments as on some delicious dream. I now come to the change. I have lingered on my childish reminiscences, my bright and happy youth, and now I must tell the rest—the blight and the sorrow.

It was Christmas, always a joyful and a hospitable time in the country, especially in such an old hall as our home, where quaint customs and frolics were much clung to, as part and parcel of the very dwelling itself. The hall was full of guests—so full, indeed, that there was great difficulty in providing sleeping accommodation for all. Several narrow and dark chambers in the turrets—mere pigeon-holes, as we irreverently called what had been thought good enough for the stately gentlemen of Elizabeth's reign—were now allotted to bachelor visitors, after having been empty for a century. All the spare rooms in the body and wings of the hall were occupied, of course; and the servants who had been brought down were lodged at the farm and at the keeper's, so great was the demand for space. At last the unexpected arrival of an elderly relative, who had been asked months before, but scarcely expected, caused great commotion. My aunts went about wringing their hands distractedly. Lady Speldhurst was a personage of some consequence; she was a distant cousin, and had been for years on cool terms with us all, on account of some fancied affront or slight when she had paid her LAST visit, about the time of my christening. She was seventy years old; she was infirm, rich, and testy; moreover, she was my godmother, though I had forgotten the fact; but it seems that though I had formed no expectations of a legacy in my favour, my aunts had done so for me. Aunt Margaret was especially eloquent on the subject. 'There isn't a room left,' she said; 'was ever anything so unfortunate! We cannot put Lady Speldhurst into the turrets, and yet where IS she to sleep? And Rosa's godmother, too! Poor, dear child, how dreadful! After all these years of estrangement, and with a hundred thousand in the funds, and no comfortable, warm room at her own unlimited disposal—and Christmas, of all times in the year!' What WAS to be done? My aunts could not resign their own chambers to Lady Speldhurst, because they had already given them up to some of the married guests. My father was the most hospitable of men, but he was rheumatic, gouty, and methodical. His sisters-in-law dared not propose to shift his quarters; and, indeed, he would have far sooner dined on prison fare than have been translated to a strange bed. The matter ended in my giving up my room. I had a strange reluctance to making the offer, which surprised myself. Was it a boding of evil to come? I cannot say. We are strangely and wonderfully made. It MAY have been. At any rate, I do not think it was any selfish unwillingness to make an old and infirm lady comfortable by a trifling sacrifice. I was perfectly healthy and strong. The weather was not cold for the time of the year. It was a dark, moist Yule—not a snowy one, though snow brooded overhead in the darkling clouds. I DID make the offer, which became me, I said with a laugh, as the youngest. My sisters laughed too, and made a jest of my evident wish to propitiate my godmother. 'She is a fairy godmother, Rosa,' said Minnie; 'and you know she was affronted at your christening, and went away muttering vengeance. Here she is coming back to see you; I hope she brings golden gifts with her.'

I thought little of Lady Speldhurst and her possible golden gifts. I cared nothing for the wonderful fortune in the funds that my aunts whispered and nodded about so mysteriously. But since then I have wondered whether, had I then showed myself peevish or obstinate—had I refused to give up my room for the expected kinswoman—it would not have altered the whole of my life? But then Lucy or Minnie would have offered in my stead, and been sacrificed—what do I say?—better that the blow should have fallen as it did than on those dear ones.

The chamber to which I removed was a dim little triangular room in the western wing, and was only to be reached by traversing the picture-gallery, or by mounting a little flight of stone stairs which led directly upward from the low-browed arch of a door that opened into the garden. There was one more room on the same landing-place, and this was a mere receptacle for broken furniture, shattered toys, and all the lumber that WILL accumulate in a country-house. The room I was to inhabit for a few nights was a tapestry-hung apartment, with faded green curtains of some costly stuff, contrasting oddly with a new carpet and the bright, fresh hangings of the bed, which had been hurriedly erected. The furniture was half old, half new; and on the dressing-table stood a very quaint oval mirror, in a frame of black wood—unpolished ebony, I think. I can remember the very pattern of the carpet, the number of chairs, the situation of the bed, the figures on the tapestry. Nay, I can recollect not only the colour of the dress I wore on that fated evening, but the arrangement of every scrap of lace and ribbon, of every flower, every jewel, with a memory but too perfect.

Scarcely had my maid finished spreading out my various articles of attire for the evening (when there was to be a great dinner-party) when the rumble of a carriage announced that Lady Speldhurst had arrived. The short winter's day drew to a close, and a large number of guests were gathered together in the ample drawing-room, around the blaze of the wood-fire, after dinner. My father, I recollect, was not with us at first. There were some squires of the old, hard-riding, hard-drinking stamp still lingering over their port in the dining-room, and the host, of course, could not leave them. But the ladies and all the younger gentlemen—both those who slept under our roof, and those who would have a dozen miles of fog and mire to encounter on their road home—were all together. Need I say that Reginald was there? He sat near me—my accepted lover, my plighted future husband. We were to be married in the spring. My sisters were not far off; they, too, had found eyes that sparkled and softened in meeting theirs, had found hearts that beat responsive to their own. And, in their cases, no rude frost nipped the blossom ere it became the fruit; there was no canker in their flowerets of young hope, no cloud in their sky. Innocent and loving, they were beloved by men worthy of their esteem.

The room—a large and lofty one, with an arched roof—had somewhat of a sombre character, from being wainscoted and ceiled with polished black oak of a great age. There were mirrors, and there were pictures on the walls, and handsome furniture, and marble chimney-pieces, and a gay Tournay carpet; but these merely appeared as bright spots on the dark background of the Elizabethan woodwork. Many lights were burning, but the blackness of the walls and roof seemed absolutely to swallow up their rays, like the mouth of a cavern. A hundred candles could not have given that apartment the cheerful lightness of a modern drawing room. But the gloomy richness of the panels matched well with the ruddy gleam from the enormous wood-fire, in which, crackling and glowing, now lay the mighty Yule log. Quite a blood-red lustre poured forth from the fire, and quivered on the walls and the groined roof. We had gathered round the vast antique hearth in a wide circle. The quivering light of the fire and candles fell upon us all, but not equally, for some were in shadow. I remember still how tall and manly and handsome Reginald looked that night, taller by the head than any there, and full of high spirits and gayety. I, too, was in the highest spirits; never had my bosom felt lighter, and I believe it was my mirth that gradually gained the rest, for I recollect what a blithe, joyous company we seemed. All save one. Lady Speldhurst, dressed in grey silk and wearing a quaint head-dress, sat in her armchair, facing the fire, very silent, with her hands and her sharp chin propped on a sort of ivory-handled crutch that she walked with (for she was lame), peering at me with half-shut eyes. She was a little, spare old woman, with very keen, delicate features of the French type. Her grey silk dress, her spotless lace, old-fashioned jewels, and prim neatness of array, were well suited to the intelligence of her face, with its thin lips, and eyes of a piercing black, undimmed by age. Those eyes made me uncomfortable, in spite of my gayety, as they followed my every movement with curious scrutiny. Still I was very merry and gay; my sisters even wondered at my ever-ready mirth, which was almost wild in its excess. I have heard since then of the Scottish belief that those doomed to some great calamity become fey, and are never so disposed for merriment and laughter as just before the blow falls. If ever mortal was fey, then I was so on that evening.

Still, though I strove to shake it off, the pertinacious observation of old Lady Speldhurst's eyes DID make an impression on me of a vaguely disagreeable nature. Others, too, noticed her scrutiny of me, but set it down as a mere eccentricity of a person always reputed whimsical, to say the least of it.

However, this disagreeable sensation lasted but a few moments. After a short pause my aunt took her part in the conversation, and we found ourselves listening to a weird legend, which the old lady told exceedingly well. One tale led to another. Everyone was called on in turn to contribute to the public entertainment, and story after story, always relating to demonology and witchcraft, succeeded. It was Christmas, the season for such tales; and the old room, with its dusky walls and pictures, and vaulted roof, drinking up the light so greedily, seemed just fitted to give effect to such legendary lore. The huge logs crackled and burned with glowing warmth; the blood-red glare of the Yule log flashed on the faces of the listeners and narrator, on the portraits, and the holly wreathed about their frames, and the upright old dame, in her antiquated dress and trinkets, like one of the originals of the pictures, stepped from the canvas to join our circle. It threw a shimmering lustre of an ominously ruddy hue upon the oaken panels. No wonder that the ghost and goblin stories had a new zest. No wonder that the blood of the more timid grew chill and curdled, that their flesh crept, that their hearts beat irregularly, and the girls peeped fearfully over their shoulders, and huddled close together like frightened sheep, and half fancied they beheld some impish and malignant face gibbering at them from the darkling corners of the old room. By degrees my high spirits died out, and I felt the childish tremors, long latent, long forgotten, coming over me. I followed each story with painful interest; I did not ask myself if I believed the dismal tales. I listened, and fear grew upon me— the blind, irrational fear of our nursery days. I am sure most of the other ladies present, young or middle-aged, were affected by the circumstances under which these traditions were heard, no less than by the wild and fantastic character of them. But with them the impression would die out next morning, when the bright sun should shine on the frosted boughs, and the rime on the grass, and the scarlet berries and green spikelets of the holly; and with me— but, ah! what was to happen ere another day dawn? Before we had made an end of this talk my father and the other squires came in, and we ceased our ghost stories, ashamed to speak of such matters before these new-comers—hard-headed, unimaginative men, who had no sympathy with idle legends. There was now a stir and bustle.

Servants were handing round tea and coffee, and other refreshments. Then there was a little music and singing. I sang a duet with Reginald, who had a fine voice and good musical skill. I remember that my singing was much praised, and indeed I was surprised at the power and pathos of my own voice, doubtless due to my excited nerves and mind. Then I heard someone say to another that I was by far the cleverest of the Squire's daughters, as well as the prettiest. It did not make me vain. I had no rivalry with Lucy and Minnie. But Reginald whispered some soft, fond words in my ear a little before he mounted his horse to set off homeward, which DID make me happy and proud. And to think that the next time we met—but I forgave him long ago. Poor Reginald! And now shawls and cloaks were in request, and carriages rolled up to the porch, and the guests gradually departed. At last no one was left but those visitors staying in the house. Then my father, who had been called out to speak with the bailiff of the estate, came back with a look of annoyance on his face.

'A strange story I have just been told,' said he; 'here has been my bailiff to inform me of the loss of four of the choicest ewes out of that little flock of Southdowns I set such store by, and which arrived in the north but two months since. And the poor creatures have been destroyed in so strange a manner, for their carcasses are horribly mangled.'

Most of us uttered some expression of pity or surprise, and some suggested that a vicious dog was probably the culprit.

'It would seem so,' said my father; 'it certainly seems the work of a dog; and yet all the men agree that no dog of such habits exists near us, where, indeed, dogs are scarce, excepting the shepherds' collies and the sporting dogs secured in yards. Yet the sheep are gnawed and bitten, for they show the marks of teeth. Something has done this, and has torn their bodies wolfishly; but apparently it has been only to suck the blood, for little or no flesh is gone.'

'How strange!' cried several voices. Then some of the gentlemen remembered to have heard of cases when dogs addicted to sheep-killing had destroyed whole flocks, as if in sheer wantonness, scarcely deigning to taste a morsel of each slain wether.

My father shook his head. 'I have heard of such cases, too,' he said; 'but in this instance I am tempted to think the malice of some unknown enemy has been at work. The teeth of a dog have been busy, no doubt, but the poor sheep have been mutilated in a fantastic manner, as strange as horrible; their hearts, in especial, have been torn out, and left at some paces off, half-gnawed. Also, the men persist that they found the print of a naked human foot in the soft mud of the ditch, and near it—this.' And he held up what seemed a broken link of a rusted iron chain.

Many were the ejaculations of wonder and alarm, and many and shrewd the conjectures, but none seemed exactly to suit the bearings of the case. And when my father went on to say that two lambs of the same valuable breed had perished in the same singular manner three days previously, and that they also were found mangled and gore-stained, the amazement reached a higher pitch. Old Lady Speldhurst listened with calm, intelligent attention, but joined in none of our exclamations. At length she said to my father, 'Try and recollect—have you no enemy among your neighbours?' My father started, and knit his brows. 'Not one that I know of,' he replied; and indeed he was a popular man and a kind landlord. 'The more lucky you,' said the old dame, with one of her grim smiles. It was now late, and we retired to rest before long. One by one the guests dropped off. I was the member of the family selected to escort old Lady Speldhurst to her room—the room I had vacated in her favour. I did not much like the office. I felt a remarkable repugnance to my godmother, but my worthy aunts insisted so much that I should ingratiate myself with one who had so much to leave that I could not but comply. The visitor hobbled up the broad oaken stairs actively enough, propped on my arm and her ivory crutch. The room never had looked more genial and pretty, with its brisk fire, modern furniture, and the gay French paper on the walls. 'A nice room, my dear, and I ought to be much obliged to you for it, since my maid tells me it is yours,' said her ladyship; 'but I am pretty sure you repent your generosity to me, after all those ghost stories, and tremble to think of a strange bed and chamber, eh?' I made some commonplace reply. The old lady arched her eyebrows. 'Where have they put you, child?' she asked; 'in some cock-loft of the turrets, eh? or in a lumber-room—a regular ghost-trap? I can hear your heart beating with fear this moment. You are not fit to be alone.' I tried to call up my pride, and laugh off the accusation against my courage, all the more, perhaps, because I felt its truth. 'Do you want anything more that I can get you, Lady Speldhurst?' I asked, trying to feign a yawn of sleepiness. The old dame's keen eyes were upon me. 'I rather like you, my dear,' she said, 'and I liked your mamma well enough before she treated me so shamefully about the christening dinner. Now, I know you are frightened and fearful, and if an owl should but flap your window to-night, it might drive you into fits. There is a nice little sofa-bed in this dressing closet—call your maid to arrange it for you, and you can sleep there snugly, under the old witch's protection, and then no goblin dare harm you, and nobody will be a bit the wiser, or quiz you for being afraid.' How little I knew what hung in the balance of my refusal or acceptance of that trivial proffer! Had the veil of the future been lifted for one instant! but that veil is impenetrable to our gaze.

I left her door. As I crossed the landing a bright gleam came from another room, whose door was left ajar; it (the light) fell like a bar of golden sheen across my path. As I approached the door opened and my sister Lucy, who had been watching for me, came out. She was already in a white cashmere wrapper, over which her loosened hair hung darkly and heavily, like tangles of silk. 'Rosa, love,' she whispered, 'Minnie and I can't bear the idea of your sleeping out there, all alone, in that solitary room— the very room too Nurse Sherrard used to talk about! So, as you know Minnie has given up her room, and come to sleep in mine, still we should so wish you to stop with us to-night at any rate, and I could make up a bed on the sofa for myself or you—and—' I stopped Lucy's mouth with a kiss. I declined her offer. I would not listen to it. In fact, my pride was up in arms, and I felt I would rather pass the night in the churchyard itself than accept a proposal dictated, I felt sure, by the notion that my nerves were shaken by the ghostly lore we had been raking up, that I was a weak, superstitious creature, unable to pass a night in a strange chamber. So I would not listen to Lucy, but kissed her, bade her good-night, and went on my way laughing, to show my light heart. Yet, as I looked back in the dark corridor, and saw the friendly door still ajar, the yellow bar of light still crossing from wall to wall, the sweet, kind face still peering after me from amidst its clustering curls, I felt a thrill of sympathy, a wish to return, a yearning after human love and companionship. False shame was strongest, and conquered. I waved a gay adieu. I turned the corner, and peeping over my shoulder, I saw the door close; the bar of yellow light was there no longer in the darkness of the passage. I thought at that instant that I heard a heavy sigh. I looked sharply round. No one was there. No door was open, yet I fancied, and fancied with a wonderful vividness, that I did hear an actual sigh breathed not far off, and plainly distinguishable from the groan of the sycamore branches as the wind tossed them to and fro in the outer blackness. If ever a mortal's good angel had cause to sigh for sorrow, not sin, mine had cause to mourn that night. But imagination plays us strange tricks and my nervous system was not over-composed or very fitted for judicial analysis. I had to go through the picture-gallery. I had never entered this apartment by candle-light before and I was struck by the gloomy array of the tall portraits, gazing moodily from the canvas on the lozenge-paned or painted windows, which rattled to the blast as it swept howling by. Many of the faces looked stern, and very different from their daylight expression. In others a furtive, flickering smile seemed to mock me as my candle illumined them; and in all, the eyes, as usual with artistic portraits, seemed to follow my motions with a scrutiny and an interest the more marked for the apathetic immovability of the other features. I felt ill at ease under this stony gaze, though conscious how absurd were my apprehensions; and I called up a smile and an air of mirth, more as if acting a part under the eyes of human beings than of their mere shadows on the wall. I even laughed as I confronted them. No echo had my short-lived laughter but from the hollow armour and arching roof, and I continued on my way in silence.

By a sudden and not uncommon revulsion of feeling I shook off my aimless terrors, blushed at my weakness, and sought my chamber only too glad that I had been the only witness of my late tremors. As I entered my chamber I thought I heard something stir in the neglected lumber-room, which was the only neighbouring apartment. But I was determined to have no more panics, and resolutely shut my eyes to this slight and transient noise, which had nothing unnatural in it; for surely, between rats and wind, an old manor- house on a stormy night needs no sprites to disturb it. So I entered my room, and rang for my maid. As I did so I looked around me, and a most unaccountable repugnance to my temporary abode came over me, in spite of my efforts. It was no more to be shaken off than a chill is to be shaken off when we enter some damp cave. And, rely upon it, the feeling of dislike and apprehension with which we regard, at first sight, certain places and people, was not implanted in us without some wholesome purpose. I grant it is irrational—mere animal instinct—but is not instinct God's gift, and is it for us to despise it? It is by instinct that children know their friends from their enemies—that they distinguish with such unerring accuracy between those who like them and those who only flatter and hate them. Dogs do the same; they will fawn on one person, they slink snarling from another. Show me a man whom children and dogs shrink from, and I will show you a false, bad man—lies on his lips, and murder at his heart. No; let none despise the heaven-sent gift of innate antipathy, which makes the horse quail when the lion crouches in the thicket—which makes the cattle scent the shambles from afar, and low in terror and disgust as their nostrils snuff the blood-polluted air. I felt this antipathy strongly as I looked around me in my new sleeping-room, and yet I could find no reasonable pretext for my dislike. A very good room it was, after all, now that the green damask curtains were drawn, the fire burning bright and clear, candles burning on the mantel-piece, and the various familiar articles of toilet arranged as usual. The bed, too, looked peaceful and inviting—a pretty little white bed, not at all the gaunt funereal sort of couch which haunted apartments generally contain.

My maid entered, and assisted me to lay aside the dress and ornaments I had worn, and arranged my hair, as usual, prattling the while, in Abigail fashion. I seldom cared to converse with servants; but on that night a sort of dread of being left alone—a longing to keep some human being near me possessed me—and I encouraged the girl to gossip, so that her duties took her half an hour longer to get through than usual. At last, however, she had done all that could be done, and all my questions were answered, and my orders for the morrow reiterated and vowed obedience to, and the clock on the turret struck one. Then Mary, yawning a little, asked if I wanted anything more, and I was obliged to answer no, for very shame's sake; and she went. The shutting of the door, gently as it was closed, affected me unpleasantly. I took a dislike to the curtains, the tapestry, the dingy pictures— everything. I hated the room. I felt a temptation to put on a cloak, run, half-dressed, to my sisters' chamber, and say I had changed my mind and come for shelter. But they must be asleep, I thought, and I could not be so unkind as to wake them. I said my prayers with unusual earnestness and a heavy heart. I extinguished the candles, and was just about to lay my head on my pillow, when the idea seized me that I would fasten the door. The candles were extinguished, but the firelight was amply sufficient to guide me. I gained the door. There was a lock, but it was rusty or hampered; my utmost strength could not turn the key. The bolt was broken and worthless. Balked of my intention, I consoled myself by remembering that I had never had need of fastenings yet, and returned to my bed. I lay awake for a good while, watching the red glow of the burning coals in the grate. I was quiet now, and more composed. Even the light gossip of the maid, full of petty human cares and joys, had done me good— diverted my thoughts from brooding. I was on the point of dropping asleep, when I was twice disturbed. Once, by an owl, hooting in the ivy outside—no unaccustomed sound, but harsh and melancholy; once, by a long and mournful howling set up by the mastiff, chained in the yard beyond the wing I occupied. A long-drawn, lugubrious howling was this latter, and much such a note as the vulgar declare to herald a death in the family. This was a fancy I had never shared; but yet I could not help feeling that the dog's mournful moans were sad, and expressive of terror, not at all like his fierce, honest bark of anger, but rather as if something evil and unwonted were abroad. But soon I fell asleep.

How long I slept I never knew. I awoke at once with that abrupt start which we all know well, and which carries us in a second from utter unconsciousness to the full use of our faculties. The fire was still burning, but was very low, and half the room or more was in deep shadow. I knew, I felt, that some person or thing was in the room, although nothing unusual was to be seen by the feeble light. Yet it was a sense of danger that had aroused me from slumber. I experienced, while yet asleep, the chill and shock of sudden alarm, and I knew, even in the act of throwing off sleep like a mantle, WHY I awoke, and that some intruder was present. Yet, though I listened intently, no sound was audible, except the faint murmur of the fire—the dropping of a cinder from the bars—the loud, irregular beatings of my own heart. Notwithstanding this silence, by some intuition I knew that I had not been deceived by a dream, and felt certain that I was not alone. I waited. My heart beat on; quicker, more sudden grew its pulsations, as a bird in a cage might flutter in presence of the hawk. And then I heard a sound, faint, but quite distinct, the clank of iron, the rattling of a chain! I ventured to lift my head from the pillow. Dim and uncertain as the light was, I saw the curtains of my bed shake, and caught a glimpse of something beyond, a darker spot in the darkness. This confirmation of my fears did not surprise me so much as it shocked me. I strove to cry aloud, but could not utter a word. The chain rattled again, and this time the noise was louder and clearer. But though I strained my eyes, they could not penetrate the obscurity that shrouded the other end of the chamber whence came the sullen clanking. In a moment several distinct trains of thought, like many-colored strands of thread twining into one, became palpable to my mental vision. Was it a robber? Could it be a supernatural visitant? Or was I the victim of a cruel trick, such as I had heard of, and which some thoughtless persons love to practice on the timid, reckless of its dangerous results? And then a new idea, with some ray of comfort in it, suggested itself. There was a fine young dog of the Newfoundland breed, a favourite of my father's, which was usually chained by night in an outhouse. Neptune might have broken loose, found his way to my room, and, finding the door imperfectly closed, have pushed it open and entered. I breathed more freely as this harmless interpretation of the noise forced itself upon me. It was—it must be—the dog, and I was distressing myself uselessly. I resolved to call to him; I strove to utter his name—'Neptune, Neptune,' but a secret apprehension restrained me, and I was mute.

Then the chain clanked nearer and nearer to the bed, and presently I saw a dusky, shapeless mass appear between the curtains on the opposite side to where I was lying. How I longed to hear the whine of the poor animal that I hoped might be the cause of my alarm. But no; I heard no sound save the rustle of the curtains and the clash of the iron chains. Just then the dying flame of the fire leaped up, and with one sweeping, hurried glance I saw that the door was shut, and, horror! it is not the dog! it is the semblance of a human form that now throws itself heavily on the bed, outside the clothes, and lies there, huge and swart, in the red gleam that treacherously died away after showing so much to affright, and sinks into dull darkness. There was now no light left, though the red cinders yet glowed with a ruddy gleam like the eyes of wild beasts. The chain rattled no more. I tried to speak, to scream wildly for help; my mouth was parched, my tongue refused to obey. I could not utter a cry, and, indeed, who could have heard me, alone as I was in that solitary chamber, with no living neighbour, and the picture-gallery between me and any aid that even the loudest, most piercing shriek could summon. And the storm that howled without would have drowned my voice, even if help had been at hand. To call aloud—to demand who was there—alas! how useless, how perilous! If the intruder were a robber, my outcries would but goad him to fury; but what robber would act thus? As for a trick, that seemed impossible. And yet, WHAT lay by my side, now wholly unseen? I strove to pray aloud as there rushed on my memory a flood of weird legends—the dreaded yet fascinating lore of my childhood. I had heard and read of the spirits of the wicked men forced to revisit the scenes of their earthly crimes—of demons that lurked in certain accursed spots—of the ghoul and vampire of the east, stealing amidst the graves they rifled for their ghostly banquets; and then I shuddered as I gazed on the blank darkness where I knew it lay. It stirred—it moaned hoarsely; and again I heard the chain clank close beside me—so close that it must almost have touched me. I drew myself from it, shrinking away in loathing and terror of the evil thing—what, I knew not, but felt that something malignant was near.

And yet, in the extremity of my fear, I dared not speak; I was strangely cautious to be silent, even in moving farther off; for I had a wild hope that it—the phantom, the creature, whichever it was—had not discovered my presence in the room. And then I remembered all the events of the night—Lady Speldhurst's ill-omened vaticinations, her half-warnings, her singular look as we parted, my sister's persuasions, my terror in the gallery, the remark that 'this was the room nurse Sherrard used to talk of'. And then memory, stimulated by fear, recalled the long-forgotten past, the ill-repute of this disused chamber, the sins it had witnessed, the blood spilled, the poison administered by unnatural hate within its walls, and the tradition which called it haunted. The green room—I remembered now how fearfully the servants avoided it—how it was mentioned rarely, and in whispers, when we were children, and how we had regarded it as a mysterious region, unfit for mortal habitation. Was It—the dark form with the chain—a creature of this world, or a spectre? And again—more dreadful still—could it be that the corpses of wicked men were forced to rise and haunt in the body the places where they had wrought their evil deeds? And was such as these my grisly neighbour? The chain faintly rattled. My hair bristled; my eyeballs seemed starting from their sockets; the damps of a great anguish were on my brow. My heart laboured as if I were crushed beneath some vast weight. Sometimes it appeared to stop its frenzied beatings, sometimes its pulsations were fierce and hurried; my breath came short and with extreme difficulty, and I shivered as if with cold; yet I feared to stir. IT moved, it moaned, its fetters clanked dismally, the couch creaked and shook. This was no phantom, then—no air-drawn spectre. But its very solidity, its palpable presence, were a thousand times more terrible. I felt that I was in the very grasp of what could not only affright but harm; of something whose contact sickened the soul with deathly fear. I made a desperate resolve: I glided from the bed, I seized a warm wrapper, threw it around me, and tried to grope, with extended hands, my way to the door. My heart beat high at the hope of escape. But I had scarcely taken one step before the moaning was renewed—it changed into a threatening growl that would have suited a wolf's throat, and a hand clutched at my sleeve. I stood motionless. The muttering growl sank to a moan again, the chain sounded no more, but still the hand held its grip of my garment, and I feared to move. It knew of my presence, then. My brain reeled, the blood boiled in my ears, and my knees lost all strength, while my heart panted like that of a deer in the wolf's jaws. I sank back, and the benumbing influence of excessive terror reduced me to a state of stupor.

When my full consciousness returned I was sitting on the edge of the bed, shivering with cold, and barefooted. All was silent, but I felt that my sleeve was still clutched by my unearthly visitant. The silence lasted a long time. Then followed a chuckling laugh that froze my very marrow, and the gnashing of teeth as in demoniac frenzy; and then a wailing moan, and this was succeeded by silence. Hours may have passed—nay, though the tumult of my own heart prevented my hearing the clock strike, must have passed—but they seemed ages to me. And how were they passed? Hideous visions passed before the aching eyes that I dared not close, but which gazed ever into the dumb darkness where It lay—my dread companion through the watches of the night. I pictured It in every abhorrent form which an excited fancy could summon up: now as a skeleton; with hollow eye-holes and grinning, fleshless jaws; now as a vampire, with livid face and bloated form, and dripping mouth wet with blood. Would it never be light! And yet, when day should dawn I should be forced to see It face to face. I had heard that spectre and fiend were compelled to fade as morning brightened, but this creature was too real, too foul a thing of earth, to vanish at cock-crow. No! I should see it—the Horror—face to face! And then the cold prevailed, and my teeth chattered, and shiverings ran through me, and yet there was the damp of agony on my bursting brow. Some instinct made me snatch at a shawl or cloak that lay on a chair within reach, and wrap it round me. The moan was renewed, and the chain just stirred. Then I sank into apathy, like an Indian at the stake, in the intervals of torture. Hours fled by, and I remained like a statue of ice, rigid and mute. I even slept, for I remember that I started to find the cold grey light of an early winter's day was on my face, and stealing around the room from between the heavy curtains of the window.

Shuddering, but urged by the impulse that rivets the gaze of the bird upon the snake, I turned to see the Horror of the night. Yes, it was no fevered dream, no hallucination of sickness, no airy phantom unable to face the dawn. In the sickly light I saw it lying on the bed, with its grim head on the pillow. A man? Or a corpse arisen from its unhallowed grave, and awaiting the demon that animated it? There it lay—a gaunt, gigantic form, wasted to a skeleton, half-clad, foul with dust and clotted gore, its huge limbs flung upon the couch as if at random, its shaggy hair streaming over the pillows like a lion's mane. His face was toward me. Oh, the wild hideousness of that face, even in sleep! In features it was human, even through its horrid mask of mud and half-dried bloody gouts, but the expression was brutish and savagely fierce; the white teeth were visible between the parted lips, in a malignant grin; the tangled hair and beard were mixed in leonine confusion, and there were scars disfiguring the brow.

Round the creature's waist was a ring of iron, to which was attached a heavy but broken chain—the chain I had heard clanking. With a second glance I noted that part of the chain was wrapped in straw to prevent its galling the wearer. The creature —I cannot call it a man—had the marks of fetters on its wrists, the bony arm that protruded through one tattered sleeve was scarred and bruised; the feet were bare, and lacerated by pebbles and briers, and one of them was wounded, and wrapped in a morsel of rag. And the lean hands, one of which held my sleeve, were armed with talons like an eagle's. In an instant the horrid truth flashed upon me—I was in the grasp of a madman. Better the phantom that scares the sight than the wild beast that rends and tears the quivering flesh—the pitiless human brute that has no heart to be softened, no reason at whose bar to plead, no compassion, naught of man save the form and the cunning. I gasped in terror. Ah! the mystery of those ensanguined fingers, those gory, wolfish jaws! that face, all besmeared with blackening blood, is revealed!

The slain sheep, so mangled and rent—the fantastic butchery—the print of the naked foot—all, all were explained; and the chain, the broken link of which was found near the slaughtered animals—it came from his broken chain—the chain he had snapped, doubtless, in his escape from the asylum where his raging frenzy had been fettered and bound, in vain! in vain! Ah me! how had this grisly Samson broken manacles and prison bars—how had he eluded guardian and keeper and a hostile world, and come hither on his wild way, hunted like a beast of prey, and snatching his hideous banquet like a beast of prey, too! Yes, through the tatters of his mean and ragged garb I could see the marks of the seventies, cruel and foolish, with which men in that time tried to tame the might of madness. The scourge—its marks were there; and the scars of the hard iron fetters, and many a cicatrice and welt, that told a dismal tale of hard usage. But now he was loose, free to play the brute—

the baited, tortured brute that they had made him—now without the cage, and ready to gloat over the victims his strength should overpower. Horror! horror! I was the prey—the victim—already in the tiger's clutch; and a deadly sickness came over me, and the iron entered into my soul, and I longed to scream, and was dumb! I died a thousand deaths as that morning wore on. I DARED NOT faint. But words cannot paint what I suffered as I waited—waited till the moment when he should open his eyes and be aware of my presence; for I was assured he knew it not. He had entered the chamber as a lair, when weary and gorged with his horrid orgy; and he had flung himself down to sleep without a suspicion that he was not alone. Even his grasping my sleeve was doubtless an act done betwixt sleeping and waking, like his unconscious moans and laughter, in some frightful dream.

Hours went on; then I trembled as I thought that soon the house would be astir, that my maid would come to call me as usual, and awake that ghastly sleeper. And might he not have time to tear me, as he tore the sheep, before any aid could arrive? At last what I dreaded came to pass—a light footstep on the landing—there is a tap at the door. A pause succeeds, and then the tapping is renewed, and this time more loudly. Then the madman stretched his limbs, and uttered his moaning cry, and his eyes slowly opened—very slowly opened and met mine. The girl waited a while ere she knocked for the third time. I trembled lest she should open the door unbidden—see that grim thing, and bring about the worst.

I saw the wondering surprise in his haggard, bloodshot eyes; I saw him stare at me half vacantly, then with a crafty yet wondering look; and then I saw the devil of murder begin to peep forth from those hideous eyes, and the lips to part as in a sneer, and the wolfish teeth to bare themselves. But I was not what I had been. Fear gave me a new and a desperate composure—a courage foreign to my nature. I had heard of the best method of managing the insane; I could but try; I DID try.

Calmly, wondering at my own feigned calm, I fronted the glare of those terrible eyes. Steady and undaunted was my gaze— motionless my attitude. I marvelled at myself, but in that agony of sickening terror I was OUTWARDLY firm. They sink, they quail, abashed, those dreadful eyes, before the gaze of a helpless girl; and the shame that is never absent from insanity bears down the pride of strength, the bloody cravings of the wild beast. The lunatic moaned and drooped his shaggy head between his gaunt, squalid hands.

I lost not an instant. I rose, and with one spring reached the door, tore it open, and, with a shriek, rushed through, caught the wondering girl by the arm, and crying to her to run for her life, rushed like the wind along the gallery, down the corridor, down the stairs. Mary's screams filled the house as she fled beside me. I heard a long-drawn, raging cry, the roar of a wild animal mocked of its prey, and I knew what was behind me. I never turned my head—I flew rather than ran. I was in the hall already; there was a rush of many feet, an outcry of many voices, a sound of scuffling feet, and brutal yells, and oaths, and heavy blows, and I fell to the ground crying, 'Save me!' and lay in a swoon. I awoke from a delirious trance. Kind faces were around my bed, loving looks were bent on me by all, by my dear father and dear sisters; but I scarcely saw them before I swooned again.

When I recovered from that long illness, through which I had been nursed so tenderly, the pitying looks I met made me tremble. I asked for a looking-glass. It was long denied me, but my importunity prevailed at last—a mirror was brought. My youth was gone at one fell swoop. The glass showed me a livid and haggard face, blanched and bloodless as of one who sees a spectre; and in the ashen lips, and wrinkled brow, and dim eyes, I could trace nothing of my old self. The hair, too, jetty and rich before, was now as white as snow; and in one night the ravages of half a century had passed over my face. Nor have my nerves ever recovered their tone after that dire shock. Can you wonder that my life was blighted, that my lover shrank from me, so sad a wreck was I?

I am old now—old and alone. My sisters would have had me to live with them, but I chose not to sadden their genial homes with my phantom face and dead eyes. Reginald married another. He has been dead many years. I never ceased to pray for him, though he left me when I was bereft of all. The sad weird is nearly over now. I am old, and near the end, and wishful for it. I have not been bitter or hard, but I cannot bear to see many people, and am best alone. I try to do what good I can with the worthless wealth Lady Speldhurst left me, for, at my wish, my portion was shared between my sisters. What need had I of inheritance?—I, the shattered wreck made by that one night of horror!

The Open Door

Margaret Oliphant

I TOOK THE house of Brentwood on my return from India in 18—, for the temporary accommodation of my family, until I could find a permanent home for them. It had many advantages which made it peculiarly appropriate. It was within reach of Edinburgh; and my boy Roland, whose education had been considerably neglected, could go in and out to school; which was thought to be better for him than either leaving home altogether or staying there always with a tutor. The first of these expedients would have seemed preferable to me; the second commended itself to his mother. The doctor, like a judicious man, took the midway between. 'Put him on his pony, and let him ride into the High School every morning; it will do him all the good in the world,' Dr Simson said; 'and when it is bad weather, there is the train.' His mother accepted this solution of the difficulty more easily than I could have hoped; and our pale-faced boy, who had never known anything more invigorating than Simla, began to encounter the brisk breezes of the North in the subdued severity of the month of May. Before the time of the vacation in July we had the satisfaction of seeing him begin to acquire something of the brown and ruddy complexion of his schoolfellows. The English system did not commend itself to Scotland in these days. There was no little Eton at Fettes; nor do I think, if there had been, that a genteel exotic of that class would have tempted either my wife or me. The lad was doubly precious to us, being the only one left us of many; and he was fragile in body, we believed, and deeply sensitive in mind. To keep him at home, and yet to send him to school,—to combine the advantages of the two systems,—seemed to be everything that could be desired. The two girls also found at Brentwood everything they wanted. They were near enough to Edinburgh to have masters and lessons as many as they required for completing that never-ending education which the young people seem to require nowadays. Their mother married me when she was younger than Agatha; and I should like to see them improve upon their mother! I myself was then no more than twenty-five,—an age at which I see the young fellows now groping about them, with no notion what they are going to do with their lives. However; I suppose every generation has a conceit of itself which elevates it, in its own opinion, above that which comes after it.

Brentwood stands on that fine and wealthy slope of country—one of the richest in Scotland—which lies between the Pentland Hills and the Firth. In clear weather you could see the blue gleam—like a bent bow, embracing the wealthy fields and scattered houses—of the great estuary on one side of you, and on the other the blue heights, not gigantic like those we had been used to, but just high enough for all the glories of the atmosphere, the play of clouds, and sweet reflections, which give to a hilly country an interest and a charm which nothing else can emulate. Edinburgh—with its two lesser heights, the Castle and the Calton Hill, its spires and towers piercing through the smoke, and Arthur's Seat lying crouched behind, like a guardian no longer very needful, taking his repose beside the well-beloved charge, which is now, so to speak, able to take care of itself without him—lay at our right hand. From the lawn and drawing-room windows we could see all these varieties of landscape. The colour was sometimes a little chilly, but sometimes, also, as animated and full of vicissitude as a drama. I was never tired of it. Its colour and freshness revived the eyes which had grown weary of arid plains and blazing skies. It was always cheery, and fresh, and full of repose.

The village of Brentwood lay almost under the house, on the other side of the deep little ravine, down which a stream—which ought to have been a lovely, wild, and frolicsome little river— flowed between its rocks and trees. The river, like so many in that district, had, however, in its earlier life been sacrificed to trade, and was grimy with paper-making. But this did not affect our pleasure in it so much as I have known it to affect other streams. Perhaps our water was more rapid; perhaps less clogged with dirt and refuse. Our side of the dell was charmingly *accidenté*, and clothed with fine trees, through which various paths wound down to the river-side and to the village bridge which crossed the stream. The village lay in the hollow, and climbed, with very prosaic houses, the other side. Village architecture does not flourish in Scotland. The blue slates and the grey stone are sworn foes to the picturesque; and though I do not, for my own part, dislike the interior of an old-fashioned hewed and galleried church, with its little family settlements on all sides, the square box outside, with its bit of a spire like a handle to lift it by, is not an improvement to the landscape. Still a cluster of houses on differing elevations, with scraps of garden coming in between, a hedgerow with clothes laid out to dry, the opening of a street with its rural sociability, the women at their doors, the slow wagon lumbering along, gives a centre to the landscape. It was cheerful to look at, and convenient in a hundred ways. Within ourselves we had walks in plenty, the glen being always beautiful in all its phases, whether the woods were green in the spring or ruddy in the autumn. In the park which surrounded the house were the ruins of the former mansion of

Brentwood,—a much smaller and less important house than the solid Georgian edifice which we inhabited. The ruins were picturesque, however, and gave importance to the place. Even we, who were but temporary tenants, felt a vague pride in them, as if they somehow reflected a certain consequence upon ourselves. The old building had the remains of a tower,—an indistinguishable mass of mason-work, over-grown with ivy; and the shells of walls attached to this were half filled up with soil. I had never examined it closely, I am ashamed to say. There was a large room, or what had been a large room, with the lower part of the windows still existing, on the principal floor, and underneath other windows, which were perfect, though half filled up with fallen soil, and waving with a wild growth of brambles and chance growths of all kinds. This was the oldest part of all. At a little distance were some very commonplace and disjointed fragments of building, one of them suggesting a certain pathos by its very commonness and the complete wreck which it showed. This was the end of a low gable, a bit of grey wall, all incrusted with lichens, in which was a common door-way. Probably it had been a servants' entrance, a backdoor, or opening into what are called 'the offices' in Scotland. No offices remained to be entered,—pantry and kitchen had all been swept out of being; but there stood the door-way open and vacant, free to all the winds, to the rabbits, and every wild creature. It struck my eye, the first time I went to Brentwood, like a melancholy comment upon a life that was over. A door that led to nothing,— closed once, perhaps, with anxious care, bolted and guarded, now void of any meaning. It impressed me, I remember, from the first; so perhaps it may be said that my mind was prepared to attach to it an importance which nothing justified.

The summer was a very happy period of repose for us all. The warmth of Indian suns was still in our veins. It seemed to us that we could never have enough of the greenness, the dewiness, the freshness of the northern landscape. Even its mists were pleasant to us, taking all the fever out of us, and pouring in vigour and refreshment. In autumn we followed the fashion of the time, and went away for change which we did not in the least require. It was when the family had settled down for the winter, when the days were short and dark, and the rigorous reign of frost upon us, that the incidents occurred which alone could justify me in intruding upon the world my private affairs. These incidents were, however, of so curious a character, that I hope my inevitable references to my own family and pressing personal interests will meet with a general pardon.

I was absent in London when these events began. In London an old Indian plunges back into the interests with which all his previous life has been associated, and meets old friends at every step. I had been circulating among some half-dozen of these,— enjoying the return to my former life in shadow, though I had been so thankful in substance to throw it aside,—and had missed some of my home letters, what with going down from Friday to Monday to old Benbow's place in the country, and stopping on the way back to dine and sleep at Sellar's and to take a look into Cross's stables, which occupied another day. It is never safe to miss one's letters. In this transitory life, as the Prayer-book says, how can one ever be certain what is going to happen? All was well at home. I knew exactly (I thought) what they would have to say to me: 'The weather has been so fine, that Roland has not once gone by train, and he enjoys the ride beyond anything.' 'Dear papa, be sure that you don't forget anything, but bring us so-and-so, and so-and-so,'—a list as long as my arm. Dear girls and dearer mother! I would not for the world have forgotten their commissions, or lost their little letters, for all the Benbows and Crosses in the world.

But I was confident in my home-comfort and peacefulness. When I got back to my club, however, three or four letters were lying for one, upon some of which I noticed the 'immediate,' 'urgent,' which old-fashioned people and anxious people still believe will influence the post-office and quicken the speed of the mails. I was about to open one of these, when the club porter brought me two telegrams, one of which, he said, had arrived the night before. I opened, as was to be expected, the last first, and this was what I read: 'Why don't you come or answer? For God's sake, come. He is much worse.' This was a thunderbolt to fall upon a man's head who had one only son, and lie the light of his eyes! The other telegram, which I opened with hands trembling so much that I lost time by my haste, was to much the same purport: 'No better; doctor afraid of brain-fever. Calls for you day and night. Let nothing detain you.' The first thing I did was to look up the time-tables to see if there was any way of getting off sooner than by the night-train, though I knew well enough there was not; and then I read the letters, which furnished, alas! too clearly, all the details. They told me that the boy had been pale for some time, with a scared look. His mother had noticed it before I left home, but would not say anything to alarm me. This look had increased day by day: and soon it was observed that Roland came home at a wild gallop through the park, his pony panting and in foam, himself 'as white as a sheet,' but with the perspiration streaming from his forehead. For a long time he had resisted all questioning, but at length had developed such strange changes of mood, showing a reluctance to go to school, a desire to be fetched in the carriage at night,—which was a ridiculous piece of luxury,—an unwillingness to go out into the grounds, and nervous start at every sound, that his mother had insisted upon an explanation. When the boy—our boy Roland, who had never known what fear was—began to talk to her of voices he had heard in the park, and shadows that had appeared to him among the ruins, my wife promptly put him to bed and sent for Dr Simson, which, of course, was the only thing to do.

I hurried off that evening, as may be supposed, with an anxious heart. How I got through the hours before the starting of the train, I cannot tell. We must all be thankful for the quickness of the railway when in anxiety; but to have thrown myself into a post-chaise as soon as horses could be put to, would have been a relief. I got to Edinburgh very early in the blackness of the winter morning, and scarcely dared look the man in the face, at whom I gasped, 'What news?' My wife had sent the brougham for me, which I concluded, before the man spoke, was a bad sign. His answer was that stereotyped answer which leaves the imagination so wildly free,—'Just the same.' Just the same! What might that mean? The horses seemed to me to creep along the long dark country road. As we dashed through the park, I thought I heard someone moaning among the trees, and clenched my fist at him (whoever he might be) with fury. Why had the fool of a woman at the gate allowed any one to come in to disturb the quiet of the place? If I had not been in such hot haste to get home, I think I should have stopped the carriage and got out to see what tramp it was that had made an entrance, and chosen my grounds, of all places in the world,— when my boy was ill!—to grumble and groan in. But I had no reason to complain of our slow pace here. The horses flew like lightning along the intervening path, and drew up at the door all panting, as if they had run a race. My wife stood waiting to receive me, with a pale face, and a candle in her hand, which made her look paler still as the wind blew the flame about. 'He is sleeping,' she said in a whisper, as if her voice might wake him. And I replied, when I could find my voice, also in a whisper, as though the jingling of the horses' furniture and the sound of their hoofs must not have been more dangerous. I stood on the steps with her a moment, almost afraid to go in, now that I was here; and it seemed to me that I saw without observing, if I may say so, that the horses were unwilling to turn round, though their stables lay that way, or that the men were unwilling. These things occurred to me afterwards, though at the moment I was not capable of anything but to ask questions and to hear of the condition of the boy.

I looked at him from the door of his room, for we were afraid to go near, lest we should disturb that blessed sleep. It looked like actual sleep, not the lethargy into which my wife told me he would sometimes fall. She told me everything in the next room, which communicated with his, rising now and then and going to the door of communication; and in this there was much that was very startling and confusing to the mind. It appeared that ever since the winter began—since it was early dark, and night had fallen before his return from school—he had been hearing voices among the ruins: at first only a groaning, he said, at which his pony was as much alarmed as he was, but by degrees a voice. The tears ran down my wife's cheeks as she described to me how he would start up in the night and cry out, 'Oh, mother, let me in! oh, mother, let me in!' with a pathos which rent her heart. And she sitting there all the time, only longing to do everything his heart could desire! But though she would try to soothe him, crying, 'You are at home, my darling. I am here. Don't you know me? Your mother is here!' he would only stare at her, and after a while spring up again with the same cry. At other times he would be quite reasonable, she said, asking eagerly when I was coming, but declaring that he must go with me as soon as I did so, 'to let them in'. 'The doctor thinks his nervous system must have received a shock,' my wife said. 'Oh, Henry, can it be that we have pushed him on too much with his work—a delicate boy like Roland? And what is his work in comparison with his health? Even you would think little of honours or prizes if it hurt the boy's health.' Even I!—as if I were an inhuman father sacrificing my child to my ambition. But I would not increase her trouble by taking any notice. After awhile they persuaded me to lie down, to rest, and to eat, none of which things had been possible since I received their letters. The mere fact of being on the spot, of course, in itself was a great thing; and when I knew that I could be called in a moment, as soon as he was awake and wanted me, I felt capable, even in the dark, chill morning twilight, to snatch an hour or two's sleep. As it happened, I was so worn out with the strain of anxiety, and he so quieted and consoled by knowing I had come, that I was not disturbed till the afternoon, when the twilight had again settled down. There was just daylight enough to see his face when I went to him; and what a change in a fortnight! He was paler and more worn, I thought, than even in those dreadful days in the plains before we left India. His hair seemed to me to have grown long and lank; his eyes were like blazing lights projecting out of his white face. He got hold of my hand in a cold and tremulous clutch, and waved to everybody to go away. 'Go away—even mother,' he said; 'go away.' This went to her heart; for she did not like that even I should have more of the boy's confidence than herself; but my wife has never been a woman to think of herself, and she left us alone. 'Are they all gone?' he said eagerly. 'They would not let me speak. The doctor treated me as if I were a fool. You know I am not a fool, papa.'

'Yes, yes, my boy, I know. But you are ill, and quiet is so necessary. You are not only not a fool, Roland, but you are reasonable and understand. When you are ill you must deny yourself; you must not do everything that you might do being well.'

He waved his thin hand with a sort of indignation. 'Then, father, I am not ill,' he cried. 'Oh, I thought when you came you would not stop me,—you would see the sense of it! What do you think is the matter with me, all of you? Simson is well enough; but he is only a doctor. What do you think is the matter with me? I am no more ill than you are. A doctor, of course, he thinks you are ill the moment he looks at you—that's what he's there for—and claps you into bed.'

'Which is the best place for you at present, my dear boy.'

'I made up my mind,' cried the little fellow, 'that I would stand it till you came home. I said to myself, I won't frighten mother and the girls. But now, father,' he cried, half jumping out of bed, 'it's not illness: it's a secret.'

His eyes shone so wildly, his face was so swept with strong feeling, that my heart sank within me. It could be nothing but fever that did it, and fever had been so fatal. I got him into my arms to put him back into bed. 'Roland,' I said, humouring the poor child, which I knew was the only way, 'if you are going to tell me this secret to do any good, you know you must be quite quiet, and not excite yourself. If you excite yourself, I must not let you speak.'

'Yes, father,' said the boy. He was quiet directly, like a man, as if he quite understood. When I had laid him back on his pillow, he looked up at me with that grateful, sweet look with which children, when they are ill, break one's heart, the water coming into his eyes in his weakness. 'I was sure as soon as you were here you would know what to do,' he said.

'To be sure, my boy. Now keep quiet, and tell it all out like a man.' To think I was telling lies to my own child! for I did it only to humour him, thinking, poor little fellow, his brain was wrong.

'Yes, father. Father, there is some one in the park—some one that has been badly used.' 'Hush, my dear; you remember there is to be no excitement. Well, who is this somebody, and who has been ill-using him? We will soon put a stop to that.'

'Ah,' cried Roland, 'but it is not so easy as you think. I don't know who it is. It is just a cry. Oh, if you could hear it! It gets into my head in my sleep. I heard it as clear—as clear; and they think that I am dreaming, or raving perhaps,' the boy said, with a sort of disdainful smile.

This look of his perplexed me; it was less like fever than I thought. 'Are you quite sure you have not dreamed it, Roland?' I said.

'Dreamed?—that!' He was springing up again when he suddenly bethought himself, and lay down flat, with the same sort of smile on his face. 'The pony heard it, too,' he said. 'She jumped as if she had been shot. If I had not grasped at the reins—for I was frightened, father—'

'No shame to you, my boy,' said I, though I scarcely knew why.

'If I hadn't held to her like a leech, she'd have pitched me over her head, and never drew breath till we were at the door. Did the pony dream it?' he said, with a soft disdain, yet indulgence for my foolishness. Then he added slowly, 'It was only a cry the first time, and all the time before you went away. I wouldn't tell you, for it was so wretched to be frightened. I thought it might be a hare or a rabbit snared, and I went in the morning and looked; but there was nothing. It was after you went I heard it really first; and this is what he says.' He raised himself on his elbow close to me, and looked me in the face: 'Oh, mother, let me in! oh, mother, let me in!' As he said the words a mist came over his face, the mouth quivered, the soft features all melted and changed, and when he had ended these pitiful words, dissolved in a shower of heavy tears.

Was it a hallucination? Was it the fever of the brain? Was it the disordered fancy caused by great bodily weakness? How could I tell? I thought it wisest to accept it as if it were all true.

'This is very touching, Roland,' I said.

'Oh, if you had just heard it, father! I said to myself, if father heard it he would do something; but mamma, you know, she's given over to Simson, and that fellow's a doctor, and never thinks of anything but clapping you into bed.'

'We must not blame Simson for being a doctor, Roland.'

'No, no,' said my boy, with delightful toleration and indulgence; 'oh, no; that's the good of him; that's what he's for; I know that. But you—you are different; you are just father; and you'll do something—directly, papa, directly; this very night.'

'Surely,' I said. 'No doubt it is some little lost child.'

He gave me a sudden, swift look, investigating my face as though to see whether, after all, this was everything my eminence as 'father' came to,—no more than that. Then he got hold of my shoulder, clutching it with his thin hand. 'Look here,' he said, with a quiver in his voice; 'suppose it wasn't—living at all!'

'My dear boy, how then could you have heard it?' I said.

He turned away from me with a pettish exclamation,—'As if you didn't know better than that!'

'Do you want to tell me it is a ghost?' I said.

Roland withdrew his hand; his countenance assumed an aspect of great dignity and gravity; a slight quiver remained about his lips. 'Whatever it was—you always said we were not to call names. It was something—in trouble. Oh, father, in terrible trouble!'

'But, my boy,' I said (I was at my wits' end), 'if it was a child that was lost, or any poor human creature—but, Roland, what do you want me to do?'

'I should know if I was you,' said the child eagerly. 'That is what I always said to myself,—Father will know. Oh, papa, papa, to have to face it night after night, in such terrible, terrible trouble, and never to be able to do it any good! I don't want to cry; it's like a baby, I know; but what can I do else? Out there all by itself in the ruin, and nobody to help it! I can't bear it! I can't bear it!' cried my generous boy. And in his weakness he burst out, after many attempts to restrain it, into a great childish fit of sobbing and tears.

I do not know that I ever was in a greater perplexity, in my life; and afterwards, when I thought of it, there was something comic in it too. It is bad enough to find your child's mind possessed with the conviction that he has seen, or heard, a ghost; but that he should require you to go instantly and help that ghost was the most bewildering experience that had ever come my way. I am a sober man myself, and not superstitious—at least any more than everybody is superstitious. Of course I do not believe in ghosts; but I don't deny, any more than other people, that there are stories which I cannot pretend to understand. My blood got a sort of chill in my veins at the idea that Roland should be a ghost-seer; for that generally means a hysterical temperament and weak health, and all that men most hate and fear for their children. But that I should take up his ghost and right its wrongs, and save it from its trouble, was such a mission as was enough to confuse any man. I did my best to console my boy without giving any promise of this astonishing kind; but he was too sharp for me: he would have none of my caresses. With sobs breaking in at intervals upon his voice, and the rain-drops hanging on his eyelids, he yet returned to the charge.

'It will be there now!—it will be there all the night! Oh, think, papa,—think if it was me! I can't rest for thinking of it. Don't!' he cried, putting away my hand,—'don't! You go and help it, and mother can take care of me.'

'But, Roland, what can I do?'

My boy opened his eyes, which were large with weakness and fever, and gave me a smile such, I think, as sick children only know the secret of. 'I was sure you would know as soon as you came. I always said, Father will know. And mother,' he cried, with a softening of repose upon his face, his limbs relaxing, his form sinking with a luxurious ease in his bed,—'mother can come and take care of me.'

I called her, and saw him turn to her with the complete dependence of a child; and then I went away and left them, as perplexed a man as any in Scotland. I must say, however, I had this consolation, that my mind was greatly eased about Roland. He might be under a hallucination; but his head was clear enough, and I did not think him so ill as everybody else did. The girls were astonished even at the ease with which I took it. 'How do you think he is?' they said in a breath, coming round me, laying hold of me. 'Not half so ill as I expected,' I said; 'not very bad at all.' 'Oh, papa, you are a darling!' cried Agatha, kissing me, and crying upon my shoulder; while little Jeanie, who was as pale as Roland, clasped both her arms round mine, and could not speak at all. I knew nothing about it, not half so much as Simson; but they believed in me: they had a feeling that all would go right now. God is very good to you when your children look to you like that. It makes one humble, not proud. I was not worthy of it; and then I recollected that I had to act the part of a father to Roland's ghost,—which made me almost laugh, though I might just as well have cried. It was the strangest mission that ever was intrusted to mortal man.

It was then I remembered suddenly the looks of the men when they turned to take the brougham to the stables in the dark that morning. They had not liked it, and the horses had not liked it. I remembered that even in my anxiety about Roland I had heard them tearing along the avenue back to the stables, and had made a memorandum mentally that I must speak of it. It seemed to me that the best thing I could do was to go to the stables now and make a few inquiries. It is impossible to fathom the minds of rustics; there might be some devilry of practical joking, for anything I knew; or they might have some interest in getting up a bad reputation for the Brentwood avenue. It was getting dark by the time I went out, and nobody who knows the country will need to be told how black is the darkness of a November night under high laurel-bushes and yew-trees. I walked into the heart of the shrubberies two or three times, not seeing a step before me, till I came out upon the broader carriage-road, where the trees opened a little, and there was a faint grey glimmer of sky visible, under which the great limes and elms stood darkling like ghosts; but it grew black again as I approached the corner where the ruins lay. Both eyes and ears were on the alert, as may be supposed; but I could see nothing in the absolute gloom, and, so far as I can recollect, I heard nothing. Nevertheless there came a strong impression upon me that somebody was there. It is a sensation which most people have felt. I have seen when it has been strong enough to awake me out of sleep, the sense of some one looking at me. I suppose my imagination had been affected by Roland's story; and the mystery of the darkness is always full of suggestions. I stamped my feet violently on the gravel to rouse myself, and called out sharply, 'Who's there?'

Nobody answered, nor did I expect any one to answer, but the impression had been made. I was so foolish that I did not like to look back, but went sideways, keeping an eye on the gloom behind. It was with great relief that I spied the light in the stables, making a sort of oasis in the darkness. I walked very quickly into the midst of that lighted and cheerful place, and thought the clank of the groom's pail one of the pleasantest sounds I had ever heard. The coachman was the head of this little colony, and it was to his house I went to pursue my investigations. He was a native of the district, and had taken care of the place in the absence of the family for years; it was impossible but that he must know everything that was going on, and all the traditions of the place. The men, I could see, eyed me anxiously when I thus appeared at such an hour among them, and followed me with their eyes to Jarvis's house, where he lived alone with his old wife, their children being all married and out in the world. Mrs Jarvis met me with anxious questions. How was the poor young gentleman? But the others knew, I could see by their faces, that not even this was the foremost thing in my mind.

⁕

'Noises?—ou ay, there'll be noises,—the wind in the trees, and the water soughing down the glen. As for tramps, Cornel, no, there's little o' that kind o' cattle about here; and Merran at the gate's a careful body.' Jarvis moved about with some embarrassment from one leg to another as he spoke. He kept in the shade, and did not look at me more than he could help. Evidently his mind was perturbed, and he had reasons for keeping his own counsel. His wife sat by, giving him a quick look now and then, but saying nothing. The kitchen was very snug and warm and bright,—as different as could be from the chill and mystery of the night outside.

'I think you are trifling with me, Jarvis,' I said.

'Triflin', Cornel? No me. What would I trifle for? If the deevil himsel was in the auld hoose, I have no interest in 't one way or another—'

'Sandy, hold your peace!' cried his wife imperatively.

'And what am I to hold my peace for, wi' the Cornel standing there asking a' thae questions? I'm saying, if the deevil himsel—'

'And I'm telling ye hold your peace!' cried the woman, in great excitement. 'Dark November weather and lang nichts, and us that ken a' we ken. How daur ye name—a name that shouldna be spoken?' She threw down her stocking and got up, also in great agitation. 'I tellt ye you never could keep it. It's no a thing that will hide, and the haill toun kens as weel as you or me. Tell the Cornel straight out—or see, I'll do it. I dinna hold wi' your secrets, and a secret that the haill toun kens!' She snapped her fingers with an air of large disdain. As for Jarvis, ruddy and big as he was, he shrank to nothing before this decided woman. He repeated to her two or three times her own adjuration, 'Hold your peace!' then, suddenly changing his tone, cried out, 'Tell him then, confound ye! I'll wash my hands o't. If a' the ghosts in Scotland were in the auld hoose, is that ony concern o' mine?'

After this I elicited without much difficulty the whole story. In the opinion of the Jarvises, and of everybody about, the certainty that the place was haunted was beyond all doubt. As Sandy and his wife warmed to the tale, one tripping up another in their eagerness to tell everything, it gradually developed as distinct a superstition as I ever heard, and not without poetry and pathos. How long it was since the voice had been heard first, nobody could tell with certainty. Jarvis's opinion was that his father, who had been coachman at Brentwood before him, had never heard anything about it, and that the whole thing had arisen within the last ten years, since the complete dismantling of the old house; which was a wonderfully modern date for a tale so well authenticated. According to these witnesses, and to several whom I questioned afterwards, and who were all in perfect agreement, it was only in the months of November and December that 'the visitation' occurred. During these months, the darkest of the year, scarcely a night passed without the recurrence of these inexplicable cries. Nothing, it was said, had ever been seen,—at least, nothing that could be identified. Some people, bolder or more imaginative than the others, had seen the darkness moving, Mrs Jarvis said, with unconscious poetry. It began when night fell, and continued, at intervals, till day broke. Very often it was only all inarticulate cry and moaning, but sometimes the words which had taken possession of my poor boy's fancy had been distinctly audible,—'Oh, mother, let me in!' The Jarvises were not aware that there had ever been any investigation into it. The estate of Brentwood had lapsed into the hands of a distant branch of the family, who had lived but little there; and of the many people who had taken it, as I had done, few had remained through two Decembers. And nobody had taken the trouble to make a very close examination into the facts. 'No, no,' Jarvis said, shaking his head, 'No, no, Cornel. Wha wad set themsels up for a laughin'-stock to a' the country-side, making a wark about a ghost? Naebody believes in ghosts. It bid to be the wind in the trees, the last gentleman said, or some effec' o' the water wrastlin' among the rocks. He said it was a' quite easy explained; but he gave up the hoose. And when you cam, Cornel, we were awfu' anxious you should never hear. What for should I have spoiled the bargain and hairmed the property for no-thing?'

'Do you call my child's life nothing?' I said in the trouble of the moment, unable to restrain myself. 'And instead of telling this all to me, you have told it to him,—to a delicate boy, a child unable to sift evidence or judge for himself, a tender-hearted young creature—'

I was walking about the room with an anger all the hotter that I felt it to be most likely quite unjust. My heart was full of bitterness against the stolid retainers of a family who were content to risk other people's children and comfort rather than let a house be empty. If I had been warned I might have taken precautions, or left the place, or sent Roland away, a hundred things which now I could not do; and here I was with my boy in a brain-fever, and his life, the most precious life on earth, hanging in the balance, dependent on whether or not I could get to the reason of a commonplace ghost-story! I paced about in high wrath, not seeing what I was to do; for to take Roland away, even if he were able to travel, would not settle his agitated mind; and I feared even that a scientific explanation of refracted sound or reverberation, or any other of the easy certainties with which we elder men are silenced, would have very little effect upon the boy.

'Cornel,' said Jarvis solemnly, 'and *she'll* bear me witness,— the young gentleman never heard a word from me—no, nor from either groom or gardener; I'll gie ye my word for that. In the first place, he's no a lad that invites ye to talk. There are some that are, and some that arena. Some will draw ye on, till ye've tellt them a' the clatter of the toun, and a' ye ken, and whiles mair. But Maister Roland, his mind's fu' of his books. He's aye civil and kind, and a fine lad; but no that sort. And ye see it's for a' our interest, Cornel, that you should stay at Brentwood. I took it upon me mysel to pass the word,—'No a syllable to Maister Roland, nor to the young leddies—no a syllable.' The women-servants, that have little reason to be out at night, ken little or nothing about it. And some think it grand to have a ghost so long as they're no in the way of coming across it. If you had been tellt the story to begin with, maybe ye would have thought so yourself.'

This was true enough, though it did not throw any light upon my perplexity. If we had heard of it to start with, it is possible that all the family would have considered the possession of a ghost a distinct advantage. It is the fashion of the times. We never think what a risk it is to play with young imaginations, but cry out, in the fashionable jargon, 'A ghost!—nothing else was wanted to make it perfect.' I should not have been above this myself.

I should have smiled, of course, at the idea of the ghost at all, but then to feel that it was mine would have pleased my vanity. Oh, yes, I claim no exemption. The girls would have been delighted. I could fancy their eagerness, their interest, and excitement. No; if we had been told, it would have done no good,—we should have made the bargain all the more eagerly, the fools that we are. 'And there has been no attempt to investigate it,' I said, 'to see what it really is?'

'Eh, Cornel,' said the coachman's wife, 'wha would investigate, as ye call it, a thing that nobody believes in? Ye would be the laughin'-stock of a' the country-side, as my man says.'

'But you believe in it,' I said, turning upon her hastily. The woman was taken by surprise. She made a step backward out of my way.

'Lord, Cornel, how ye frichten a body! Me!—there's awfu' strange things in this world. An unlearned person doesna ken what to think. But the minister and the gentry they just laugh in your face. Inquire into the thing that is not! Na, na, we just let it be.'

'Come with me, Jarvis,' I said hastily, 'and we'll make an attempt at least. Say nothing to the men or to anybody. I'll come back after dinner, and we'll make a serious attempt to see what it is, if it is anything. If I hear it,—which I doubt,—you may be sure I shall never rest till I make it out. Be ready for me about ten o'clock.'

'Me, Cornel!' Jarvis said, in a faint voice. I had not been looking at him in my own preoccupation, but when I did so, I found that the greatest change had come over the fat and ruddy coachman. 'Me, Cornel!' he repeated, wiping the perspiration from his brow. His ruddy face hung in flabby folds, his knees knocked together, his voice seemed half extinguished in his throat. Then he began to rub his hands and smile upon me in a deprecating, imbecile way. 'There's nothing I wouldna do to pleasure ye, Cornel,' taking a step further back. 'I'm sure *she* kens

I've aye said I never had to do with a mair fair, weel-spoken gentleman—' Here Jarvis came to a pause, again looking at me, rubbing his hands.

'Well?' I said.

'But eh, sir!' he went on, with the same imbecile yet insinuating smile, 'if ye'll reflect that I am no used to my feet. With a horse atween my legs, or the reins in my hand, I'm maybe nae worse than other men; but on fit, Cornel—It's no the—bogles—but I've been cavalry, ye see,' with a little hoarse laugh, 'a' my life. To face a thing ye dinna understan'—on your feet, Cornel.'

'Well, sir, if *I* do it,' said I tartly, 'why shouldn't you?'

'Eh, Cornel, there's an awfu' difference. In the first place, ye tramp about the haill countryside, and think naething of it; but a walk tires me mair than a hunard miles' drive; and then ye're a gentleman, and do your ain pleasure; and you're no so auld as me; and it's for your ain bairn, ye see, Cornel; and then—'

'He believes in it, Cornel, and you dinna believe in it,' the woman said.

'Will you come with me?' I said, turning to her.

She jumped back, upsetting her chair in her bewilderment. 'Me!' with a scream, and then fell into a sort of hysterical laugh. 'I wouldna say but what I would go; but what would the folk say to hear of Cornel Mortimer with an auld silly woman at his heels?'

The suggestion made me laugh too, though I had little inclination for it. 'I'm sorry you have so little spirit, Jarvis,' I said. 'I must find some one else, I suppose.'

Jarvis, touched by this, began to remonstrate, but I cut him short. My butler was a soldier who had been with me in India, and was not supposed to fear anything,—man or devil,—certainly not the former; and I felt that I was losing time. The Jarvises were too thankful to get rid of me. They attended me to the door with the most anxious courtesies. Outside, the two grooms stood close by, a little confused by my sudden exit. I don't know if perhaps they had been listening,—as least standing as near as possible, to catch any scrap of the conversation. I waved my hand to them as I went past, in answer to their salutations, and it was very apparent to me that they also were glad to see me go.

And it will be thought very strange, but it would be weak not to add, that I myself, though bent on the investigation I have spoken of, pledged to Roland to carry it out, and feeling that my boy's health, perhaps his life, depended on the result of my inquiry,—I felt the most unaccountable reluctance to pass these ruins on my way home. My curiosity was intense; and yet it was all my mind could do to pull my body along. I daresay the scientific people would describe it the other way, and attribute my cowardice to the state of my stomach. I went on; but if I had followed my impulse, I should have turned and bolted. Everything in me seemed to cry out against it: my heart thumped, my pulses all began, like sledge-hammers, beating against my ears and every sensitive part. It was very dark, as I have said; the old house, with its shapeless tower, loomed a heavy mass through the darkness, which was only not entirely so solid as itself. On the other hand, the great dark cedars of which we were so proud seemed to fill up the night. My foot strayed out of the path in my confusion and the gloom together, and I brought myself up with a cry as I felt myself knock against something solid. What was it? The contact with hard stone and lime and prickly bramble-bushes restored me a little to myself. 'Oh, it's only the old gable,' I said aloud, with a little laugh to reassure myself. The rough feeling of the stones reconciled me. As I groped about thus, I shook off my visionary folly. What so easily explained as that I should have strayed from the path in the darkness? This brought me back to common existence, as if I had been shaken by a wise hand out of all the silliness of superstition. How silly it was, after all! What did it matter which path I took? I laughed again, this time with better heart, when suddenly, in a moment, the blood was chilled in my veins, a shiver stole along my spine, my faculties seemed to forsake me. Close by me, at my side, at my feet, there was a sigh. No, not a groan, not a moaning, not anything so tangible,—a perfectly soft, faint, inarticulate sigh. I sprang back, and my heart stopped beating. Mistaken! no, mistake was impossible. I heard it as clearly as I hear myself speak; a long, soft, weary sigh, as if drawn to the utmost, and emptying out a load of sadness that filled the breast. To hear this in the solitude, in the dark, in the night (though it was still early), had an effect which I cannot describe. I feel it now,—something cold creeping over me, up into my hair, and down to my feet, which refused to move. I cried out, with a trembling voice, 'Who is there?' as I had done before; but there was no reply.

I got home I don't quite know how; but in my mind there was no longer any indifference as to the thing, whatever it was, that haunted these ruins. My scepticism disappeared like a mist. I was as firmly determined that there was something as Roland was. I did not for a moment pretend to myself that it was possible I could be deceived; there were movements and noises which I understood all about,—cracklings of small branches in the frost, and little rolls of gravel on the path, such as have a very eerie sound sometimes, and perplex you with wonder as to who has done it, *when there is no real mystery*; but I assure you all these little movements of nature don't affect you one bit *when there is something*. I understood *them*. I did not understand the sigh. That was not simple nature; there was meaning in it, feeling, the soul of a creature invisible. This is the thing that human nature trembles at,—a creature invisible, yet with sensations, feelings, a power somehow of expressing itself. I had not the same sense of unwillingness to turn my back upon the scene of the mystery which I had experienced in going to the stables; but I almost ran home, impelled by eagerness to get everything done that had to be done, in order to apply myself to finding it out. Bagley was in the hall as usual when I went in. He was always there in the afternoon, always with the appearance of perfect occupation, yet, so far as I know, never doing anything. The door was open, so that I hurried in without any pause, breathless; but the sight of his calm regard, as he came to help me off with my overcoat, subdued me in a moment. Anything out of the way, anything incomprehensible, faded to nothing in the presence of Bagley. You saw and wondered how *he* was made: the parting of his hair, the tie of his white neckcloth, the fit of his trousers, all perfect as works of art; but you could see how they were done, which makes all the difference. I flung myself upon him, so to speak, without waiting to note the extreme unlikeness of the man to anything of the kind I meant. 'Bagley,' I said, 'I want you to come out with me tonight to watch for—'

'Poachers, Colonel?' he said, a gleam of pleasure running all over him.

'No, Bagley; a great deal worse,' I cried.

'Yes, Colonel; at what hour, sir?' the man said; but then I had not told him what it was.

It was ten o'clock when we set out. All was perfectly quiet indoors. My wife was with Roland, who had been quite calm, she said, and who (though, no doubt, the fever must run its course) had been better ever since I came. I told Bagley to put on a thick greatcoat over his evening coat, and did the same myself, with strong boots; for the soil was like a sponge, or worse. Talking to him, I almost forgot what we were going to do. It was darker even than it had been before, and Bagley kept very close to me as we went along. I had a small lantern in my hand, which gave us a partial guidance. We had come to the corner where the path turns. On one side was the bowling-green, which the girls had taken possession of for their croquet-ground,—a wonderful enclosure surrounded by high hedges of holly, three hundred years old and more; on the other, the ruins. Both were black as night; but before we got so far, there was a little opening in which we could just discern the trees and the lighter line of the road. I thought it best to pause there and take breath. 'Bagley,' I said, 'there is something about these ruins I don't understand.

It is there I am going. Keep your eyes open and your wits about you. Be ready to pounce upon any stranger you see,— anything, man or woman. Don't hurt, but seize anything you see.' 'Colonel,' said Bagley, with a little tremor in his breath, 'they do say there's things there—as is neither man nor woman.' There was no time for words. 'Are you game to follow me, my man? that's the question,' I said. Bagley fell in without a word, and saluted. I knew then I had nothing to fear.

We went, so far as I could guess, exactly as I had come; when I heard that sigh. The darkness, however, was so complete that all marks, as of trees or paths, disappeared. One moment we felt our feet on the gravel, another sinking noiselessly into the slippery grass, that was all. I had shut up my lantern, not wishing to scare any one, whoever it might be. Bagley followed, it seemed to me, exactly in my footsteps as I made my way, as I supposed, towards the mass of the ruined house. We seemed to take a long time groping along seeking this; the squash of the wet soil under our feet was the only thing that marked our progress. After a while I stood still to see, or rather feel, where we were. The darkness was very still, but no stiller than is usual in a winter's night. The sounds I have mentioned—the crackling of twigs, the roll of a pebble, the sound of some rustle in the dead leaves, or creeping creature on the grass—were audible when you listened, all mysterious enough when your mind is disengaged, but to me cheering now as signs of the livingness of nature, even in the death of the frost. As we stood still there came up from the trees in the glen the prolonged hoot of an owl. Bagley started with alarm, being in a state of general nervousness, and not knowing what he was afraid of. But to me the sound was encouraging and pleasant, being so comprehensible.

'An owl,' I said, under my breath. 'Y—es, Colonel,' said Bagley, his teeth chattering. We stood still about five minutes, while it broke into the still brooding of the air, the sound widening out in circles, dying upon the darkness. This sound, which is not a cheerful one, made me almost gay. It was natural, and relieved the tension of the mind. I moved on with new courage, my nervous excitement calming down.

When all at once, quite suddenly, close to us, at our feet, there broke out a cry. I made a spring backwards in the first moment of surprise and horror, and in doing so came sharply against the same rough masonry and brambles that had struck me before. This new sound came upwards from the ground,—a low, moaning, wailing voice, full of suffering and pain. The contrast between it and the hoot of the owl was indescribable,— the one with a wholesome wildness and naturalness that hurt nobody; the other, a sound that made one's blood curdle, full of human misery. With a great deal of fumbling,—for in spite of everything I could do to keep up my courage my hands shook,— I managed to remove the slide of my lantern. The light leaped out like something living, and made the place visible in a moment. We were what would have been inside the ruined building had anything remained but the gable-wall which I have described. It was close to us, the vacant door-way in it going out straight into the blackness outside. The light showed the bit of wall, the ivy glistening upon it in clouds of dark green, the bramble-branches waving, and below, the open door,—a door that led to nothing. It was from this the voice came which died out just as the light flashed upon this strange scene. There was a moment's silence, and then it broke forth again. The sound was so near, so penetrating, so pitiful, that, in the nervous start I gave, the light fell out of my hand. As I groped for it in the dark my hand was clutched by Bagley, who, I think, must have dropped upon his knees; but I was too much perturbed myself to think much of this. He clutched at me in the confusion of his terror, forgetting all his usual decorum. 'For God's sake, what is it, sir?' he gasped. If I yielded, there was evidently an end of both of us. 'I can't tell,' I said, 'any more than you; that's what we've got to find out. Up, man, up!' I pulled him to his feet. 'Will you go round and examine the other side, or will you stay here with the lantern?' Bagley gasped at me with a face of horror. 'Can't we stay together, Colonel?' he said; his knees were trembling under him. I pushed him against the corner of the wall, and put the light into his hands. 'Stand fast till I come back; shake yourself together, man; let nothing pass you,' I said. The voice was within two or three feet of us; of that there could be no doubt.

I went myself to the other side of the wall, keeping close to it. The light shook in Bagley's hand, but, tremulous though it was, shone out through the vacant door, one oblong block of light marking all the crumbling corners and hanging masses of foliage. Was that something dark huddled in a heap by the side of it? I pushed forward across the light in the door-way, and fell upon it with my hands; but it was only a juniper-bush growing close against the wall. Meanwhile, the sight of my figure crossing the door-way had brought Bagley's nervous excitement to a height: he flew at me, gripping my shoulder. 'I've got him, Colonel! I've got him!' he cried, with a voice of sudden exultation. He thought it was a man, and was at once relieved. But at that moment the voice burst forth again between us, at our feet,— more close to us than any separate being could be. He dropped off from me, and fell against the wall, his jaw dropping as if he were dying. I suppose, at the same moment, he saw that it was me whom he had clutched. I, for my part, had scarcely more command of myself. I snatched the light out of his hand, and flashed it all about me wildly. Nothing,—the juniper-bush which I thought I had never seen before, the heavy growth of the glistening ivy, the brambles waving. It was close to my ears now, crying, crying, pleading as if for life. Either I heard the same words Roland had heard, or else, in my excitement, his imagination got possession of mine. The voice went on, growing into distinct articulation, but wavering about, now from one point, now from another, as if the owner of it were moving slowly back and forward. 'Mother! mother!' and then an outburst of wailing. As my mind steadied, getting accustomed (as one's mind gets accustomed to anything), it seemed to me as if some uneasy, miserable creature was pacing up and down before a closed door. Sometimes—but that must have been excitement—I thought I heard a sound like knocking, and then another burst, 'Oh, mother! mother!' All this close, close to the space where I was standing with my lantern, now before me, now behind me: a creature restless, unhappy, moaning, crying, before the vacant door-way, which no one could either shut or open more.

'Do you hear it, Bagley? do you hear what it is saying?' I cried, stepping in through the door-way. He was lying against the wall, his eyes glazed, half dead with terror. He made a motion of his lips as if to answer me, but no sounds came; then lifted his hand with a curious imperative movement as if ordering me to be silent and listen. And how long I did so I cannot tell. It began to have an interest, an exciting hold upon me, which I could not describe. It seemed to call up visibly a scene any one could understand,—a something shut out, restlessly wandering to and fro; sometimes the voice dropped, as if throwing itself down, sometimes wandered off a few paces, growing sharp and clear. 'Oh, mother, let me in! oh, mother, mother, let me in! oh, let me in!' Every word was clear to me. No wonder the boy had gone wild with pity. I tried to steady my mind upon Roland, upon his conviction that I could do something, but my head swam with the excitement, even when I partially overcame the terror. At last the words died away, and there was a sound of sobs and moaning. I cried out, 'In the name of God, who are you?' with a kind of feeling in my mind that to use the name of God was profane, seeing that I did not believe in ghosts or anything supernatural; but I did it all the same, and waited, my heart giving a leap of terror lest there should be a reply. Why this should have been I cannot tell, but I had a feeling that if there was an answer it would be more than I could bear. But there was no answer; the moaning went on, and then, as if it had been real, the voice rose a little higher again, the words recommenced, 'Oh, mother, let me in! oh, mother, let me in!' with an expression that was heart-breaking to hear.

As if it had been real! What do I mean by that? I suppose I got less alarmed as the thing went on. I began to recover the use of my senses,—I seemed to explain it all to myself by saying that this had once happened, that it was a recollection of a real scene. Why there should have seemed something quite satisfactory and composing in this explanation I cannot tell, but so it was. I began to listen almost as if it had been a play, forgetting Bagley, who, I almost think, had fainted, leaning against the wall. I was startled out of this strange spectatorship that had fallen upon me by the sudden rush of something which made my heart jump once more, a large black figure in the door-way waving its arms. 'Come in! come in! come in!' it shouted out hoarsely at the top of a deep bass voice, and then poor Bagley fell down senseless across the threshold. He was less sophisticated than I,—he had not been able to bear it any longer. I took him for something supernatural, as he took me, and it was some time before I awoke to the necessities of the moment. I remembered only after, that from the time I began to give my attention to the man, I heard the other voice no more. It was some time before I brought him to. It must have been a strange scene: the lantern making a luminous spot in the darkness, the man's white face lying on the black earth, I over him, doing what I could for him, probably I should have been thought to be murdering him had any one seen us. When at last I succeeded in pouring a little brandy down his throat, he sat up and looked about him wildly. 'What's up?' he said; then recognizing me, tried to struggle to his feet with a faint 'Beg your pardon, Colonel.' I got him home as best I could, making him lean upon my arm. The great fellow was as weak as a child. Fortunately he did not for some time remember what had happened. From the time Bagley fell the voice had stopped, and all was still.

———••👁••———

'You've got an epidemic in your house, Colonel,' Simson said to me next morning. 'What's the meaning of it all? Here's your butler raving about a voice. This will never do, you know; and so far as I can make out, you are in it too.'

'Yes, I am in it, Doctor. I thought I had better speak to you. Of course you are treating Roland all right, but the boy is not raving, he is as sane as you or me. It's all true.'

'As sane as—I—or you. I never thought the boy insane. He's got cerebral excitement, fever. I don't know what you've got. There's something very queer about the look of your eyes.'

'Come,' said I, 'you can't put us all to bed, you know. You had better listen and hear the symptoms in full.'

The Doctor shrugged his shoulders, but he listened to me patiently. He did not believe a word of the story, that was clear; but he heard it all from beginning to end. 'My dear fellow,' he said, 'the boy told me just the same. It's an epidemic. When one person falls a victim to this sort of thing, it's as safe as can be,— there's always two or three.'

'Then how do you account for it?' I said.

'Oh, account for it!—that's a different matter; there's no accounting for the freaks our brains are subject to. If it's delusion, if it's some trick of the echoes or the winds,—some phonetic disturbance or other—'

'Come with me to-night, and judge for yourself,' I said.

Upon this he laughed aloud, then said, 'That's not such a bad idea; but it would ruin me forever if it were known that John Simson was ghost-hunting.'

'There it is,' said I; 'you dart down on us who are unlearned with your phonetic disturbances, but you daren't examine what the thing really is for fear of being laughed at. That's science!'

'It's not science,—it's common-sense,' said the Doctor. 'The thing has delusion on the front of it. It is encouraging an unwholesome tendency even to examine. What good could come of it? Even if I am convinced, I shouldn't believe.'

'I should have said so yesterday; and I don't want you to be convinced or to believe,' said I. 'If you prove it to be a delusion, I shall be very much obliged to you for one. Come; somebody must go with me.'

'You are cool,' said the Doctor. 'You've disabled this poor fellow of yours, and made him—on that point—a lunatic for life; and now you want to disable me. But, for once, I'll do it. To save appearance, if you'll give me a bed, I'll come over after my last rounds.'

It was agreed that I should meet him at the gate, and that we should visit the scene of last night's occurrences before we came to the house, so that nobody might be the wiser. It was scarcely possible to hope that the cause of Bagley's sudden illness should not somehow steal into the knowledge of the servants at least, and it was better that all should be done as quietly as possible. The day seemed to me a very long one. I had to spend a certain part of it with Roland, which was a terrible ordeal for me, for what could I say to the boy? The improvement continued, but he was still in a very precarious state, and the trembling vehemence with which he turned to me when his mother left the room filled me with alarm. 'Father?' he said quietly. 'Yes, my boy, I am giving my best attention to it; all is being done that I can do. I have not come to any conclusion—yet. I am neglecting nothing you said,' I cried. What I could not do was to give his active mind any encouragement to dwell upon the mystery. It was a hard predicament, for some satisfaction had to be given him. He looked at me very wistfully, with the great blue eyes which shone so large and brilliant out of his white and worn face. 'You must trust me,' I said. 'Yes, father. Father understands,' he said to himself, as if to soothe some inward doubt. I left him as soon as I could. He was about the most precious thing I had on earth, and his health my first thought; but yet somehow, in the excitement of this other subject, I put that aside, and preferred not to dwell upon Roland, which was the most curious part of it all.

That night at eleven I met Simson at the gate. He had come by train, and I let him in gently myself. I had been so much absorbed in the coming experiment that I passed the ruins in going to meet him, almost without thought, if you can understand that. I had my lantern; and he showed me a coil of taper which he had ready for use. 'There is nothing like light,' he said, in his scoffing tone. It was a very still night, scarcely a sound, but not so dark. We could keep the path without difficulty as we went along. As we approached the spot we could hear a low moaning, broken occasionally by a bitter cry. 'Perhaps that is your voice,' said the Doctor; 'I thought it must be something of the kind. That's a poor brute caught in some of these infernal traps of yours; you'll find it among the bushes somewhere.' I said nothing. I felt no particular fear, but a triumphant satisfaction in what was to follow. I led him to the spot where Bagley and I had stood on the previous night. All was silent as a winter night could be,—so silent that we heard far off the sound of the horses in the stables, the shutting of a window at the house. Simson lighted his taper and went peering about, poking into all the corners. We looked like two conspirators lying in wait for some unfortunate traveller; but not a sound broke the quiet. The moaning had stopped before we came up; a star or two shone over us in the sky, looking down as if surprised at our strange proceedings. Dr Simson did nothing but utter subdued laughs under his breath. 'I thought as much,' he said. 'It is just the same with tables and all other kinds of ghostly apparatus; a sceptic's presence stops everything. When I am present nothing ever comes off. How long do you think it will be necessary to stay here? Oh, I don't complain; only when *you* are satisfied, *I* am-quite.'

I will not deny that I was disappointed beyond measure by this result. It made me look like a credulous fool. It gave the Doctor such a pull over me as nothing else could. I should point to all his morals for years to come; and his materialism, his scep-ticism, would be increased beyond endurance. 'It seems, indeed,' I said, 'that there is to be no—' 'Manifestation,' he said, laughing; 'that is what all the mediums say. No manifestations, in consequence of the presence of an unbeliever.' His laugh sounded very uncomfortable to me in the silence; and it was now near midnight. But that laugh seemed the signal; before it died away the moaning we had heard before was resumed. It started from some distance off, and came towards us, nearer and nearer, like some one walking along and moaning to himself. There could be no idea now that it was a hare caught in a trap. The approach was slow, like that of a weak person, with little halts and pauses. We heard it coming along the grass straight towards the vacant door-way. Simson had been a little startled by the first sound. He said hastily, 'That child has no business to be out so late.' But he felt, as well as I, that this was no child's voice. As it came nearer, he grew silent, and, going to the door-way with his taper, stood looking out towards the sound. The taper being unprotected blew about in the night air, though there was scarcely any wind. I threw the light of my lantern steady and white across the same space. It was in a blaze of light in the midst of the blackness. A little icy thrill had gone over me at the first sound, but as it came close, I confess that my only feeling was satisfaction. The scoffer could scoff no more. The light touched his own face, and showed a very perplexed countenance. If he was afraid, he concealed it with great success, but he was perplexed. And then all that had happened on the previous night was enacted once more. It fell strangely upon me with a sense of repetition. Every cry, every sob seemed the same as before. I listened almost without any emotion at all in my own person, thinking of its effect upon Simson. He maintained a very bold front, on the whole. All that coming and going of the voice was, if our ears could be trusted, exactly in front of the vacant, blank door-way, blazing full of light, which caught and shone in the glistening leaves of the great hollies at a little distance. Not a rabbit could have crossed the turf without being seen; but there was nothing. After a time, Simson, with a certain caution and bodily reluctance, as it seemed to me, went out with his roll of taper into this space. His figure showed against the holly in full outline. Just at this moment the voice sank, as was its custom, and seemed to fling itself down at the door. Simson recoiled violently, as if some one had come up against him, then turned, and held his taper low, as if examining something. 'Do you see anybody?' I cried in a whisper, feeling the chill of nervous panic steal over me at this action. 'It's nothing but a—confounded juniper-bush,' he said. This I knew very well to be nonsense, for the juniper-bush was on the other side. He went about after this round and round, poking his taper everywhere, then returned to me on the inner side of the wall. He scoffed no longer; his face was contracted and pale. 'How long does this go on?' he whispered to me, like a man who does not wish to interrupt some one who is speaking. I had become too much perturbed myself to remark whether the successions and changes of the voice were the same as last night. It suddenly went out in the air almost as he was speaking, with a soft reiterated sob dying away. If there had been anything to be seen, I should have said that the person was at that moment crouching on the ground close to the door.

We walked home very silent afterwards. It was only when we were in sight of the house that I said, 'What do you think of it?' 'I can't tell what to think of it,' he said quickly. He took—though he was a very temperate man—not the claret I was going to offer him, but some brandy from the tray, and swallowed it almost undiluted. 'Mind you, I don't believe a word of it,' he said, when he had lighted his candle; 'but I can't tell what to think,' he turned round to add, when he was half-way upstairs.

All of this, however, did me no good with the solution of my problem. I was to help this weeping, sobbing thing, which was already to me as distinct a personality as anything I knew; or what should I say to Roland? It was on my heart that my boy would die if I could not find some way of helping this creature. You may be surprised that I should speak of it in this way. I did not know if it was man or woman; but I no more doubted that it was a soul in pain than I doubted my own being; and it was my business to soothe this pain,—to deliver it, if that was possible. Was ever such a task given to an anxious father trembling for his only boy? I felt in my heart, fantastic as it may appear, that I must fulfil this somehow, or part with my child; and you may conceive that rather than do that I was ready to die. But even my dying would not have advanced me, unless by bringing me into the same world with that seeker at the door.

--------••✿••--------

Next morning Simson was out before breakfast, and came in with evident signs of the damp grass on his boots, and a look of worry and weariness, which did not say much for the night he had passed. He improved a little after breakfast, and visited his two patients,—for Bagley was still an invalid. I went out with him on his way to the train, to hear what he had to say about the boy. 'He is going on very well,' he said; 'there are no complications as yet. But mind you, that's not a boy to be trifled with, Mortimer. Not a word to him about last night.' I had to tell him then of my last interview with Roland, and of the impossible demand he had made upon me, by which, though he tried to laugh, he was much discomposed, as I could see. 'We must just perjure ourselves all round,' he said, 'and swear you exorcised it;' but the man was too kind-hearted to be satisfied with that. 'It's frightfully serious for you, Mortimer. I can't laugh as I should like to. I wish I saw a way out of it, for your sake. By the way,' he added shortly, 'didn't you notice that juniper-bush on the left-hand side?' 'There was one on the right hand of the door. I noticed you made that mistake last night.' 'Mistake!' he cried, with a curious low laugh, pulling up the collar of his coat as though he felt the cold,—'there's no juniper there this morning, left or right. Just go and see.' As he stepped into the train a few minutes after, he looked back upon me and beckoned me for a parting word. 'I'm coming back tonight,' he said.

I don't think I had any feeling about this as I turned away from that common bustle of the railway which made my private preoccupations feel so strangely out of date. There had been a distinct satisfaction in my mind before, that his scepticism had been so entirely defeated. But the more serious part of the matter pressed upon me now. I went straight from the railway to the manse, which stood on a little plateau on the side of the river opposite to the woods of Brentwood. The minister was one of a class which is not so common in Scotland as it used to be. He was a man of good family, well educated in the Scotch way, strong in philosophy, not so strong in Greek, strongest of all in experience,—a man who had 'come across,' in the course of his life, most people of note that had ever been in Scotland, and who was said to be very sound in doctrine, without infringing the toleration with which old men, who are good men, are generally endowed. He was old-fashioned; perhaps he did not think so much about the troublous problems of theology as many of the young men, nor ask himself any hard questions about the Confession of Faith; but he understood human nature, which is perhaps better. He received me with a cordial welcome.

'Come away, Colonel Mortimer,' he said; 'I'm all the more glad to see you, that I feel it's a good sign for the boy. He's doing well?—God be praised,—and the Lord bless him and keep him. He has many a poor body's prayers, and that can do nobody harm.'

'He will need them all, Dr Moncrieff,' I said, 'and your counsel too.' And I told him the story,—more than I had told Simson. The old clergyman listened to me with many suppressed exclamations, and at the end the water stood in his eyes.

'That's just beautiful,' he said. 'I do not mind to have heard anything like it; it's as fine as Burns when he wished deliverance to one—that is prayed for in no kirk. Ay, ay! so he would have you console the poor lost spirit? God bless the boy! There's something more than common in that, Colonel Mortimer. And also the faith of him in his father!—I would like to put that into a sermon.' Then the old gentleman gave me an alarmed look, and said, 'No, no; I was not meaning a sermon; but I must write it down for the "Children's Record".' I saw the thought that passed through his mind. Either he thought, or he feared I would think, of a funeral sermon. You may believe this did not make me more cheerful.

I can scarcely say that Dr Moncrieff gave me any advice. How could any one advise on such a subject? But he said, 'I think I'll come too. I'm an old man; I'm less liable to be frightened than those that are further off the world unseen. It behooves me to think of my own journey there. I've no cut-and-dry beliefs on the subject. I'll come too; and maybe at the moment the Lord will put into our heads what to do.'

This gave me a little comfort,—more than Simson had given me. To be clear about the cause of it was not my grand desire. It was another thing that was in my mind,—my boy. As for the poor soul at the open door, I had no more doubt, as I have said, of its existence than I had of my own. It was no ghost to me. I knew the creature, and it was in trouble. That was my feeling about it, as it was Roland's. To hear it first was a great shock to my nerves, but not now; a man will get accustomed to anything. But to do something for it was the great problem; how was I to be serviceable to a being that was invisible, that was mortal no longer? 'Maybe at the moment the Lord will put it into our heads.' This is very old-fashioned phraseology, and a week before, most likely, I should have smiled (though always with kindness) at Dr Moncrieff's credulity; but there was a great comfort, whether rational or otherwise I cannot say, in the mere sound of the words.

The road to the station and the village lay through the glen, not by the ruins; but though the sunshine and the fresh air, and the beauty of the trees, and the sound of the water were all very soothing to the spirits, my mind was so full of my own subject that I could not refrain from turning to the right hand as I got to the top of the glen, and going straight to the place which I may call the scene of all my thoughts. It was lying full in the sunshine, like all the rest of the world. The ruined gable looked due east, and in the present aspect of the sun the light streamed down through the door-way as our lantern had done, throwing a flood of light upon the damp grass beyond. There was a strange suggestion in the open door,—so futile, a kind of emblem of vanity: all free around, so that you could go where you pleased, and yet that semblance of an enclosure,—that way of entrance, unnecessary, leading to nothing. And why any creature should pray and weep to get in-to nothing, or be kept out—by nothing, you could not dwell upon it, or it made your brain go round. I remembered, however, what Simson said about the juniper, with a little smile on my own mind as to the inaccuracy of recollection which even a scientific man will be guilty of. I could see now the light of my lantern gleaming upon the wet glistening surface of the spiky leaves at the right hand,—and he ready to go to the stake for it that it was the left! I went round to make sure. And then I saw what he had said. Right or left there was no juniper at all! I was confounded by this, though it was entirely a matter of detail nothing at all,—a bush of brambles waving, the grass growing up to the very walls. But after all, though it gave me a shock for a moment, what did that matter? There were marks as if a number of footsteps had been up and down in front of the door, but these might have been our steps; and all was bright and peaceful and still. I poked about the other ruin—the larger ruins of the old house—for some time, as I had done before. There were marks upon the grass here and there— I could not call them footsteps—all about; but that told for nothing one way or another. I had examined the ruined rooms closely the first day. They were half filled up with soil and *debris*, withered brackens and bramble,—no refuge for any one there. It vexed me that Jarvis should see me coming from that spot when he came up to me for his orders. I don't know whether my nocturnal expeditions had got wind among the servants, but there was a significant look in his face. Something in it I felt was like my own sensation when Simson in the midst of his scepticism was struck dumb. Jarvis felt satisfied that his veracity had been put beyond question. I never spoke to a servant of mine in such a peremptory tone before. I sent him away 'with a flea in his lug,' as the man described it afterwards. Interference of any kind was intolerable to me at such a moment.

But what was strangest of all was, that I could not face Roland. I did not go up to his room, as I would have naturally done, at once. This the girls could not understand. They saw there was some mystery in it. 'Mother has gone to lie down,' Agatha said; 'he has had such a good night.' 'But he wants you so, papa!' cried little Jeanie, always with her two arms embracing mine in a pretty way she had. I was obliged to go at last, but what could I say? I could only kiss him, and tell him to keep still,—that I was doing all I could. There is something mystical about the patience of a child. 'It will come all right, won't it, father?' he said. 'God grant it may! I hope so, Roland.' 'Oh, yes, it will come all right.' Perhaps he understood that in the midst of my anxiety I could not stay with him as I should have done otherwise. But the girls were more surprised than it is possible to describe. They looked at me with wondering eyes. 'If I were ill, papa, and you only stayed with me a moment, I should break my heart,' said Agatha. But the boy had a sympathetic feeling. He knew that of my own will I would not have done it. I shut myself up in the library, where I could not rest, but kept pacing up and down like a caged beast. What could I do? and if I could do nothing, what would become of my boy? These were the questions that, without ceasing, pursued each other through my mind.

Simson came out to dinner, and when the house was all still, and most of the servants in bed, we went out and met Dr Moncrieff, as we had appointed, at the head of the glen. Simson, for his part, was disposed to scoff at the Doctor. 'If there are to be any spells, you know, I'll cut the whole concern,' he said. I did not make him any reply. I had not invited him; he could go or come as he pleased. He was very talkative, far more so than suited my humour, as we went on. 'One thing is certain, you know; there must be some human agency,' he said. 'It is all bosh about apparitions. I never have investigated the laws of sound to any great extent, and there's a great deal in ventriloquism that we don't know much about.' 'If it's the same to you,' I said, 'I wish you'd keep all that to yourself, Simson. It doesn't suit my state of mind.' 'Oh, I hope I know how to respect idiosyncrasy,' he said. The very tone of his voice irritated me beyond measure. These scientific fellows, I wonder people put up with them as they do, when you have no mind for their cold-blooded confidence. Dr Moncrieff met us about eleven o'clock, the same time as on the previous night. He was a large man, with a venerable countenance and white hair,— old, but in full vigour, and thinking less of a cold night walk than many a younger man. He had his lantern, as I had. We were fully provided with means of lighting the place, and we were all of us resolute men. We had a rapid consultation as we went up, and the result was that we divided to different posts. Dr Moncrieff remained inside the wall—if you can call that inside where there was no wall but one. Simson placed himself on the side next the ruins, so as to intercept any communication with the old house, which was what his mind was fixed upon. I was posted on the other side. To say that nothing could come near without being seen was self-evident. It had been so also on the previous night. Now, with our three lights in the midst of the darkness, the whole place seemed illuminated. Dr Moncrieff's lantern, which was a large one, without any means of shutting up,—an old-fashioned lantern with a pierced and ornamental top,—shone steadily, the rays shooting out of it upward into the gloom. He placed it on the grass, where the middle of the room, if this had been a room, would have been. The usual effect of the light streaming out of the door-way was prevented by the illumination which Simson and I on either side supplied. With these differences, everything seemed as on the previous night.

And what occurred was exactly the same, with the same air of repetition, point for point, as I had formerly remarked. I declare that it seemed to me as if I were pushed against, put aside, by the owner of the voice as he paced up and down in his trouble,— though these are perfectly futile words, seeing that the stream of light from my lantern, and that from Simson's taper, lay broad and clear, without a shadow, without the smallest break, across the entire breadth of the grass. I had ceased even to be alarmed, for my part. My heart was rent with pity and trouble,—pity for the poor suffering human creature that moaned and pleaded so, and trouble for myself and my boy. God! if I could not find any help,—and what help could I find?—Roland would die.

We were all perfectly still till the first outburst was exhausted, as I knew, by experience, it would be. Dr Moncrieff, to whom it was new, was quite motionless on the other side of the wall, as we were in our places. My heart had remained almost at its usual beating during the voice. I was used to it; it did not rouse all my pulses as it did at first. But just as it threw itself sobbing at the door (I cannot use other words), there suddenly came something which sent the blood coursing through my veins, and my heart into my mouth. It was a voice inside the wall,—the minister's well-known voice. I would have been prepared for it in any kind of adjuration, but I was not prepared for what I heard. It came out with a sort of stammering, as if too much moved for utterance. 'Willie, Willie! Oh, God preserve us! is it you?'

These simple words had an effect upon me that the voice of the invisible creature had ceased to have. I thought the old man, whom I had brought into this danger, had gone mad with terror. I made a dash round to the other side of the wall, half crazed myself with the thought. He was standing where I had left him, his shadow thrown vague and large upon the grass by the lantern which stood at his feet. I lifted my own light to see his face as I rushed forward. He was very pale, his eyes wet and glistening, his mouth quivering with parted lips. He neither saw nor heard me. We that had gone through this experience before, had crouched towards each other to get a little strength to bear it. But he was not even aware that I was there. His whole being seemed absorbed in anxiety and tenderness. He held out his hands, which trembled, but it seemed to me with eagerness, not fear. He went on speaking all the time. 'Willie, if it is you,—and it's you, if it is not a delusion of Satan,—Willie, lad! why come ye here frighting them that know you not? Why came ye not to me?'

He seemed to wait for an answer. When his voice ceased, his countenance, every line moving, continued to speak. Simson gave me another terrible shock, stealing into the open door-way with his light, as much awe-stricken, as wildly curious, as I. But the minister resumed, without seeing Simson, speaking to some one else. His voice took a tone of expostulation:—

'Is this right to come here? Your mother's gone with your name on her lips. Do you think she would ever close her door on her own lad? Do ye think the Lord will close the door, ye faint-hearted creature? No!—I forbid ye! I forbid ye!' cried the old man. The sobbing voice had begun to resume its cries. He made a step forward, calling out the last words in a voice of command. 'I forbid ye! Cry out no more to man. Go home, ye wandering spirit! go home! Do you hear me?—me that christened ye, that have struggled with ye, that have wrestled for ye with the Lord!' Here the loud tones of his voice sank into tenderness. 'And her too, poor woman! poor woman! her you are calling upon.

She's not here. You'll find her with the Lord. Go there and seek her, not here. Do you hear me, lad? go after her there. He'll let you in, though it's late. Man, take heart! if you will lie and sob and greet, let it be at heaven's gate, and not your poor mother's ruined door.'

He stopped to get his breath; and the voice had stopped, not as it had done before, when its time was exhausted and all its repetitions said, but with a sobbing catch in the breath as if overruled. Then the minister spoke again, 'Are you hearing me, Will? Oh, laddie, you've liked the beggarly elements all your days. Be done with them now. Go home to the Father—the Father! Are you hearing me?' Here the old man sank down upon his knees, his face raised upwards, his hands held up with a tremble in them, all white in the light in the midst of the darkness. I resisted as long as I could, though I cannot tell why; then I, too, dropped upon my knees. Simson all the time stood in the door-way, with an expression in his face such as words could not tell, his under lip dropped, his eyes wild, staring. It seemed to be to him, that image of blank ignorance and wonder, that we were praying. All the time the voice, with a low arrested sobbing, lay just where he was standing, as I thought.

'Lord,' the minister said,—'Lord, take him into Thy ever-lasting habitations. The mother he cries to is with Thee. Who can open to him but Thee? Lord, when is it too late for Thee, or what is too hard for Thee? Lord, let that woman there draw him inower! Let her draw him inower!'

I sprang forward to catch something in my arms that flung itself wildly within the door. The illusion was so strong, that I never paused till I felt my forehead graze against the wall and my hands clutch the ground,—for there was nobody there to save from falling, as in my foolishness I thought. Simson held out his hand to me to help me up. He was trembling and cold, his lower lip hanging, his speech almost inarticulate. 'It's gone,' he said, stammering,—'it's gone!' We leaned upon each other for a moment, trembling so much, both of us, that the whole scene trembled as if it were going to dissolve and disappear; and yet as long as I live I will never forget it,—the shining of the strange lights, the blackness all round, the kneeling figure with all the whiteness of the light concentrated on its white venerable head and uplifted hands. A strange solemn stillness seemed to close all round us. By intervals a single syllable, 'Lord! Lord!' came from the old minister's lips. He saw none of us, nor thought of us. I never knew how long we stood, like sentinels guarding him at his prayers, holding our lights in a confused dazed way, not knowing what we did. But at last he rose from his knees, and standing up at his full height, raised his arms, as the Scotch manner is at the end of a religious service, and solemnly gave the apostolical benediction,—to what? to the silent earth, the dark woods, the wide breathing atmosphere; for we were but spectators gasping an Amen!

It seemed to me that it must be the middle of the night, as we all walked back. It was in reality very late. Dr Moncrieff put his arm into mine. He walked slowly, with an air of exhaustion. It was as if we were coming from a death-bed. Something hushed and solemnized the very air. There was that sense of relief in it which there always is at the end of a death-struggle. And nature, persistent, never daunted, came back in all of us, as we returned into the ways of life. We said nothing to each other, indeed, for a time; but when we got clear of the trees and reached the opening near the house, where we could see the sky, Dr Moncrieff himself was the first to speak. 'I must be going,' he said; 'it's very late, I'm afraid. I will go down the glen, as I came.'

'But not alone. I am going with you, Doctor.'

'Well, I will not oppose it. I am an old man, and agitation wearies more than work. Yes; I'll be thankful of your arm. Tonight, Colonel, you've done me more good turns than one.'

I pressed his hand on my arm, not feeling able to speak. But Simson, who turned with us, and who had gone along all this time with his taper flaring, in entire unconsciousness, came to himself, apparently at the sound of our voices, and put out that wild little torch with a quick movement, as if of shame. 'Let me carry your lantern,' he said; 'it is heavy.' He recovered with a spring; and in a moment, from the awe-stricken spectator he had been, became himself, sceptical and cynical. 'I should like to ask you a question,' he said. 'Do you believe in Purgatory, Doctor? It's not in the tenets of the Church, so far as I know.'

'Sir,' said Dr Moncrieff, 'an old man like me is sometimes not very sure what he believes. There is just one thing I am certain of—and that is the loving-kindness of God.'

'But I thought that was in this life. I am no theologian—'

'Sir,' said the old man again, with a tremor in him which I could feel going over all his frame, 'if I saw a friend of mine within the gates of hell, I would not despair but his Father would take him by the hand still, if he cried like *you*.'

'I allow it is very strange, very strange. I cannot see through it. That there must be human agency, I feel sure. Doctor, what made you decide upon the person and the name?'

The minister put out his hand with the impatience which a man might show if he were asked how he recognized his brother. 'Tuts!' he said, in familiar speech; then more solemnly, 'How should I not recognize a person that I know better—far better— than I know you?'

'Then you saw the man?'

Dr Moncrieff made no reply. He moved his hand again with a little impatient movement, and walked on, leaning heavily on my arm. And we went on for a long time without another word, threading the dark paths, which were steep and slippery with the damp of the winter. The air was very still,—not more than enough to make a faint sighing in the branches, which mingled with the sound of the water to which we were descending. When we spoke again, it was about indifferent matters,—about the height of the river, and the recent rains. We parted with the minister at his own door, where his old housekeeper appeared in great perturbation, waiting for him. 'Eh, me, minister! the young gentleman will be worse?' she cried.

'Far from that—better. God bless him!' Dr Moncrieff said.

I think if Simson had begun again to me with his questions, I should have pitched him over the rocks as we returned up the glen; but he was silent, by a good inspiration. And the sky was clearer than it had been for many nights, shining high over the trees, with here and there a star faintly gleaming through the wilderness of dark and bare branches. The air, as I have said, was very soft in them, with a subdued and peaceful cadence. It was real, like every natural sound, and came to us like a hush of peace and relief. I thought there was a sound in it as of the breath of a sleeper, and it seemed clear to me that Roland must be sleeping, satisfied and calm. We went up to his room when we went in. There we found the complete hush of rest. My wife looked up out of a doze, and gave me a smile: 'I think he is a great deal better; but you are very late,' she said in a whisper, shading the light with her hand that the Doctor might see his patient. The boy had got back something like his own colour. He woke as we stood all round his bed. His eyes had the happy, half-awakened look of childhood, glad to shut again, yet pleased with the interruption and glimmer of the light. I stooped over him and kissed his forehead, which was moist and cool. 'All is well, Roland,' I said. He looked up at me with a glance of pleasure, and took my hand and laid his cheek upon it, and so went to sleep.

For some nights after, I watched among the ruins, spending all the dark hours up to midnight patrolling about the bit of wall which was associated with so many emotions; but I heard nothing, and saw nothing beyond the quiet course of nature;

nor, so far as I am aware, has anything been heard again. Dr Moncrieff gave me the history of the youth, whom he never hesitated to name. I did not ask, as Simson did, how he recognized him. He had been a prodigal,—weak, foolish, easily imposed upon, and 'led away,' as people say. All that we had heard had passed actually in life, the Doctor said. The young man had come home thus a day or two after his mother died,— who was no more than the housekeeper in the old house,—and distracted with the news, had thrown himself down at the door and called upon her to let him in. The old man could scarcely speak of it for tears. To me it seemed as if—Heaven help us, how little do we know about anything!—a scene like that might impress itself somehow upon the hidden heart of nature. I do not pretend to know how, but the repetition had struck me at the time as, in its terrible strangeness and incomprehensibility, almost mechanical,—as if the unseen actor could not exceed or vary, but was bound to re-enact the whole. One thing that struck me, however, greatly, was the likeness between the old minister and my boy in the manner of regarding these strange phenomena. Dr Moncrieff was not terrified, as I had been myself, and all the rest of us. It was no 'ghost,' as I fear we all vulgarly considered it, to him,—but a poor creature whom he knew under these conditions, just as he had known him in the flesh, having no doubt of his identity. And to Roland it was the same. This spirit in pain,—if it was a spirit,—this voice out of the unseen,—was a poor fellow-creature in misery, to be succoured and helped out of his trouble, to my boy. He spoke to me quite frankly about it when he got better. 'I knew father would find out some way,' he said. And this was when he was strong and well, and all idea that he would turn hysterical or become a seer of visions had happily passed away.

———— ⋅∘⋅ ————

I must add one curious fact, which does not seem to me to have any relation to the above, but which Simson made great use of, as the human agency which he was determined to find somehow. We had examined the ruins very closely at the time of these occurrences; but afterwards, when all was over, as we went casually about them one Sunday afternoon in the idleness of that unemployed day, Simson with his stick penetrated an old window which had been entirely blocked up with fallen soil. He jumped down into it in great excitement, and called me to follow. There we found a little hole,—for it was more a hole than a room,—entirely hidden under the ivy and ruins, in which there was a quantity of straw laid in a corner, as if someone had made a bed there, and some remains of crusts about the floor. Someone had lodged there, and not very long before, he made out; and that this unknown being was the author of all the mysterious sounds we heard he is convinced. 'I told you it was human agency,' he said triumphantly. He forgets, I suppose, how he and I stood with our lights, seeing nothing, while the space between us was audibly traversed by something that could speak, and sob, and suffer. There is no argument with men of this kind. He is ready to get up a laugh against me on this slender ground. 'I was puzzled myself,—I could not make it out,—but I always felt convinced human agency was at the bottom of it. And here it is,—and a clever fellow he must have been,' the Doctor says.

Bagley left my service as soon as he got well. He assured me it was no want of respect, but he could not stand 'them kind of things;' and the man was so shaken and ghastly that I was glad to give him a present and let him go. For my own part, I made a point of staying out the time—two years—for which I had taken Brentwood; but I did not renew my tenancy. By that time we had settled, and found for ourselves a pleasant home of our own.

I must add, that when the Doctor defies me, I can always bring back gravity to his countenance, and a pause in his railing, when I remind him of the juniper-bush. To me that was a matter of little importance. I could believe I was mistaken. I did not care about it one way or other; but on his mind the effect was different. The miserable voice, the spirit in pain, he could think of as the result of ventriloquism, or reverberation, or—anything you please: an elaborate prolonged hoax, executed somehow by the tramp that had found a lodging in the old tower; but the juniper-bush staggered him. Things have effects so different on the minds of different men.

The Body-Snatcher

Robert Louis Stevenson

EVERY NIGHT IN the year, four of us sat in the small parlour of the *George* at Debenham—the undertaker, and the landlord, and Fettes, and myself. Sometimes there would be more; but blow high, blow low, come rain or snow or frost, we four would be each planted in his own particular armchair. Fettes was an old drunken Scotsman, a man of education obviously, and a man of some property, since he lived in idleness. He had come to Debenham years ago, while still young, and by a mere continuance of living had grown to be an adopted townsman. His blue camlet cloak was a local antiquity, like the church-spire. His place in the parlour at the *George*, his absence from church, his old, crapulous, disreputable vices, were all things of course in Debenham. He had some vague Radical opinions and some fleeting infidelities, which he would now and again set forth and emphasize with tottering slaps upon the table. He drank rum—five glasses regularly every evening; and for the greater portion of his nightly visit to the *George* sat, with his glass in his right hand, in a state of melancholy alcoholic saturation. We called him the Doctor, for he was supposed to have some special knowledge of medicine, and had been known upon a pinch, to set a fracture or reduce a dislocation; but, beyond these slight particulars, we had no knowledge of his character and antecedents.

One dark winter night—it had struck nine some time before the landlord joined us—there was a sick man in the *George*, a great neighbouring proprietor suddenly struck down with apoplexy on his way to Parliament; and the great man's still greater London doctor had been telegraphed to his bedside. It was the first time that such a thing had happened in Debenham, for the railway was but newly open, and we were all proportionately moved by the occurrence.

'He's come,' said the landlord, after he had filled and lighted his pipe.

'He?' said I. 'Who?—not the doctor?'

'Himself,' replied our host.

'What is his name?'

'Dr Macfarlane,' said the landlord.

Fettes was far through his third tumbler, stupidly fuddled, now nodding over, now staring mazily around him; but at the last word he seemed to awaken, and repeated the name 'Macfarlane' twice, quietly enough the first time, but with sudden emotion at the second.

'Yes,' said the landlord, 'that's his name, Doctor Wolfe Macfarlane.'

Fettes became instantly sober: his eyes awoke, his voice became clear, loud, and steady, his language forcible and earnest. We were all startled by the transformation, as if a man had risen from the dead.

'I beg your pardon,' he said, 'I am afraid I have not been paying much attention to your talk. Who is this Wolfe Macfarlane?' And then, when he had heard the landlord out, 'It cannot be, it cannot be,' he added; 'and yet I would like well to see him face to face.'

'Do you know him, Doctor?' asked the undertaker, with a gasp.

'God forbid!' was the reply. 'And yet the name is a strange one; it were too much to fancy two. Tell me, landlord, is he old?'

'Well,' said the host, 'he's not a young man, to be sure, and his hair is white; but he looks younger than you.'

'He is older, though; years older. But,' with a slap upon the table, 'it's the rum you see in my face—rum and sin. This man, perhaps, may have an easy conscience and a good digestion. Conscience! Hear me speak. You would think I was some good, old, decent Christian, would you not? But no, not I; I never canted. Voltaire might have canted if he'd stood in my shoes; but the brains'—with a rattling fillip on his bald head—'the brains were clear and active, and I saw and made no deductions'.

'If you know this doctor,' I ventured to remark, after a somewhat awful pause, 'I should gather that you do not share the landlord's good opinion.'

Fettes paid no regard to me.

'Yes,' he said, with sudden decision, 'I must see him face to face.' There was another pause, and then a door was closed rather sharply on the first floor, and a step was heard upon the stair.

'That's the doctor,' cried the landlord. 'Look sharp, and you can catch him.'

It was but two steps from the small parlour to the door of the old *George* inn; the wide oak staircase landed almost in the street; there was room for a Turkey rug and nothing more between the threshold and the last round of the descent; but this little space was every evening brilliantly lit up, not only by the light upon the stair and the great signal-lamp below the sign, but by the warm radiance of the bar-room window. The *George* thus brightly advertised itself to passers-by in the cold street. Fettes walked steadily to the spot, and we, who were hanging behind, beheld the two men meet, as one of them had phrased it, face to face. Dr Macfarlane was alert and vigorous. His white hair set off his pale and placid, although energetic, countenance.

He was richly dressed in the finest of broadcloth and the whitest of linen, with a great gold watchchain, and studs and spectacles of the same precious material. He wore a broad-folded tie, white and speckled with lilac, and he carried on his arm a comfortable driving-coat of fur. There was no doubt but he became his years, breathing as he did, of wealth and consideration; and it was a surprising contrast to see our parlour sot—bald, dirty, pimpled, and robed in his old camlet cloak—confront him at the bottom of the stairs.

'Macfarlane!' he said somewhat loudly, more like a herald than a friend.

The great doctor pulled up short on the fourth step, as though the familiarity of the address surprised and somewhat shocked his dignity.

'Toddy Macfarlane!' repeated Fettes.

The London man almost staggered. He stared for the swiftest of seconds at the man before him, glanced behind him with a sort of scare, and then in a startled whisper, 'Fettes!' he said, 'you!'

'Ay,' said the other, 'me! Did you think I was dead too? We are not so easy shut of our acquaintance.'

'Hush, hush!' exclaimed the doctor. 'Hush, hush! this meeting is so unexpected—I can see you are unmanned. I hardly knew you, I confess, at first; but I am overjoyed—overjoyed to have this opportunity. For the present it must be how-d'ye-do and goodbye in one, for my fly is waiting, and I must not fail the train; but you shall—let me see—yes—you shall give me your address, and you can count on early news of me. We must do something for you, Fettes. I fear you are out at elbows; but we must see to that for auld lang syne, as once we sang at suppers.'

'Money!' cried Fettes; 'money from you! The money that I had from you is lying where I cast it in the rain.'

Dr Macfarlane had talked himself into some measure of superiority and confidence, but the uncommon energy of this refusal cast him back into his first confusion.

A horrible, ugly look came and went across his almost venerable countenance. 'My dear fellow,' he said, 'be it as you please; my last thought is to offend you. I would intrude on none. I will leave you my address, however—'

'I do not wish it—I do not wish to know the roof that shelters you,' interrupted the other. 'I heard your name; I feared it might be you; I wished to know if, after all, there were a God; I know now that there is none. Begone!'

He still stood in the middle of the rug, between the stair and the doorway; and the great London physician, in order to escape, would be forced to step to one side. It was plain that he hesitated before the thought of this humiliation. White as he was, there was a dangerous glitter in his spectacles; but while he still paused uncertain, he became aware that the driver of his fly was peering in from the street at this unusual scene and caught a glimpse at the same time of our little body from the parlour, huddled by the corner of the bar. The presence of so many witnesses decided him at once to flee. He crouched together, brushing on the wainscot, and made a dart like a serpent, striking for the door. But his tribulation was not yet entirely at an end, for even as he was passing Fettes clutched him by the arm and these words came in a whisper, and yet painfully distinct, 'Have you seen it again?'

The great rich London doctor cried out aloud with a sharp, throttling cry; he dashed his questioner across the open space, and, with his hands over his head, fled out of the door like a detected thief. Before it had occurred to one of us to make a movement, the fly was already rattling toward the station. The scene was over like a dream, but the dream had left proofs and traces of its passage. Next day the servant found the fine gold spectacles broken on the threshold, and that very night we were all standing breathless by the bar-room window, and Fettes at our side, sober, pale, and resolute in look.

'God protect us, Mr Fettes!' said the landlord, coming first into possession of his customary senses. 'What in the universe is all this? These are strange things you have been saying.'

Fettes turned toward us; he looked us each in succession in the face. 'See if you can hold your tongues,' said he. 'That man Macfarlane is not safe to cross; those that have done so already have repented it too late.'

And then, without so much as finishing his third glass, far less waiting for the other two, he bade us goodbye and went forth, under the lamp of the hotel, into the black night.

We three turned to our places in the parlour, with the big red fire and four clear candles; and as we recapitulated what had passed the first chill of our surprise soon changed into a glow of curiosity. We sat late; it was the latest session I have known in the old *George*. Each man, before we parted, had his theory that he was bound to prove; and none of us had any nearer business in this world than to track out the past of our condemned companion, and surprise the secret that he shared with the great London doctor. It is no great boast, but I believe I was a better hand at worming out a story than either of my fellows at the *George*; and perhaps there is now no other man alive who could narrate to you the following foul and unnatural events.

In his young days Fettes studied medicine in the schools of Edinburgh. He had talent of a kind, the talent that picks up swiftly what it hears and readily retails it for its own. He worked little at home; but he was civil, attentive, and intelligent in the presence of his masters. They soon picked him out as a lad who listened closely and remembered well; nay, strange as it seemed to me when I first heard it, he was in those days well favoured, and pleased by his exterior. There was, at that period, a certain extramural teacher of anatomy, whom I shall here designate by the letter K. His name was subsequently too well known. The man who bore it skulked through the streets of Edinburgh in disguise, while the mob that applauded at the execution of Burke called loudly for the blood of his employer. But Mr K—

was then at the top of his vogue; he enjoyed a popularity due partly to his own talent and address, partly to the incapacity of his rival, the university professor. The students, at least, swore by his name, and Fettes believed himself, and was believed by others, to have laid the foundations of success when he had acquired the favour of this meteorically famous man. Mr K— was a *bon vivant* as well as an accomplished teacher; he liked a sly allusion no less than a careful preparation. In both capacities Fettes enjoyed and deserved his notice, and by the second year of his attendance he held the half-regular position of second demonstrator or sub-assistant in his class.

In this capacity, the charge of the theatre and lecture-room devolved in particular upon his shoulders. He had to answer for the cleanliness of the premises and the conduct of the other students, and it was a part of his duty to supply, receive, and divide the various subjects. It was with a view to this last—at that time very delicate—affair that he was lodged by Mr K— in the same wynd, and at last in the same building, with the dissecting-rooms. Here, after a night of turbulent pleasures, his hand still tottering, his sight still misty and confused, he would be called out of bed in the black hours before the winter dawn by the unclean and desperate interlopers who supplied the table. He would open the door to these men, since infamous throughout the land. He would help them with their tragic burthen, pay them their sordid price, and remain alone, when they were gone, with the unfriendly relics of humanity. From such a scene he would return to snatch another hour or two of slumber, to repair the abuses of the night, and refresh himself for the labours of the day.

Few lads could have been more insensible to the impressions of a life thus passed among the ensigns of mortality. His mind was closed against all general considerations. He was incapable of interest in the fate and fortunes of another, the slave of his own desires and low ambitions. Cold, light, and selfish in the last resort, he had that modicum of prudence, miscalled morality, which keeps a man from inconvenient drunkenness or punishable theft. He coveted, besides, a measure of consideration from his masters and his fellow-pupils, and he had no desire to fail conspicuously in the external parts of life. Thus he made it his pleasure to gain some distinction in his studies, and day after day rendered unimpeachable eye-service to his employer, Mr K——. For his day of work he indemnified himself by nights of roaring, blackguardly enjoyment; and when that balance had been struck, the organ that he called his conscience declared itself content.

The supply of subjects was a continual trouble to him as well as to his master. In that large and busy class, the raw material of the anatomists kept perpetually running out; and the business thus rendered necessary was not only unpleasant in itself, but threatened dangerous consequences to all who were concerned. It was the policy of Mr K—— to ask no questions in his dealings with the trade. 'They bring the boy, and we pay the price,' he used to say, dwelling on the alliteration—*quid pro quo*. And, again, and somewhat profanely, 'Ask no questions,' he would tell his assistants, 'for conscience' sake.' There was no understanding that the subjects were provided by the crime of murder. Had that idea been broached to him in words, he would have recoiled in horror; but the lightness of his speech upon so grave a matter was, in itself, an offence against good manners, and a temptation to the men with whom he dealt. Fettes, for instance, had often remarked to himself upon the singular freshness of the bodies. He had been struck again and again by the hang-dog, abominable looks of the ruffians who came to him before the dawn; and, putting things together clearly in his private thoughts, he perhaps attributed a meaning too immoral and too categorical to the unguarded counsels of his master. He understood his duty, in short, to have three branches: to take what was brought, to pay the price, and to avert the eye from any evidence of crime.

One November morning this policy of silence was put sharply to the test. He had been awake all night with a racking toothache—pacing his room like a caged beast or throwing himself in fury on his bed—and had fallen at last into that profound, uneasy slumber that so often follows on a night of pain, when he was awakened by the third or fourth angry repetition of the concerted signal. There was a thin, bright moonshine: it was bitter cold, windy, and frosty; the town had not yet awakened, but an indefinable stir already preluded the noise and business of the day. The ghouls had come later than usual, and they seemed more than usually eager to be gone. Fettes, sick with sleep, lighted them upstairs. He heard their grumbling Irish voices through a dream; and as they stripped the sack from their sad merchandise he leaned dozing, with his shoulder propped against the wall; he had to shake himself to find the men their money. As he did so his eyes lighted on the dead face. He started; he took two steps nearer, with the candle raised.

'God Almighty!' he cried. 'That is Jane Galbraith!'

The men answered nothing, but they shuffled nearer the door.

'I know her, I tell you,' he continued. 'She was alive and hearty yesterday. It's impossible she can be dead; it's impossible you should have got this body fairly.'

'Sure, sir, you're mistaken entirely,' said one of the men.

But the other looked Fettes darkly in the eyes, and demanded the money on the spot.

It was impossible to misconceive the threat or to exaggerate the danger. The lad's heart failed him. He stammered some excuses, counted out the sum, and saw his hateful visitors depart. No sooner were they gone than he hastened to confirm his doubts. By a dozen unquestionable marks he identified the girl he had jested with the day before. He saw, with horror, marks upon her body that might well betoken violence. A panic seized him, and he took refuge in his room. There he reflected at length over the discovery that he had made; considered soberly the bearing of Mr K——'s instructions and the danger to himself of interference in so serious a business, and at last, in sore perplexity, determined to wait for the advice of his immediate superior, the class assistant.

This was a young doctor, Wolfe Macfarlane, a high favourite among all the reckless students, clever, dissipated, and unscrupulous to the last degree. He had travelled and studied abroad. His manners were agreeable and a little forward. He was an authority on the stage, skilful on the ice or the links with skate or golf-club; he dressed with nice audacity, and, to put the finishing touch upon his glory, he kept a gig and a strong trotting-horse. With Fettes he was on terms of intimacy; indeed their relative positions called for some community of life; and when subjects were scarce the pair would drive far into the country in Macfarlane's gig, visit and desecrate some lonely graveyard, and return before dawn with their booty to the door of the dissecting-room.

On that particular morning Macfarlane arrived somewhat earlier than his wont. Fettes heard him, and met him on the stairs, told him his story, and showed him the cause of his alarm. Macfarlane examined the marks on her body.

'Yes', he said with a nod, 'it looks fishy.'

'Well, what should I do?' asked Fettes.

'Do?' repeated the other. 'Do you want to do anything? Least said soonest mended, I should say.'

'Someone else might recognize her,' objected Fettes. 'She was as well known as the Castle Rock.'

'We'll hope not,' said Macfarlane, 'and if anybody does— well, you didn't, don't you see, and there's an end. The fact is, this has been going on too long. Stir up the mud, and you'll get K—— into the most unholy trouble; you'll be in a shocking box yourself. So will I, if you come to that. I should like to know how any one of us would look, or what the devil we should have to say for ourselves, in any Christian witness-box. For me, you know there's one thing certain—that, practically speaking, all our subjects have been murdered.'

'Macfarlane!' cried Fettes.

'Come now!' sneered the other. 'As if you hadn't suspected it yourself!'

'Suspecting is one thing—'

'And proof another. Yes, I know; and I'm as sorry as you are this should have come here,' tapping the body with his cane. 'The next best thing for me is not to recognize it; and,' he added coolly, 'I don't. You may, if you please. I don't dictate, but I think a man of the world would do as I do; and I may add, I fancy that is what K— would look for at our hands. The question is, Why did he choose us two for his assistants? And I answer, because he didn't want old wives.'

This was the tone of all others to affect the mind of a lad like Fettes. He agreed to imitate Macfarlane. The body of the unfortunate girl was duly dissected, and no one remarked or appeared to recognize her.

One afternoon, when his day's work was over, Fettes dropped into a popular tavern and found Macfarlane sitting with a stranger. This was a small man, very pale and dark, with coal-black eyes. The cut of his features gave a promise of intellect and refinement which was but feebly realized in his manners, for he proved, upon a nearer acquaintance, coarse, vulgar, and stupid. He exercised, however, a very remarkable control over Macfarlane; issued orders like the Great Bashaw; became inflamed at the least discussion or delay, and commented rudely on the servility with which he was obeyed. This most offensive person took a fancy to Fettes on the spot, plied him with drinks, and honoured him with unusual confidences on his past career. If a tenth part of what he confessed were true, he was a very loathsome rogue; and the lad's vanity was tickled by the attention of so experienced a man.

'I'm a pretty bad fellow myself,' the stranger remarked, 'but Macfarlane is the boy—Toddy Macfarlane I call him. Toddy, order your friend another glass.' Or it might be, 'Toddy, you jump up and shut the door.' 'Toddy hates me,' he said again. 'Oh, yes, Toddy, you do!'

'Don't you call me that confounded name,' growled Macfarlane.

'Hear him! Did you ever see the lads play knife? He would like to do that all over my body,' remarked the stranger.

'We medicals have a better way than that,' said Fettes. 'When we dislike a dead friend of ours, we dissect him.'

Macfarlane looked up sharply, as though this jest was scarcely to his mind.

The afternoon passed. Gray, for that was the stranger's name, invited Fettes to join them at dinner, ordered a feast so sumptuous that the tavern was thrown in commotion, and when all was done commanded Macfarlane to settle the bill. It was late before they separated; the man Gray was incapably drunk. Macfarlane, sobered by his fury, chewed the cud of the money he had been forced to squander and the slights he had been obliged to swallow. Fettes, with various liquors singing in his head, returned home with devious footsteps and a mind entirely in abeyance. Next day Macfarlane was absent from the class, and Fettes smiled to himself as he imagined him still squiring the intolerable Gray from tavern to tavern. As soon as the hour of liberty had struck he posted from place to place in quest of his last night's companions. He could find them, however, nowhere; so returned early to his rooms, went early to bed, and slept the sleep of the just.

At four in the morning he was awakened by the well-known signal. Descending to the door, he was filled with astonishment to find Macfarlane with his gig, and in the gig one of those long and ghastly packages with which he was so well acquainted.

'What?' he cried. 'Have you been out alone? How did you manage?'

But Macfarlane silenced him roughly, bidding him turn to business. When they had got the body upstairs and laid it on the table, Macfarlane made at first as if he were going away. Then he paused and seemed to hesitate; and then, 'You had better look at the face,' said he, in tones of some constraint. 'You had better,' he repeated, as Fettes only stared at him in wonder.

'But where, and how, and when did you come by it?' cried the other.

'Look at the face,' was the only answer.

Fettes was staggered; strange doubts assailed him. He looked from the young doctor to the body, and then back again. At last, with a start, he did as he was bidden. He had almost expected the sight that met his eyes, and yet the shock was cruel. To see, fixed in the rigidity of death and naked on that coarse layer of sack-cloth, the man whom he had left well-clad and full of meat and sin upon the threshold of a tavern, awoke, even in the thoughtless Fettes, some of the terrors of the conscience. It was a *cras tibi* which re-echoed in his soul, that two whom he had known should have come to lie upon these icy tables. Yet these were only secondary thoughts. His first concern regarded Wolfe. Unprepared for a challenge so momentous, he knew not how to look his comrade in the face. He durst not meet his eye, and he had neither words nor voice at his command.

It was Macfarlane himself who made the first advance. He came up quietly behind and laid his hand gently but firmly on the other's shoulder.

'Richardson,' said he, 'may have the head.'

Now Richardson was a student who had long been anxious for that portion of the human subject to dissect. There was no answer, and the murderer resumed: 'Talking of business, you must pay me; your accounts, you see, must tally.'

Fettes found a voice, the ghost of his own: 'Pay you!' he cried, 'Pay you for that?'

'Why, yes, of course you must. By all means and on every possible account, you must,' returned the other. 'I dare not give it for nothing, you dare not take it for nothing; it would compromise us both. This is another case like Jane Galbraith's. The more things are wrong the more we must act as if all were right. Where does old K— keep his money?'

'There,' answered Fettes hoarsely, pointing to a cupboard in the corner.

'Give me the key, then,' said the other, calmly, holding out his hand.

There was an instant's hesitation, and the die was cast. Macfarlane could not suppress a nervous twitch, the infinitesimal mark of an immense relief, as he felt the key between his fingers. He opened the cupboard, brought out pen and ink and a paper-book that stood in one compartment, and separated from the funds in a drawer a sum suitable to the occasion.

'Now, look here,' he said, 'there is the payment made—first proof of your good faith: first step to your security. You have now to clinch it by a second. Enter the payment in your book, and then you for your part may defy the devil.'

The next few seconds were for Fettes an agony of thought; but in balancing his terrors it was the most immediate that triumphed. Any future difficulty seemed almost welcome if he could avoid a present quarrel with Macfarlane. He set down the candle which he had been carrying all the time, and with a steady hand entered the date, the nature, and the amount of the transaction.

'And now,' said Macfarlane, 'it's only fair that you should pocket the lucre. I've had my share already. By-the-by, when a man of the world falls into a bit of luck, has a few shillings extra in his pocket—I'm ashamed to speak of it, but there's a rule of conduct in the case. No treating, no purchase of expensive class-books, no squaring of old debts; borrow, don't lend.'

'Macfarlane,' began Fettes, still somewhat hoarsely, 'I have put my neck in a halter to oblige you.'

'To oblige me?' cried Wolfe. 'Oh, come! You did, as near as I can see the matter, what you downright had to do in self-defence. Suppose I got into trouble, where would you be? This second little matter flows clearly from the first. Mr Gray is the continuation of Miss Galbraith. You can't begin and then stop. If you begin, you must keep on beginning; that's the truth. No rest for the wicked.'

A horrible sense of blackness and the treachery of fate seized hold upon the soul of the unhappy student.

'My God!' he cried, 'but what have I done? and when did I begin? To be made a class assistant—in the name of reason, where's the harm in that? Service wanted the position; Service might have got it. Would *he* have been where *I* am now?'

'My dear fellow,' said Macfarlane, 'what a boy you are! What harm *has* come to you? What harm *can* come to you if you hold your tongue? Why, man, do you know what this life is? There are two squads of us—the lions and the lambs. If you're a lamb, you'll come to lie upon these tables like Gray or Jane Galbraith; if you're a lion, you'll live and drive a horse like me, like K—, like all the world with any wit or courage. You're staggered at the first. But look at K—! My dear fellow, you're clever, you have pluck. I like you, and K— likes you. You were born to lead the hunt; and I tell you, on my honour and my experience of life, three days from now you'll laugh at all these scarecrows like a high-school boy at a farce.'

And with that Macfarlane took his departure and drove off up the wynd in his gig to get under cover before daylight. Fettes was thus left alone with his regrets. He saw the miserable peril in which he stood involved. He saw, with inexpressible dismay, that there was no limit to his weakness, and that, from concession to concession, he had fallen from the arbiter of Macfarlane's destiny to his paid and helpless accomplice. He would have given the world to have been a little braver at the time, but it did not occur to him that he might still be brave. The secret of Jane Galbraith and the cursed entry in the day-book closed his mouth.

Hours passed; the class began to arrive; the members of the unhappy Gray were dealt out to one and to another, and received without remark. Richardson was made happy with the head; and before the hour of freedom rang Fettes trembled with exultation to perceive how far they had already gone toward safety.

For two days he continued to watch, with increasing joy, the dreadful process of disguise.

On the third day Macfarlane made his appearance. He had been ill, he said; but he made up for lost time by the energy with which he directed the students. To Richardson in particular he extended the most valuable assistance and advice, and that student, encouraged by the praise of the demonstrator, burned high with ambitious hopes, and saw the medal already in his grasp.

Before the week was out Macfarlane's prophecy had been fulfilled. Fettes had outlived his terrors and had forgotten his baseness. He began to plume himself upon his courage, and had so arranged the story in his mind that he could look back on these events with an unhealthy pride. Of his accomplice he saw but little. They met, of course, in the business of the class; they received their orders together from Mr K——. At times they had a word or two in private, and Macfarlane was from first to last particularly kind and jovial. But it was plain that he avoided any reference to their common secret; and even when Fettes whispered to him that he had cast in his lot with the lions and forsworn the lambs, he only signed to him smilingly to hold his peace.

At length an occasion arose which threw the pair once more into a closer union. Mr K—— was again short of subjects; pupils were eager, and it was a part of this teacher's pretensions to be always well supplied. At the same time there came the news of a burial in the rustic graveyard of Glencorse. Time has little changed the place in question. It stood then, as now, upon a cross-road, out of call of human habitations, and buried fathom deep in the foliage of six cedar trees. The cries of the sheep upon the neighbouring hills, the streamlets upon either hand, one loudly singing among pebbles, the other dripping furtively from pond to pond, the stir of the wind in mountainous old flowering chestnuts, and once in seven days the voice of the bell and the old tunes of the precentor, were the only sounds that disturbed the silence around the rural church. The Resurrection Man—to use a by-name of the period—was not to be deterred by any of the sanctities of customary piety. It was part of his trade to despise and desecrate the scrolls and trumpets of old tombs, the paths worn by the feet of worshippers and mourners, and the offerings and the inscriptions of bereaved affection. To rustic neighbourhoods, where love is more than commonly tenacious, and where some bonds of blood or fellowship unite the entire society of a parish, the body-snatcher, far from being repelled by natural respect, was attracted by the ease and safety of the task. To bodies that had been laid in earth, in joyful expectation of a far different awakening, there came that hasty, lamp-lit, terror-haunted resurrection of the spade and mattock. The coffin was forced, the cerements torn, and the melancholy relics, clad in sackcloth, after being rattled for hours on moonless by-ways, were at length exposed to uttermost indignities before a class of gaping boys.

Somewhat as two vultures may swoop upon a dying lamb, Fettes and Macfarlane were to be let loose upon a grave in that green and quiet resting-place. The wife of a farmer, a woman who had lived for sixty years, and been known for nothing but good butter and a godly conversation, was to be rooted from her grave at midnight and carried, dead and naked, to that far-away city that she had always honoured with her Sunday best; the place beside her family was to be empty till the crack of doom; her innocent and almost venerable members to be exposed to that last curiosity of the anatomist.

Late one afternoon the pair set forth, well wrapped in cloaks and furnished with a formidable bottle. It rained without remission

—a cold, dense, lashing rain. Now and again there blew a puff of wind, but these sheets of falling water kept it down. Bottle and all, it was a sad and silent drive as far as Penicuik, where they were to spend the evening. They stopped once, to hide their implements in a thick bush not far from the churchyard, and once again at the Fisher's Tryst, to have a toast before the kitchen fire and vary their nips of whisky with a glass of ale. When they reached their journey's end the gig was housed, the horse was fed and comforted, and the two young doctors in a private room sat down to the best dinner and the best wine the house afforded. The lights, the fire, the beating rain upon the window, the cold, incongruous work that lay before them, added zest to their enjoyment of the meal. With every glass their cordiality increased. Soon Macfarlane handed a little pile of gold to his companion.

'A compliment,' he said. 'Between friends these little d—d accommodations ought to fly like pipe-lights.'

Fettes pocketed the money, and applauded the sentiment to the echo. 'You are a philosopher,' he cried. 'I was an ass till I knew you. You and K— between you, by the Lord Harry! but you'll make a man of me.'

'Of course we shall,' applauded Macfarlane. 'A man? I tell you, it required a man to back me up the other morning. There are some big, brawling, forty-year-old cowards who would have turned sick at the look of the d—d thing; but not you—you kept your head. I watched you.'

'Well, and why not?' Fettes thus vaunted himself. 'It was no affair of mine. There was nothing to gain on the one side but disturbance, and on the other I could count on your gratitude, don't you see?' And he slapped his pocket till the gold pieces rang.

Macfarlane somehow felt a certain touch of alarm at these unpleasant words. He may have regretted that he had taught his young companion so successfully, but he had no time to interfere, for the other noisily continued in this boastful strain:

'The great thing is not to be afraid. Now, between you and me I don't want to hang—that's practical; but for all cant, Macfarlane, I was born with a contempt. Hell, God, Devil, right, wrong, sin, crime, and all the old gallery of curiosities—they may frighten boys, but men of the world, like you and me, despise them. Here's to the memory of Gray!'

It was by this time growing somewhat late. The gig, according to order, was brought round to the door with both lamps brightly shining, and the young men had to pay their bill and take the road. They announced that they were bound for Peebles, and drove in that direction till they were clear of the last houses of the town; then, extinguishing the lamps, returned upon their course, and followed a by-road toward Glencorse. There was no sound but that of their own passage, and the incessant, strident pouring of the rain. It was pitch dark; here and there a white gate or a white stone in the wall guided them for a short space across the night; but for the most part it was at a foot pace, and almost groping, that they picked their way through that resonant blackness to their solemn and isolated destination. In the sunken woods that traverse the neighbourhood of the burying-ground the last glimmer failed them, and it became necessary to kindle a match and reillumine one of the lanterns of the gig. Thus, under the dripping trees, and environed by huge and moving shadows, they reached the scene of their unhallowed labours.

They were both experienced in such affairs, and powerful with the spade; and they had scarce been twenty minutes at their task before they were rewarded by a dull rattle on the coffin lid. At the same moment Macfarlane, having hurt his hand upon a stone, flung it carelessly above his head. The grave, in which they now stood almost to the shoulders, was close to the edge of the plateau of the graveyard; and the gig lamp had been propped, the better to illuminate theirs labours, against a tree, and on the immediate verge of the steep bank descending to the stream. Chance had taken a sure aim with the stone. Then came a clang of broken glass; night fell upon them; sounds alternately dull and ringing announced the bounding of the lantern down the bank, and its occasional collision with the trees. A stone or two, which it had dislodged in its descent, rattled behind it into the profundities of the glen; and then silence, like night, resumed its sway; and they might bend their hearing to its utmost pitch, but naught was to be heard except the rain, now marching to the wind, now steadily falling over miles of open country.

They were so nearly at an end of their abhorred task that they judged it wisest to complete it in the dark. The coffin was exhumed and broken open; the body inserted in the dripping sack and carried between them to the gig; one mounted to keep it in its place, and the other, taking the horse by the mouth, groped along by wall and bush until they reached the wider road by the Fisher's Tryst. Here was a faint, diffused radiancy, which they hailed like daylight; by that they pushed the horse to a good pace and began to rattle along merrily in the direction of the town.

They had both been wetted to the skin during their operations, and now, as the gig jumped among the deep ruts, the thing that stood propped between them fell now upon one and now upon the other. At every repetition of the horrid contact each instinctively repelled it with greater haste; and the process, natural although it was, began to tell upon the nerves of the companions. Macfarlane made some ill-favoured jest about the farmer's wife, but it came hollowly from his lips, and was allowed to drop in silence. Still their unnatural burthen bumped from side to side; and now the head would be laid, as if in confidence, upon their shoulders, and now the drenching sackcloth would flap icily about their faces. A creeping chill began to possess the soul of Fettes. He peered at the bundle, and it seemed somehow larger than at first. All over the countryside, and from every degree of distance, the farm dogs accompanied their passage with tragic ululations; and it grew and grew upon his mind that some unnatural miracle had been accomplished, that some nameless change had befallen the dead body, and that it was in fear of their unholy burden that the dogs were howling.

'For God's sake,' said he, making a great effort to arrive at speech, 'for God's sake, let's have a light!'

Seemingly Macfarlane was affected in the same direction; for though he made no reply, he stopped the horse, passed the reins to his companion, got down, and proceeded to kindle the remaining lamp. They had by that time got no further than the cross-road down to Auchendinny. The rain still poured as though the deluge were returning, and it was no easy matter to make a light in such a world of wet and darkness. When at last the flickering blue flame had been transferred to the wick and began to expand and clarify, and shed a wide circle of misty brightness round the gig, it became possible for the two young men to see each other and the thing they had along with them. The rain had moulded the rough sacking to the outlines of the body underneath; the head was distinct from the trunk, the shoulders plainly modelled; something at once spectral and human riveted their eyes upon the ghastly comrade of their drive.

For some time Macfarlane stood motionless, holding up the lamp. A nameless dread was swathed, like a wet sheet, about the body, and tightened the white skin upon the face of Fettes; a fear that was meaningless, a horror of what could not be, kept mounting to his brain. Another beat of the watch, and he had spoken. But his comrade forestalled him.

'That is not a woman,' said Macfarlane, in a hushed voice.

'It was a woman when we put her in,' whispered Fettes.

'Hold that lamp,' said the other. 'I must see her face.'

And as Fettes took the lamp his companion untied the fastenings of the sack and drew down the cover from the head. The light fell very clear upon the dark, well-moulded features and smooth-shaven cheeks of a too familiar countenance, often beheld in dreams of both of these young men. A wild yell rang up into the night; each leaped from his own side into the road-way; the lamp fell, broke, and was extinguished; and the horse, terrified by this unusual commotion, bounded and went off toward Edinburgh at a gallop, bearing along with it, sole occupant of the gig, the body of the dead and long-dissected Gray.

The Captain of the *Pole-star*

Sir Arthur Conan Doyle

[Being an extract from the journal of JOHN MCALISTER RAY, student of medicine, kept by him during the six months' voyage in the Arctic Seas, of the steam-whaler *Pole-star*, of Dundee, Captain Nicholas Craigie.]

September 11th. Lat. 81° 40' N.; Long. 2° E.—Still lying-to amid enormous ice fields. The one which stretches away to the north of us, and to which our ice-anchor is attached, cannot be smaller than an English county. To the right and left unbroken sheets extend to the horizon. This morning the mate reported that there were signs of pack ice to the southward. Should this form of sufficient thickness to bar our return, we shall be in a position of danger, as the food, I hear, is already running somewhat short. It is late in the season and the nights are beginning to reappear. This morning I saw a star twinkling just over the foreyard—the first since the beginning of May. There is considerable discontent among the crew, many of whom are anxious to get back home to be in time for the herring season, when labour always commands a high price upon the Scotch coast. As yet their displeasure is only signified by sullen countenances and black looks, but I heard from the second mate this afternoon that they contemplated sending a deputation to the Captain to explain their grievance. I much doubt how he will receive it, as he is a man of fierce temper, and very sensitive about anything approaching to an infringement of his rights. I shall venture after dinner to say a few words to him upon the subject. I have always found that he will tolerate from me what he would resent from any other member of the crew. Amsterdam Island, at the north-west corner of Spitzbergen, is visible upon our starboard quarter—a rugged line of volcanic rocks, intersected by white seams, which represent glaciers. It is curious to think that at the present moment there is probably no human being nearer to us than the Danish settlements in the south of Greenland—a good nine hundred miles as the crow flies. A captain takes a great responsibility upon himself when he risks his vessel under such circumstances. No whaler has ever remained in these latitudes till so advanced a period of the year.

9 P.M. I have spoken to Captain Craigie, and though the result has been hardly satisfactory, I am bound to say that he listened to what I had to say very quietly and even deferentially. When I had finished he put on that air of iron determination which I have frequently observed upon his face, and paced rapidly backwards and forwards across the narrow cabin for some minutes. At first I feared that I had seriously offended him, but he dispelled the idea by sitting down again, and putting his hand upon my arm with a gesture which almost amounted to a caress. There was a depth of tenderness too in his wild dark eyes which surprised me considerably. 'Look here, Doctor', he said, 'I'm sorry I ever took you—I am indeed—and I would give fifty pounds this minute to see you standing safe upon the Dundee quay. It's hit or miss with me this time. There are fish to the north of us. How dare you shake your head, sir, when I tell you I saw them blowing from the masthead!'—this in a sudden burst of fury, though I was not conscious of having shown any signs

of doubt. 'Two and twenty fish in as many minutes as I am a living man, and not one under ten foot.* Now, Doctor, do you think I can leave the country when there is only one infernal strip of ice between me and my fortune. If it came on to blow from the north tomorrow we could fill the ship and be away before the frost could catch us. If it came on to blow from the south—well, I suppose, the men are paid for risking their lives, and as for myself it matters but little to me, for I have more to bind me to the other world than to this one. I confess that I am sorry for *you,* though. I wish I had old Angus Tait who was with me last voyage, for he was a man that would never be missed, and you—you said once that you were engaged, did you not?'

'Yes,' I answered, snapping the spring of the locket which hung from my watch-chain, and holding up the little vignette of Flora.

'Blast you!' he yelled, springing out of his seat, with his very beard bristling with passion. 'What is your happiness to me? What have I to do with her that you must dangle her photograph before my eyes?' I almost thought that he was about to strike me in the frenzy of his rage, but with another imprecation he dashed open the door of the cabin and rushed out upon deck, leaving me considerably astonished at his extraordinary violence. It is the first time that he has ever shown me anything but courtesy and kindness. I can hear him pacing excitedly up and down overhead as I write these lines.

I should like to give a sketch of the character of this man, but it seems presumptuous to attempt such a thing upon paper, when the idea in my own mind is at best a vague and uncertain one. Several times I have thought that I grasped the clue which might explain it, but only to be disappointed by his presenting himself in some new light which would upset all my conclusions.

---

* A whale is measured among whalers not by the length of its body, but by the length of its whalebone.

It may be that no human eye but my own shall ever rest upon these lines, yet as a psychological study I shall attempt to leave some record of Captain Nicholas Craigie.

A man's outer case generally gives some indication of the soul within. The Captain is tall and well formed, with dark, handsome face, and a curious way of twitching his limbs, which may arise from nervousness, or be simply an outcome of his excessive energy. His jaw and whole cast of countenance is manly and resolute, but the eyes are the distinctive feature of his face. They are of the very darkest hazel, bright and eager, with a singular mixture of recklessness in their expression, and of something else which I have sometimes thought was more allied with horror than any other emotion. Generally the former predominated, but on occasions, and more particularly when he was thoughtfully inclined, the look of fear would spread and deepen until it imparted a new character to his whole countenance. It is at these times that he is most subject to tempestuous fits of anger, and he seems to be aware of it, for I have known him lock himself up so that no one might approach him until his dark hour was passed. He sleeps badly, and I have heard him shouting during the night, but his room is some little distance from mine, and I could never distinguish the words which he said.

This is one phase of his character, and the most disagreeable one. It is only through my close association with him, thrown together as we are day after day, that I have observed it. Otherwise he is an agreeable companion, well read and entertaining, and as gallant a seaman as ever trod a deck. I shall not easily forget the way in which he handled the ship when we were caught by a gale among the loose ice at the beginning of April. I have never seen him so cheerful, and even hilarious, as he was that night as he paced backwards and forwards upon the bridge amid the flashing of the lightning and the howling of the wind. He has told me several times that the thought of death was a pleasant one to him, which is a sad thing for a young man to say; he cannot be much more than thirty, though his hair and moustache are already slightly grizzled. Some great sorrow must have overtaken him and blighted his whole life. Perhaps I should be the same if I lost my Flora—God knows! I think if it were not for her that I should care very little whether the wind blew from the north or the south tomorrow. There, I hear him come down the companion and he has locked himself up in his room, which shows that he is still in an amiable mood. And so to bed, as old Pepys would say, for the candle is burning down (we have to use them now since the nights are closing in), and the steward has turned in, so there are no hopes of another one.

September 12th. Calm clear day, and still lying in the same position. What wind there is comes from the south-east, but it is very slight. Captain is in a better humour, and apologized to me at breakfast for his rudeness. He still looks somewhat *distrait*, however, and retains that wild look in his eyes which in a Highlander would mean that he was 'fey'—at least so our chief engineer remarked to me, and he has some reputation among the Celtic portion of our crew as a seer and expounder of omens.

It is strange that superstition should have obtained such mastery over this hard-headed and practical race. I could not have believed to what an extent it is carried had I not observed it for myself. We have had a perfect epidemic of it this voyage, until I have felt inclined to serve out rations of sedatives and nerve tonics with the Saturday allowance of grog. The first symptom of it was that shortly after leaving Shetland the men at the wheel used to complain that they heard plaintive cries and screams in the wake of the ship, as if something were following it and were unable to overtake it. This fiction has been kept up during the whole voyage, and on dark nights at the beginning of the seal-fishing it was only with great difficulty that men could be induced to do their spell. No doubt what they heard was either the creaking of the rudder-chains, or the cry of some passing sea-bird. I have been fetched out of bed several times to listen to it, but I need hardly say that I was never able to distinguish anything unnatural. The men, however, are so absurdly positive upon the subject that it is hopeless to argue with them. I mentioned the matter to the Captain once, but to my surprise he took it very gravely, and indeed appeared to be considerably disturbed by what I told him. I should have thought that he at least would have been above such vulgar delusions.

All this disquisition upon superstition leads me up to the fact that Mr Manson, our second mate, saw a ghost last night—or, at least, says that he did, which of course is the same thing. It is quite refreshing to have some new topic of conversation after the eternal routine of bears and whales which has served us for so many months. Manson swears the ship is haunted, and that he would not stay in her a day if he had any other place to go to. Indeed the fellow is honestly frightened, and I had to give him some chloral and bromide of potassium this morning to steady him down. He seemed quite indignant when I suggested that he had been having an extra glass the night before, and I was obliged to pacify him by keeping as grave a countenance as possible during his story, which he certainly narrated in a very straightforward and matter-of-fact way.

'I was on the bridge,' he said, 'about four bells in the middle watch, just when the night was at its darkest. There was a bit of a moon, but the clouds were blowing across it so that you couldn't see far from the ship. John McLeod, the harpooner, came aft from the foc'sle-head and reported a strange noise on the starboard bow. I went forrard and we both heard it, sometimes like a bairn crying and sometimes like a wench in pain. I've been seventeen years to the country and I never heard seal, old or young, make a sound like that. As we were standing there on the foc'sle-head the moon came out from behind a cloud, and we both saw a sort of white figure moving across the ice field in the same direction that we had heard the cries. We lost sight of it for a while, but it came back on the port bow, and we could just make it out like a shadow on the ice. I sent a hand aft for the rifles, and McLeod and I went down on to the pack, thinking that maybe it might be a bear. When we got on the ice I lost sight of McLeod, but I pushed on in the direction where I could still hear the cries. I followed them for a mile or maybe more, and then running round a hummock I came right on to the top of it standing and waiting for me seemingly. I don't know what it was. It wasn't a bear any way. It was tall and white and straight, and if it wasn't a man nor a woman, I'll stake my davy it was something worse. I made for the ship as hard as I could run, and precious glad I was to find myself aboard. I signed articles to do my duty by the ship, and on the ship I'll stay, but you don't catch me on the ice again after sundown.'

That is his story given as far as I can in his own words. I fancy what he saw must in spite of his denial, have been a young bear erect upon its hind legs, an attitude which they often assume when alarmed. In the uncertain light this would bear a resemblance to a human figure, especially to a man whose nerves were already somewhat shaken. Whatever it may have been, the occurrence is unfortunate, for it has produced a most unpleasant effect upon the crew. Their looks are more sullen than before and their discontent more open. The double grievance of being debarred from the herring fishing and of being detained in what they choose to call a haunted vessel, may lead them to do something rash. Even the harpooners, who are the oldest and steadiest among them, are joining in the general agitation.

Apart from this absurd outbreak of superstition, things are looking rather more cheerful. The pack which was forming to the south of us has partly cleared away, and the water is so warm as to lead me to believe that we are lying in one of those branches of the gulf-stream which run up between Greenland and Spitzbergen. There are numerous small Medusæ and sealemons about the ship, with abundance of shrimps, so that there is every possibility of 'fish' being sighted. Indeed one was seen blowing about dinner-time, but in such a position that it was impossible for the boats to follow it.

September 13th. Had an interesting conversation with the chief mate Mr Milne upon the bridge. It seems that our Captain is as great an enigma to the seamen, and even to the owners of the vessel, as he has been to me. Mr Milne tells me that when the ship is paid off, upon returning from a voyage, Captain Craigie disappears, and is not seen again until the approach of another season, when he walks quietly into the office of the company, and asks whether his services will be required. He has no friend in Dundee, nor does anyone pretend to be acquainted with his early history. His position depends entirely upon his skill as a seaman, and the name for courage and coolness which he had earned in the capacity of mate, before being entrusted with a separate command. The unanimous opinion seems to be that he is not a Scotchman, and that his name is an assumed one. Mr Milne thinks that he has devoted himself to whaling simply for the reason that it is the most dangerous occupation which he could select, and that he courts death in every possible manner. He mentioned several instances of this, one of which is rather curious, if true. It seems that on one occasion he did not put in an appearance at the office, and a substitute had to be selected in his place. That was at the time of the last Russian and Turkish war. When he turned up again next spring he had a puckered wound in the side of his neck which he used to endeavour to conceal with his cravat. Whether the mate's inference that he had been engaged in the war is true or not I cannot say. It was certainly a strange coincidence.

The wind is veering round in an easterly direction, but is still very slight. I think the ice is lying closer than it did yesterday. As far as the eye can reach on every side there is one wide expanse of spotless white, only broken by an occasional rift or the dark shadow of a hummock. To the south there is the narrow lane of blue water which is our sole means of escape, and which is closing up every day. The Captain is taking a heavy responsibility upon himself. I hear that the tank of potatoes has been finished, and even the biscuits are running short, but he preserves the same impossible countenance and spends the greater part of the day at the crow's nest, sweeping the horizon with his glass. His manner is very variable, and he seems to avoid my society, but there has been no repetition of the violence which he showed the other night.

7.30 P.M. My deliberate opinion is that we are commanded by a madman. Nothing else can account for the extraordinary vagaries of Captain Craigie. It is fortunate that I have kept this journal of our voyage, as it will serve to justify us in case we have to put him under any sort of restraint, a step which I should only consent to as a last resource. Curiously enough it was he himself who suggested lunacy and not mere eccentricity as the secret of his strange conduct. He was standing upon the bridge about an hour ago, peering as usual through his glass, while I was walking up and down the quarterdeck. The majority of the men were below at their tea, for the watches have not been regularly kept of late. Tired of walking, I leaned against the bulwarks, and admired the mellow glow cast by the sinking sun upon the great ice fields which surround us. I was suddenly aroused from the reverie into which I had fallen by a hoarse voice at my elbow, and starting round I found that the Captain had descended and was standing by my side. He was staring out over the ice with an expression in which horror, surprise, something approaching to joy were contending for the mastery. In spite of the cold, great drops of perspiration were coursing down his forehead and he was evidently fearfully excited. His limbs twitched like those of a man upon the verge of an epileptic fit, and the lines about his mouth were drawn and hard.

'Look!' he gasped, seizing me by the wrist, but still keeping his eyes upon the distant ice, and moving his head slowly in a horizontal direction, as if following some object which was moving across the field of vision. 'Look! There, man, there! Between the hummocks! Now coming out from behind the far one! You see her, you *must* see her! There still! Flying from me, by God, flying from me—and gone!'

He uttered the last two words in a whisper of concentrated agony which shall never fade from my remembrance. Clinging to the ratlines he endeavoured to climb up upon the top of the bulwarks as if in the hope of obtaining a last glance at the departing object. His strength was not equal to the attempt, however, and he staggered back against the saloon skylights, where he leaned panting and exhausted. His face was so livid that I expected him to become unconscious, so lost no time leading him down the companion, and stretching him upon one of the sofas in the cabin. I then poured him out some brandy which I held to his lips, and which had a wonderful effect upon him, bringing the blood back into his white face and steadying his poor shaking limbs. He raised himself up upon his elbow, and looking round to see that we were alone, he beckoned to me to come and sit beside him.

'You saw it, didn't you?' he asked, still in the same subdued awesome tone so foreign to the nature of the man.

'No, I saw nothing.'

His head sank back again upon the cushions. 'No, he wouldn't without the glass,' he murmured. 'He couldn't. It was the glass that showed her to me, and then the eyes of love—the eyes of love. I say, Doc, don't let the steward in! He'll think I'm mad. Just bolt the door, will you!'

I rose and did what he had commanded.

He lay quiet for a little, lost in thought apparently, and then raised himself up upon his elbow again, and asked for some more brandy.

'You don't think I am, do you, Doc?' he asked as I was putting the bottle back into the after-locker. 'Tell me now, as man to man, do you think that I am mad?'

'I think you have something on your mind,' I answered, 'which is exciting you and doing you a good deal of harm.'

'Right there, lad!' he cried, his eyes sparkling from the effects of the brandy. 'Plenty on my mind—plenty! But I can work out the latitude and the longitude, and I can handle my sextant and manage my logarithms. You couldn't prove me mad in a court of law, could you, now?' It was curious to hear the man lying back and coolly arguing out the question of his own sanity.

'Perhaps not,' I said, 'but still I think you would be wise to get home as soon as you can and settle down to a quiet life for a while.'

'Get home, eh?' he muttered with a sneer upon his face. 'One word for me and two for yourself, lad. Settle down with Flora—pretty little Flora. Are bad dreams signs of madness?'

'Sometimes,' I answered.

'What else? what would be the first symptoms?'

'Pains in the head, noises in the ears, flashes before the eyes, delusions—'

'Ah! what about them?' he interrupted. 'What would you call a delusion?'

'Seeing a thing which is not there is a delusion.'

'But she *was* there!' he groaned to himself. 'She *was* there!' and rising, he unbolted the door and walked with slow and uncertain steps to his own cabin, where I have no doubt that he will remain until tomorrow morning. His system seems to have received a terrible shock, whatever it may have been that he imagined himself to have seen. The man becomes a greater mystery every day, though I fear that the solution which he has himself suggested is the correct one, and that his reason is affected. I do not think that a guilty conscience has anything to do with his behaviour. The idea is a popular one among the officers, and, I believe, the crew; but I have seen nothing to support it. He has not the air of a guilty man, but of one who has had terrible usage at the hands of fortune, and who should be regarded as a martyr rather than a criminal.

The wind is veering round to the south tonight. God help us if it blocks that narrow pass which is our only road to safety! Situated as we are on the edge of the main Arctic pack, or the 'barrier' as it is called by the whalers, any wind from the north has the effect of shredding out the ice around us and allowing our escape, while a wind from the south blows up all the loose ice behind us and hems us in between two packs. God help us, I say again!

September 14th.—Sunday, and a day of rest. My fears have been confirmed, and the thin strip of blue water has disappeared from the southward. Nothing but the great motionless ice fields around us, with their weird hummocks and fantastic pinnacles. There is a deathly silence over their wide expanse which is horrible. No lapping of the waves now, no cries of seagulls or straining of sails, but one deep universal silence in which the murmurs of the seamen, and the creak of their boots upon the white shining deck, seem discordant and out of place. Our only visitor was an Arctic fox, a rare animal upon the pack, though common enough upon the land. He did not come near the ship, however, but after surveying us from a distance fled rapidly across the ice. This was curious conduct, as they generally know nothing of man, and being of an inquisitive nature become so familiar that they are easily captured. Incredible as it may seem, even this little incident produced a bad effect upon the crew. 'Yon puir beastie kens mair, aye an' sees mair nor you nor me!' was the comment of one of the leading harpooners, and the others nodded their acquiescence. It is vain to attempt to argue against such puerile superstition. They have made up their minds that there is a curse upon the ship, and nothing will ever persuade them to the contrary.

The Captain remained in seclusion all day except for about half an hour in the afternoon, when he came out upon the quarterdeck. I observed that he kept his eye fixed upon the spot where the vision of yesterday had appeared, and was quite prepared for another outburst, but none such came. He did not seem to see me although I was standing close beside him. Divine service was read as usual by the chief engineer. It is a curious thing that in whaling vessels the Church of England Prayer-book is always employed, although there is never a member of that Church among either officers or crew. Our men are all Roman Catholics or Presbyterians, the former predominating. Since a ritual is used which is foreign to both, neither can complain that the other is preferred to them, and they listen with all attention and devotion, so that the system has something to recommend it.

A glorious sunset, which made the great fields of ice look like a lake of blood. I have never seen a finer and at the same time more ghastly effect. Wind is veering round. If it will blow twenty-four hours from the north all will yet be well.

September 15th. Today is Flora's birthday. Dear lass! it is well that she cannot see her boy, as she used to call me, shut up among the ice fields with a crazy captain and a few weeks' provisions. No doubt she scans the shipping list in the *Scotsman* every morning to see if we are reported from Shetland. I have to set an example to the men and look cheery and unconcerned; but God knows my heart is very heavy at times.

The thermometer is at nineteen Fahrenheit today. There is but little wind, and what there is comes from an unfavourable quarter. Captain is in an excellent humour; I think he imagines he has seen some other omen or vision, poor fellow, during the night, for he came into my room early in the morning, and stooping down over my bunk whispered, 'It wasn't a delusion, Doc, it's all right!' After breakfast he asked me to find out how much food was left, which the second mate and I proceeded to do. It is even less than we had expected. Forward they have half a tank full of biscuits, three barrels of salt meat, and a very limited supply of coffee beans and sugar. In the after-hold and lockers there are a good many luxuries such as tinned salmon, soups, haricot mutton, etc., but they will go a very short way among a crew of fifty men. There are two barrels of flour in the store-room, and an unlimited supply of tobacco. Altogether there is about enough to keep the men on half rations for eighteen or twenty days—certainly not more. When we reported the state of things to the Captain, he ordered all hands to be piped, and addressed them from the quarterdeck. I never saw him to better advantage. With his tall, well-knit figure and dark animated face, he seemed a man born to command, and he discussed the situation in a cool sailor-like way which showed that while appreciating the danger he had an eye for every loophole of escape.

'My lads,' he said, 'no doubt you think I brought you into this fix, if it is a fix, and maybe some of you feel bitter against me on account of it. But you must remember that for many a season no ship that comes to the country has brought in as much oil-money as the old *Pole-star*, and every one of you has had his share of it. You can leave your wives behind you in comfort while other poor fellows come back to find their lasses on the parish. If you have to thank me for the one you have to thank me for the other, and we may call it quits. We've tried a bold venture before this and succeeded, so now that we've tried one and failed we've no cause to cry out about it. If the worst comes to the worst, we can make the land across the ice, and lay in a stock of seals which will keep us alive until the spring. It won't come to that, though, for you'll see the Scotch coast again before three weeks are out. At present every man must go on half rations, share and share alike, and no favour to any. Keep up your hearts and you'll pull through this as you've pulled through many a danger before.' These few simple words of his had a wonderful effect upon the crew. His former unpopularity was forgotten, and the old harpooner whom I have already mentioned for his superstition, led off three cheers, which were heartily joined in by all hands.

September 16th.—The wind has veered round to the north during the night, and the ice shows some symptoms of opening out. The men are in a good humour in spite of the short allowance upon which they have been placed. Steam is kept up in the engine-room, that there may be no delay should an opportunity for escape present itself. The Captain is in exuberant spirits, though he still retains that wild 'fey' expression which I have already remarked upon. This burst of cheerfulness puzzles me more than his former gloom. I cannot understand it. I think I mentioned in an early part of this journal that one of his oddities is that he never permits any person to enter his cabin, but insists upon making his own bed, such as it is, and performing every other office for himself. To my surprise he handed me the key today and requested me to go down there and take the time by his chronometer while he measured the altitude of the sun at noon. It is a bare little room containing a washing-stand and a few books, but little else in the way of luxury, except some pictures upon the walls. The majority of these are small cheap oleographs, but there was one water-colour sketch of the head of a young lady which arrested my attention. It was evidently a portrait, and not one of those fancy types of female beauty which sailors particularly affect. No artist could have evolved from his own mind such a curious mixture of character and weakness. The languid, dreamy eyes with their drooping lashes, and the broad, low brow unruffled by thought or care, were in strong contrast with the clean-cut, prominent jaw, and the resolute set of the lower lip. Underneath it in one of the corners was written 'M. B., æt. 19'. That any one in the short space of nineteen years of existence could develop such strength of will as was stamped upon her face seemed to me at the time to be well-nigh incredible. She must have been an extraordinary woman. Her features have thrown such a glamour over me that though I had but a fleeting glance at them, I could, were I a draughtsman, reproduce them line for line upon this page of the journal. I wonder what part she has played in our Captain's life. He has hung her picture at the end of his berth so that his eyes continually rest upon it. Were he a less reserved man I should make some remark upon the subject. Of the other things in his cabin there was nothing worthy of mention—uniform coats, a camp stool, small looking-glass, tobacco box and numerous pipes, including an oriental hookah—which by-the-bye gives some colour to Mr Milne's story about his participation in the war, though the connection may seem rather a distant one.

11.20 p.m. Captain just gone to bed after a long and interesting conversation on general topics. When he chooses he can be a most fascinating companion, being remarkably well read, and having the power of expressing his opinion forcibly without appearing to be dogmatic. I hate to have my intellectual toes trod upon. He spoke about the nature of the soul and sketched out the views of Aristotle and Plato upon the subject in a masterly manner. He seems to have a leaning for metempsychosis and the doctrines of Pythagoras. In discussing them we touched upon modern spiritualism, and I made some joking allusion to the impostures of Slade, upon which, to my surprise, he warned me most impressively against confusing the innocent with the guilty, and argued that it would be as logical to brand Christianity as an error, because Judas who professed that religion was a villain. He shortly afterwards bade me goodnight and retired to his room.

The wind is freshening up, and blows steadily from the north. The nights are as dark now as they are in England. I hope tomorrow may set us free from our frozen fetters.

September 17th. The Bogie again. Thank Heaven that I have strong nerves! The superstition of these poor fellows, and the circumstantial accounts which they give, with the utmost earnestness and self conviction, would horrify any man not accustomed to their ways. There are many versions of the matter, but the sum-total of them all is that something uncanny has been flitting round the ship all night, and that Sandie McDonald of Peterhead and 'lang' Peter Williamson of Shetland saw it, as also did Mr Milne on the bridge—so having three witnesses, they can make a better case of it than the second mate did. I spoke to Milne after breakfast and told him that he should be above such nonsense, and that as an officer he ought to set the men a better example. He shook his weatherbeaten head ominously, but answered with characteristic caution, 'Mebbe aye, mebbe na, Doctor,' he said; 'I didna ca' it a ghaist. I canna' say I preen my faith in sea bogles an' the like, though there's a mony as claims to ha' seen a' that and waur. I'm no easy feared, but may be your ain bluid would run a bit cauld, mun, if instead o' speerin' aboot it in daylicht ye were wi' me last night, an' seed an awfu' like shape, white an' gruesome, whiles here, whiles there, an' it greetin' and ca'ing in the darkness like a bit lambie that hae lost its mither. Ye would na' be sae ready to put it a' doon to auld wives' clavers then, I'm thinkin'.' I saw it was hopeless to reason with him, so contented myself with begging him as a personal favour to call me up the next time the spectre appeared—a request to which he acceded with many ejaculations expressive of his hopes that such an opportunity might never arise.

As I had hoped, the white desert behind us has become broken by many thin streaks of water which intersect it in all directions. Our latitude today was 80° 52' N., which shows that there is a strong southerly drift upon the pack. Should the wind continue favourable it will break up as rapidly as it formed. At present we can do nothing but smoke and wait and hope for the best. I am rapidly becoming a fatalist. When dealing with such uncertain factors as wind and ice a man can be nothing else. Perhaps it was the wind and sand of the Arabian deserts which gave the minds of the original followers of Mahomet their tendency to bow to kismet.

These spectral alarms have a very bad effect upon the Captain. I feared that it might excite his sensitive mind, and endeavoured to conceal the absurd story from him, but unfortunately he overheard one of the men making an allusion to it, and insisted upon being informed about it. As I had expected, it brought out all his latent lunacy in an exaggerated form. I can hardly believe that this is the same man who discoursed philosophy last night with the most critical acumen, and coolest judgement. He is pacing backwards and forwards upon the quarterdeck like a caged tiger, stopping now and again to throw out his hands with a yearning gesture, and stare impatiently out over the ice. He keeps up a continual mutter to himself, and once he called out, 'But a little time, love—but a little time!' Poor fellow, it is sad to see a gallant seaman and accomplished gentleman reduced to such a pass, and to think that imagination and delusion can cow a mind to which real danger was but the salt of life. Was ever a man in such a position as I, between a demented captain and a ghost-seeing mate? I sometimes think I am the only really sane man aboard the vessel—except perhaps the second engineer, who is a kind of ruminant and would care nothing for all the fiends in the Red Sea, so long as they would leave him alone and not disarrange his tools.

The ice is still opening rapidly, and there is every probability of our being able to make a start tomorrow morning. They will think I am inventing when I tell them at home all the strange things that have befallen me.

12 P.M. I have been a good deal startled, though I feel steadier now, thanks to a stiff glass of brandy. I am hardly myself yet however as this handwriting will testify. The fact is that I have gone through a very strange experience, and am beginning to doubt whether I was justified in branding everyone on board as madmen, because they professed to have seen things which did not seem reasonable to my understanding. Pshaw! I am a fool to let such a trifle unnerve me, and yet coming as it does after all these alarms, it has an additional significance, for I cannot doubt either Mr Manson's story or that of the mate, now that I have experienced that which I used formerly to scoff at.

After all it was nothing very alarming—a mere sound, and that was all. I cannot expect that anyone reading this, if anyone ever should read it, will sympathize with my feelings, or realize the effect which it produced upon me at the time. Supper was over and I had gone on deck to have a quiet pipe before turning in. The night was very dark—so dark that standing under the quarter boat, I was unable to see the officer upon the bridge. I think I have already mentioned the extraordinary silence which prevails in these frozen seas. In other parts of the world, be they ever so barren, there is some slight vibration of the air— some faint hum, be it from the distant haunts of men, or from the leaves of the trees, or the wings of the birds, or even the faint rustle of the grass that covers the ground. One may not actively perceive the sound, and yet if it were withdrawn it would be missed. It is only here in these Arctic seas that stark, unfathomable stillness obtrudes itself upon you in all its gruesome reality. You find your tympanum straining to catch some little murmur and dwelling eagerly upon every accidental sound within the vessel. In this state I was leaning against the bulwarks when there arose from the ice almost directly underneath me, a cry, sharp and shrill, upon the silent air of the night, beginning, as it seemed to me, at a note such as prima donna never reached, and mounting from that ever higher and higher until it culminated in a long wail of agony, which might have been the last cry of a lost soul. The ghastly scream is still ringing in my ears. Grief, unutterable grief, seemed to be expressed in it and a great longing, and yet through it all there was an occasional wild note of exultation. It seemed to come from close beside me, and yet as I glared into the darkness I could make out nothing. I waited some little time, but without hearing any repetition of the sound, so I came below, more shaken than I have ever been in my life before. As I came down the companion I met Mr Milne coming up to relieve the watch. 'Weel, Doctor,' he said, 'may be that's auld wives' clavers tae? Did ye no hear it skirling? Maybe thats a supersteetion?

what d'ye think o't noo?' I was obliged to apologize to the honest fellow, and acknowledge that I was as puzzled by it as he was. Perhaps tomorrow things may look different. At present I dare hardly write all that I think. Reading it again in days to come, when I have shaken off all these associations, I should despise myself for having been so weak.

September 18th.—Passed a restless and uneasy night still haunted by that strange sound. The Captain does not look as if he had had much repose either, for his face is haggard and his eyes bloodshot. I have not told him of my adventure of last night, nor shall I. He is already restless and excited, standing up, sitting down, and apparently utterly unable to keep still.

A fine lead appeared in the pack this morning, as I had expected, and we were able to cast off our ice-anchor, and steam about twelve miles in a west-sou'-westerly direction. We were then brought to a halt by a great floe as massive as any which we have left behind us. It bars our progress completely, so we can do nothing but anchor again and wait until it breaks up, which it will probably do within twenty-four hours, if the wind holds. Several bladder-nosed seals were seen swimming in the water, and one was shot, an immense creature more than eleven feet long. They are fierce, pugnacious animals, and are said to be more than a match for a bear. Fortunately they are slow and clumsy in their movements, so that there is little danger in attacking them upon the ice.

The Captain evidently does not think we have seen the last of our troubles, though why he should take a gloomy view of the situation is more than I can fathom, since everyone else on board considers that we have had a miraculous escape, and are sure now to reach the open sea.

'I suppose you think it's all right now, Doctor?' he said as we sat together after dinner.

'I hope so,' I answered.

'We mustn't be too sure—and yet no doubt you are right.

We'll all be in the arms of our own true loves before long, lad, won't we? But we mustn't be too sure—we mustn't be too sure.'

He sat silent a little, swinging his leg thoughtfully backwards and forwards. 'Look here,' he continued. 'It's a dangerous place this, even at its best—a treacherous, dangerous place. I have known men cut off very suddenly in a land like this. A slip would do it sometimes—a single slip, and down you go through a crack and only a bubble on the green water to show where it was that you sank. It's a queer thing.' he continued with a nervous laugh, 'but all the years I've been in this country I never once thought of making a will—not that I have anything to leave in particular, but still when a man is exposed to danger he should have everything arranged and ready—don't you think so?'

'Certainly,' I answered, wondering what on earth he was driving at.

'He feels better for knowing it's all settled,' he went on. 'Now if anything should ever befall me, I hope that you will look after things for me. There is very little in the cabin, but such as it is I should like it to be sold, and the money divided in the same proportion as the oil-money among the crew. The chronometer I wish you to keep yourself as some slight remembrance of our voyage. Of course all this is a mere precaution, but I thought I would take the opportunity of speaking to you about it. I suppose I might rely upon you if there were any necessity?'

'Most assuredly,' I answered; 'and since you are taking this step, I may as well—'

'You! you!' he interrupted. *You're* all right. What the devil is the matter with *you*? There, I didn't mean to be peppery, but I don't like to hear a young fellow, that has hardly began life, speculating about death. Go up on deck and get some fresh air into your lungs instead of talking nonsense in the cabin, and encouraging me to do the same.'

The more I think of this conversation of ours the less do I like it. Why should the man be settling his affairs at the very time when we seem to be emerging from all danger? There must be some method in his madness. Can it be that he contemplates suicide? I remember that upon one occasion he spoke in a deeply reverent manner of the heinousness of the crime of self-destruction. I shall keep my eye upon him however, and though I cannot obtrude upon the privacy of his cabin, I shall at least make a point of remaining on deck as long as he stays up.

Mr Milne pooh-poohs my fears, and says it is only the 'skipper's little way'. He himself takes a very rosy view of the situation. According to him we shall be out of the ice by the day after tomorrow, pass Jan Meyen two days after that, and sight Shetland in little more than a week. I hope he may not be too sanguine. His opinion may be fairly balanced against the gloomy precautions of the Captain, for he is an old and experienced seaman, and weights his words well before uttering them.

The long-impending catastrophe has come at least. I hardly know what to write about it. The Captain is gone. He may come back to us again alive, but I fear me—I fear me. It is now seven o'clock of the morning of the 19th of September. I have spent the whole night traversing the great ice-floe in front of us with a party of seamen in the hope of coming upon some trace of him, but in vain. I shall try to give some account of the circumstances which attended upon his disappearance. Should anyone ever chance to read the words which I put down, I trust they will remember that I do not write from conjecture or from hearsay, but that I, a sane and educated man, am describing accurately what actually occurred before my very eyes. My inferences are my own but I shall be answerable for the facts.

The Captain remained in excellent spirits after the conversation which I have recorded. He appeared to be nervous and impatient however, frequently changing his position, and moving his limbs in an aimless choreic way which is characteristic of him at times. In a quarter of an hour he went upon deck seven times, only to descend after a few hurried paces. I followed him each time, for there was something about his face which confirmed my resolution of not letting him out of my sight. He seemed to observe the effect which his movements had produced, for he endeavoured by an over-done hilarity, laughing boisterously at the very smallest of jokes, to quiet my apprehensions.

After supper he went on to the poop once more, and I with him. The night was dark and very still, save for the melancholy soughing of the wind among the spars. A thick cloud was coming up from the northwest, and the ragged tentacles which it threw out in front of it were drifting across the face of the moon, which only shone now and again through a rift in the wrack. The Captain paced rapidly backwards and forwards, and then seeing me still dogging him he came across and hinted that he thought I should be better below—which I need hardly say had the effect of strengthening my resolution to remain on deck.

I think he forgot about my presence after this, for he stood silently leaning over the taffrail, and peering out across the great desert of snow, part of which lay in shadow, while part glittered mistily in the moonlight. Several times I could see by his movements that he was referring to his watch, and once he muttered a short sentence of which I could only catch the one word 'ready'. I confess to having felt an eerie feeling creeping over me as I watched the loom of his tall figure through the darkness, and noted how completely he fulfilled the idea of a man who is keeping a tryst. A tryst with whom? Some vague perception began to dawn upon me as I pieced one fact with another, but I was utterly unprepared for the sequel.

By the sudden intensity of his attitude I felt that he saw something. I crept up behind him. He was staring with an eager questioning gaze at what seemed to be a wreath of mist, blown swiftly in a line with the ship. It was a dim nebulous body devoid of shape, sometimes more, sometimes less apparent, as the light fell on it. The moon was dimmed in its brilliancy at the moment by a canopy of thinnest cloud, like the coating of an anemone.

'Coming, lass, coming,' cried the skipper, in a voice of unfathomable tenderness and compassion, like one who soothes a beloved one by some favour long looked for, and as pleasant to bestow as to receive.

What followed, happened in an instant. I had no power to interfere. He gave one spring to the top of the bulwarks, and another which took him on to the ice, almost to the feet of the pale misty figure. He held out his hands as if to clasp it, and so ran into the darkness with outstretched arms and loving words. I still stood rigid and motionless, straining my eyes after his retreating form, until his voice died away in the distance. I never thought to see him again, but at that moment the moon shone out brilliantly through a chink in the cloudy heaven, and illuminated the great field of ice. Then I saw his dark figure already a very long way off, running with prodigious speed across the frozen plain. That was the last glimpse which we caught of him—perhaps the last we ever shall. A party was organized to follow him, and I accompanied them, but the men's hearts were not in the work, and nothing was found. Another will be formed within a few hours. I can hardly believe I have not been dreaming, or suffering from some hideous nightmare as I write these things down.

7.30 P.M.—Just returned dead beat and utterly tired out from a second unsuccessful search for the Captain. The floe is of enormous extent, for though we have traversed at least twenty miles of its surface, there has been no sign of its coming to an end. The frost has been so severe of late that the overlying snow is frozen as hard as granite, otherwise we might have had the footsteps to guide us. The crew are anxious that we should cast off and steam round the floe and so to the southward, for the ice has opened up during the night, and the sea is visible upon the horizon. They argue that Captain Craigie is certainly dead, and that we are all risking our lives to no purpose by remaining when we have an opportunity of escape. Mr Milne and I have had the greatest difficulty in persuading them to wait until tomorrow night, and have been compelled to promise that we will not under any circumstances delay our departure longer than that. We propose therefore to take a few hour's sleep and then to start upon a final search.

September 20th, evening.—I crossed the ice this morning with a party of men exploring the southern part of the floe, while Mr Milne went off in a northerly direction. We pushed on for ten or twelve miles without seeing a trace of any living thing except a single bird, which fluttered a great way over our heads, and which by its flight I should judge to have been a falcon. The southern extremity of the ice field tapered away into a long narrow spit which projected out into the sea. When we came to the base of this promontory, the men halted, but I begged them to continue to the extreme end of it that we might have the satisfaction of knowing that no possible chance had been neglected.

We had hardly gone a hundred yards before McDonald of Peterhead cried out that he saw something in front of us, and began to run. We all got a glimpse of it and ran too. At first it was only a vague darkness against the white ice, but as we raced along together it took the shape of a man, and eventually of the man of whom we were in search. He was lying face downwards upon a frozen bank. Many little crystals of ice and feathers of snow had drifted on to him as he lay, and sparkled upon his dark seaman's jacket. As we came up some wandering puff of wind caught these tiny flakes in its vortex, and they whirled up into the air, partially descended again, and then, caught once more in the current, sped rapidly away in the direction of the sea. To my eyes it seemed but a snow-drift, but many of my companions averred that it started up in the shape of a woman, stooped over the corpse and kissed it, and then hurried away across the floe. I have learned never to ridicule any man's opinion, however strange it may seem. Sure it is that Captain Nicholas Craigie had met with no painful end, for there was a bright smile upon his blue pinched features, and his hands were still outstretched as though grasping at the strange visitor which had summoned him away into the dim world that lies beyond the grave.

We buried him the same afternoon with the ship's ensign around him, and a thirty-two pound shot at his feet. I read the burial service, while the rough sailors wept like children, for these were many who owed much to his kind heart, and who showed now the affection which his strange ways had repelled during his lifetime. He went off the grating with a dull, sullen splash, and as I looked into the green water I saw him go down, down, down, until he was but a little flickering patch of white hanging upon the outskirts of eternal darkness. Then even that faded away and he was gone. There he shall lie, with his secret and his sorrows and his mystery all still buried in his breast, until that great day when the sea shall give up its dead, and Nicholas Craigie come out from among the ice with the smile upon his face, and his stiffened arms outstretched in greeting. I pray that his lot may be a happier one in that life than it has been in this.

I shall not continue my journal. Our road to home lies plain and clear before us, and the great ice field will soon be but a remembrance of the past. It will be some time before I get over the shock produced by recent events. When I began this record of our voyage I little thought of how I should be compelled to finish it. I am writing these final words in the lonely cabin, still starting at times and fancying I hear the quick nervous step of the dead man upon the deck above me. I entered his cabin tonight as was my duty, to make a list of his effects in order that they might be entered in the official log. All was as it had been upon my previous visit, save that the picture which I have described as having hung at the end of his bed had been cut out of its frame, as with a knife, and was gone. With this last link in a strange chain of evidence I close my diary of the voyage of the *Pole-star*.

————— ·◦⟨۞⟩◦· —————

[NOTE by Dr John McAlister Ray, senior. 'I have read over the strange events connected with the death of the Captain of the *Pole-star*, as narrated in the journal of my son. That everything occurred exactly as he describes it I have the fullest confidence, and, indeed, the most positive certainty, for I know him to be a strong-nerved and unimaginative man, with the strictest regard for veracity. Still, the story is, on the face of it, so vague and so improbable, that I was long opposed to its publication. Within the last few days, however, I have had independent testimony upon the subject which throws a new light upon it. I had run down to Edinburgh to attend a meeting of the British Medical Association, when I chanced to come across Dr P—, an old college chum of mine, now practising at Saltash, in Devonshire. Upon my telling him of this experience of my son's, he declared to me that he was familiar with the man, and proceeded, to my no small surprise, to give me a description of him, which tallied remarkably well with that given in the journal, except that he depicted him as a younger man. According to his account, he had been engaged to a young lady of singular beauty residing upon the Cornish coast. During his absence at sea his betrothed had died under circumstances of peculiar horror.]

The Grey Cavalier of Penterton Hall

Guy Boothby

CHRISTMAS AT PENTERTON HALL was, like the rite of matrimony, a thing not to be taken in hand 'wantonly or unadvisedly'. It was a festive season which few, who had participated in it, are ever likely to forget.

In the first place the old Squire was not the sort of man to stand any nonsense. He invited you, meaning that you should have a good time while you were with him; he welcomed you with the same intention; he looked after your comfort and amusements from the day that you entered his hospitable doors until you left them again; and if, when that sad moment arrived, you departed with the opinion that Christmas at Penterton was not what it had been described, well then, you did what no other man had been known to do before you, and deserved to suffer as such.

Why, the mere sight of the Squire's jolly red face was sufficient to make a man enjoy himself, to say nothing of his cheery voice and inexhaustible fund of anecdotes, which everyone had heard before, but which all longed to hear again. As a host he was one man in a thousand, and when you come to his housekeeper and niece, pretty Winifred Dycie, well, all you can say is that she is just one in a million, and I don't mind who knows that I say so.

How it came about that the Squire had never married has never been properly explained; between ourselves, however, I fancy there is some mystery in the matter. There are not wanting people indeed who assert that the Squire and his brother both loved and wooed Winifred's mother; that the younger was successful, and that the Squire, like the trump he always was, and always will be, acted up to his principles, held out his hand to his rival and wished him joy.

When, five years later, Winifred's father met his death on the field of battle, and his wife died of a broken heart on receiving the news, he took the little orphan girl to live with him, and gave her every scrap of his great heart. No one will ever realise how much that couple loved each other, but many who have stayed at Penterton can hazard a very good guess.

If you were to listen to the old Squire you would hear the most absurd stories about his darling. He would tell you how, when she was only a tiny dot of five, she would accompany him on his visits to the kennels, and pick out old Rover and Roysterer from fifteen couple or more, and never cry or even whimper when the great beasts fawned about her, and endeavoured to put their paws upon her shoulder and try to lick her face.

He would tell you the most extraordinary stories about her prowess in the saddle, how, 'by Gad, sir,' she had ridden his own pet hunter, Nimrod, on a certain, ever to be remembered day, when the hounds met at Pinkly Gorse, 'and fairly floored the field, sir.' And if the telling happened to be at night, it's a thousand pounds to a sixpence that he would order up another bottle of port, one of the very particular, by the way, and drink to the health of the sweetest maid who ever wore a habit.

I don't think I should be very far wrong in saying that, before she was twenty, she had never given the Squire a moment's unhappiness. That, unfortunately, was to come, and it was the coming of it that constitutes this story.

Needless to say, old Squire Dycie's niece was not likely to

lack admirers. As a matter of fact, they flocked in from all directions, until the Squire began to think that it would be wiser were he to issue orders that no male should be admitted within his gates without a written permit from himself. To the Squire's great joy, however, they invariably went away disconsolate. How were they to know that Winifred's heart was already given, and, as is so often the case, to the very man of all others of whom the Squire was least likely to approve?

Handsome, devil-may-care Dick Beverley, the ruined Squire of Blicksford, was a charming companion, of irreproachable birth and manners; as a setoff, however, against these advantages, it was well known that he had squandered his patrimony, had been rusticated from Cambridge, and was, in consequence, the horror of virtuous mothers with marriageable daughters for many miles around.

That he should have fallen in love with pretty Winifred Dycie seemed only natural, for they all did, but that she should have reciprocated his affections, and have promised to be his wife, seemed to be out of the proper order of things. However, it was a fact, and one that was likely to cause a considerable amount of trouble for all parties concerned in the near future. One day the young man screwed up his courage and rode over to the Hall for an interview with the Squire. The latter listened to him patiently, and then spoke his mind.

'Impossible,' he said, 'quite impossible. What you ask is out of the question.'

'You mean, I suppose, that you have heard all sorts of things about me. That I am hard up and have been a bit wild. I don't deny it, but if I give you my word that I will reform, and that I will not marry your niece until I have set the old place on its feet again, will you accept that as sufficient proof of my love, and sanction our engagement?'

'I can sanction nothing,' the Squire answered. 'I can only repeat that what you ask is impossible.'

'Entreaty will not move you?'

'Nothing will move me,' the other replied. 'My mind is made up.'

Seeing that it was useless to say anything further, Dick bade him goodbye, and that night, at a stolen meeting in a wood behind the Hall, informed Winifred of what had occurred at the interview. Some meddlesome person told the Squire of the meeting, and he spoke to his niece upon the subject. She confessed her love, and vowed that without young Beverley life for her would be a blank. Then the Squire lost his temper, and said things for which I can assure you he was sorry afterwards.

The result was a misunderstanding and a tiff, which, on the Squire's part, took the form of a letter to the young man in question, warning him to have no intercourse with the lady in question, under the pain of his, the Squire's, severest displeasure. In less than a month he had come to hate the young man as he had never hated anyone in his life before. His very name was an abomination to him. What was more, he shepherded his niece more closely than ever, and seldom allowed her out of his sight.

In consequence, the lovers were not permitted to meet, and Winifred began to look pale and heavy-eyed, and life at the Hall was the reverse of cheerful. There could be no doubt that the affair was causing the dear old Squire a great amount of misery. He was not the same man at all. He had no desire to be unjust, nor, had he considered young Beverley a suitable match, would he have stood in the way for a moment. As a matter of fact, he did not know much about him personally, and what little he did know was told him by busybodies who doubtless had their own reasons for desiring to prove the young fellow a villain of the deepest dye.

On one pitiable occasion, he was driven into saying something which, at any other time, he would rather have cut his tongue out than have uttered. When he left the drawing-room, where the interview had taken place, and returned to his own room Gregory, his ancient butler, informed him that Mrs Gibbs, the housekeeper, desired to speak to him.

'Send her in, send her in,' said the Squire a little sharply, for he was not in the humour for domestic worries. Then to himself, he added, 'What on earth can the woman have to say to me?'

It turned out that Mrs Gibbs' errand was of a peculiar nature. A domestic crisis was imminent, and chaos reigned in the servants' hall. Put into plain words it amounted to this: the Grey Cavalier, the famous Penterton ghost, who was known to pace the quadrangle at the back of the house when any great trouble was about to happen to the family, had made his appearance on three occasions of late, and had been plainly seen by a footman, a lady's maid, and a housemaid.

The footman had been reduced to a state of Collapse, the females to a condition of idiocy. According to their statements he was standing in the moonlit quadrangle at the time, gazing sadly at the house. Then, with a wave of his hand, he had disappeared in the direction of the chapel, back to his tomb behind the altar. They indignantly denied any possibility of their having been mistaken. They had seen his great grey boots, his love locks, his lace ruffles, and his grey beaver hat, and, as a result, nothing could induce them to stay after their month was up, or to cross the quadrangle after dark.

'Your maids are a pack of fools, and the footman is something worse,' cried the irritable Squire, not, however, without a thrill of satisfaction as he thought of the story he would now be able to tell concerning the famous spectre. However, he sent Mrs Gibbs about her business, and then sat down at his writing table to pen a letter to his best friend in the world. He told him of his difficulty regarding young Beverley, of his niece's state of health, and asked his advice.

Two days later an answer arrived, and in it the old Colonel promised to do his best to exorcise the fatal passion that had taken possession of the pretty Winifred, and, for this reason, he would spend Christmas at the Hall, and bring as many of his young friends as he could collect with him. Now, if the Colonel knew one eligible young man he knew a dozen, the respectability, wealth, and culture of whom he was prepared to guarantee with his life.

What was more he knew half-a-dozen girls of transcendent beauty and accomplishments, who would act as excellent foils and would put Winifred upon her mettle. With such a force at his back it would be strange indeed, he argued, if they were unable to rout Beverley, and drive him from the field never to return. Although Winifred protested against such an invasion, the necessary invitations were despatched, and in due course accepted by the parties concerned. In the meantime Beverley was supposed to be in London, and Winifred's heart was about as sad as it was possible for the heart of a maiden to be.

Indeed, the only person who seemed to be enjoying the festive season at all was the grey ghost of Sir Michael, who, within the previous month, had been twice seen on his accustomed promenade. The result was so upsetting from a domestic point of view that instead of venerating him as he had been brought up to do, the Squire began to look upon his supernatural relative as a nuisance second only to Beverley himself. Though he protested that it was all fancy, and those who declared that they had seen the apparition must have dreamt it, I have an idea that he was no more disposed to pay a visit to the quadrangle at night than were the maidservants themselves. What was more he confined his visits to the Chapel to daylight, and anxiously looked forward to the time when his visitors should arrive, and by so doing create a diversion.

At last the great day arrived, and the stables found their time fully taken up meeting trains and conveying guests to the Hall. Holly and mistletoe decorated the corridors, great logs spluttered on the fires, and all was gaiety and merrymaking. The Squire, to all appearances, was jollity itself. He had a warm welcome for each new arrival, a joke for the men, and, well, if the truth must be told, a kiss for the girls.

The seeds of some promising flirtations were sown at afternoon tea, and by the time the dressing gong sounded for dinner, all was as merry as a marriage bell. Indeed, it was not until late in the evening, just as the bedroom candlesticks made their appearance, that a damper was cast upon the spirits of the party. Then one young lady, more courageous than the rest, turned to the Squire and asked if it were true, as her maid had told her, that the Grey Cavalier had been making his appearance rather too frequently of late?

The Squire gazed at her in amazement. The temerity of the young lady staggered him. As a rule the Grey Cavalier was never mentioned, save with bated breath, and never by any chance within an hour of bedtime. He noticed also that Winifred's hand trembled, and that she turned deathly pale. He remembered the fact that she had always entertained a great fear of the spectre, and his warm old heart went out to the girl for that reason, and, perhaps, if the truth must be told, for still another. He was well aware that she loved young Beverley, and he was filled with sorrow that it should have fallen to his lot to have been compelled to differ with her as to the merits of the man of her choice. However, as the matter stood it was impossible for him to draw back, and accordingly he was forced not only to let her suffer, but to suffer himself at the same time. He thought of this when his guests had departed to their various bedrooms, and he and Winifred stood at the bottom of the great staircase, bidding each other goodnight. His old heart was troubled, and it was made none the easier when Winifred clasped her arms about his neck and said, 'Dear old uncle, you must try to think better of me. You have been so good to me, and I have repaid your kindness so poorly. You will never know how grateful I am to you for it all.'

'Pooh, pooh,' said the Squire, 'you mustn't talk nonsense,

little girl. Run away to bed and come down to breakfast in the morning with the roses on your cheeks.'

He noticed that the girl heaved a heavy sigh as she turned to go upstairs, and, though he could not understand the reason, he was even more upset than before. He began to wonder whether young Beverley might not, with encouragement, turn out better than he expected, and if he should give him the chance. This led him to think of his dear, dead brother, and of Winifred's mother, both of whom at that very moment were perhaps watching him and sighing at his treatment of their orphan child.

He accordingly heaved another heavy sigh, more doleful than the first, and accompanied old Gregory on his locking-up operations with an even sadder heart than ever. He had not retired to his couch more than a couple of hours, however, a sleepless couple, by the way, when the unmistakeable click of an iron latch in the quadrangle below reached his ears. What could it mean?

He sprang out of the bed and hastened to the window. He was only just in time, for there, crossing the open space, was a tall, grey figure, habited in the costume of a Cavalier. It was a frosty night, and the moon shone so cold and clear that every detail of his costume was plainly observable, even to the love locks and the long grey boots. For the first time in his life the Squire was looking upon the apparition whose appearance was supposed to foretell death or disaster to his family.

Suddenly, however, something struck him as being somewhat singular, and when he had seen the figure disappear by the small door into the chapel on the other side, he left the window and began to dress. Then, taking a candle, he departed from his chamber, and set off on a tour of inspection.

The house was in total darkness, and as silent as a grave. He did not hesitate, however, but pushed on, passed the billiard room, passed his own study, until he reached the door in the long corridor, which opened into the Chapel itself.

Once there he blew out the light, and softly opened the door. Creeping in he found the worshipping place of his ancestors in total darkness save where it was lighted by the moonbeams which entered through the lancet windows on the further side. The marble effigies of his long departed relatives showed stiff and dark above their tombs, but in the centre of the aisle stood two figures whom he clearly recognised.

One was the Grey Cavalier, the other Winifred, his niece. From his place of vantage he could plainly overhear all that they were saying. Their conversation ran somewhat as follows:

'Are you sure, Dick dear, that you mean what you say?' whispered the girl, who, by the way, had her arms round the Cavalier's neck.

'Quite sure,' the ghost of the Grey Cavalier replied. 'The old man loves you, and though he doesn't trust me, I'll be dashed if I'll be such a mean cad as to carry you off and break his heart, while there's a chance of winning him round to our way of thinking. He'll like me all the better when he sees how hard I'm trying to be worthy of you, and, on the other hand, just think what life here would be to him without you, little woman.'

'I wish, Dick dear, he knew you as you are. He has only heard the things evil disposed people have said about you. He doesn't know how good you really are.'

'Not very good, I'm afraid,' the other replied. 'If I've improved a bit of late, I owe it all to you and your gentle influence. But I am trying to pull up, and that at least is something. And now I must be off. You say there is a ball on Boxing night, so I suppose I must wait until another night to see you.'

'Cannot you come then?'

'What, the Grey Cavalier make his appearance on such a festive occasion? If you think you could manage to slip away for a quarter of an hour I might try.'

'I am sure I could. At any rate I'll do my best. But isn't it a great risk to run?'

'Risk, not a bit of it. In that case the Spectre will be seen at midnight precisely.'

The Squire waited to hear no more, but, softly opening the door, picked up his candle, and fled to his own room to think over all he had heard. So far as that particular night was concerned his rest was not likely to be disturbed. In the morning, however, he was a different being; he had come to an understanding with himself, and was brighter in consequence.

His face at breakfast said as much. Never had such a Christmas Day been known at Penterton Hall. The Squire was like a new man; he proposed everyone's health at lunch, and conducted himself like an amiable lunatic during the remainder of the day. Boxing Day arrived in due course, and discovered no change in his condition.

Winifred scarcely knew what to make of his behaviour. Poor child, the dance of that evening presented no chance of enjoyment for her. Before dusk the Squire summoned the Colonel and two or three of the young men to his study, and kept them there for upwards of an hour. It was to be observed that when they emerged they seemed to be staggering under the weight of a great responsibility.

Of all the balls that have taken place at Penterton that of which I am about to attempt a description will always be considered the most remarkable. One of the most noticeable features was the fact that shortly before midnight the Colonel and the young men aforesaid disappeared from the ball room. Winifred followed their example a little later. The Squire also was not to be seen.

The clock in the belfry had scarcely struck twelve before the door of the ball room opened and the Squire entered, escorting his niece. She was very pale, and seemed much put out about something. Almost at the same moment the door at the further end of the room opened, and a singular figure, attired after the manner of the reign of the first Charles, entered, escorted by the

Colonel and his stalwart aides. Winifred, on seeing him, uttered a cry, and would have run towards him but that the Squire held her back.

'Ladies and gentlemen,' the dear old fellow began, looking round at those present as he spoke, 'all of you have heard of the famous Grey Cavalier of Penterton Hall. You will in the future be able to say that you have seen him face to face, and that he is not so terrible as you have been led to suppose. At last the Spectre has been laid by the heels, and in saying that I have to make a confession to you. My dear friends, I feel that I am very much to blame. For a long time past I have listened to the voice of public opinion, and refused to hear that of love. The first I am about to put on one side; upon the other for the future I will pin my faith.

'Mr Beverley, you have played me a trick in the matter of the Grey Cavalier, but I am sure if I give you my darling's hand, you will show me that my confidence has not been misplaced. From this moment we will let bygones be bygones, and now' (here he turned to the musicians) 'play up; let us have some music.'

Of course, we all knew the story of the unhappy love affair, and we were all, or at any rate those of us who were married, delighted at the denouement. Winifred's face was a picture to see, and as for the Ghost, well, if ever the Grey Cavalier was half as happy as he appeared to be as he whirled his lady love over the ball room floor, he must have been as jolly a spectre as could have been found throughout the length and breadth of the land.

They are to be married in three months' time, and the Squire has commanded our presence at the ceremony. Everyone agrees that Beverley is a reformed character, and if he is at all grateful for his happiness, he must surely reflect that he owes it to the lucky thought which induced him to take upon himself the role of the Grey Cavalier of Penterton Hall.

Keeping His Promise

Algernon Blackwood

IT WAS ELEVEN o'clock at night, and young Marriott was locked into his room, cramming as hard as he could cram. He was a 'Fourth Year Man' at Edinburgh University and he had been ploughed for this particular examination so often that his parents had positively declared they could no longer supply the funds to keep him there.

His rooms were cheap and dingy, but it was the lecture fees that took the money. So Marriott pulled himself together at last and definitely made up his mind that he would pass or die in the attempt, and for some weeks now he had been reading as hard as mortal man can read. He was trying to make up for lost time and money in a way that showed conclusively he did not understand the value of either. For no ordinary man—and Marriott was in every sense an ordinary man—can afford to drive the mind as he had lately been driving his, without sooner or later paying the cost.

Among the students he had few friends or acquaintances, and these few had promised not to disturb him at night, knowing he was at last reading in earnest. It was, therefore, with feelings a good deal stronger than mere surprise that he heard his doorbell ring on this particular night and realised that he was to have a visitor. Some men would simply have muffled the bell and gone on quietly with their work. But Marriott was not this sort. He was nervous. It would have bothered and pecked at his mind all night long not to know who the visitor was and what he wanted. The only thing to do, therefore, was to let him in—and out again—as quickly as possible.

The landlady went to bed at ten o'clock punctually, after which hour nothing would induce her to pretend she heard the bell, so Marriott jumped up from his books with an exclamation that augured ill for the reception of his caller, and prepared to let him in with his own hand.

The streets of Edinburgh town were very still at this late hour—it was late for Edinburgh—and in the quiet neighbourhood of F—— Street, where Marriott lived on the third floor, scarcely a sound broke the silence. As he crossed the floor, the bell rang a second time, with unnecessary clamour, and he unlocked the door and passed into the little hallway with considerable wrath and annoyance in his heart at the insolence of the double interruption.

'The fellows all know I'm reading for this exam. Why in the world do they come to bother me at such an unearthly hour?'

The inhabitants of the building, with himself, were medical students, general students, poor Writers to the Signet, and some others whose vocations were perhaps not so obvious. The stone staircase, dimly lighted at each floor by a gas-jet that would not turn above a certain height, wound down to the level of the street with no pretence at carpet or railing. At some levels it was cleaner than at others. It depended on the landlady of the particular level.

The acoustic properties of a spiral staircase seem to be peculiar. Marriott, standing by the open door, book in hand, thought every moment the owner of the footsteps would come into view. The sound of the boots was so close and so loud that they seemed to travel disproportionately in advance of their cause. Wondering who it could be, he stood ready with all manner of sharp greetings for the man who dared thus to disturb his work. But the man did not appear. The steps sounded almost under his nose, yet no one was visible.

A sudden queer sensation of fear passed over him—a faintness and a shiver down the back. It went, however, almost as soon as it came, and he was just debating whether he would call aloud to his invisible visitor, or slam the door and return to his books, when the cause of the disturbance turned the corner very slowly and came into view.

It was a stranger. He saw a youngish man short of figure and very broad. His face was the colour of a piece of chalk and the eyes, which were very bright, had heavy lines underneath them. Though the cheeks and chin were unshaven and the general appearance unkempt, the man was evidently a gentleman, for he was well dressed and bore himself with a certain air. But, strangest of all, he wore no hat, and carried none in his hand; and although rain had been falling steadily all the evening, he appeared to have neither overcoat nor umbrella.

A hundred questions sprang up in Marriott's mind and rushed to his lips, chief among which was something like 'Who in the world are you?' and 'What in the name of heaven do you come to me for?' But none of these questions found time to express themselves in words, for almost at once the caller turned his head a little so that the gas light in the hall fell upon his features from a new angle. Then in a flash Marriott recognised him.

'Field! Man alive! Is it you?' he gasped.

The Fourth Year Man was not lacking in intuition, and he perceived at once that here was a case for delicate treatment. He divined, without any actual process of thought, that the catastrophe often predicted had come at last, and that this man's father had turned him out of the house. They had been at a private school together years before, and though they had hardly met once since, the news had not failed to reach him from time to time with considerable detail, for the family lived near his own and between certain of the sisters there was great intimacy. Young Field had gone wild later, he remembered hearing about it all—drink, a woman, opium, or something of the sort—he could not exactly call to mind.

'Come in,' he said at once, his anger vanishing. 'There's been something wrong, I can see. Come in, and tell me all about it and perhaps I can help—' He hardly knew what to say, and stammered a lot more besides. The dark side of life, and the horror of it, belonged to a world that lay remote from his own select little atmosphere of books and dreamings. But he had a man's heart for all that.

He led the way across the hall, shutting the front door carefully behind him, and noticed as he did so that the other, though certainly sober, was unsteady on his legs, and evidently much exhausted. Marriott might not be able to pass his examinations, but he at least knew the symptoms of starvation—acute starvation, unless he was much mistaken—when they stared him in the face.

'Come along,' he said cheerfully, and with genuine sympathy in his voice. 'I'm glad to see you. I was going to have a bite of something to eat, and you're just in time to join me.'

The other made no audible reply, and shuffled so feebly with his feet that Marriott took his arm by way of support. He noticed for the first time that the clothes hung on him with pitiful looseness. The broad frame was literally hardly more than a frame. He was as thin as a skeleton. But, as he touched him, the sensation of faintness and dread returned. It only lasted a moment, and then passed off, and he ascribed it not unnaturally to the distress and shock of seeing a former friend in such a pitiful plight.

'Better let me guide you. It's shamefully dark—this hall. I'm always complaining,' he said lightly, recognising by the weight upon his arm that the guidance was sorely needed, 'but the old cat never does anything except promise.' He led him to the sofa, wondering all the time where he had come from and how he had found out the address. It must be at least seven years since those days at the private school when they used to be such close friends.

'Now, if you'll forgive me for a minute,' he said, 'I'll get supper ready—such as it is. And don't bother to talk. Just take it easy on the sofa. I see you're dead tired. You can tell me about it afterwards, and we'll make plans.'

The other sat down on the edge of the sofa and stared in silence, while Marriott got out the brown loaf, scones, and huge pot of marmalade that Edinburgh students always keep in their cupboards. His eyes shone with a brightness that suggested drugs, Marriott thought, stealing a glance at him from behind the cupboard door. He did not like yet to take a full square look. The fellow was in a bad way, and it would have been so like an examination to stare and wait for explanations. Besides, he was evidently almost too exhausted to speak. So, for reasons of delicacy—and for another reason as well which he could not exactly formulate to himself—he let his visitor rest apparently unnoticed, while he busied himself with the supper. He lit the spirit lamp to make cocoa, and when the water was boiling he drew up the table with the good things to the sofa, so that Field need not have even the trouble of moving to a chair.

'Now, let's tuck in,' he said, 'and afterwards we'll have a pipe and a chat. I'm reading for an exam, you know, and I always have something about this time. It's jolly to have a companion.'

He looked up and caught his guest's eyes directed straight upon his own. An involuntary shudder ran through him from head to foot. The face opposite him was deadly white and wore a dreadful expression of pain and mental suffering.

'By Gad!' he said, jumping up, 'I quite forgot. I've got some whisky somewhere. What an ass I am. I never touch it myself when I'm working like this.'

He went to the cupboard and poured out a stiff glass which the other swallowed at a single gulp and without any water. Marriott watched him while he drank it, and at the same time noticed something else as well—Field's coat was all over dust, and on one shoulder was a bit of cobweb. It was perfectly dry; Field arrived on a soaking wet night without hat, umbrella, or overcoat, and yet perfectly dry, even dusty. Therefore he had been under cover. What did it all mean? Had he been hiding in the building? ...

It was very strange. Yet he volunteered nothing; and Marriott had pretty well made up his mind by this time that he would not ask any questions until he had eaten and slept. Food and sleep were obviously what the poor devil needed most and first—he was pleased with his powers of ready diagnosis—and it would not be fair to press him till he had recovered a bit.

They ate their supper together while the host carried on a running one-sided conversation, chiefly about himself and his exams and his 'old cat' of a landlady, so that the guest need not utter a single word unless he really wished to—which he evidently did not! But, while he toyed with his food, feeling no desire to eat, the other ate voraciously. To see a hungry man devour cold scones, stale oatcake, and brown bread laden with marmalade was a revelation to this inexperienced student who had never known what it was to be without at least three meals a day. He watched in spite of himself, wondering why the fellow did not choke in the process.

But Field seemed to be as sleepy as he was hungry. More than once his head dropped and he ceased to masticate the food in his mouth. Marriott had positively to shake him before he would go on with his meal. A stronger emotion will overcome a weaker, but this struggle between the sting of real hunger and the magical opiate of overpowering sleep was a curious sight to the student, who watched it with mingled astonishment and alarm. He had heard of the pleasure it was to feed hungry men, and watch them eat, but he had never actually witnessed it, and he had no idea it was like this. Field ate like an animal—gobbled, stuffed, gorged. Marriott forgot his reading, and began to feel something very much like a lump in his throat.

'Afraid there's been awfully little to offer you, old man,' he managed to blurt out when at length the last scone had disappeared, and the rapid, one-sided meal was at an end. Field still made no reply, for he was almost asleep in his seat. He merely looked up wearily and gratefully.

'Now you must have some sleep, you know,' he continued, 'or you'll go to pieces. I shall be up all night reading for this blessed exam. You're more than welcome to my bed. Tomorrow we'll have a late breakfast and—and see what can be done—and make plans—I'm awfully good at making plans, you know,' he added with an attempt at lightness.

Field maintained his 'dead sleepy' silence, but appeared to acquiesce, and the other led the way into the bedroom, apologising as he did so to this half-starved son of a baronet—whose own home was almost a palace—for the size of the room. The weary guest, however, made no pretence of thanks or politeness. He merely steadied himself on his friend's arm as he staggered across the room, and then, with all his clothes on, dropped his exhausted body on the bed. In less than a minute he was to all appearances sound asleep.

For several minutes Marriott stood in the open door and watched him; praying devoutly that he might never find himself in a like predicament, and then fell to wondering what he would do with his unbidden guest on the morrow. But he did not stop long to think, for the call of his books was imperative, and happen what might, he must see to it that he passed that examination.

Having again locked the door into the hall, he sat down to his books and resumed his notes on *materia medica* where he had left off when the bell rang. But it was difficult for some time to concentrate his mind on the subject. His thoughts kept wandering to the picture of that white-faced, strange-eyed fellow, starved and dirty, lying in his clothes and boots on the bed. He recalled their schooldays together before they had drifted apart, and how they had vowed eternal friendship—and all the rest of it. And now! What horrible straits to be in. How could any man let the love of dissipation take such hold upon him?

But one of their vows together Marriott, it seemed, had completely forgotten. Just now, at any rate, it lay too far in the background of his memory to be recalled.

Through the half-open door—the bedroom led out of the sitting-room and had no other door—came the sound of deep, long-drawn breathing, the regular, steady breathing of a tired man, so tired that, even to listen to it made Marriott almost want to go to sleep himself.

'He needed it,' reflected the student, 'and perhaps it came only just in time!'

Perhaps so; for outside the bitter wind from across the Forth howled cruelly and drove the rain in cold streams against the window-panes, and down the deserted streets. Long before Marriott settled down again properly to his reading, he heard distantly, as it were, through the sentences of the book, the heavy, deep breathing of the sleeper in the next room.

A couple of hours later, when he yawned and changed his books, he still heard the breathing, and went cautiously up to the door to look round.

At first the darkness of the room must have deceived him, or else his eyes were confused and dazzled by the recent glare of the reading lamp. For a minute or two he could make out nothing at all but dark lumps of furniture, the mass of the chest of drawers by the wall, and the white patch where his bath stood in the centre of the floor.

Then the bed came slowly into view. And on it he saw the outline of the sleeping body gradually take shape before his eyes, growing up strangely into the darkness, till it stood out in marked relief—the long black form against the white counterpane.

He could hardly help smiling. Field had not moved an inch. He watched him a moment or two and then returned to his books. The night was full of the singing voices of the wind and rain. There was no sound of traffic; no hansoms clattered over the cobbles, and it was still too early for the milk carts. He worked on steadily and conscientiously, only stopping now and again to change a book, or to sip some of the poisonous stuff that kept him awake and made his brain so active, and on these occasions Field's breathing was always distinctly audible in the room. Outside, the storm continued to howl, but inside the house all was stillness. The shade of the reading lamp threw all the light upon the littered table, leaving the other end of the room in comparative darkness. The bedroom door was exactly opposite him where he sat. There was nothing to disturb the worker, nothing but an occasional rush of wind against the windows, and a slight pain in his arm.

This pain, however, which he was unable to account for, grew once or twice very acute. It bothered him; and he tried to remember how, and when, he could have bruised himself so severely, but without success.

At length the page before him turned from yellow to grey, and there were sounds of wheels in the street below. It was four o'clock. Marriott leaned back and yawned prodigiously. Then he drew back the curtains. The storm had subsided and the Castle Rock was shrouded in mist. With another yawn he turned away from the dreary outlook and prepared to sleep the remaining four hours till breakfast on the sofa. Field was still breathing heavily in the next room, and he first tip-toed across the floor to take another look at him.

Peering cautiously round the half-opened door his first glance fell upon the bed now plainly discernible in the grey light of morning. He stared hard. Then he rubbed his eyes. Then he rubbed his eyes again and thrust his head farther round the edge of the door. With fixed eyes he stared harder still, and harder.

But it made no difference at all. He was staring into an empty room.

The sensation of fear he had felt when Field first appeared upon the scene returned suddenly, but with much greater force. He became conscious, too, that his left arm was throbbing violently and causing him great pain. He stood wondering, and staring, and trying to collect his thoughts. He was trembling from head to foot.

By a great effort of the will he left the support of the door and walked forward boldly into the room.

There, upon the bed, was the impress of a body, where Field had lain and slept. There was the mark of the head on the pillow, and the slight indentation at the foot of the bed where the boots had rested on the counterpane. And there, plainer than ever—for he was closer to it—was *the breathing*!

Marriott tried to pull himself together. With a great effort he found his voice and called his friend aloud by name!

'Field! Is that you? Where are you?' There was no reply; but the breathing continued without interruption, coming directly from the bed. His voice had such an unfamiliar sound that Marriott did not care to repeat his questions, but he went down on his knees and examined the bed above and below, pulling the mattress off finally, and taking the coverings away separately one by one. But though the sounds continued there was no visible sign of Field, nor was there any space in which a human being, however small, could have concealed itself. He pulled the bed out from the wall, but the sound *stayed where it was*. It did not move with the bed.

Marriott, finding self-control a little difficult in his weary condition, at once set about a thorough search of the room. He went through the cupboard, the chest of drawers, the little alcove where the clothes hung—everything. But there was no sign of anyone. The small window near the ceiling was closed; and, anyhow, was not large enough to let a cat pass. The sitting-room door was locked on the inside; he could not have got out that way. Curious thoughts began to trouble Marriott's mind, bringing in their train unwelcome sensations. He grew more and more excited; he searched the bed again till it resembled the scene of a pillow fight; he searched both rooms, knowing all the time it was useless,—and then he searched again. A cold perspiration broke out all over his body; and the sound of heavy breathing, all this time, never ceased to come from the corner where Field had lain down to sleep.

Then he tried something else. He pushed the bed back exactly into its original position—and himself lay down upon it just where his guest had lain. But the same instant he sprang up again in a single bound. The breathing was close beside him, almost on his cheek, and between him and the wall! Not even a child could have squeezed into the space.

He went back into his sitting-room, opened the windows, welcoming all the light and air possible, and tried to think the whole matter over quietly and clearly. Men who read too hard, and slept too little, he knew were sometimes troubled with very vivid hallucinations. Again he calmly reviewed every incident of the night; his accurate sensations; the vivid details; the emotions stirred in him; the dreadful feast—no single hallucination could ever combine all these and cover so long a period of time. But with less satisfaction he thought of the recurring faintness, and curious sense of horror that had once or twice come over him, and then of the violent pains in his arm. These were quite unaccountable.

Moreover, now that he began to analyse and examine, there was one other thing that fell upon him like a sudden revelation: *During the whole time Field had not actually uttered a single word!* Yet, as though in mockery upon his reflections, there came ever from that inner room the sound of the breathing, long-drawn, deep, and regular. The thing was incredible. It was absurd.

Haunted by visions of brain fever and insanity, Marriott put on his cap and macintosh and left the house. The morning air on Arthur's Seat would blow the cobwebs from his brain; the scent of the heather, and above all, the sight of the sea. He roamed over the wet slopes above Holyrood for a couple of hours, and did not return until the exercise had shaken some of the horror out of his bones, and given him a ravening appetite into the bargain.

As he entered he saw that there was another man in the room, standing against the window with his back to the light. He recognised his fellow-student Greene, who was reading for the same examination.

'Read hard all night, Marriott,' he said, 'and thought I'd drop in here to compare notes and have some breakfast. You're out early?' he added, by way of a question. Marriott said he had a headache and a walk had helped it, and Greene nodded and said 'Ah!' But when the girl had set the steaming porridge on the table and gone out again, he went on with rather a forced tone, 'Didn't know you had any friends who drank, Marriott?'

This was obviously tentative, and Marriott replied drily that he did not know it either.

'Sounds just as if some chap were "sleeping it off" in there, doesn't it, though?' persisted the other, with a nod in the direction of the bedroom, and looking curiously at his friend. The two men stared steadily at each other for several seconds, and then Marriott said earnestly—'Then you hear it too, thank God!'

'Of course I hear it. The door's open. Sorry if I wasn't meant to.'

'Oh, I don't mean that,' said Marriott, lowering his voice. 'But I'm awfully relieved. Let me explain. Of course, if you hear it too, then it's all right; but really it frightened me more than I can tell you. I thought I was going to have brain fever, or something, and you know what a lot depends on this exam. It always begins with sounds, or visions, or some sort of beastly hallucination, and I—'

'Rot!' ejaculated the other impatiently.

'What are you talking about?'

'Now, listen to me, Greene,' said Marriott, as calmly as he could, for the breathing was still plainly audible, 'and I'll tell you what I mean, only don't interrupt.' And thereupon he related exactly what had happened during the night, telling everything, even down to the pain in his arm. When it was over he got up from the table and crossed the room.

'You hear the breathing now plainly, don't you?' he said. Greene said he did. 'Well, come with me, and we'll search the room together.' The other, however, did not move from his chair.

'I've been in already,' he said sheepishly; 'I heard the sounds and thought it was you. The door was ajar—so I went in.'

Marriott made no comment, but pushed the door open as wide as it would go. As it opened, the sound of breathing grew more and more distinct.

'*Someone* must be in there,' said Greene under his breath.

'*Someone* is in there, but *where?*' said Marriott. Again he urged his friend to go in with him. But Greene refused point-blank; said he had been in once and had searched the room and there was nothing there. He would not go in again for a good deal.

They shut the door and retired into the other room to talk it all over with many pipes. Greene questioned his friend very closely, but without illuminating result, since questions cannot alter facts.

'The only thing that ought to have a proper, a logical, explanation is the pain in my arm,' said Marriott, rubbing that member with an attempt at a smile. 'It hurts so infernally and aches all the way up. I can't remember bruising it, though.'

'Let me examine it for you," said Greene. "I'm awfully good at bones in spite of the examiners' opinion to the contrary.'

It was a relief to play the fool a bit, and Marriott took his coat off and rolled up his sleeve.

'By George, though, I'm bleeding!' he exclaimed. 'Look here! What on earth's this?'

On the forearm, quite close to the wrist, was a thin red line. There was a tiny drop of apparently fresh blood on it. Greene came over and looked closely at it for some minutes. Then he sat back in his chair, looking curiously at his friend's face.

'You've scratched yourself without knowing it,' he said presently.

'There's no sign of a bruise. It must be something else that made the arm ache.'

Marriott sat very still, staring silently at his arm as though the solution of the whole mystery lay there actually written upon the skin.

'What's the matter? I see nothing very strange about a scratch,' said Greene, in an unconvincing sort of voice. 'It was your cuff links probably. Last night in your excitement—'

But Marriott, white to the very lips, was trying to speak. The sweat stood in great beads on his forehead. At last he leaned forward close to his friend's face.

'Look,' he said, in a low voice that shook a little. 'Do you see that red mark? I mean *underneath* what you call the scratch?'

Greene admitted he saw something or other, and Marriott wiped the place clean with his handkerchief and told him to look again more closely.

'Yes, I see,' returned the other, lifting his head after a moment's careful inspection. 'It looks like an old scar.'

'It is an old scar,' whispered Marriott, his lips trembling. 'Now it all comes back to me.'

'All what?' Greene fidgeted on his chair. He tried to laugh, but without success. His friend seemed bordering on collapse.

'Hush! Be quiet, and—I'll tell you,' he said. '*Field made that scar.*'

For a whole minute the two men looked each other full in the face without speaking.

'Field made that scar!' repeated Marriott at length in a louder voice.

'Field! You mean—last night?'

'No, not last night. Years ago —at school, with his knife. And I made a scar in his arm with mine.' Marriott was talking rapidly now.

'We exchanged drops of blood in each other's cuts. He put a drop into my arm and I put one into his—'

'In the name of heaven, what for?'

'It was a boys' compact. We made a sacred pledge, a bargain. I remember it all perfectly now. We had been reading some dreadful book and we swore to appear to one another—I mean, whoever died first swore to show himself to the other. And we sealed the compact with each other's blood. I remember it all so well—the hot summer afternoon in the playground, seven years ago—and one of the masters caught us and confiscated the knives—and I have never thought of it again to this day—'

'And you mean—' stammered Greene.

But Marriott made no answer. He got up and crossed the room and lay down wearily upon the sofa, hiding his face in his hands.

Greene himself was a bit non-plussed. He left his friend alone for a little while, thinking it all over again. Suddenly an idea seemed to strike him. He went over to where Marriott still lay motionless on the sofa and roused him. In any case it was better to face the matter, whether there was an explanation or not. Giving in was always the silly exit.

'I say, Marriott,' he began, as the other turned his white face up to him. 'There's no good being so upset about it. I mean—if it's all an hallucination we know what to do. And if it isn't— well, we know what to think, don't we?'

'I suppose so. But it frightens me horribly for some reason,' returned his friend in a hushed voice. 'And that poor devil—'

'But, after all, if the worst is true and—and that chap *has* kept his promise—well, he has, that's all, isn't it?'

Marriott nodded.

'There's only one thing that occurs to me,' Greene went on, 'and that is, are you quite sure that—that he really ate like that—I mean that he actually *ate anything at all?*" he finished, blurting out all his thought.

Marriott stared at him for a moment and then said he could easily make certain. He spoke quietly. After the main shock no lesser surprise could affect him.

'I put the things away myself,' he said, 'after we had finished. They are on the third shelf in that cupboard. No one's touched 'em since.'

He pointed without getting up, and Greene took the hint and went over to look.

'Exactly,' he said, after a brief examination; 'just as I thought. It was partly hallucination, at any rate. The things haven't been touched. Come and see for yourself.'

Together they examined the shelf. There was the brown loaf, the plate of stale scones, the oatcake, all untouched. Even the glass of whisky Marriott had poured out stood there with the whisky still in it.

'You were feeding—no one,' said Greene 'Field ate and drank nothing. He was not there at all!'

'But the breathing?' urged the other in a low voice, staring with a dazed expression on his face.

Greene did not answer. He walked over to the bedroom, while Marriott followed him with his eyes. He opened the door, and listened. There was no need for words. The sound of deep, regular breathing came floating through the air. There was no hallucination about that, at any rate. Marriott could hear it where he stood on the other side of the room.

Greene closed the door and came back. 'There's only one thing to do,' he declared with decision. 'Write home and find out about him, and meanwhile come and finish your reading in my rooms. I've got an extra bed.'

'Agreed,' returned the Fourth Year Man; 'there's no hallucination about that exam; I must pass that whatever happens.'

And this was what they did.

It was about a week later when Marriott got the answer from his sister. Part of it he read out to Greene—

'It is curious,' she wrote, 'that in your letter you should have enquired after Field. It seems a terrible thing, but you know only a short while ago Sir John's patience became exhausted, and he turned him out of the house, they say without a penny. Well, what do you think? He has killed himself. At least, it looks like suicide. Instead of leaving the house, he went down into the cellar and simply starved himself to death. . . . They're trying to suppress it, of course, but I heard it all from my maid, who got it from their footman. . . . They found the body on the 14th and the doctor said he had died about twelve hours before. . . . He was dreadfully thin.'

'Then he died on the 13th,' said Greene.

Marriott nodded.

'That's the very night he came to see you.' Marriott nodded again.

The Lass with the Delicate Air

Eileen Bigland

EARLY IN 1949 I underwent a rather severe operation. Convalescence was a slow process and being an impatient sort of man I asked the specialist if he couldn't hurry matters along. A dour but kindly Scot, he said merely, 'Humph! You know a deal about machinery, don't you?'

'I ought to—after all, I'm an engineer.'

'Then you know that major repairs to a broken-down machine may take a considerable time?'

'Of course, but . . .'

'You're the machine,' he interrupted dryly, 'and you've consistently overworked yourself the past four years. Have you ever taken a holiday since you came back from the war?'

'Oh, a weekend here and there.' I began to explain that after my long absence in North Africa and Italy my business had required every minute I could spend on it, but again he cut across my speech.

'And now you've let yourself in for a six months' job.' In blunt terms he told me that my only chance of regaining complete health lay in giving up work until the autumn. 'You've got partners and you can afford it financially,' he ended abruptly.

He was right. Inwardly I had known, though I had refused to admit it, that both my mind and body were worn out, and now I felt strangely grateful for his confirmation. Despite difficult conditions business was flourishing and there was no reason why I should not leave the running of it to my colleagues. 'But where could I go?' I asked feebly.

'Scotland—it's a soothing country though you may not believe it. You fish a bit, don't you, and can handle a gun? Take a wee house somewhere in the Highlands and live outdoors as much as possible.' Ushering me to the door he added, 'Try McTavish in Union Street, Inverness. He's a sound agent.'

Feeling slightly bewildered I paused on the steps and looked up and down Harley Street. Perhaps if it had not been one of those cruelly brilliant April mornings when the light emphasizes the dinginess of town houses I might not have accepted the specialist's advice, but as I blinked in the sunshine I thought suddenly of the shining firths of the north, the cloud-dappled hills, the scented forests of fir and pine. Four days later I reached Inverness, booked a room in the Station Hotel, and went in search of McTavish.

He was a pleasant elderly man, but shook his head when I told him what I wanted. 'I doubt there's nothing nearer than Nairnside,' he said.

I replied eagerly that when stationed near Nairn early in the war I had developed quite an affection for the district, whereupon he looked relieved and suggested driving me there that very afternoon. We took the coast road that runs by the Moray Firth, turned inland at Gollanfield, climbed towards Cawdor woods and the wine-dark peat moss behind them. Glancing back I saw the silver stretch of water, the black humps of the soutars guarding the entrance to Cromarty harbour, the glittering white cap of Wyvis rising beyond. If the house mentioned by McTavish commanded such a view I'd take it at any price!

But it turned out to be a grim, small-windowed building set in a hollow ringed by trees so tall that all view was blotted out. McTavish was apologetic, and when I demanded if he knew of anywhere from which the firth and the Black Isle could be seen he eyed me warily. 'Would you be afraid of ghosts?' he asked.

I burst out laughing. 'Good heavens, no!'

'Well,' his voice was hesitant, 'there's Auchindoune; you get a rare view from its windows. But you see, during the '45 Rebellion it was a farmhouse where Charlie's men sheltered after Culloden. The red-coats caught and shot them—the marks are on the kitchen-garden wall to this day—and the crofters say that come the back-end of every year you'll hear the skirl of the pipes and the tramp of the clansmen's feet. Back in the war I sold the place to a rich man from Glasgow, but inside of three months he rushed into my office as if the devil were after him, roaring that the house was haunted, that he never wished to see it again, and that I could let it furnished at any rental I could get. I've let it twice,' he added lugubriously, 'but the folk didn't stay.'

'Because of the ghosts of Charlie's men?' I asked idly.

A queerly evasive expression crossed McTavish's face. 'Maybe,' he said, 'or maybe . . .' his voice tailed off.

But I wasn't in the mood to listen to any more superstitious nonsense and turned towards the car. 'Let's have a look at it.' As McTavish drove on up the hill I grinned at the notion of anyone asking a hard-headed, middle-aged business man like myself if he was afraid of ghosts.

Auchindoune was a square, comfortable-looking house, its garden well tended and gay with spring flowers, its big high-ceilinged rooms furnished with good solid stuff (whatever the man from Glasgow's failings he had had taste), and the view was superb. We were shown round by an old couple called Cameron who were resident caretakers and before our tour of inspection was over I said I would take the place for six months. While we discussed details Mrs Cameron stood primly, hands crossed above her spotless white apron, but her husband regarded me suspiciously. 'Would you be alone?' he demanded.

'Yes, I'm a bachelor. Maybe the house is too large for my needs but I like it. It has an—an air about it.' Then I stopped aghast. Whatever had possessed me to say those last words?

'It has that,' answered Cameron, and I fancied his expression was distinctly more favourable. 'The wife could do for you.'

So it was arranged and I settled into Auchindoune the following day. It was glorious weather and for the first week I saw little of the Camerons—which was just as well, I reflected, being aware that to the inhabitants of these parts anybody hailing from outside a twenty-mile radius was a foreigner, an enemy one to boot. Mrs Cameron thawed first under compliments on her excellent cooking but I gave her husband a fairly wide berth until a morning when I came across him in the yard plaiting withy baskets and paused to inquire about trout-fishing prospects. He gave me particulars civilly enough, then shot a glance at some primroses in my buttonhole and jerked a thumb towards the rounded wooded hill at the back of the house. 'Have you been up the Doune?'

I nodded. 'It's my favourite after-breakfast walk. The air tastes like wine on the tongue up there, and as for the primroses in that mossy hollow on the top,' I touched my buttonhole, 'they're better than you'd find in most gardens.'

A funny smile flickered on his lips and was gone. 'Ay,' he said softly, 'they grow well for ones they love.' But before I could ask his meaning he switched the subject back to fishing and, to my surprise, suggested accompanying me to the stream up on the peat moss that afternoon.

I soon discovered that where trout were concerned I was a tyro compared to Cameron. I found too that he was surprisingly well informed about world affairs, on which he discoursed at length. As we walked homewards he regaled me with legendary tales of fishermen in the far-off days of his youth, yet despite the friendliness in his soft Highland voice I could not rid myself of the feeling that behind his talk lay a certain hostility. This, I thought, was understandable enough. He was an old man, he loved Auchindoune, he resented its occupation by a mere Sassenach; when he grew more used to my company he would thaw as his wife had done.

After a delicious high tea (Mrs Cameron had grilled our catch to perfection) I wandered up to my sitting-room on the first floor feeling happily, healthily tired and looking forward with an eagerness long forgotten to the reading of a new biography which had just arrived from the library. As I opened the door I heard a slight noise—like the swish of a woman's skirts—and drew back instinctively. Who on earth could be in my room? Not Mrs Cameron, for I had just left her clearing the dining-room table. I pushed the door wide. The room was empty, the long curtains by the open windows billowed in the breeze—then I smelt the fragrance of primroses and could have sworn that someone drifted past me.

'Pull yourself together,' I muttered, closing the door sharply behind me. 'You've been listening to too many tall Highland tales.' Settling myself in my chair I opened my book but I hadn't read more than a few pages before another sound made me lift my head. Outside in the garden someone was whistling a sad, plaintive tune impossible to describe, for though the notes were soft and sweet they held a throbbing urgency so disturbing that I leapt to my feet and leaned far out over the window-sill.

There was nobody in sight. The garden lay dreaming under the pale evening sky, yet that inexpressibly poignant whistling rose on the still air from the lawn directly beneath me. Presently it grew fainter, as if the whistler was retreating round the corner of the house in the direction of the Doune, and suddenly I *knew*

I had to follow, had to trace the origin of that tragic little tune. Reluctant that the Camerons should see me I crept downstairs, let myself out of the front door, and took the wooded path leading up the Doune. The whistling floated back to me, but though I broke into a half-trot and kept peering ahead through the young green branches of the mountain-ash I could see no sign of the whistler. Panting, my feet slipping on the smooth path, I gained the top of the hill at last and paused on the lip of the mossy hollow. Below me, bending above the primroses, was the figure of a girl in a faded blue print frock. For a moment I paused, feeling extraordinarily foolish. Whatever was this village lass, for such I judged her to be, going to think of a middle-aged stranger, breathless and red-faced, interrupting her primrose-picking? Besides, ten to one she had come to keep tryst with some local lad, probably the mysterious whistler, who would imagine I was pursuing his beloved. It was an infernally awkward situation but as I teetered on the lip of the hollow wondering how I could retreat without rousing her attention the girl lifted her head. . . .

She had a face I had dreamed of sometimes but never encountered, its perfect oval shape framed in tumbled hair of bright chestnut. The eyes beneath the arched brows were grey and wide-set, the nose small and straight, the mouth generously curved. Even as I stared at her she stood erect, her hands full of starry blossoms, and I saw her dress was ragged, her slim feet bare and brown. Then she began to walk towards me, her every movement holding ineffable grace, and as she came closer I saw such anguish in her eyes that for a moment I could neither speak nor move.

Somehow I found my voice. 'What is wrong? Do you want help?'

She made no answer but nodded slightly and for an instant I thought a smile touched her mouth. Only then did I notice her extreme pallor. 'But you're ill,' I babbled stupidly. 'Look, sit down and rest, then tell me where you live and I will take you home,' and I stepped forward to take her by the arm. What happened next made the blood freeze in my veins, for when I tried to grasp her elbow my hand closed upon itself—*there was no arm to take hold of.* Yet still in front of me, only about two feet away, stood this amazingly beautiful creature with the tortured eyes.

From somewhere in the distance I heard myself say hoarsely, 'There are no such things as ghosts—you can't be one.' She gave a second little nod, threw her arms wide in a gesture of despair so that the primroses scattered on the ground, and darted to the far lip of the hollow. So swiftly had she moved that by the time I had collected myself and scrambled after her she was running downhill through the trees. Strangely enough my spasm of fear had left me and as I followed the glint of her blue frock in the gathering dusk I remember murmuring confusedly, 'Phantom or human: human or phantom she's in dreadful trouble. I've *got* to catch up with her and learn her story.' But it was easier to say than to do, for there was no path this side of the Doune, and while I slithered and stumbled through the undergrowth the girl ahead skimmed along like a bird, her feet seeming scarcely to touch the ground.

My heart was pounding in my chest before she paused in her flight, rested her hand against the bole of a mountain-ash and gazed back at me out of those sorrowful grey eyes. When I neared her she threw back her head and looked upwards through the branches as though in search of something. I too looked up, then as quickly looked back—the girl had gone. Furiously I blundered on another hundred yards or so and found I had reached the edge of the wood. Before me the broad fields of Nairnside stretched in the twilight but strain my sight as I might I could catch no glimpse of a blue frock against their misty green. In that split second of time at the mountain-ash the girl had completely vanished.

Laboriously I clambered up the Doune again, arguing with myself as I went. She couldn't be a ghost, it was ridiculous nonsense even to imagine it. Ah, but she hadn't spoken and there was something about the lift of her head, the pallor of her skin, the incredible grace of her movements. Rubbish, ghosts didn't pick primroses . . . suddenly I stopped. Those primroses she had dropped. *There* was proof! I struggled on till I reached the mossy hollow, walked round it, went down on my knees and scanned the ground. There was still enough light but as an extra precaution I ran my hands over the moss. Not a single loose primrose could I find.

How long I crouched by the hollow I do not know, but by the time I swung down the hill towards Auchindoune a sickle moon hung high in the sky. From the shadowy drive Cameron's voice hailed me. 'I've been waiting on Sutherland the keeper from Clunis who said he'd be over the night. Did you see him up the Doune, sir? A big man with a brown jacket and leggings.'

Somehow I felt this visit of Sutherland to be a fiction and a wild, unreasoning anger filled me. 'I saw nobody,' I snapped, 'good night!'

In my sitting-room I poured myself a large whisky and soda and took up my book. But the drink tasted bitter on my tongue and between my eyes and the printed page came the lovely oval face of the girl in blue. Was that old devil Cameron trying to witch me? Was I going daft? Was the girl real or was she a figment of the imagination induced perhaps by all those new-fangled drugs they had given me in hospital? Suddenly I jerked upright in the chair at a familiar melancholy sound. In two strides I was at the window. 'Cameron, I shouted, 'stop that confounded whistling!'

A minute or so later Mrs Cameron put her head round the door. 'Were you wanting something, sir?' she asked anxiously.

'No—yes—where's your husband?'

'In his bed this past half-hour, sir.' Her russet-apple face creased into lines of such perplexity that I knew she was telling the truth. With a muttered apology I dismissed her and swallowed the rest of my drink at a gulp. There was, there must be, some perfectly reasonable explanation of the evening's happenings. In the morning I'd go into Inverness and ask McTavish exactly why the man from Glasgow and others had left Auchindoune. Not that I was afraid of . . . the glass slid from my hand and shivered to pieces in the empty fireplace. It had just come to me that I was far from being afraid. Whoever or whatever the girl in blue was I had fallen in love for the first time in my forty-three years.

I didn't go to Inverness the following day. Instead, like any love-sick boy, I spent the next three weeks haunting the Doune. I walked right round the base of the hill, climbed it from all angles, searched the tangles of blackberry, gorse and bog myrtle for possible caves or other hiding-places, sat for hours in the mossy hollow where the primroses grew; but not once did I see the girl whose beauty and anguish now so obsessed me that I thought of her by day and dreamed of her by night, nor did I hear the whistler's plaintive tune. Mrs Cameron sighed over the tears and rents in my flannel trousers and her husband eyed me curiously when I refused to go fishing with him. People to whom I had been given introductions sent me invitations to which I returned evasive replies, and when a friend telegraphed saying he was in Inverness and would like to come and stay I flew into such a state of panic that I borrowed the Cawdor grocer's bicycle and pedalled the twelve miles into town to put him off.

After all it was McTavish who gave me the first clue. He arrived unexpectedly one afternoon and inquired so courteously about my comfort that I could do no less than ask him to tea. We chatted idly of this and that; then he said, 'My Glasgow client is delighted you took the house.'

Almost without volition I demanded, 'What made him leave? What did he see here—maybe Charlie's men, or maybe . . . ?' McTavish looked acutely uncomfortable.

'It wasn't seeing exactly, it was—well—hearing. Mind you,' he hurried on, 'he was a skeery fellow and it's my opinion he gossiped too much with the Nairnside folk, but he said that come every new moon he heard whistling . . .'

But I was out of my chair and shaking him by the shoulder. '*Whistling*! From the garden, you mean?'

Poor McTavish cowered back. 'I don't know, just whistling. Oh, sir, don't say you've heard it too?'

'I have,' I said grimly, 'but it's not driving me away, I want to find out its origin.'

He shook his head. 'There are always scores of stories about old houses like this but the people hereabouts are so close-mouthed that all I can find out is that about fifty years ago the farmer who lived here had a beautiful daughter who ran off with a tinker lad. Some say he got himself shot, others that he sickened and died. Anyway the girl went out of her mind with grief and didn't live long after him. I'd not be knowing any more.' he finished feebly. 'I've heard tell old Cameron has the whole history but when I asked him he swore he'd never heard of it.'

At the moment the significance of that last remark escaped me—I was too busy trying to remember when there was a new moon, and before McTavish's car was out of the drive I was leafing the pages of my diary. The date was six days ahead.

Thereafter I lived for the new moon. During my first six days of waiting I kept away from the Doune and passed the long drowsy hours in the garden conning over in my mind the sparse information given me by McTavish. Several times I thought of eking this out by tactful questioning of the Cawdor villagers but I felt a strange reluctance to do so and a positive recoil from the idea of approaching Cameron on the subject, for somehow instinct told me he was antagonistic to the figure I had met with on the Doune; several times I tried to laugh myself out of the whole absurd business of imagining I was in love with a being, earthly or unearthly, whose appearance was heralded by a whistled tune, but self-mockery did not work—I was too much in thrall, worldly individual though I was.

And the new moon did not fail me. Just after sunset I heard the whistling and, trembling with excitement, followed it up the Doune. There in the hollow was the girl in blue, but this time she stood facing me with outstretched arms, a smile on her lips. 'So you've come back,' I whispered, 'come back because I love you so utterly, my very dear.' But to my horror, as I stepped towards her the arms fell slackly to her sides and she stared at me sadly, shaking her head. The next moment she had fled down the far side of the hill and, as before, I raced after her, saw her rest her hand on the mountain-ash and gaze up into its branches, lost her entirely just short of the edge of the wood. . . .

So elusive an encounter, yet as I walked homewards I was filled with an ecstasy not even the presence of Cameron in the yard could dispel.

June passed, and July, and half of August. Looking back it seems as if I dreamed through those two and a half months, waking only when the date on the calendar told me my love would return that night—then I would wait in a fever of impatience for the summer day to close. It had been April when I first saw her and I remember awakening on the morning of 16th August and thinking: 'Tonight we shall meet again but this fifth time she will tell me what troubles her, and I shall destroy or exorcize whatever it may be, and she will stay warm and sweet in my arms.'

But to my dismay her face was drawn with grief when I found her in the hollow and I shall never forget the piteous appeal in her grey eyes. As usual she ran from me and I followed, but when she reached the mountain-ash she not only looked up but pointed to the green berries beginning to cluster on its branches. I stepped forward, pointing, also, and the sorrow died in her eyes and she nodded. Just for a minute she stood so close I could see the rise and fall of her breast, then suddenly she was gone and I was staring at the still bole of the tree. . . .

That was the end of dreaming, for day and night I was haunted by the memory of her tragic face and by the knowledge that in some way I had failed to give her something she wanted desperately, something without which she was compelled to suffer time without end.

The moon was in its last quarter when Mrs Cameron lingered after setting my luncheon dishes on the table. 'If you please, sir, Cameron's asking could you come and see him.'

I glanced up in bewilderment. 'See him? Why, can't he come and see me?'

She gave a little snuffle. 'He's been in his bed a week, sir. I had the Doctor out from Nairn. He says it's the pneumonia and gave me a fair talking-to for not sending for him earlier.'

My sense of guilt must have shown in my flushed face. Ever since that April evening when he had told me that cock-and-bull story about a visit from Sutherland the keeper I had kept out of Cameron's way, spoken to him tersely when obliged. Then I had grown conscious that he kept a vigilant eye on me around the time of the new moon and been convinced of his enmity towards both myself and the girl of the Doune. For the past three weeks I had been so absorbed I had entirely failed to notice his disappearance from garden or yard. Now, looking at his wife's worried, wrinkled countenance, I felt all kinds of a cad.

'Of course, I'll come,' I said, giving her shoulder an awkward pat, 'but why on earth didn't you tell me when he was first taken ill?'

'You look gey sick yourself, sir.' Then her voice dropped, 'And Cameron said he thought you were against him.'

So Cameron had been aware of my feelings and—what was it McTavish had said—Cameron had the whole history of the farmer's daughter who had run away with a tinker lad. My lunch went untouched and despite the heat of the day I sat shivering in my chair. Was I on the fringe of discovering what ailed my unhappy love—and did I want to know the truth? For the first time in months the materialist in me came uppermost. These damned Highlanders had bewitched me with their hints of spooks and such-like nonsense and I was a fool ever to have meddled. . . .

'Would you be ready now, sir?' said Mrs Cameron from behind me.

I followed her along the stone passage leading to the kitchen quarters conscious only of the violent conflict in my mind. One side cried urgently to know the secret behind my lovely girl's wanderings: the other shied desperately away from any possible proof that she belonged to a world not our own, for selfishly it clung to the hope that some day, somehow, she and I might find normal human happiness together.

Mrs Cameron pushed open a door. 'In here, sir.'

Cameron lay propped up on pillows in a wide bed. One glance sufficed to tell me he was very ill indeed and while I murmured conventional sympathy his faded eyes regarded me in mute entreaty. He waited until his wife had left us before saying in a thread-like whisper, 'She came to you every new moon, didn't she?'

This time I could not lie. 'Yes,' I said.

He sighed. 'She came to me but the once, yon was my punishment. Fifty years I've lived with my sin and before I go I must tell you the ways of it. Her name was Elspeth Munro and she lived here in Auchindoune. Such a delicate lass she was with her chestnut hair, and her big grey eyes, and her walk that was like running water. Her father Hamish was a hard man, set on his only child making a fine marriage, and when I came here from the Lochiel country and began to court her he was gey pleased.'

His gnarled hands twitched, restlessly on the white coverlet. 'It's hard to believe, but I had money in those days, most of it made in ways I don't like to remember. A cattle and sheep dealer

I was, but the real money came from distilling whisky—there wasn't a lad in the Cameron country who could jink the Excisemen as cleverly as I did. Well, I bought a farm over Culloden way, a lonely place with a barn just suited to my purpose, for I distilled the whisky in a hut up on the peat moss and stored the casks in the barn under the grain. The moment I set eyes on Elspeth I knew she was the lass for me and by the year's end we were betrothed. She hated me, I know that now. When I kissed her she fluttered in my arms like a bird—but I was a masterful man and a cruel one and I was set on bending her to my will. The wedding day was fixed for September but the spring before a tinker came to my door asking for work. They called him Logie, a heigho-heugho lad he was with a gipsy face and a quick bright smile—and I gave him the job of minding my sheep up on the peat moss.

'I never heard a lad whistle like Logie. I used to hear it echoing down the glen of an evening, but what I didn't know was that Elspeth heard it too until the April night I found them lying in the hollow on the Doune top. I thrashed the lad within an inch of his life, took Elspeth home and told her father to keep her under lock and key till her wedding-day. She grew pale and wisht but I didn't care for she was like a fever in my blood and all I minded was to have her for my own. Come August a shepherd from the west told me Logie was working at Achnasheen and that was good news for it was a long journey from Nairnside at that time.

'We were married in Cawdor church, and I mind how beautiful Elspeth looked in her long white silk dress as she came up the aisle with her father. One sorrowful glance she gave me that went through me like a knife, but then the service began and all I thought of was the presents I would give her to win her round, to make her love me.'

Cameron's thready voice petered out and he closed his eyes for a moment, then went on: 'It was when we came out of the church that it happened. I could feel Elspeth trembling on my arm but I was so proud of showing her to the crowd that had gathered that I did not hear the whistling—at first. It was only when I was about to hand her into the fine carriage I had hired that she broke from me, and it was then I heard the tune that Logie had always whistled. The next instant Elspeth was running through the Castle gates and up the path leading through Cawdor woods to the peat moss, her dress kilted up above her knees, her long white veil streaming behind her. I started after her, but she moved too quick . . .' Cameron's head turned from side to side on the pillow and when he spoke again I had to bend closer to hear the words.

'Logie must have been waiting for her in the woods, but though Hamish and I searched for a week we never saw sign of them. I doubt it was my pride was hurt the most, but I wouldn't admit that. Back home I went, shut myself up, and drank my own whisky. Half fuddled I was all and every day, but never too drunk to walk up the Doune each night. It was there they had first loved each other and I had the feeling they'd come back so I always carried my gun. It was a year to the day of my marriage I found them. They were sitting beneath a rowan tree and it broke my heart to see Elspeth, for she wore a ragged blue dress and had no shoes to her feet and she was burned as black as Logie. Laughing they were and teasing each other with great bunches of the scarlet berries. They neither saw nor heard me as I drew nearer and raised my gun.

'I mind the blood spurting from Logie's mouth, spattering his shirt with great red blotches, and Elspeth kneeling beside him. Then she lifted her head and when I saw the hate blazing from her eyes I was off down the hill like the coward I was. But I couldn't keep away. In the gloaming I went back. Elspeth had gone but Logie's body was still there and I carried it—I was a strong man then—up the Doune to the edge of the hollow. I covered him with bracken and went home for a spade. I knew

I'd be safe, for not a single crofter would climb the Doune after dusk for fear of the ghosts of Charlie's men. Late that night I buried him—you'll mind what I told you, primroses grow well for those they love?

'Next day two of Hamish's men found Elspeth wandering on the Doune side and brought her home to Auchindoune. Her wits were gone and never a word did she say till the day I rode over to see her. Sane or mad I wanted to claim her as my wife but when she saw me she raised herself up in bed and pointed, "Red as rowan berries," she said. "Red as rowan berries".'

The old man's head lolled forward. 'There's little else to tell,' he muttered. 'She died three months later and they buried her in Cawdor churchyard. I aye think Hamish knew the truth for a year later he put the Excisemen on to me, but when I came out of gaol he too had died and all I wanted was to forget. I wasn't allowed to do that. Everywhere I went I heard Logie's whistle and saw Elspeth's eyes. I tried to leave the place—something kept me tied to it. When I married I came here to Auchindoune for I thought maybe if I tended her home she'd forgive me. It didn't work out that way . . .' He slumped back, his breath coming in shallow gasps.

I leaned over him and gripped his shoulder. 'Tell me, tell me, what is it that Elspeth wants so desperately?'

His eyelids flickered. 'Red as rowan berries,' he muttered, 'red as rowan berries!'

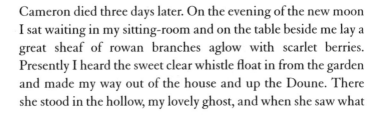

Cameron died three days later. On the evening of the new moon I sat waiting in my sitting-room and on the table beside me lay a great sheaf of rowan branches aglow with scarlet berries. Presently I heard the sweet clear whistle float in from the garden and made my way out of the house and up the Doune. There she stood in the hollow, my lovely ghost, and when she saw what

I bore in my arms a look of radiance overspread her face. I bent down and strewed the rowans on Logie's makeshift grave and as I straightened she stretched out her hands. I took them in my own and they were, I swear, warm living hands. I drew her towards me, and as we kissed I knew that for one wild, wonderful moment the real Elspeth Munro belonged to me; then she retreated, but now the colour glowed in her cheeks and as she reached the far lip of the hollow she turned and gave me a joyous wave of the hand . . .

Deliberately I extended my tenancy of Auchindoune for a further month and told McTavish I wished to rent it the following summer. But though I waited in the sitting-room on new moon evenings I never heard the whistle of Logie again, never saw the blue-clad Elspeth standing in the hollow. Sad though I was—for I shall always love her—I knew in my heart I had done the only thing possible, I had given her peace.

Consanguinity

Ronald Duncan

THE *Flying Scotsman* was two hours late. That used to happen frequently during the war, especially when the Heinkels had been over during the night. The train was blacked out, the lights were dim; two officers sat opposite each other in a first-class compartment. One of them was reading *The Idiot*; the other, a Major of about thirty-five, sat huddled in a corner staring intently in front of him as though examining a scene which lay behind his eyes. He smoked continuously. Neither of the men had spoken for four hours; they had been in the train for four hours five minutes. Even then their conversation had been restricted, and omitted any introductions. Captain Maclean of the Seaforth Highlanders had permitted himself to remark that 'it was a perfect bore carrying these bloody gasmasks around', and in reply Major Buckle of the Black Watch had grunted. Their reticence was, however, not due to the notices displayed above their seats to the effect that 'Idle chatter helps Hitler', but to the fact that neither had any curiosity about the other. Perhaps both had seen too much of their fellow men to want to get to know another. That was true of Captain Maclean at least, who had just endured nine weeks of a crowded troop-ship. To him, understandably, silence now seemed a luxury and solitude an indulgence.

He planned to spend his leave in complete privacy. It was unlikely that his sister, who kept house for him in Edinburgh, would do anything to spoil his brief retreat. But as a precaution he had delayed informing her of his arrival, and merely sent her a wire from King's Cross. He did not wish to be met at Waverley Station by a gathering of the clan.

The train jolted suddenly to a standstill. A cloud of steam from the vacuum brakes oozed into the compartment.

'Signals, I suppose,' Maclean said, putting down his book and glancing at the blind over the window. 'This will make us later than ever.'

Major Buckle looked at his watch. Comment was unnecessary. A stop was unlikely to hasten their arrival.

But after about ten minutes the express edged its way forward again and eventually sidled unobtrusively into a station. This moment always provided an opening gambit for conversation during the war, which even Captain Maclean could not resist.

'Where are we?' he asked, peering round the blind at the completely darkened platform.

'God knows,' Buckle replied. 'It looks like hell. Maybe it is hell. I think I recognize it. I used to go to the St Leger occasionally. This will be Doncaster.'

They both remarked almost simultaneously that they should have been eighty miles nearer Edinburgh by this time, after which observation they felt almost old friends. Nothing joins people together so quickly as a mutual complaint.

'It's bloody rough,' Maclean muttered, 'catching a train that's half a day late when you've only got a fortnight's leave.'

'Been overseas?' Buckle asked, without the slightest interest.

'Singapore.' The reply was curt but not rude.

'Tough.' The comment was sympathetic without sentiment.

Not a word more was said. The fact that Maclean's regiment

had retreated for four months through the Malayan jungle only to be practically annihilated on the docks at Singapore, and that he was the only officer of his brigade alive to tell the tale, was no excuse for him to do so. It was not shame that kept him silent; he would have been just as reticent if he had taken part in a victory. One did not talk shop.

'Seen any good shows in London recently?' he asked.

'Rattigan's play wasn't bad.'

'But that came off months ago.'

'Did it?'

'Yes. Time passes.'

'Does it?' Buckle asked pointedly.

Maclean looked embarrassed, sensing some philosophical edge behind the question. Then suddenly he smiled with relief.

'Ah, of course, I see what you mean. Time certainly does drag in a train.'

'That's not what I meant.'

'Oh.'

Maclean picked up his book. Within five minutes, both officers were sleeping. The train tore through the night, carrying its ungainly passengers forward while they crawled back into their dreams. Dreams of a severed hand like a glove on the floor. Dreams of a Negress with a necklace of breasts. But Maclean remembered neither when he awoke in the half-light with a crick in his neck. Quickly he straightened his tie and combed his hair.

'What we need is a cup of char,' he said.

'We've just passed through Peebles,' Buckle told him. 'We should be in in about half an hour.'

One could not say that the two officers had slept together, but the fact that they had sprawled within the same compartment seemed to ease their relationship. The morning found them much more talkative than they had been the night before.

'Do you live in Edinburgh too?' Maclean asked.

'No, but I used to. That's why I'm going there.'

Paradoxes always annoyed Maclean. He was afraid that somebody was pulling his leg.

'You mean you live just outside the city?' he asked, hoping to clear up the apparent contradiction.

'No, I don't live anywhere now,' Buckle answered without a note of regret.

Immediately three garish pictures floated into the Captain's mind: First, he visualized the Major standing beside a bombed-out house, smouldering in ruins, where lay the bodies of his entire family. For some reason a rocking-horse and a Teddy-bear were to the fore in this image. The second visual headline showed the Major driving his tank through the approaches to Benghazi. A dispatch rider hands him a cable. It is from his wife. Maclean could read it clearly over Major Buckle's shoulder. 'I am sleeping occasionally with the postman, but I am pregnant by the milkman. When you get this I shall be living with the dustman. Your loving wife.'

'War's a bloody bore, the way it uproots chaps,' he said.

Then the third picture came into his mind. He saw his sister Angela standing waiting on the platform, her mouth as full of questions as his nanny's used to be of pins.

'If you've nowhere to stay in Edinburgh, my sister and I would be awfully pleased to put you up.'

Thank you. I should be glad of your hospitality for a night or two.'

'And, of course, your wife, if . . .'

'No, I am alone.'

The second image flashed like a film trailer across Maclean's mind.

'I am not married.'

It faded. And the third picture, of his sister standing on the platform, came into focus. He had not the slightest doubt that she was there waiting.

Everything about Angela was a compromise, even her sex.

With her cairn puppy waiting beside her and her smart, crocodile handbag tucked under her arm, she looked completely unobtrusive. Her whole appearance was a compromise, for though Angela knew that her looks were striking, and wished to be the centre of attraction, yet she dressed so tastefully and stood so demurely that you would not pause as you passed her or notice what she wore. Her rather chic hat suggested a femininity and gaiety which the severity of her tweeds contradicted. In one hand she twirled a pretty French parasol, but her stance was that of a man. Nobody had ever told her that she had beautiful legs and a pretty instep, but she knew. Perhaps that was why she wore the sheerest silk stockings, and the flattest and heaviest of brogues to ruin the effect, Just as nature had failed to make up its mind, giving her straight, dull hair (whereas her brother's was naturally curly), and the prettiest eyes and mouth above a rather too heavy chin. Her hips were distinctly boyish, but not even the tightest bra could hide her breasts. Though Angela was nearly thirty she was as embarrassed by her breasts as she had been when they first leaned out from their boyish tree. Alex had laughed at her then; she still feared his derision and wished her womanhood away. For it was that which confused their relationship. Ever since their mother's death she had been both mother and sister to Alex. For the last ten years she had been wife in all but shame. She was, of course, quite unaware of any incestuous leanings; she merely liked Alex more than any other man, and had turned away the attention of several admirers because any surrender to them had made her feel unfaithful to him. They were happy living together in the old house in Randal Crescent. They could read books at table, they could sit on the edge of each other's bed.

She had counted the days, the hours, till this train should bring him back to her. And as it steamed into the platform and she saw him stepping down from his compartment, she felt entire again for the first time in twelve months. First her eyes, then her feet, ran to meet him, as though she would embrace him and erase the months of anxiety she had endured but dared not show. He was all the world to her—or almost. For the rest, perhaps one day she would adopt one.

'Alex!' she cried. But there was no embrace. The cairn on the lead took one hand and the parasol the other. 'Here's Boxer to see you. He's awfully patient. Your train's hours late.'

Alex was both officer and gentleman. He gave his sister a smile, but kissed and fondled the dog.

Then, turning, he introduced her to the Major. But Angela had no eyes for him; she was wholly absorbed in her brother. Like any woman, though, she was more observant than she was curious, and noticed detail when she was not looking for it. In the cursory but polite glance she gave Major Buckle as he shook her hand, Angela formed an indelible impression. She saw him as a lonely, shy and pathetic figure, and was not in the least taken in by his strong build and hearty manner. His light-blue eyes gave him a remoteness, a coldness which attracted her, while his lips, which seemed unnaturally red against the pallor of his skin, gave his mouth a sensuousness and warmth which repelled her. She also noticed that his batman had ironed the wrong side of his tie.

Buckle, on the other hand, had every opportunity to look at Angela while she chatted away so excitedly to her brother. And though his eyes grazed over her closely, he saw only her wet lower lip, her breasts and her narrow hips, and was quite unaware of the colour of her eyes and hair, or what she was wearing. By the time they had reached the ticket barrier, he knew that he wanted to sleep with her. It was a bore that he would be her brother's guest.

The next few days were the happiest in Angela's life. She did not know why. Historians maintain that wars are caused by economics. They are wrong. Economics is their excuse; the reason for war is that it destroys that which we all want destroyed: the *status quo*, with which we identify our own inhibitions. War alone releases our personal relationships. It is not a necessary evil but a necessary pleasure. If we were honest, we would admit that all the slaughter, cruelty and suffering which war entails remain for us merely a matter of regrettable statistics. What means something to us is that war provides us with that sense of insecurity which is life, when peace has seemed as respectable and as dull as death. It is true that a drunken orgy might provide a similar release, but it is quite difficult to remain completely drunk for several years and impossible to indulge in the briefest fling without some curious sense of remorse. In war, we can release ourselves without guilt; indeed, our excuses become duties and any behaviour is condoned under the blanket of the great sacrifice which we curse publicly, but enjoy privately. National disasters can be borne with comfortable fortitude; it is personal sorrow, not grief for another but a lack in our own life, which is so unbearable. It is a burden we would put down though a million men fall with it.

Angela sang as she skipped about the kitchen in dressing-gown and mules getting the breakfast. Angela sang as she carried first one tray and then the other up to the two men's rooms. She had got up early and done all the housework and prepared a picnic. Now as she ran her bath and admired her figure in the mirror above it, she was radiant with happiness. It was nice having two men to fuss over again. She had not felt so useful since her father had died. It was nice getting up early to cut sandwiches, make a salad and iron shirts; and what doubled her pleasure was that she could now indulge her affection for her brother with a certain sense of virtue, or even sacrifice. His leave was short: it was right he should have breakfast in bed. And the presence of a guest in the house gave another excuse for any of the luxuries she planned. As she stepped into the bath she decided she would give them salmon for supper. Then she remembered she had not locked the bathroom door. She got out of the bath to do so. Still singing gaily, she stepped into the water again. The door remained ajar.

'I'll sling this sponge at you, Alex, if you rinse your razor in my bath. It's a filthy trick.'

There was a note of soft petulance in her voice, the tone women use when they complain about those masculine habits which are so endearing to them.

'Hurry up and get out of that. Buckle will want a bath too.' Alex dipped his razor beside her, and turned to lather his face.

Angela lay full length, swishing the water together with her legs so that it flopped up over her flat tummy. It was a sort of aid to meditation she had employed since childhood.

'Alex, do you like him?'

Her casual voice betrayed the fact that the question meant a great deal to her.

'Immensely,' he replied.

Angela sat up, relieved, and began soaping herself energetically. His answer had meant everything to her.

'We seem to get on so well together,' she said. 'I can hardly believe you only met him in a train three days ago. And yet he's so reticent. I hardly know a thing about him.'

'Do you need to?' Alex mumbled, his face contorted beneath his blade.

'Not if you like him.'

The trio passed the next few days very idly, without plan or purpose, driving out for a picnic during the day and pubcrawling in the evening. This was to please Alex, who still had literary aspirations. Edinburgh is probably the only city in the British Isles where writers still congregate at their regular tavern, and not even the war dispersed this coterie of affable but garrulous cadgers. Angela liked to hear her brother talk; after a couple of whiskies she, too, was convinced of his talent. She felt as proud as a mother, and listened as indulgently as a wife while he told the synopsis of a play he intended to write one fine day to a Scottish Nationalist poet who accepted Drambuie and beer in strict rotation. Angela knew the plot better than Alex, prompted him here and there, and remarked that a scene reminded her of a play by Bridie she had seen years ago at the King's. After all, she was his sister.

Throughout these sessions Major Buckle sat content, yet contributed little to the conversation beyond an admission that he had not read whatever book they happened to be discussing. But he seldom took his eyes off Alex, and though he himself had no literary pretensions and did nothing to express his own personality, he was plainly impressed by that of his friend. It was the shadow-like loyalty to her brother that made Angela warm to Peter Buckle. He didn't attract her physically. Both his appearance and her responses were far too vague, nebulous and undefined for her to have any feeling as precise as that. On the other hand, his features were regular and inconspicuous and his personality so passive that she could not possibly find him objectionable. It was, she felt, as if she now had two brothers, and the better they got on together, the fonder she became of each.

As they walked home after the third evening spent in the Green Dragon, Angela slipped her right arm through her brother's and, since Buckle was on her left, she gave him the other. After the fifth evening, she kissed her brother good night, and since Buckle was sitting beside Alex, she gave him a peck too. They seemed such good friends it was only right they should share her favours. After the seventh evening spent in precisely the same fashion, and following the consumption of half a dozen whiskies, Angela and Buckle found themselves alone in the back of a car. Sometimes the suggestive environment can be mistaken for personal feeling. Major Buckle took the initiative. He smudged her lips and undid the buttons of her blouse, only withdrawing when the intricacies of her bra defeated his fumbling fingers. By the end of a fortnight, it was agreed that there was some sort of understanding between them, though

223

neither could have told precisely what was understood. It certainly was not love; it looked dangerously like the imminence of marriage. Events moved quickly in war and nobody looked too closely. It was agreed that the three of them should go to London and see a few shows.

As her relationship with Buckle developed, Angela relaxed. She took to wandering in and out of her brother's bedroom clad in her undies, or precariously swathed in a bath-towel. Their rooms in the hotel adjoined; she used to sit for hours gossiping to Alex as he lay in bed. Buckle's room was only across the corridor. But he remained undisturbed. Nevertheless, his presence there was an indispensable catalyst, Angela felt that, now she had a man of her own as it were, there was nothing to inhibit her enjoying such harmless intimacies with her brother. Another factor, of course, was that she knew her brother's leave would soon be over. No one knew when or whether they would see each other again. In those circumstances, when there were air-raids every night to remind people how transient their moment was, despair was often mistaken for desire. Sometimes desire found its own desperation.

Buckle proposed to Angela while she lay beside him on the platform of Lancaster Gate tube station. It seemed the decent thing to do, though even Major Buckle, who was not sufficiently a realist to have a sense of humour, recognized something slightly inappropriate in making plans for the future in the middle of a series of air-raids which had already destroyed several square miles of the city. Perhaps their horizontal position on the asphalt floor compensated for the less romantic aspects of the occasion.

They had been forced to seek shelter in the tube on their way back to their hotel from the Mercury Theatre. That was four hours ago. The all-clear had not sounded. Alex lay beside them sleeping. The rest of the platform was covered with ungainly bodies slunked in sleep and each covered by a single blanket. These were the regulars, timid termites who had taken to sleeping in the tubes every night. Trains did not wake them, passengers walking by did not disturb them, nothing embarrassed them. Couples old and young lay under the slot machines and wire refuse baskets, and even on the stairs, as though in the privacy of their own bedrooms. Though the English are supposed to be prudes, once they are horizontal, in parks or on the beach, they lose all modesty and have less inhibitions in public than they have in the privacy of their homes. Many a man now walking in the sun was begotten on the steps of an escalator in the full glare of a neon light.

In such an environment, Angela could hardly have refused. Death was in the air and birth, or something extraordinarily like it lay about her. She snuggled up to Buckle and smiled over his shoulder at her brother. They were joined in holy wedlock two days later by special licence at Caxton Hall. Alex gave her away and Buckle received her, both slightly hilarious and a little drunk. Only Angela was serious or sober.

After the sordid civic ceremony, where the officializing bureaucrat apes a clergyman by intoning the regulations with his hands clasped together, and gives you a receipt with all the unction of handing you a sacrament, the couple drove straight to Victoria Station. Alex accompanied them on to the platform to put them in the train to Brighton. He stood by the window talking to his sister. There were tears in her eyes. Only four days of his leave remained. She could not bear to leave him.

'Couldn't Alex come too?' she pleaded, turning to her husband.

Together they dragged him into the carriage just as the train started. Alex felt rather an intruder and a little foolish, holding a bag of confetti in his pocket. He could scarcely open it now, and fling it over them before sitting beside them for the rest of the journey.

'I've only got a platform ticket,' he said.

'Let's go along to the bar and have a drink,' Buckle suggested.

The two friends immediately left the compartment. Angela smiled indulgently after them, then glanced into her compact and powdered her nose. It all seemed a dream to her. She glanced at the ring on her finger. Like any virgin, she was terribly frightened. She knew she was going to lose something she had preserved but did not want. It was like going to the dentist. But it was nice that Alex had come too. She used her lipstick with deliberation, then crossed her legs and looked out of the window, counting the telegraph posts which passed in a minute. She knew that they stood fifty yards apart, and from that data could compute the speed of the train. It was a trick she had learned from her father.

Angela awoke the next morning, but before she was conscious of the light she was aware of her dream. Before opening her eyes, she tried to recall it. . . .

She had been out hunting, but instead of riding a horse she had dreamed she was sitting astride a giraffe. The animal had galloped, quite out of control, through a forest where every tree was on fire, each separate limb of timber blossoming with a flame. Having recalled her dream, she remembered, and raising her thighs, removed the bath-towel beneath her. She got out of bed and carried it into the bathroom. Buckle was not in bed, neither was he in the bath. She frowned, then dimly remembered that he had said something or other about going downstairs to get an evening paper. But that, she realized, must have been last night. He must have returned since then. There was proof of that. She rang for her coffee, got back into bed and lit a cigarette. Probably her husband and Alex had gone for a dip. The hotel was by the beach. At any rate she did not feel like bathing: she felt very refreshed. She had never slept so deeply or woken so well. For an hour she lay enjoying the sensation of heaviness in her limbs. It was to her as if her youth had been a drought and now it had rained and she was the rain and she was the river. But for all that she could recall nothing of the storm, nor did she try. It was enough to lie there enjoying the sensation of being quenched. Her limbs had drunk from her own desire. Her thighs and her breasts felt heavy, and yet it was this that at the same time made her feel so light as though she might float. It was the first time that Angela had been aware of her own body as an instrument of pleasure. She had previously regarded it as a vehicle for health.

She had her breakfast and then decided for once in her life not to take a bath. She did not want to wash this feeling away. She looked carefully at her nakedness in the mirror. She looked just the same.

Appearance can be deceptive, she thought, and stretched like a cat.

She dressed quickly and went along the corridor to her brother's room expecting to find her husband jawing to him. Alex was alone; he lay in bed reading.

'Have you and Peter been out for a bathe?' Angela asked him.

Alex shook his head.

'I wonder where he's gone?'

'Probably for a walk?'

Angela nodded.

For the next hour, neither gave Buckle a thought. But when they went downstairs Angela asked the hotel porter if he had seen Major Buckle. The man was not helpful. He had not seen anyone go out, and since he had not been on duty the previous evening when Angela and her husband had arrived, he would not have recognized him anyhow.

'If he didn't have breakfast with you upstairs he must have been into the dining-room,' Alex suggested.

But the head waiter assured them that nobody had been to Angela's table that morning.

They decided that Buckle had gone for a bathe or taken a walk, and set out to wander along the front. At first they tried to see if they could spot him among the bathers who already sported themselves on the beach, but after a few moments their own conversation became absorbing; they forgot their search, thinking they would find Buckle at the hotel when they got back. They walked for about three miles along the front, stopped and had coffee and then returned leisurely to their hotel.

'Have you seen my husband?' Angela asked the porter as he handed her the key to her room.

'No, madam,' the man replied cheerfully, as if reassuring her.

'That fool thinks we're having an affair, and that you're frightened your husband will come and catch us red-handed,' Alex joked as they went up in the lift.

Angela said nothing. She was not amused.

Her room was empty. There was no note or message from Buckle. For some reason, neither Angela nor her brother thought of looking in the bathroom or on the dressing-table to see whether Buckle's shaving kit or hair brushes were still there. But when he did not appear for lunch, or turn up during the afternoon, they decided that he had probably been called up to London by the War Office on some urgent business and had been delayed longer than he expected.

'That sort of thing often happens these days,' Alex told his sister. 'A chap in our regiment got called off on some secret mission the first day of his leave.'

'He could have phoned.'

'Maybe he did when we were out.'

'Then there'd have been a message.'

'If he's in London, he's bound to have lunched at the club. I'll ring and ask if they've seen him.'

Alex shook his head as he returned from the kiosk. They sat

for a few minutes in silence.

'I'll go and pack,' Angela said.

She was now very worried. So was her brother, but with more reason. He had not told her that when he had inquired for her husband, the secretary of the club had blandly replied that Buckle was dead. Of course Alex realized that there must have been two members with the same name. Still, it had been a shock to him.

Early next morning, Alex accompanied his sister to the War Office. A Colonel Hutchison received them. Alex explained: if Buckle had been recalled to his unit or dispatched on some mission, it was only fair that his wife should be told of his whereabouts, especially in these circumstances. . . .

'What circumstances?' the Colonel asked sympathetically,

'We were on our honeymoon,' Angela said; 'we were only married yesterday afternoon.'

'You did say Major Peter Buckle of the Black Watch?' the Colonel asked.

'Yes, sir,' Alex replied rather shortly.

'Are you sure there's not some mistake?'

'A woman's hardly likely to forget her husband's name,' Angela said.

The Colonel rang a bell on his desk.

'Bring me the army list of the Black Watch,' he told the secretary.

When this was handed to him he glanced rapidly down the list of names. Then he got up and looked out of the window, 'I thought it was unlikely. But there was just a chance that there were two officers of the same name and rank in the same regiment.'

He turned and faced the brother and sister.

'As I said, there must be some mistake. Major Buckle was blown to pieces before my eyes six months ago.'

'Impossible!' Angela blurted out.

'A mine exploded under his car. Very little was left of Buckle, but quite enough to identify him. The man whom you married yesterday must have been masquerading as Major Buckle.'

'I'm sure he was genuine,' Maclean said. 'I'd have spotted it if he wasn't.'

'I'm sorry, Captain, but I doubt it. There are plenty of these people who pass themselves off as officers these days. We must trace this Major Buckle of yours. Intelligence will want to question him. I suppose you've got a photograph of him? Did he look remotely like this?'

The Colonel produced a photograph from the drawer of his desk.

'Yes, that's Peter,' Angela said.

'That's impossible I'm afraid, madam. If you have a photograph of your husband you can compare it with this. I am sure you will see that the likeness is only enough to justify the impostor in his attempt. Have you such a photograph?'

Angela shook her head sadly, and then remembered.

'Oh yes, I took several snaps of my brother and my husband at a picnic we had outside Edinburgh a couple of weeks ago.'

'May I see them?'

'The film hasn't been developed yet,' Alex explained.

'Then go and get it immediately, Captain, and we'll have it developed here.'

Half an hour later, Alex returned with the camera and handed it to the Colonel. Then he took his sister into the canteen while the film was developed. They waited.

Colonel Hutchison looked hopelessly embarrassed as he placed the six prints on the table before them.

'Your brother looks quite a film star,' he muttered, then immediately regretted the remark.

Angela stared at the prints. There were six photographs of her brother, but no trace of any figure, however dim, standing beside him.

The Drowned Rose

George Mackay Brown

THERE WAS A sudden fragrance, freshness, coldness in the room. I looked up from my book. A young woman in a red dress had come in, breathless, eager, ready for laughter. The summer twilight of the far north was just beginning; it was late in the evening, after ten o'clock. The girl peered at me where I sat in the shadowy window-seat. 'You're not Johnny,' she said, more than a bit disappointed.

'No,' I said, 'that isn't my name.'

She was certainly a very beautiful girl, with her abundant black hair and hazel eyes and small sweet sensuous mouth. Who was she—the merchant's daughter from across the road, perhaps? A girl from one of the farms? She was a bit too old to be one of my future pupils.

'Has he been here?' she cried. 'Has he been and gone again? The villain. He promised to wait for me. We're going up the hill to watch the sunset.' Again the flash of laughter in her eyes.

'I'm sorry,' I said, 'I'm a stranger. I only arrived this afternoon. But I assure you nobody has called here this evening.'

'Well now, and just who are you?' she said. 'And what are you doing here?

'My name is William Reynolds, I said. 'I'm the new school-master.'

She gave me a look of the most utter sweet astonishment. 'The new—!' she shook her head. 'I'm most terribly confused,' she said. 'I really am. The queerest things are happening.'

'Sit down and tell me about it,' I said. For I liked the girl immensely. Blast that Johnny whoever-he-is, I thought; some fellows have all the luck. Here, I knew at once, was one of the few young women it was a joy to be with. I wished she would stay for supper. My mouth began to frame the invitation.

'He'll have gone to the hill without me,' she said. 'I'll wring his neck. The sun'll be down in ten minutes. I'd better hurry.'

She was gone as suddenly as she had come. The fragrance went with her. I discovered, a bit to my surprise, that I was shivering, even though it was a mild night and there was a decent fire burning in the grate.

'Goodnight,' I called after her.

No answer came back.

Blast that Johnny. I wouldn't mind stumbling to the top of a hill, breathless, with a rare creature like her, on such a beautiful night, I thought. I returned regretfully to my book. It was still light enough to read when I got to the end of the chapter. I looked out of the window at the russet-and-primrose sky. Two figures were silhouetted against the sunset on a rising crest of the hill. They stood there hand in hand. I was filled with happiness and envy.

I went to bed before midnight, in order to be fresh for my first morning in the new school.

———•◦⟡◦•———

I had grown utterly sick and tired of teaching mathematics in the junior secondary school in the city; trying to insert logarithms and trigonometry into the heads of louts whose only wish, like mine, was to be rid of the institution for ever. I read an advertisement in the educational journal for a male teacher—'required urgently'— for a one-teacher island school in the north. There was only a month of the summer term to go. I sent in my application at once, and was appointed without even having to endure an interview. Two days later I was in an aeroplane flying over the snow-scarred highlands of Scotland. The mountains gave way to moors and firths. Then I looked down at the sea stretching away to a huge horizon; a dark swirling tide-race; an island neatly ruled into tilth and pasture. Other islands tilted towards us. The plane settled lightly on a runway set in a dark moor. An hour later I boarded another smaller plane, and after ten merry minutes flying level with kittiwakes and cormorants I was shaking hands with the island representative of the education committee. This was the local minister. I liked the Reverend Donald Barr at once. He was, like myself, a young bachelor, but he gave me a passable tea of ham-and-eggs at the manse before driving me to the school. We talked easily and well together all the time. 'They're like every other community in the world,' he said, 'the islanders of Quoylay. They're good and bad and middling—mostly middling. There's not one really evil person in the whole island. If there's a saint I haven't met him yet. One and all, they're enormously hospitable in their farms—they'll share with you everything they have. The kids—they're a delight, shy and gentle and biddable. You've made a good move, mister, coming here, if the loneliness doesn't kill you. Sometimes it gets me down, especially on a Sunday morning when I find myself preaching to half-a-dozen unmoved faces. They were very religious once, now they're reverting to paganism as fast as they can. The minister is more or less a nonentity, a useless appendage. Changed days, my boy. We used to wield great power, we ministers. We were second only to the laird, and the schoolmaster got ten pounds a year. Your remote predecessor ate the scraps from my predecessor's table. Changed days, right enough. Enjoy yourself, Bill. I know you will, for a year or two anyway.'

By this time the manse car had brought me home with my luggage, and we were seated at either side of a newly-lighted fire in the school-house parlour. Donald Barr went away to prepare his sermon. I picked a novel at random from the bookcase, and had read maybe a half-dozen pages when I had my first visitor, the girl with the abundant black hair and laughter-lighted face; the loved one; the slightly bewildered one; the looker into sunsets.

The pupils descended on the playground, and swirled round like a swarm of birds, just before nine o'clock next morning. There were twenty children in the island school, ranging in age from five to twelve. So, they had to be arranged in different sections in the single large class-room. The four youngest were learning to read from the new phonetic script. Half-a-dozen or so of the eldest pupils would be going after the summer holidays to the senior secondary school in Kirkwall; they were making a start on French and Geometry. In between, and simultaneously, the others worked away at history, geography, reading, drawing, sums. I found the variety a bit bewildering, that first day.

Still, I enjoyed it. Everything that the minister had said about the island children was true. The impudence and indifference that the city children offered you in exchange for your labours, the common currency of my previous class-rooms, these were absent here. Instead, they looked at me and everything I did with a round-eyed wonderment. I expected that this would not last beyond the first weekend. Only once, in the middle of the afternoon, was there any kind of ruffling of the bright surface. With the six oldest ones I was going through a geometry theorem on the blackboard. A tall boy stood up. 'Please sir,' he said, 'that's not the way Miss McKillop taught us to do it.'

The class-room had been murmurous as a beehive. Now there was silence, as if a spell had been laid on the school.

'Please, sir, on Thursday afternoons Miss McKillop gave us nature study.' This from a ten-year-old girl with hair like a bronze bell. She stood up and blurted it out, bravely and a little resentfully.

'And what exactly did this nature study consist of?' I said.

'Please, sir,' said a boy whose head was like a hayrick and whose face was a galaxy of freckles, 'we would go to the beach for shells, and sometimes, please, sir, to the marsh for wild flowers.'

'Miss McKillop took us all,' said another boy. 'Please, sir.' Miss McKillop . . . Miss McKillop . . . Miss McKillop . . . The name scattered softly through the school as if a rose had shed its petals. Indeed last night's fragrance seemed to be everywhere in the class-room. A dozen mouths uttered the name. They looked at me, but they looked at me as if somebody else was sitting at the high desk beside the blackboard.

'I see,' I said. 'Nature study on Thursday afternoons. I don't see anything against it, except that I'm a great duffer when it comes to flowers and birds and such-like. Still, I'm sure none of us will be any the worse of a stroll through the fields on a Thursday afternoon. But this Thursday, you see, I'm new here, I'm feeling my way, and I'm pretty ignorant of what should be, so I think for today we'd just better carry on the way we're doing.

The spell was broken. The fragrance was withdrawn.

They returned to their phonetics and history and geometry. Their heads bent obediently once more over books and jotters. I lifted the pointer, and noticed that my fist was blue with cold. And the mouth of the boy who had first mentioned the name of Miss McKillop trembled, in the heart of that warm summer afternoon, as he gave me the proof of the theorem.

<hr />

'Thank God for that,' said Donald Barr. He brought a chessboard and a box of chessmen from the cupboard. He blew a spurt of dust from them. 'We'd have grown to hate each other after a fortnight, trying to warm each other up with politics and island gossip.' He arranged the pieces on the board. 'I'm very glad also that you're only a middling player, same as me. We can spend our evenings in an amiable silence.'

We were very indifferent players indeed. None of our games took longer than an hour to play. No victory came about through strategy, skill, or foresight. All without exception that first evening were lost by some incredible blunder (followed by muted cursings and the despairing fall of a fist on the table).

'You're right,' I said after the fourth game, 'silence is the true test of friendship.'

We had won two games each. We decided to drink a jar of ale and smoke our pipes before playing the decider. Donald Barr made his own beer, a nutty potent brew that crept through your veins and overcame you after ten minutes or so with a drowsy contentment. We smoked and sipped mostly in silence; yet fine companionable thoughts moved through our minds and were occasionally uttered.

'I am very pleased so far,' I said after a time, 'with this island and the people in it. The children are truly a delight. Mrs Sinclair who makes the school dinner has a nice touch with stew. There is also the young woman who visited me briefly last night. She was looking for somebody else, unfortunately. I hope she comes often.'

'What young woman?' said the minister drowsily.

'She didn't say her name,' I said. 'She's uncommonly good looking, what the teenagers in my last school would call a rare chick.'

'Describe this paragon,' said Donald Barr.

I am no great shakes at describing things, especially beautiful young women. But I did my best, between puffs at my pipe. The mass of black hair. The wide hazel eyes. The red restless laughing mouth. 'It was,' I said, 'as if she had come straight into the house out of a rose garden. She asked for Johnny.'

Something had happened to the Rev. Donald Barr. My words seemed to wash the drowsiness from his face; he was like a sleeper on summer hills overcome with rain. He sat up in his chair and looked at me. He was really agitated. He knocked the ember of tobacco out of his pipe. He took a deep gulp of ale from his mug. Then he walked to the window and looked out at the thickening light. The clock on the mantelshelf ticked on beyond eleven o'clock.

'And so,' I said, 'may she come back often to the school-house, if it's only to look for this Johnny.'

From Donald Barr, no answer. Silence is a test of friendship but I wanted very much to learn the name of my visitor; or rather I was seeking for a confirmation.

Donald Barr said, 'A ghost is the soul of a dead person who is earth-bound. That is, it is much attached to the things of this world that it is unwilling to let go of them. It cannot believe it is dead.

'It cannot accept for one moment that its body has been gathered back into the four elements. It refuses to set out on the only road it can take now, into the kingdom of the dead. No, it is in love too much with what it has been and known. It will not leave its money and possessions. It will not forgive the wrongs that were done to it while it was alive. It clings on desperately to love.'

'I was not speaking about any ghost,' I said. 'I was trying to tell you about this very delightful lovely girl.'

'If I was a priest,' said Donald Barr, 'instead of a minister, I might tell you that a ghost is a spirit lost between this world and purgatory. It refuses to shed its earthly appetites. It will not enter the dark gate of suffering.'

The northern twilight thickened in the room while we spoke. Our conversation was another kind of chess. Yet each knew what the other was about.

'I hope she's there tonight,' I said. 'I might even prevail on her to make me some toast and hot chocolate. For it seems I'm going to get no supper in the manse.'

237

'You're not scared?' said Donald Barr from the window.

'No,' I said. 'I'm not frightened of that kind of ghost. It seemed to me, when we were speaking together in the schoolhouse last night, this girl and I, that I was the wan lost one, the squeaker and gibberer, and she was a part of the ever-springing fountain.'

'Go home then to your ghost,' said Donald Barr. 'We won't play any more chess tonight. She won't harm you, you're quite right there.'

We stood together at the end of his garden path.

'Miss McKillop,' I murmured to the dark shape that was fumbling for the latch of the gate.

'Sandra McKillop,' said Donald, 'died the twenty-third of May this year. I buried her on the third of June, herself and John Germiston, in separate graves.

'Tell me,' I said.

'No,' said Donald, 'for I do not know the facts. Never ask me for a partial account. It seemed to me they were happy. I refuse to wrong the dead. Go in peace.'

There was no apparition in the school-house that night. I went to bed and slept soundly, drugged with fresh air, ale, fellowship; and a growing wonderment.

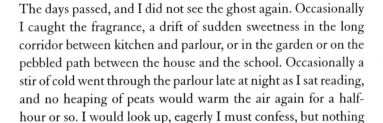

The days passed, and I did not see the ghost again. Occasionally I caught the fragrance, a drift of sudden sweetness in the long corridor between kitchen and parlour, or in the garden or on the pebbled path between the house and the school. Occasionally a stir of cold went through the parlour late at night as I sat reading, and no heaping of peats would warm the air again for a half-hour or so. I would look up, eagerly I must confess, but nothing trembled into form and breathing out of the expectant air.

It was as if the ghost had grown shy and uncertain, indicated her presence only by hints and suggestions. And in the class-room too things quietened down, and the island pupils and I worked out our regime together as the summer days passed. Only occasionally a five-year-old would whisper something about Miss McKillop, and smile, and then look sad; and it was like a small scattering of rose-petals. Apart from that everything proceeded smoothly to the final closing of books at the end of the school year.

———·•✿•·———

One man in the island I did not like, and that was Henrikson who kept the island store and garage, my neighbour. A low wall separated the school garden from Henrikson's land, which was usually untidy with empty lemonade cases, oil drums, sodden cardboard boxes. Apart from the man's simple presence, which he insisted on inflicting on me, I was put out by things in his character. For example, he showed an admiration for learning and university degrees that amounted to sycophancy; and this I could not abide, having sprung myself from a race of labourers and miners and railwaymen, good people all, more solid and sound and kindly than most university people, in my experience. But the drift of Henrikson's talk was that farmers and such like, including himself, were poor creatures indeed compared to their peers who had educated themselves and got into the professions and so risen in the world. This was bad enough; but soon he began to direct arrows of slander at this person and that in the island. 'Arrows' is too open and forthright a word for it; it was more the work of 'the smiler with the knife'. Such-and-such a farmer, he told me, was in financial difficulties, we wouldn't be seeing him in Quoylay much longer. This other young fellow had run his motor-cycle for two years now without a licence; maybe somebody should do something about it; he himself had no objection to sending anonymous letters to the authorities in such a case. Did I see that half-ruined croft down at the shore?

Two so-called respectable people in this island—he would mention no names—had spent a whole weekend together there at show time last summer, a married man and a farmer's daughter. The straw they had lain on hadn't even been cleaned out . . . This was the kind of talk that went on over the low wall between school and store on the late summer evenings. It was difficult to avoid the man; as soon as he saw me weeding the potato patch, or watering the pinks, out he came with his smirkings and cap-touchings, and leaned confidentially over the wall. It is easy to say I could simply have turned my back on him; but in many ways I am a coward; and even the basest of the living can coerce me to some extent. One evening his theme was the kirk and the minister. 'I'm not wanting to criticise any friend of yours,' he said. 'I've seen him more than once in the school-house and I've heard that you visit him in the manse, and it's no business of mine, but that man is not a real minister, if you ask me. We're used with a different kind of preaching in this island, and a different kind of pastoral behaviour too, I assure you of that. I know for a fact that he brews—he bought two tins of malt, and hops, from the store last month. The old ministers were one and all very much against drink. What's a minister for if he doesn't keep people's feet on the true path, yes, if he doesn't warn them and counsel them in season and out of season, you know, in regard to their conduct? The old ministers that were here formerly had a proper understanding of their office. But this Mr Barr, he closes his eyes to things that are a crying scandal to the whole island. For example—'

'Mr Barr is a very good friend of mine,' I said.

'O, to be sure,' he cried. 'I know. He's an educated man and so are you too, Mr Reynolds. I spoke out of place, I'm sorry. I'm just a simple countryman, brought up on the shorter catechism and the good book. Times are changing fast. I'm sure people who have been to the university have a different way of looking at things from an old country chap. No offence, Mr Reynolds, I hope.'

A few moths were out, clinging to the stones, fluttering and birring softly on the kitchen window. I turned and went in without saying goodnight to Mr Henrikson.

And as I went along the corridor, with a bad taste in my mouth from that holy old creep across the road, I heard it, a low reluctant weeping from above, from the bedroom. I ran upstairs and threw open the door. The room was empty, but it was as cold as the heart of an iceberg, and the unmistakable fragrance clung about the window curtains and the counterpane. There was the impression of a head on the pillow, as if someone had knelt beside the bed for a half-hour to sort out her troubles in silence.

My ghost was being pierced by a slow wondering sadness.

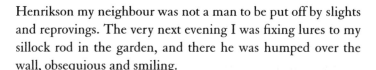

Henrikson my neighbour was not a man to be put off by slights and reprovings. The very next evening I was fixing lures to my sillock rod in the garden, and there he was humped over the wall, obsequious and smiling.

It had been a fine day, hadn't it? And now that the school was closed for the summer, would I not be thinking of going off to Edinburgh or Brighton or Majorca for a bit of a holiday? Well, that was fine, that I liked the island so much. To tell the truth, most of the folk in Quoylay were very glad to have a quiet respectable man like me in the school, after the wild goings-on that had been just before I arrived . . .

I was sick and tired of this man, and yet I knew that now I was to hear, in a very poisoned and biased version, the story of Sandra McKillop the school-mistress and Johnny. Donald Barr, out of compassion for the dead, would never have told me. So I threw my arms companionably over the wall and I offered Henrikson my tobacco pouch and I said, 'What kind of goings-on would that be now, Mr Henrikson?'

———••✦❦✦••———

Miss Sandra McKillop had come to the island school straight from the teachers' training college in Scotland two years before. (I am paraphrasing Henrikson's account, removing most of the barbs, trying to imagine a rose here and there.) She was a great change from the previous teacher, a finicky perjink old maid, and that for a start warmed the hearts of the islanders to her. But it was in the school itself that she scored her great success; the children of all ages took to her at once. She was a born teacher. Every day she held them in thrall from the first bell to the last. And even after school there was a dancing cluster of them round her all the way to her front door. The stupid ones and the ugly ones adored her especially, because she made them feel accepted. She enriched their days.

She was a good-looking girl. ('I won't deny that,' said Henrikson, 'as bonny a young woman as ever I saw.') More than one of the island bachelors hung about the school gate from time to time, hoping for a word with her. Nothing doing; she was pleasant and open with them and with everybody, but love did not enter her scheme of things; at least, not yet. She was a sociable girl, and was invited here and there among the farms for supper. She gave one or two talks to the Rural Institute, about her holidays abroad and life in her training college. She went to church every Sunday morning and sang in the choir, and afterwards taught in the Sunday school. But mostly she stayed at home. New bright curtains appeared in all the windows. She was especially fond of flowers; the little glass porch at the front of the house was full all the year round with flowering plants; the school garden, that first summer after she came, was a delight. All the bees in the island seemed to forage in those flowers.

How she first met John Germiston, nobody knows. It was almost certainly during one of those long walks she took in the summer evenings of her second year. John Germiston kept a croft on the side of the Ward Hill, a poor enough place with a couple of cows and a scatter of hens. Three years before he had courted a girl from the neighbouring island of Hellya. He had sailed across and got married in the kirk there and brought his bride home, a shy creature whose looks changed as swiftly as the summer loch. And there in his croft he installed her. And she would be seen from time to time feeding the hens at the end of the house, or hanging out washing, or standing at the road-end with her basket waiting for the grocery van. But she never became part of the community. With the coming of winter she was seen less and less—a wide-eyed face in the window, a figure against the skyline looking over the sound towards Hellya. The doctor began to call regularly once a week at the croft. John Germiston let it be known in the smithy that his wife was not keeping well.

There is a trouble in the islands that is called *morbus orcadensis*.

It is a darkening of the mind, a progressive flawing and thickening of the clear lens of the spirit. It is said to be induced in sensitive people by the long black overhang of winter; the howl and sob of the wind over the moors that goes on sometimes for days on end; the perpetual rain that makes of tilth and pasture one indiscriminate bog; the unending gnaw of the sea at the crags.

Soon after the new year they took the stricken girl to a hospital in the south.

Of course everyone in Quoylay was sorry for John Germiston. It is a hard thing for a young handsome man to work a croft by himself. And yet these things happen from time to time. There are a few cheerful old men in the folds of the hills, or down by the shore, who have been widowers since their twenties.

Somewhere on the hill, one evening in spring, John Germiston met Sandra McKillop. They spoke together. He brought her to his house. She stood in the door and saw the desolation inside; the rusted pot, the torn curtains, the filthy hearth. The worm had bored deep into that rose.

From that first meeting everything proceeded swiftly and inevitably. No sooner was school over for the day than Miss McKillop shook the adoring children off and was away to the croft of Stanebreck on the hill with a basket of bannocks or a bundle of clean washing. She stayed late into the evening. Sometimes they would be seen wandering together along the edge of the crags, while far below the Atlantic fell unquietly among shelving rocks and hollow caves; on and on they walked into the sunset, while near and far the crofts watched and speculated.

Night after night, late, as April brightened into May, she would come home alone. A light would go on in the schoolhouse kitchen. She would stand in the garden for a while among her hosts of blossoms. Then she would go in and lock the door. Her bedroom window was briefly illuminated. Then the whole house was dark.

'I suppose,' said Henrikson, 'nobody could have said a thing if it had stopped there. There was suspicion—well, what do you expect, a young woman visiting a married man night after night, and her a school-teacher with a position to keep up—but I don't suppose anybody could have done a thing about it.

'But in the end the two of them got bold. They got careless. It wasn't enough for this hussy to visit her fancy-man in his croft —O no, the bold boy takes to sallying down two or three times a week to the school-house for his supper, if you please.

'Still nobody could make a move. A person is entitled to invite another person to the house for supper, even though on one occasion at least they don't draw the curtain and I can see from my kitchen their hands folded together in the middle of the table and all that laughter going on between them.

'Mr Reynolds, I considered it my duty to watch, yes, and to report to the proper quarters if necessary.

'One Friday evening Germiston arrives at the schoolhouse at nine o'clock. A fine evening at the beginning of May it was. The light went on in the parlour. The curtain was drawn. After an hour or so the light goes on in her bedroom. "Ah ha", say I to myself, "I've missed their farewells tonight, I've missed all the kissing in the door." . . . But I was wrong, Mr Reynolds. Something far worse was happening. At half past five in the morning I got up to stock the van, and I saw him going home over the hill, black against the rising sun. At half past five in the morning.

'That same day, being an elder, I went to the manse. Mr Barr refused to do a thing about it. "Miss McKillop is a member of my church. If she's in trouble of any sort she'll come to me," he said. "I will not act on slanderous rumours. There's more than one crofter on the hill at half past five in the morning." . . . There's your modern ministers for you. And I don't care if he is your friend, Mr Reynolds, I must speak my mind about this business.

'By now the whole island was a hive of rumour.

'Neither John Germiston nor Miss McKillop could stir without some eye being on them and some tongue speculating. And yet they went on meeting one another, quite open and shameless, as if they were the only living people in an island of ghosts. They would wander along the loch shore together, hand in hand, sometimes stopping to watch the swans or the eiders, not caring at all that a dozen croft windows were watching their lingerings and kissings. Then, arm about one another, they would turn across the fields in the direction of the school-house.

'Ay, but the dog of Stanebreck was a lonely dog till the sun got up, all that month of May.

'One Tuesday morning she arrived late for school, at a quarter past nine. She arrived with the mud of the hill plastered over her stockings, and half-dead with sleep. "Hurrah", cried the bairns congregated round the locked door of the school. They knew no better, the poor innocent things. They shouted half with delight and half with disappointment when she gave them the morning off, told them to come back in the afternoon. They were not to know what manner of thing had made their teacher so exhausted.

'Of course it was no longer possible to have a woman like her for the island teacher.

'I had written to this person and that. Enquiries were under way, discreetly, you know, so as not to cause any undue sensation. I think in the end pressure would have been put on her to resign. But as things turned out it wasn't necessary.

'One night they both disappeared. They vanished as if they had been swept clean off the face of the island. The school door remained locked all the next week. John Germiston's unmilked cow bellowed in its steep field. "Ah ha," said the men in the smithy, "so it's come to this, they've run away together . . ."

'Ten days later a fishing boat drew up the two bodies a mile west of Hellya. Their arms were round each other. The fishermen had trouble separating the yellow hair from the black hair.'

Henrikson was having difficulty with his breathing; his voice dropped and quavered and choked so that I could hardly hear his last three words. 'They were naked,' he mouthed venomously.

Moths flickered between us. The sea boomed and hushed from the far side of the hill. In a nearby croft a light came on.

'And so,' said Henrikson, 'we decided that we didn't want a woman teacher after that. That's why you're here, Mr Reynolds.'

We drifted apart, Henrikson and I, to our separate doors. Eagerly that night I wished for the vanished passion to fill my rooms: the ghost, the chill, the scent of roses. But in the schoolhouse was only a most terrible desolation.

On fine evenings that summer, when tide and light were suitable, Donald Barr and I would fish for sillocks and cuithes from the long sloping skerry under the crag. Or we would ask the loan of a crofter's boat, if the fish were scanty there, and row out with our lines into the bay.

The evening before the agricultural show was bright and calm. We waited in the bay with dripping oars for the sun to set behind the hill. We put our rods deep into the dazzle but not one cuithe responded. Presently the sun furled itself in a cloud, and it was as if a rose had burst open over the sea's unflawed mirror. Cuithe fishing is a sport that requires little skill. Time after time we hauled our rods in burgeoning with strenuous sea fruit, until the bottom of the dinghy was a floor of unquiet gulping silver. Then the dense undersea hordes moved away, and for twenty minutes, while the rose of sunset faded and the long bay gloomed, we caught nothing.

'It must have been about here,' I said to Donald Barr, 'that they were drowned.'

He said nothing. He had never discussed the affair with me, beyond that one mention of the girl's name at the manse gate. A chill moved in from the west; breaths of night air flawed the dark sea mirror.

'The earth bound soul refuses to acknowledge its death,' said Donald. 'It is desperately in love with the things of this world—possessions, fame, lust. How, once it has tasted them, can it ever exist without them? Death is a negation of all that wonder and delight. It will not enter the dark door of the grave. It lurks, a ghost, round the places where it fed on earthly joys. It spreads a coldness about the abodes of the living. The five senses pulse through it, but fadingly, because there is nothing for the appetite to feed on, only memories and shadows. Sooner or later the soul must enter the dark door. But no—it will not—for a year or for a decade or for a century it lingers about the place of its passion, a rose garden or a turret or a crossroads. It will not acknowledge that all this loveliness of sea and sky and islands, and all the rare things that happen among them, are merely shadows of a greater reality. At last the starved soul is forced to accept it, for it finds itself utterly alone, surrounded as time goes by with strange new unloved objects and withered faces and skulls. Reluctantly it stoops under the dark lintel. All loves are forgotten then. It sets out on the quest for Love itself. For this it was created in the beginning.'

We hauled the dingy high up the beach and secured her to

a rock. A few mild summer stars glimmered. The sea was dark in the bay, under the shadow of the cliff, but the Atlantic horizon was still flushed a little with reluctant sunset, and all between was a vast slow heave of gray.

'I have a bottle of very good malt whisky in the school-house,' I said. 'I think a man could taste worse things after a long evening on the sea.'

It was then that I heard the harp-like shivering cries far out in the bay. The sea thins out the human voice, purges it of its earthiness, lends it a purity and poignancy.

'Wait for me,' cried the girl's voice. 'Where are you? You're swimming too fast.'

Donald Barr had heard the voices also. Night folded us increasingly in gloom and cold as we stood motionless under the sea-bank. He passed me his tobacco pouch. I struck a match. The flame trembled between us.

'This way,' shouted a firm strong happy voice (but attenuated on the harpstrings of the sea). 'I'm over here.'

The still bay shivered from end to end with a single glad cry. Then there was silence.

The minister and I turned. We climbed over loose stones and sandy hillocks to the road. We lashed our heavy basket of cuithes into the boot of Donald Barr's old Ford. Then we got in, one on each side, and he pressed the starter.

'Earth-bound souls enact their little dramas over and over again, but each time a little more weakly,' he said. 'The reality of death covers them increasingly with its good oblivion. You will be haunted for a month or two yet. But at last the roses will lose their scent.'

The car stopped in front of the dark school-house.

The Girl I Left Behind Me

Muriel Spark

IT WAS JUST gone quarter past six when I left the office.

'Teedle-um-tum-tum'—there was the tune again, going round my head. Mr Letter had been whistling it all throughout the day between his noisy telephone calls and his dreamy sessions. Sometimes he whistled 'Softly, Softly, Turn the Key', but usually it was 'The Girl I Left Behind Me' rendered at a brisk hornpipe tempo.

I stood in the bus line, tired out, and wondering how long I would endure Mark Letter (Screws & Nails) Ltd. Of course, after my long illness, it was experience. But Mr Letter and his tune, and his sudden moods of bounce, and his sudden lapses into lassitude, his sandy hair and little bad teeth, roused my resentment, especially when his tune barrelled round my head long after I had left the office; it was like taking Mr Letter home.

No one at the bus stop took any notice of me. Well, of course, why should they? I was not acquainted with anyone there, but that evening I felt particularly anonymous among the homegoers. Everyone looked right through me and even, it seemed, walked through me. Late autumn always sets my fancy toward sad ideas. The starlings were crowding in to roost on all the high cornices of the great office buildings. And I located, among the misty unease of my feelings, a very strong conviction that I had left something important behind me or some job incompleted at the office. Perhaps I had left the safe unlocked, or perhaps it was something quite trivial which nagged at me. I had half a mind to turn back, tired as I was, and reassure myself. But my bus came along and I piled in with the rest.

As usual, I did not get a seat. I clung to the handrail and allowed myself to be lurched back and forth against the other passengers. I stood on a man's foot, and said, 'Oh, sorry.' But he looked away without response, which depressed me. And more and more, I felt that I had left something of tremendous import at the office. 'Teedle-um-tum-tum'—the tune was a background to my worry all the way home. I went over in my mind the day's business, for I thought, now, perhaps it was a letter which I should have written and posted on my way home.

That morning I had arrived at the office to find Mark Letter vigorously at work. By fits, he would occasionally turn up at eight in the morning, tear at the post and, by the time I arrived, he would have despatched perhaps half a dozen needless telegrams; and before I could get my coat off, would deliver a whole day's instructions to me, rapidly fluttering his freckled hands in time with his chattering mouth. This habit used to jar me, and I found only one thing amusing about it; that was when he would say, as he gave instructions for dealing with each item, 'Mark letter urgent.' I thought that rather funny coming from Mark Letter, and I often thought of him, as he was in those moods, as Mark Letter Urgent.

As I swayed in the bus I recalled that morning's access of energy on the part of Mark Letter Urgent. He had been more urgent than usual, so that I still felt put out by the urgency. I felt terribly old for my twenty-two years as I raked round my mind for some clue as to what I had left unfinished. Something had been left amiss; the further the bus carried me from the office, the more certain I became of it. Not that I took my job to heart very greatly, but Mr Letter's moods of bustle were infectious, and when they occurred I felt fussy for the rest of the day; and although I consoled myself that I would feel better when I got home, the worry would not leave me.

By noon, Mr Letter had calmed down a little, and for an hour before I went to lunch he strode round the office with his hands in his pockets, whistling between his seedy brown teeth that sailors' song 'The Girl I Left Behind Me'. I lurched with the bus as it chugged out the rhythm, 'Teedle-um-tum-tum. Teedle-um . . .' Returning from lunch I had found silence, and wondered if Mr Letter was out, until I heard suddenly, from his tiny private office, his tune again, a low swift hum, trailing out toward the end. Then I knew that he had fallen into one of his afternoon daydreams.

I would sometimes come upon him in his little box of an office when these trances afflicted him. I would find him sitting in his swivel chair behind his desk. Usually he had taken off his coat and slung it across the back of his chair. His right elbow would be propped on the desk, supporting his chin, while from his left hand would dangle his tie. He would gaze at this tie; it was his main object of contemplation. That afternoon I had found him tie-gazing when I went into his room for some papers. He was gazing at it with parted lips so that I could see his small, separated discolored teeth, no larger than a child's first teeth. Through them he whistled his tune. Yesterday, it had been 'Softly, Softly, Turn the Key,' but today it was the other.

I got off the bus at my usual stop, with my fare still in my hand. I almost threw the coins away, absentmindedly thinking they were the ticket, and when I noticed them I thought how nearly no one at all I was, since even the conductor had, in his rush, passed me by.

Mark Letter had remained in his dream for two and a half hours. What was it I had left unfinished? I could not for the life of me recall what he had said when at last he emerged from his office-box. Perhaps it was then I had made tea. Mr Letter always liked a cup when he was neither in his frenzy nor in his abstraction, but ordinary and talkative. He would speak of his hobby, fretwork. I do not think Mr Letter had any home life. At forty-six he was still unmarried, living alone in a house at Roehampton. As I walked up the lane to my lodgings I recollected that Mr Letter had come in for his tea with his tie still dangling from his hand, his throat white under the open-neck shirt, and his 'Teedle-um-tum-tum' in his teeth.

At last I was home and my Yale in the lock. Softly, I said to myself, softly turn the key, and thank God I'm home. My landlady passed through the hall from kitchen to dining-room with a salt and pepper cruet in her crinkly hands. She had some new lodgers. 'My guests,' she always called them. The new guests took precedence over the old with my landlady. I felt desolate. I simply could not climb the stairs to my room to wash, and then descend to take brown soup with the new guests while my landlady fussed over them, ignoring me. I sat for a moment in the chair in the hall to collect my strength. A year's illness drains one, however young. Suddenly the repulsion of the brown soup and the anxiety about the office made me decide. I would not go upstairs to my room. I must return to the office to see what it was that I had overlooked.

'Teedle-um-tum-tum'—I told myself that I was giving way to neurosis. Many times I had laughed at my sister who, after she had gone to bed at night, would send her husband downstairs to make sure all the gas taps were turned off, all the doors locked, back and front. Very well, I was as silly as my sister, but I understood her obsession, and simply opened the door and slipped out of the house, tired as I was, making my weary way back to the bus stop, back to the office.

'Why should I do this for Mark Letter?' I demanded of myself. But really, I was not returning for his sake, it was for my own.

I was doing this to get rid of the feeling of incompletion, and that song in my brain swimming round like a damned goldfish.

I wondered, as the bus took me back along the familiar route, what I would say if Mark Letter should still be at the office. He often worked late, or at least, stayed there late, doing I don't know what, for his screw and nail business did not call for long hours. It seemed to me he had an affection for those dingy premises. I was rather apprehensive lest I should find Mr Letter at the office, standing, just as I had last seen him, swinging his tie in his hand, beside my desk. I resolved that if I should find him there, I should say straight out that I had left something behind me.

A clock struck quarter past seven as I got off the bus. I realized that again I had not paid my fare. I looked at the money in my hand for a stupid second. Then I felt reckless. 'Teedle-um-tum-tum'—I caught myself humming the tune as I walked quickly up the sad side street to our office. My heart knocked at my throat, for I was eager. Softly, softly, I said to myself as I turned the key of the outside door. Quickly, quickly, I ran up the stairs. Only outside the office door I halted, and while I found its key on my bunch it occurred to me how strangely my sister would think I was behaving.

I opened the door and my sadness left me at once. With a great joy I recognized what it was I had left behind me, my body lying strangled on the floor. I ran toward my body and embraced it like a lover.

One Night in the Library

James Robertson

ONE NIGHT IN the library, as I read by the light of a single lamp placed behind my chair, I became conscious of stirrings in the shadowed parts of the room. These fluttering sounds—as of a colony of restless bats in residence behind the ranks of books— interested rather than alarmed me. I knew that there were no bats. What was happening had happened before, in those hours of absolute stillness and quiet, when even the fire has ceased its cracking and hissing. The sounds I heard were the lives contained in all the thousands of volumes that surrounded me, shifting and settling in their paper beds.

I found this reassuring. It told me that all my years of reading had not been in vain: that through reading I had entered into other times and other worlds, experienced the lives of people separated from me by oceans and deserts and generations, and that they remained with me in the library. Thus comforted, I returned to the book in my hands.

But after a minute I stopped reading and looked up. Some other life had entered the room. I saw, dimly, the figure of a man, draped in some kind of robe, standing near the door. Yet the door was shut, and I was certain it had not opened in the last hour.

I reached up and directed the beam of the lamp towards him.

'What do you want?' I asked.

The robed figure shook his head. He wanted nothing. Then he raised a hand, shielding his vision, as I at first thought, against the brightness. But no, his forefinger touched the corner of one eye and then pointed at me, or more specifically at my book, and drew lines back and forth in the air. I understood that he wanted me to continue reading.

So I adjusted the lamp again, aware of the intensity of his gaze and something more—the wonder it contained. The books on the shelves were hushed. I thought how much noise is contained in silence. If I looked up I knew that, even if I could no longer see him, his ancient witness would still be in the library.

I Live Here Now

A Christmas Ghost Story

Ian Rankin

EVER SINCE HIS daughter's death, John Bates had all but given up.

Eunice had been seventeen, bubbly and surrounded by friends, keen to leave school behind to study history at university. She'd been a passionate cook and hockey player, not yet ready for a steady boyfriend, and loved absolutely by both her parents. But then one night she had consumed almost an entire bottle of vodka before climbing on to a parapet and leaping into a river swollen by over a week of near-constant rain.

John and his wife Emily had sat numbed for days on end as relatives and neighbours passed through the house, offering solace and paying tribute. Now, six months on, Emily was back at work at the florist's, increasingly busy as Christmas approached. Breakfasts were quiet affairs, the radio saving them from talking. They watched TV each evening and sometimes walked to the local park, where they'd see teenagers they didn't recognise sharing spliffs and cans on benches, wrapped up more warmly as the weather turned.

The shops had begun extending their hours, excepting the ones lost to the pandemic. A few media reports had suggested that Eunice's suicide had been in reaction to the virus, but Bates doubted that. Then again, she had left few clues. He had gone through her bedroom, even checking beneath the bed and at the back of the built-in wardrobes. He had eventually gained access to her computer and mobile phone—the phone itself having been left on the parapet, proving itself the nearest thing to a note that she would leave. Counselling had been offered but rejected though John sometimes caught a glimpse of Emily's tablet as she digested some online resource for bereaved parents. He thought she even belonged to a group who met via Zoom, though she was careful never to mention it, the meetings timed to take place when he was elsewhere.

He spent his afternoons in the reopened library, or a café or bar. He tried to catch up on his reading. He might get close to finishing the occasional cryptic crossword. It had been his job, many years back, to compile such crosswords for the local paper. That paper no longer existed. John had left anyway, Emily insisting that he should write full-time. The result had been one radio sitcom, a handful of plays, and two well-received serio-comic novels. One review had even compared him to Jonathan Coe. He'd hung on to that, while binning most of the others.

He had no commissions currently, his agent blaming (what else?) the pandemic. A stage producer was keen for him to write a spec script based on a 1930s whodunit, but there'd be no fee until an acceptable draft had been completed. His current book publisher appeared lukewarm, sales having not been commensurate with prize shortlistings.

'Just start writing anything, darling,' Emily had suggested one night, placing a hand on his shoulder. 'You might find it helps. God knows, something has to.'

But could he produce anything that wouldn't be read through the prism of Eunice's death? Would anyone publishing him do so as if handing over a belated Deepest Sympathy card? And what was worth writing about anyway? No one wanted comedy moulded from tragedy. Despite which, he had found himself this morning picking up his old leather-bound notebook—a gift from Emily after a trip to Venice—and walking to the café. After scanning the newspaper and ordering a second Americano he had opened the notebook, skimming its pages. There were ideas for projects, alongside character names and the odd smart one-liner, but outnumbered by doodles and crossings out. The last half of the book comprised blank pages, evidence that the creative well had been drying up long before Eunice took her life. Yet as he ran a thumb through these empty pages, he caught a sudden blur of ink. The words were in a neat hand, blue ballpoint rather than the black he favoured, and comprised a single sentence.

I live here now.

He had no memory at all of writing them. Moreover, they didn't seem like his handwriting. He flicked back to check, then took out his biro and wrote the words for himself. Definitely not his handwriting. He scoured the rest of the notebook, then snapped it shut and got to his feet.

Emily was busy at the counter, trimming the stems of a spray she was putting together with her usual skill. She didn't look up until he held the notebook open in front of her.

'Did Eunice do this?' he asked, voice shaking.

Emily slipped her glasses on. 'Could be,' she answered. 'I mean, it looks like her writing, doesn't it?'

'Does it though? I'm not sure.'

'She maybe did it to tease you—so you'd get a surprise when you reached that page.'

'Maybe,' Bates said, pretending to agree.

'Remember Peter and Barbara are coming for supper—you'll buy some wine, won't you?'

Their favoured off-licence was a few shops further along. Bates plucked a bottle of red from a shelf without really paying attention. There was a homeless man seated on the pavement next to the bank machine. Bates found a few coins in his pocket and bent at the waist to deposit them in the man's cardboard cup. He hadn't meant to establish eye contact but it happened anyway.

'Wife threw me out,' the man explained. 'Just need the price of a bed.'

'I'm sorry,' Bates said, straightening up and making to walk on.

'I live here now,' the man called to him. Bates froze.

'What did you say?'

'This street, this pavement—I live here now, don't I?'

———————•⋅⟨⟩⋅•———————

That evening, as the meal ended and his old friend Peter stepped into the garden for a cigarette, Bates joined him, holding out the notebook, open at the relevant page. Peter took it and angled it into the light, widening his eyes in an attempt to focus after the best part of a bottle and a half of red.

'I've looked at Eunice's handwriting,' Bates told him. 'It's similar but not identical.'

'Okay.'

'What do you think it means?'

'More to the point, what do *you* think it means?' Peter asked, falling back on his well-worn tactic when faced with a question he either didn't like or didn't understand.

'I don't know,' Bates said truthfully. 'Is it a sign perhaps?'

'From Eunice?' Peter puffed out his cheeks. 'Were practical jokes her thing, or are you saying she's suddenly communicating with you six months after her very beautiful funeral? Much more likely you wrote it in your cups, a prospective new title or opening line—it's intriguing enough for either.' Peter sucked in some smoke before exhaling. 'Bloody nice meal, by the way. We must return the favour.'

'You always say that.'

'And one of these days it shall come to pass, though I warn you—Barbara's not half the chef your Emily is. I'm hoping there's enough pud for one final helping . . .'

Once their visitors had gone, John did the tidying up while Emily stretched out along the sofa, the TV on and some leftover wine in her glass. He filled the dishwasher, wiped down the dining-table and put the good cotton napkins in the laundry basket. He had left the notebook open on his chair next to the sofa, hoping Emily might take another look and come up with an explanation that would put his mind at rest. When he went through, the notebook was on the floor next to her. He picked it up and saw that the page had been torn out. Emily pointed to the wastepaper-bin, its bottom covered in a layer of what could have been mistaken for confetti.

'Now it'll stop bothering you,' she snapped. 'You were in such a bloody mood at dinner.'

'Why did you do that?' He lifted out a few slivers. They appeared to be all blank. There was no way the jigsaw could be reconstructed.

'Forget about it, John. Time to move on with your life.'

'Life's not one of your sodding Zoom sessions,' he snarled, heading to the hall, snatching up his coat, and slamming the front door after him. The night was chilly, the sky clear, a few stars evident. He could see his breath in the air as he walked. How could she? It was an act of destruction, irreversible. He stuffed his fists into his pockets, his strides long and determined. At last he came to a bar he knew and walked in, ordering a whisky, gulping it down seated at a table. The place wasn't busy —bars seldom were these days. He ordered a refill and tried to concentrate on the TV. Its sound was muted. News and sport by the look of it. The onscreen chyron was detailing a story about unrest in an African country. Then he saw the same four words, clear as day – *I live here now*. Bates blinked, looked around to see if anyone else had noticed. The chyron was back to reporting the Africa story, but he would swear he wasn't mistaken. He watched and waited as a new story appeared, and another after that. Then a break for adverts. One was for a new Hollywood release, its male and female stars big names. Emily had mentioned it as a possible night out. After a few clips from the film, its title appeared, filling the screen.

I LIVE HERE NOW

Bates leapt to his feet, one hand on the table to steady himself. The advert had ended, replaced by one for yoghurt. Bates took his phone from his pocket and tapped in the names of the two leads. He was taken to the website for their latest release, *I Love Her Now*. Bates expelled a bark of laughter. The barman asked him if everything was all right. Bates just shook his head, finished his second drink, and left.

He made for the bank machine, but the homeless man was no longer there. The florist's shop was in darkness, too. Traffic was light. It was a weeknight, keeping the town centre quiet. The local art-house cinema was advertising a French film. Bates stared at the poster for the best part of a minute, daring it to change. Eventually he moved on, knowing his ultimate destination now. The river, the bridge, the parapet. No one was waiting for him there, just a few padlocks left by superstitious lovers. Eunice's friends had stopped leaving posies, though he knew they had plans to raise money for a plaque. As he stood there, staring down at the rippling water beneath, he sensed her phone resting near his left hand. He reached out but felt nothing. Nothing at all. He raised his own phone, its screen blank, and stared at it, willing something, anything to happen, willing the world around him to acknowledge his unceasing agony.

Less than a minute later, he hit the water, almost losing consciousness in the fall. The sharp iciness had him flailing at first, but then he relaxed, safe in the knowledge that the water was buoying him up. He saw the buildings above him change, town becoming suburb before petering out to a smattering of industrial units with high walls and fences, beyond which lay motorway, rolling hills and farmland. He had no idea how much time had passed by the time he clawed his way up a shallow bank. He staggered at first, but soon regained his balance, his clothes shivering and shoes squelching. The plod home through deserted streets took numbing hours. The door was unlocked so he let himself in, stripping in the hall and climbing the stairs to where she waited for him. Not the master bedroom but Eunice's. He lay down on her bed and closed his eyes.

A shadow loomed over him. It was Emily. She looked fearful as she asked him what had happened. When he opened his mouth it felt full of silt.

'I live here now,' he gurgled, beginning with painful slowness to sit up.

Biographical Notes on the Authors

JAMES HOGG, the Ettrick Shepherd (1770–1835), was a poet, novelist and essayist. As a young man he worked as a shepherd and farmhand, and he was largely self-educated through reading. He became friendly with Walter Scott when the latter sought out Hogg's mother, whose repertoire included old ballads and legends and who assisted Scott in compiling his *Minstrelsy of the Scottish Border*. In 1810, Hogg moved to Edinburgh to start a literary career. In 1813, his narrative poem *The Queen's Wake* was published to critical acclaim. His other works include *The Private Memoirs and Confessions of a Justified Sinner*, a novel and now his most famous work; *The Brownie of Bodseck*; *Songs, by the Ettrick Shepherd*; *Altrive Tales*; *Tales of the Wars of Montrose* and a memoir of Sir Walter Scott.

SIR WALTER SCOTT (1771–1832) is too famous to require introduction. His famous *Waverley* novels and poetry made him a literary figure of European stature. Scott had a long-standing interest in the paranormal, as his *Letters on Demonology and Witchcraft* testify. He wrote one of the best ghost stories ever penned, *Wandering Willie's Tale*, which forms part of his novel *Redgauntlet*. 'The Tapestried Chamber', reproduced here, is not as widely known, but equally well-written. It still gives nervous people nightmares.

ANONYMOUS: 'A Tale for Twilight' and 'Horror – A True Story'. The authors (or author) of these two accomplished ghost stories are not known. It has been suggested that Mrs Oliphant (q.v.) could have written them. This is plausible, but impossible to prove. It is, however, highly likely that the authors were women; many women authors of the period preferred to keep their identity secret, either because they did not wish others to know that they were supplementing their families' income in this way or for fear that the content might be deemed in some way controversial.

MARGARET OLIPHANT (1828–1897) wrote novels, historical writings and literary criticism. She also wrote chilling tales of the supernatural. Finding herself a young widow with children to educate, she became a successful woman of letters, sending her sons to Eton on the proceeds. Most of her work was published in *Blackwood's Magazine*. In the fashion of the day, as an author she was always known as 'Mrs Oliphant'. 'The Open Door' is set among the ruins of Colinton Castle, near Edinburgh; they stood in the grounds of her friends the publishing Blackwood family's country house (now part of Merchiston Castle School).

ROBERT LOUIS STEVENSON (1850–1894), like Scott, hardly requires any introduction. His novels, which include *Treasure Island*, *The Strange Case of Dr Jekyll and Mr Hyde* and *The Master of Ballantrae* are internationally known, as is his poetry. Stevenson also wrote accomplished short stories, some of which have a ghostly theme. 'The Body-Snatcher' first appeared in the *Pall Mall Magazine*'s Christmas Extra issue in 1884. The scandalous commerce in stolen corpses to supply Edinburgh's medical schools inspired the tale: the macabre trade was operated by criminals known as 'body-snatchers'. When legislation made it harder to steal fresh bodies from graveyards, they turned to murder. The most notorious were William Burke (hanged and dissected in 1829) and his accomplice William Hare. Having been brought up in Edinburgh, Stevenson was familiar with their story.

SIR ARTHUR CONAN DOYLE (1859–1930) is famous for his Sherlock Holmes stories and novels. Doyle was born in Edinburgh and graduated from Edinburgh University's medical school. In addition to the Holmes stories and scientific articles, he wrote distinguished historical novels, such as *The White Company* and *Sir Nigel*, set in the Middle Ages; the adventures of Brigadier Gerard, set in the Napoleonic period; and the exploits of Professor George Edward Challenger, a nineteenth-century scientist and explorer. Doyle helped to found the Society for Psychical Research, later becoming a spiritualist. His immense literary achievement included many short stories, some with supernatural themes. 'The Captain of the *Pole-star*', which involves a voyage into an unknown part of the Arctic Ocean, is one of his best. Doyle as a young man served as ship's doctor on a Dundee whaling vessel, which allowed him to invest this sea mystery with authentic detail.

GUY BOOTHBY (1867–1905) was an Australian of Scots descent. He passed most of his adult career in the UK, based in England but visiting Scotland, where he had relations living near Edinburgh. His literary output was enormous: it included sensational fiction published in a range of late nineteenth-century magazines. He wrote dozens of plays, short stories and over fifty novels. His Dr Nikola series, about an occultist criminal mastermind, and *Pharos, the Egyptian*, a tale of Egyptian mummies' curses and supernatural revenge, were very popular. He was fortunate to have Rudyard Kipling, whose style influenced his, as a friend and mentor. His tale in this collection, 'The Grey Cavalier of Penterton Hall', is not set in Scotland but it was published by *The Scotsman* newspaper as one of their long-running series of Christmas ghost stories.

ALGERNON BLACKWOOD (1869–1951) was born in Shooter's Hill, Kent. Like Guy Boothby, he was of distant Scots descent. Nevertheless Blackwood knew Scotland well; he, his father and brothers were keen hill walkers and rock climbers, so they passed many holidays in Skye, Argyll and Perthshire. Blackwood studied at Edinburgh University in 1888–89 but was removed by his father at the end of his first year; the university nevertheless regards him as a distinguished alumnus. A prolific author, especially of ghost, mystery and horror stories, he was also a popular broadcaster on radio and television. A consummate storyteller, the critics were united in his praise. The Government shared the general enthusiasm for Blackwood; in 1948 he received the CBE. In 1949 he received the Television Society Medal (the equivalent of an Oscar), as the outstanding television personality of 1948. Blackwood set one of his novels and at least two short stories in Edinburgh. 'Keeping his Promise', included in this anthology, is almost literally chilling, both from the implications of the plot and from its vivid evocation of Edinburgh on a freezing winter's night.

EILEEN BIGLAND (1898–1970) was born in Edinburgh. She was a prolific and erudite author, best known for her travel writing and biography. In the former category, *The Lake of the Royal Crocodiles*, an account of the Bemba people of Zambia and Katanga, and in the latter, her award-winning biography of Lord Byron, received critical acclaim. Other works included biographies of Marie Curie, Helen Keller, Joanna Trollope and Ouida. Her travel books included *Into China* (1940) and *In the Steps of George Borrow* (1951). She also wrote novels under the pseudonym of Anne Carstairs. She only wrote two known pieces of short fiction, 'The Lass with the Delicate Air' (1952), which is presented here, and 'Remembering Lee' (1955).

RONALD DUNCAN (1914–1982), despite his Scottish-sounding name, was of German origin and was born in Salisbury, Southern Rhodesia (now Harare, Zimbabwe). His original surname was Dunkelsbühler. In one of his memoirs Duncan claimed that his father was the illegitimate son of Crown Prince Rupprecht of Bavaria, son of Ludwig III, the last king, who was regarded as the true Jacobite Pretender to the thrones of Scotland and England; this gave Duncan a tenuous Scottish connection. Apart from that, he seems to have known Edinburgh well. Duncan was a very productive writer, whose works included poems, plays and film scripts. His short story 'Consanguinity', set in Scotland, has a darkly psychological aspect, including a suggestion of incestuous urges.

GEORGE MACKAY BROWN (1921–1996) was a poet, author and dramatist who remained closely identified with his native Orkney. He was one of the great Scots poets of the twentieth century. In an essay in the *Dictionary of Literary Biography*, David S. Robb declared that Brown was 'unique among modern British writers in the scope, nature, and integrity of his achievements . . . Another dimension that sets him apart . . . is the vision that informs his work, a vision made up of values drawn from his religion, his sense of history, his literary allegiances, and his devotion to Orkney.' Mackay Brown wrote a number of excellent ghost stories. When William Croft Dickinson died in 1963, Mackay Brown and other Scots writers took over and continued *The Scotsman* newspaper's series of Christmas ghost stories, which Dickinson had formerly written. 'The Drowned Rose' is brilliant, not well-known and deserves wider recognition.

MURIEL SPARK (1918–2006), née Camberg, was a Scots Jewish writer born in Edinburgh, who later converted to Roman Catholicism. Her best-known novel is *The Prime of Miss Jean*

Brodie (1961), set in a girls' school in interwar Edinburgh. Although a precocious child, enjoying Scott at a tender age, Spark found her literary voice comparatively late in life, at thirty-nine. She published her first novel, *The Comforters*, in 1957. The success of *Miss Jean Brodie*, its Broadway, film and television adaptations, assured her both financial security and a secure place in Scottish literature. *Miss Jean Brodie* has tended to overshadow Spark's other works, but she was a versatile writer, producing poetry, editing *The Poetry Review*, and writing essays, articles and short stories as well as novels. Like many other Scots writers, she successfully tried her hand at ghost stories; Spark's ghostly tales often have an unexpected and wryly humorous twist.

JAMES ROBERTSON (1958–) has written several collections of poetry and short stories and has published seven novels, the most recent being *News of the Dead* (2021). *Joseph Knight* (2003) was named Book of the Year in both the Saltire Society and Scottish Arts Council literary awards, and *And the Land Lay Still* was also Saltire Society Book of the Year in 2010. In 2013, setting himself a personal challenge, Robertson resolved to write a story every day for a year. Each tale was to be exactly 365 words long. Some draw on ancient myths and legends; others on history; some are fairy tales or dream memories. They were published in 2014 as *365 Stories*. 'One Night in the Library', the penultimate story in this volume, is taken from that collection.

IAN RANKIN (1960–) is one of the most highly regarded living crime writers. His Inspector Rebus novels, set mainly in Edinburgh, have been translated into several languages, while he has been the recipient of numerous awards, both official and academic. Rankin was born in Cardenden, Fife, where his father owned a grocery shop and his mother worked in a school canteen. He won a place at Edinburgh University, where he read English, graduating MA in 1982. After several years of adventures and temporary jobs in England and France he became a novelist, publishing two mainstream novels that were well-received. Rankin did not originally intend to become a crime novelist but proved to be extremely good at it; he has not looked back since publishing his first Rebus novel, *Knots and Crosses*, in 1987. Since then, thirteen of the Rebus novels and one short story have been adapted for television. Rankin's novels often make passing reference to the paranormal, to legends and gruesome crimes in Edinburgh's dark past. His ghost story, 'I Live Here Now', was first published in the Christmas edition of *The Spectator* in 2020.

A Note on the Author
of the Introduction

POSSIBLY AS A result of having lived in an old Edinburgh haunted house in his early youth, Alistair Kerr has always been interested in ghost stories and legends. One of his vivid early memories is of being shown round the University Medical Faculty's Museum by his father. Among the animal and human remains on display was a fascinating relic; the skeleton of the body-snatcher, William Burke. Beside it was a cast of his head, taken after execution; the mark of the hangman's noose was clearly visible.

Alistair has some notorious ancestors, one of whom was Dr Buck Ruxton, hanged for murder in 1936. He was a relation by marriage. During a Forensic Medicine lecture in the 1970s Alistair viewed some of the formalin-preserved remains of Mrs Ruxton, *nee* Kerr, who was one of her husband's victims, although at that time he was unaware that he and the remains were distantly related. A fellow student was Alexander McCall Smith, who became a lifelong friend and encouraged Alistair to start writing. This resulted in his first book, *Betrayal: The Murder of Robert Nairac GC* (Cambridge Academic, 2015, reprinted 2017), a military biography. Since then he has edited *Dark Encounters: A Collection of Ghost Stories* by William Croft Dickinson (Polygon, 2017; second edition 2019). *Tales for Twilight* is his third book.

Alistair has contributed articles to *Country Life, The University of Edinburgh Journal*, The Journal of the French Prefectoral Corps, The Royal United Services Institute's *RUSI Journal,* the annual journal of the Scottish Heraldry Society, *The Double Tressure* and the Cromwell Association's magazine, *The Protector's Pen*. He also writes book reviews and the occasional short story.

Alistair studied Scottish History and Law at the University of Edinburgh, which if anything encouraged his interest in ghost stories; the University and its church, Greyfriars, harbour a number of interesting ghosts. Despite having taken a degree in History and Law, Alistair did not become either a historian or a lawyer. He served in HM Diplomatic Service from 1975 to 2010. He has travelled in Europe, Africa, Asia and Australia, has survived two coup attempts and a civil war and has twice made the pilgrimage to The Holy Mountain (Mount Athos). He is a Fellow of the Royal Geographical Society.

Permissions

Every effort has been made to contact copyright holders of material reproduced in this book. We would be pleased to rectify any omissions in subsequent editions should they be drawn to our attention.

'Consanguinity' by Ronald Duncan is reproduced by permission of Eric Glass Ltd.

'The Drowned Rose' by George Mackay Brown is reproduced by permission of John Murray Press, an imprint of Hodder and Stoughton Ltd.

'The Girl I Left Behind Me' from *The Complete Short Stories* by Muriel Spark, published by Canongate, is reproduced by permission of David Higham Associates.

'One Night in the Library' from *365 Stories* by James Robertson, published by Penguin, is reproduced by permission of the author.

'I Live Here Now: A Christmas Ghost Story' by Ian Rankin. First published by *The Spectator*, December 2020. Copyright © John Rebus Ltd. Reproduced by permission of the author c/o Rogers, Coleridge & White Ltd., 20 Powis Mews, London W11 1JN

Envoi

And in yon wither'd bracken's lair,
Slumbered the wolf and shaggy bear;
Once on that lone and trackless sod
High chiefs and mail-clad warriors trod
And where the roe her bed has made,
Their last bright arms the vanquish'd laid.

The days of old have passed away
Like leaves upon the torrent grey,
And all their dreams of joy and woe,
As in yon eddy melts the snow;
And soon as far and dim behind
We too shall vanish on the wind.

—*Lays of the Deer Forest*, John Sobieski and Charles Edward Stuart